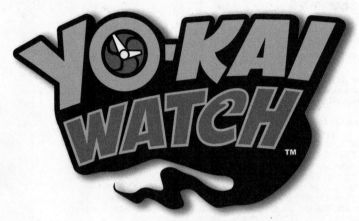

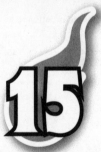

STORY AND ART BY
NORIYUKI KONISHI

ORIGINAL CONCEPT AND SUPERVISED BY LEVEL-5 INC.

YO-KAI WATCH™
Volume 15
VIZ Media Edition

Story and Art by Noriyuki Konishi
Original Concept and Supervised by LEVEL-5 Inc.

Translation/Tetsuichiro Miyaki
Lettering/John Hunt
Design/Kam Li

YO-KAI WATCH Vol. 15
by Noriyuki KONISHI
© 2013 Noriyuki KONISHI
©LEVEL-5 Inc.
Original Concept and Supervised by LEVEL-5 Inc.
All rights reserved.
Original Japanese edition published by SHOGAKUKAN.
English translation rights in the United States of America,
Canada, the United Kingdom, Ireland, Australia and New Zealand
arranged with SHOGAKUKAN.

Printed in the U.S.A.

Published by VIZ Media, LLC
P.O. Box 77010
San Francisco, CA 94107

10 9 8 7 6 5 4 3 2 1
First printing, September 2020

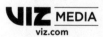
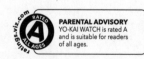

YO-KAI WATCH™

15

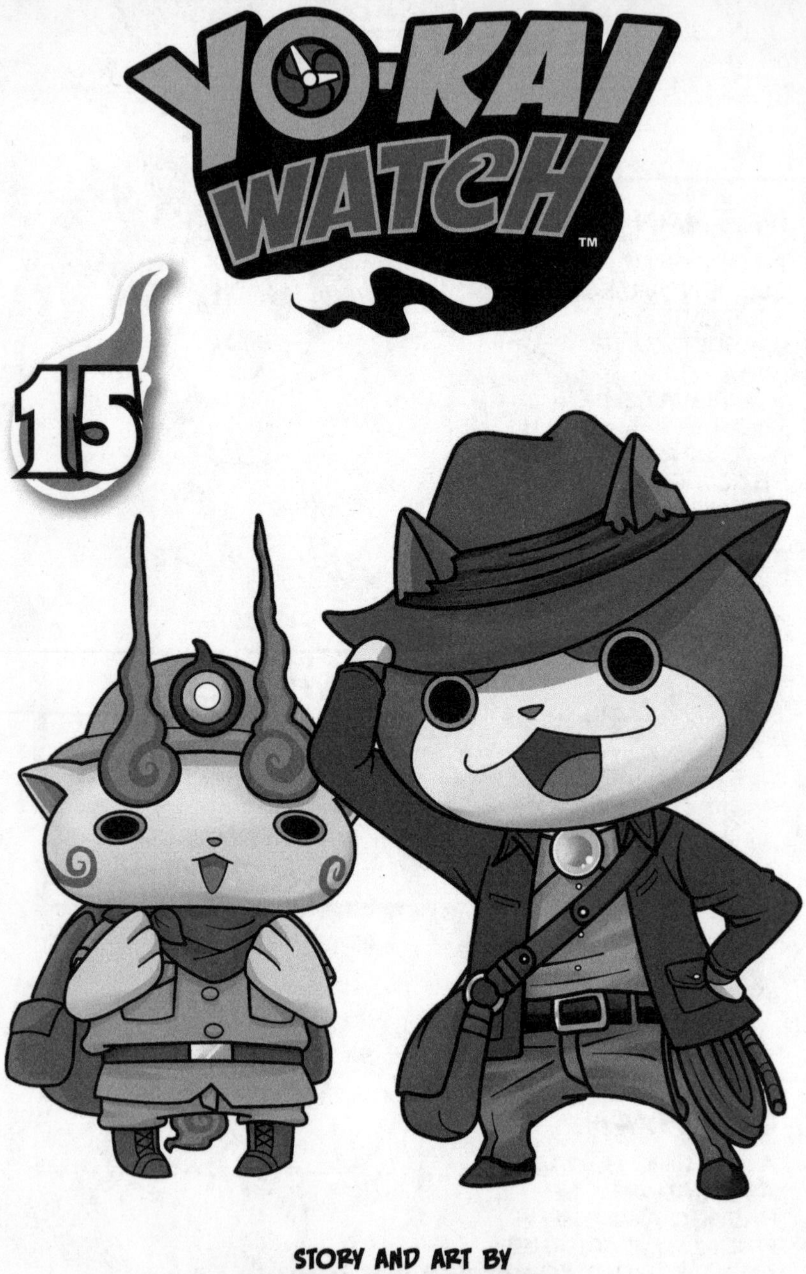

STORY AND ART BY

NORIYUKI KONISHI

ORIGINAL CONCEPT AND SUPERVISED BY LEVEL-5 INC.

CHARACTER INTRODUCTION

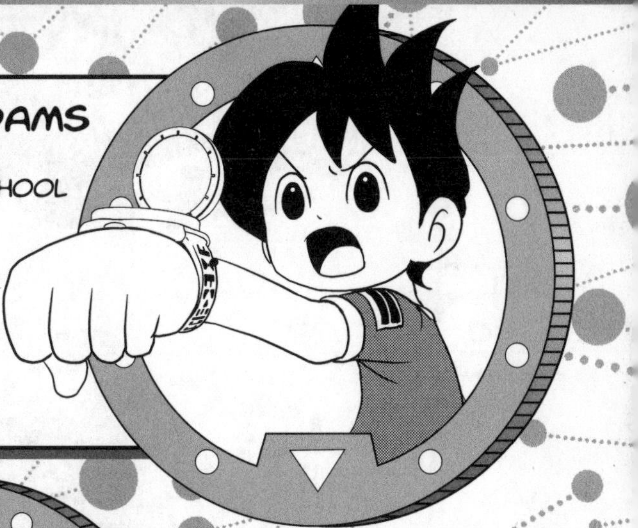

NATHAN ADAMS

AN ORDINARY ELEMENTARY SCHOOL STUDENT. WHISPER GAVE HIM THE YO-KAI WATCH, AND THEY HAVE SINCE BECOME FRIENDS.

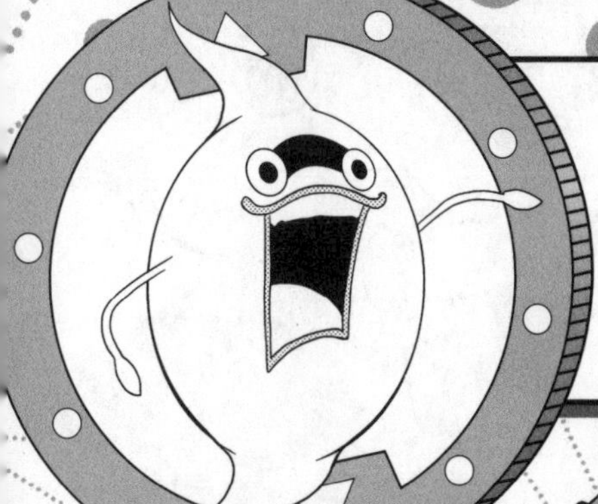

WHISPER

A YO-KAI BUTLER FREED BY NATE, WHISPER HELPS HIM WITH HIS EXTENSIVE KNOWLEDGE OF OTHER YO-KAI.

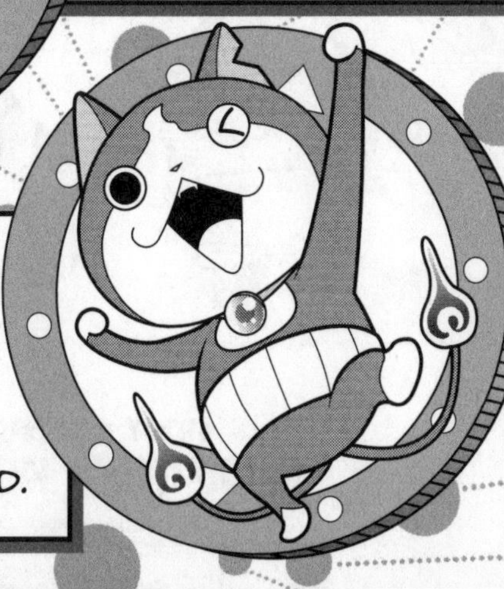

JIBANYAN

A CAT WHO BECAME A YO-KAI WHEN HE PASSED AWAY. HE IS FRIENDLY, CAREFREE, AND THE FIRST YO-KAI THAT NATE BEFRIENDED.

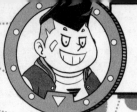

BARNABY BERNSTEIN

NATE'S CLASSMATE.
NICKNAME: BEAR.
CAN BE MISCHIEVOUS.

EDWARD ARCHER

NATE'S CLASSMATE.
NICKNAME: EDDIE.
HE ALWAYS WEARS
HEAPHONES.

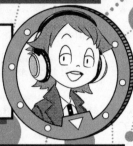

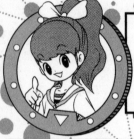

KATIE FORESTER

THE MOST POPULAR
GIRL IN NATE'S CLASS.

USAPYON

A RABBIT-LIKE YO-KAI
WEARING A SPACESUIT. HE'S
SEARCHING FOR SOMEONE.

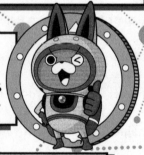

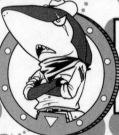

INDIANA JAWS

A VETERAN ADVENTURER
YO-KAI WHO SEARCHES
THE WORLD FOR LOST
TREASURE..

KOMASAN T

A TREASURE HUNTER WHO
WORKS WITH JIBANYAN T
AND INDIANA JAWS.

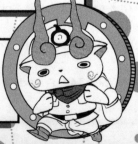

TABLE OF CONTENTS

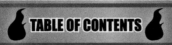

CHAPTER 135
YO-KAI WATCH BLASTERS TREASURE RAIDERS ARC: JIBANYAN T

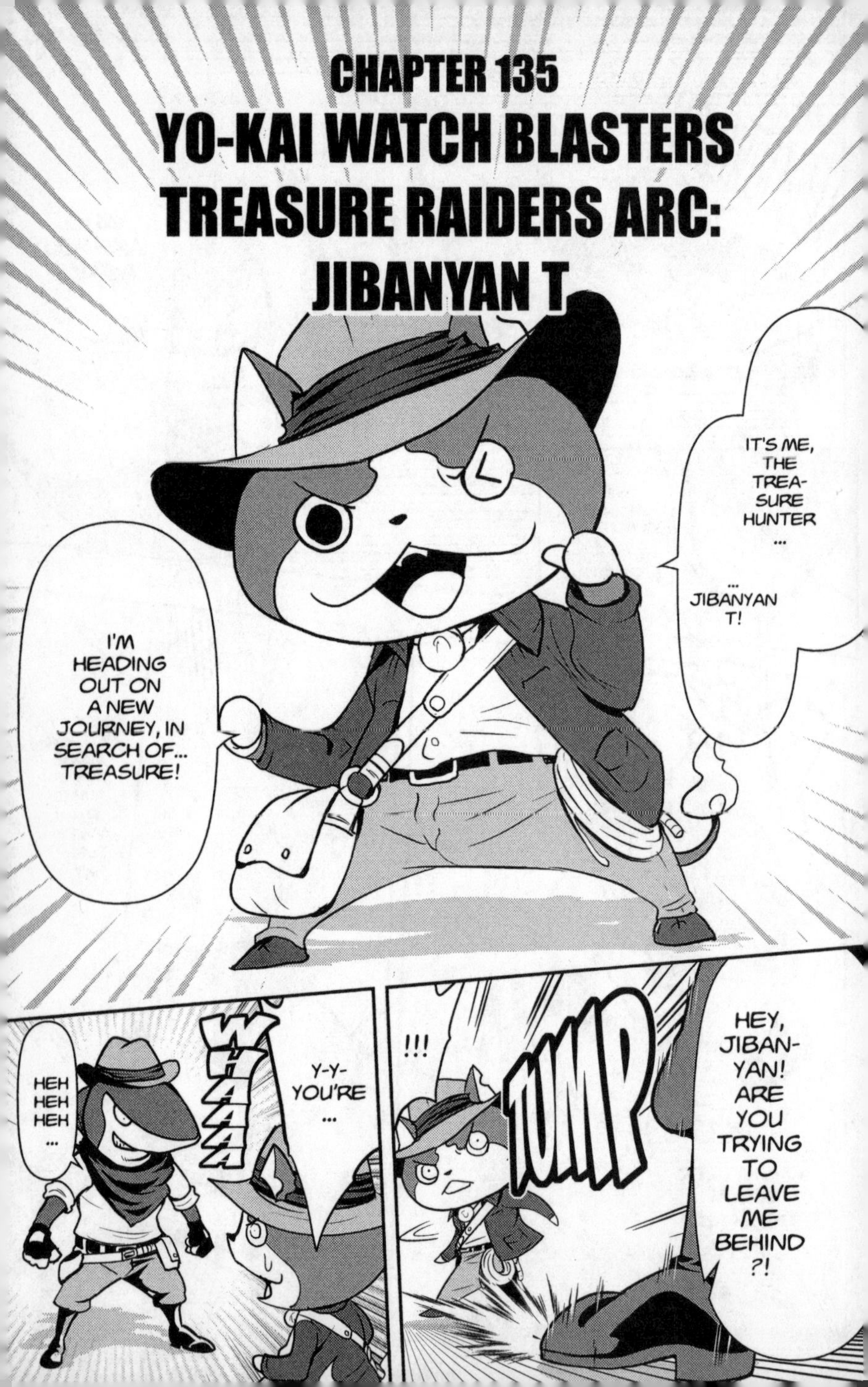
IT'S ME, THE TREASURE HUNTER... ...JIBANYAN T!
I'M HEADING OUT ON A NEW JOURNEY, IN SEARCH OF... TREASURE!
HEY, JIBANYAN! ARE YOU TRYING TO LEAVE ME BEHIND?!
TUMP
!!!
Y-Y-YOU'RE ...
WHAAAA
HEH HEH HEH ...

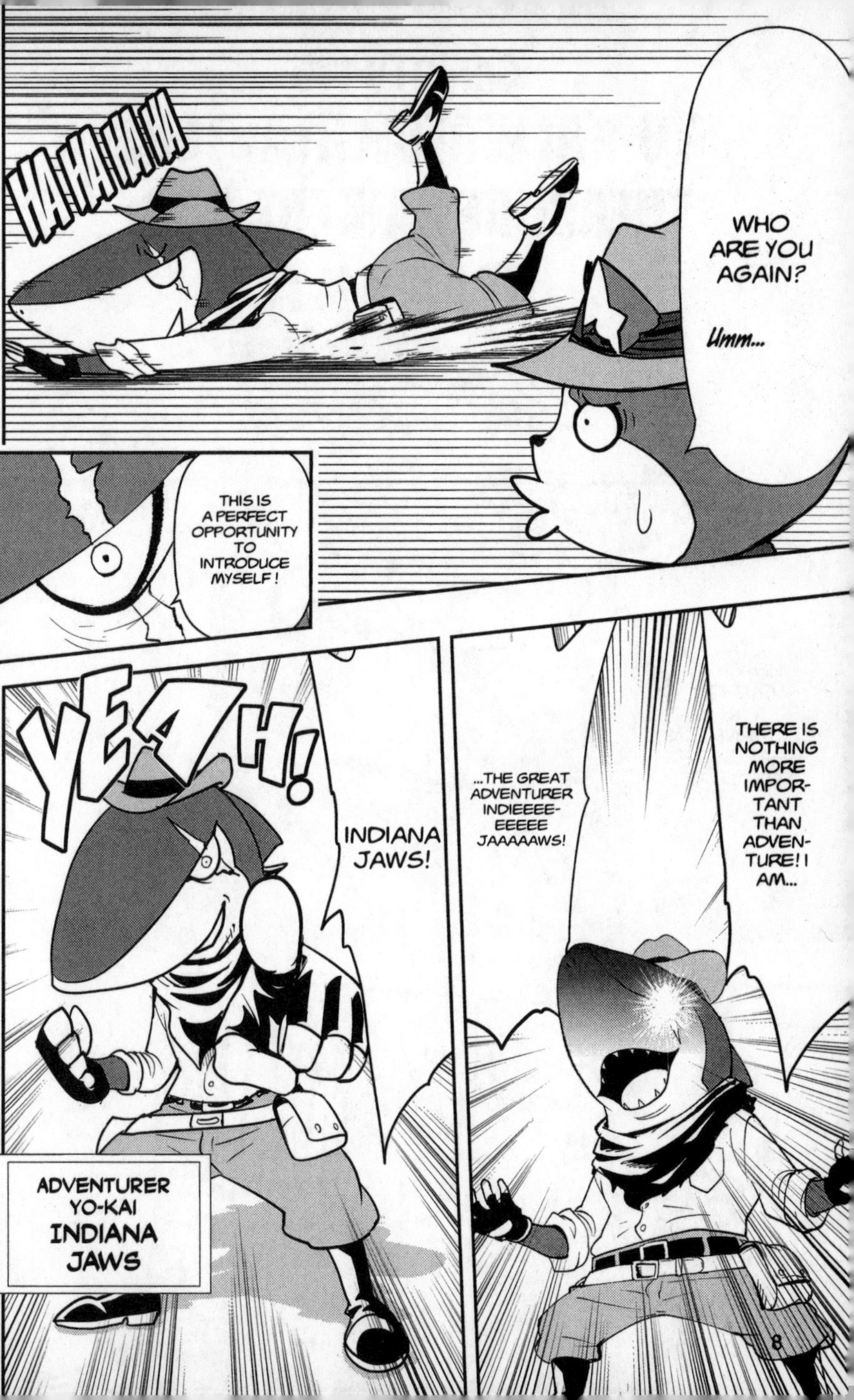
WHO ARE YOU AGAIN?
Umm...
HA HA HA HA
THIS IS A PERFECT OPPORTUNITY TO INTRODUCE MYSELF!
THERE IS NOTHING MORE IMPORTANT THAN ADVENTURE! I AM...
...THE GREAT ADVENTURER INDIEEEE-EEEEE JAAAAAWS!
INDIANA JAWS!
YEAH!
ADVENTURER YO-KAI INDIANA JAWS

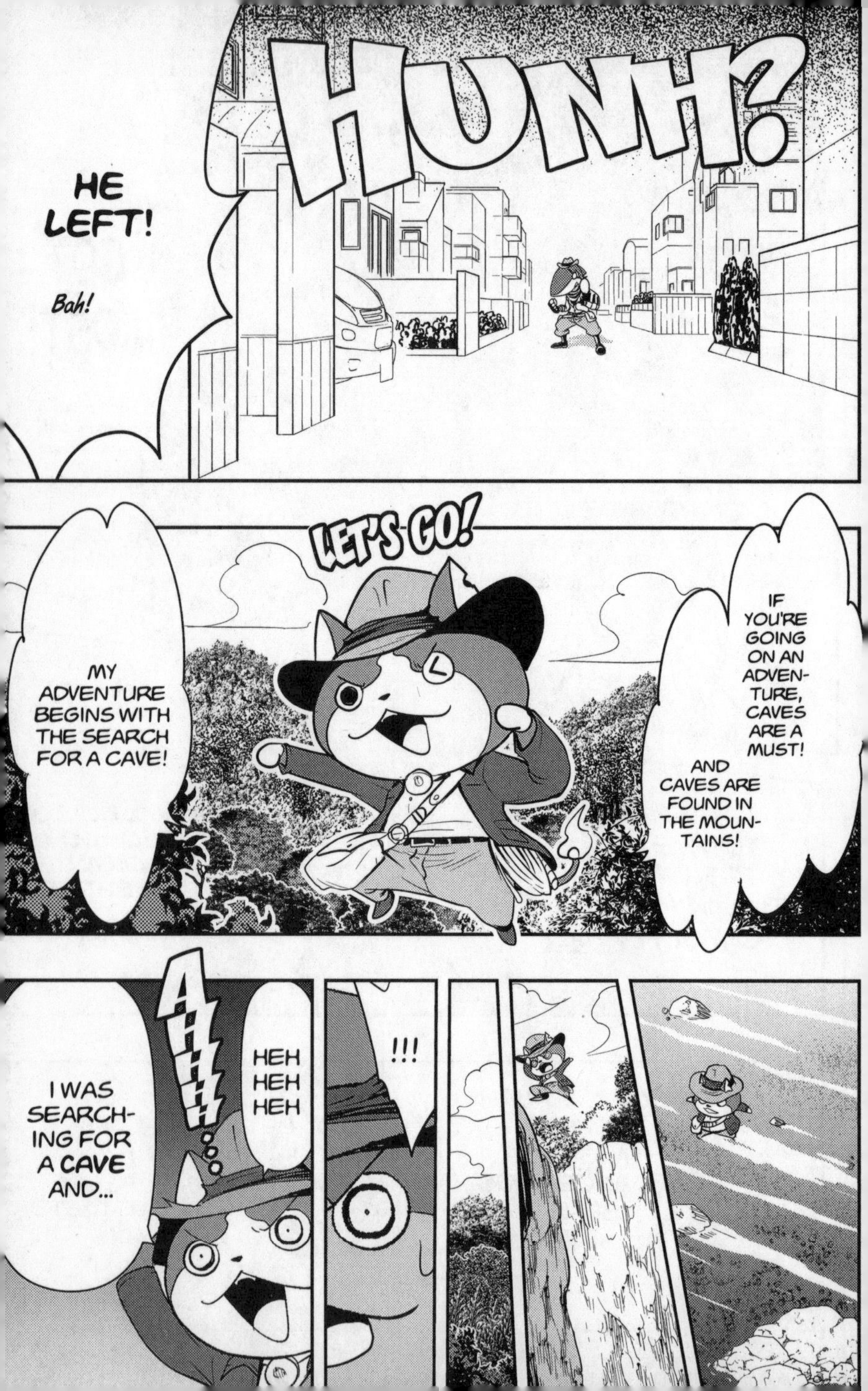
HUNH?
HE LEFT!
Bah!
IF YOU'RE GOING ON AN ADVENTURE, CAVES ARE A MUST!
AND CAVES ARE FOUND IN THE MOUNTAINS!
LET'S GO!
MY ADVENTURE BEGINS WITH THE SEARCH FOR A CAVE!
!!!
HEH HEH HEH
I WAS SEARCHING FOR A CAVE AND...

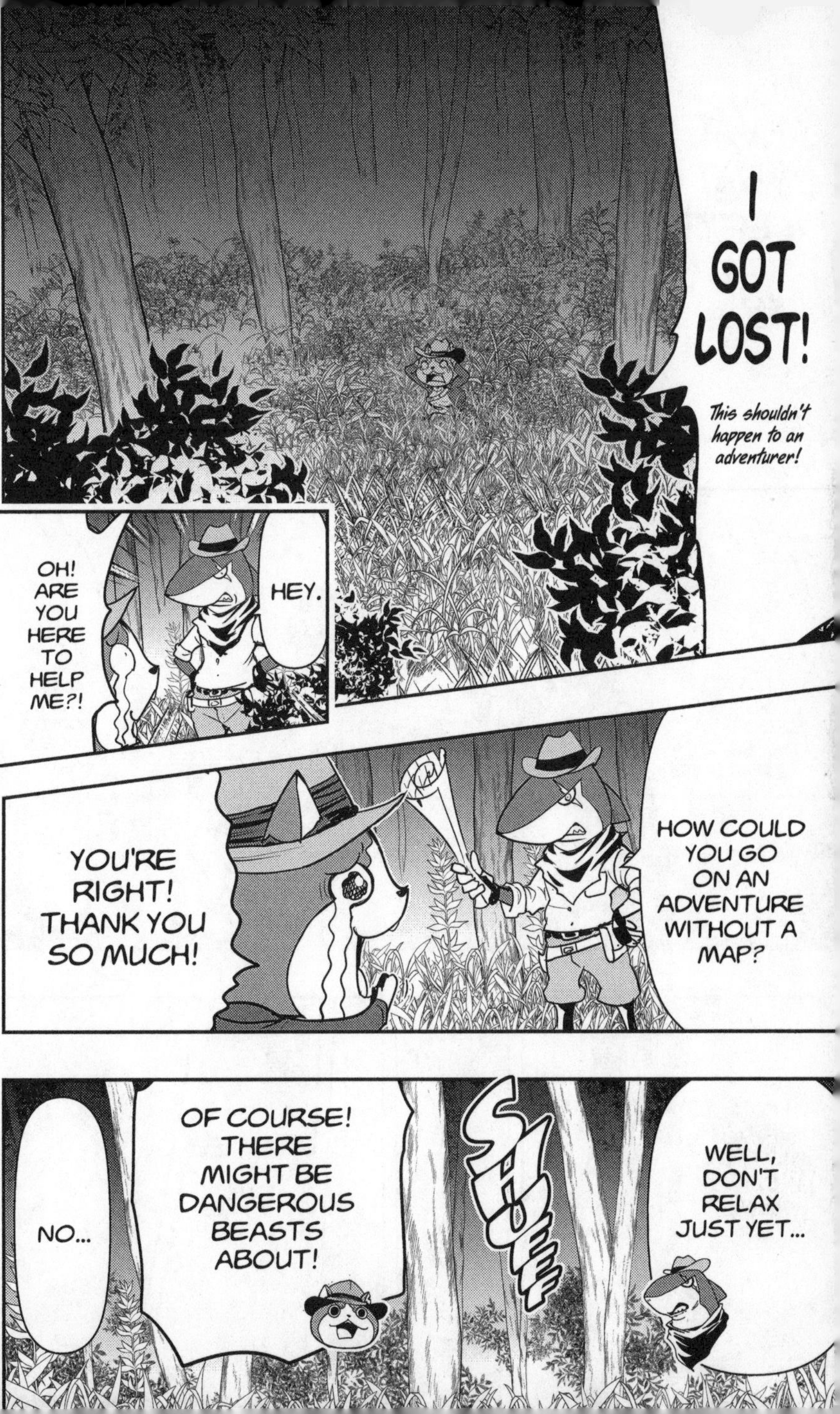
I GOT LOST!
This shouldn't happen to an adventurer!
HEY.
OH! ARE YOU HERE TO HELP ME?!
HOW COULD YOU GO ON AN ADVENTURE WITHOUT A MAP?
YOU'RE RIGHT! THANK YOU SO MUCH!
WELL, DON'T RELAX JUST YET...
OF COURSE! THERE MIGHT BE DANGEROUS BEASTS ABOUT!
NO...

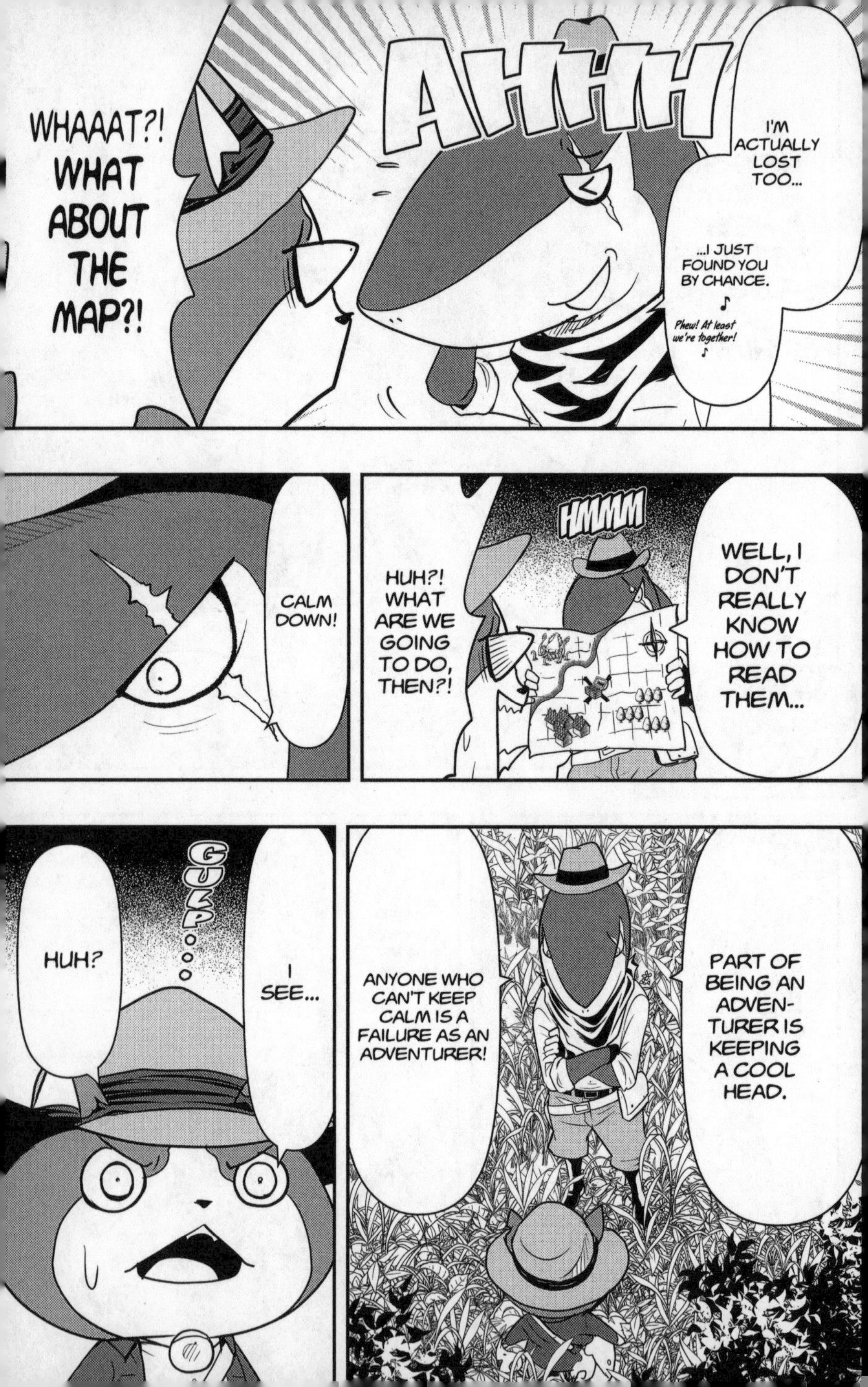
I'M ACTUALLY LOST TOO... ...I JUST FOUND YOU BY CHANCE. ♪
Phew! At least we're together! ♪
AHHHH
WHAAAT?! WHAT ABOUT THE MAP?!
HMMM
WELL, I DON'T REALLY KNOW HOW TO READ THEM...
HUH?! WHAT ARE WE GOING TO DO, THEN?!
CALM DOWN!
PART OF BEING AN ADVEN-TURER IS KEEPING A COOL HEAD.
ANYONE WHO CAN'T KEEP CALM IS A FAILURE AS AN ADVENTURER!
I SEE...
GULP...
HUH?

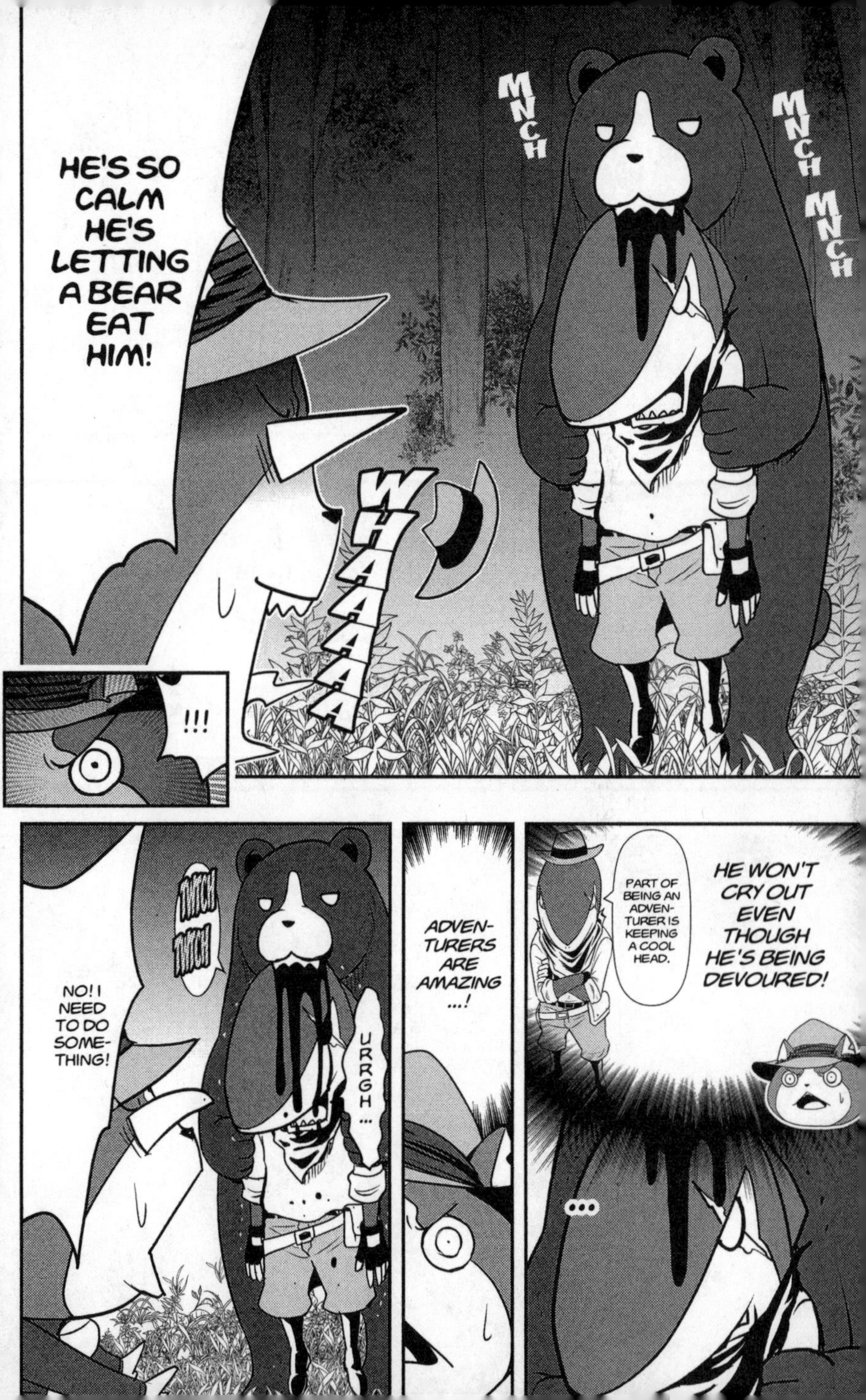
MNCH
MNCH MNCH
MNCH
HE'S SO CALM HE'S LETTING A BEAR EAT HIM!
WHAAAAAA
!!!
HE WON'T CRY OUT EVEN THOUGH HE'S BEING DEVOURED!
PART OF BEING AN ADVEN-TURER IS KEEPING A COOL HEAD.
...
ADVEN-TURERS ARE AMAZING ...!
TWITCH TWITCH
URRGH ...
NO! I NEED TO DO SOME-THING!

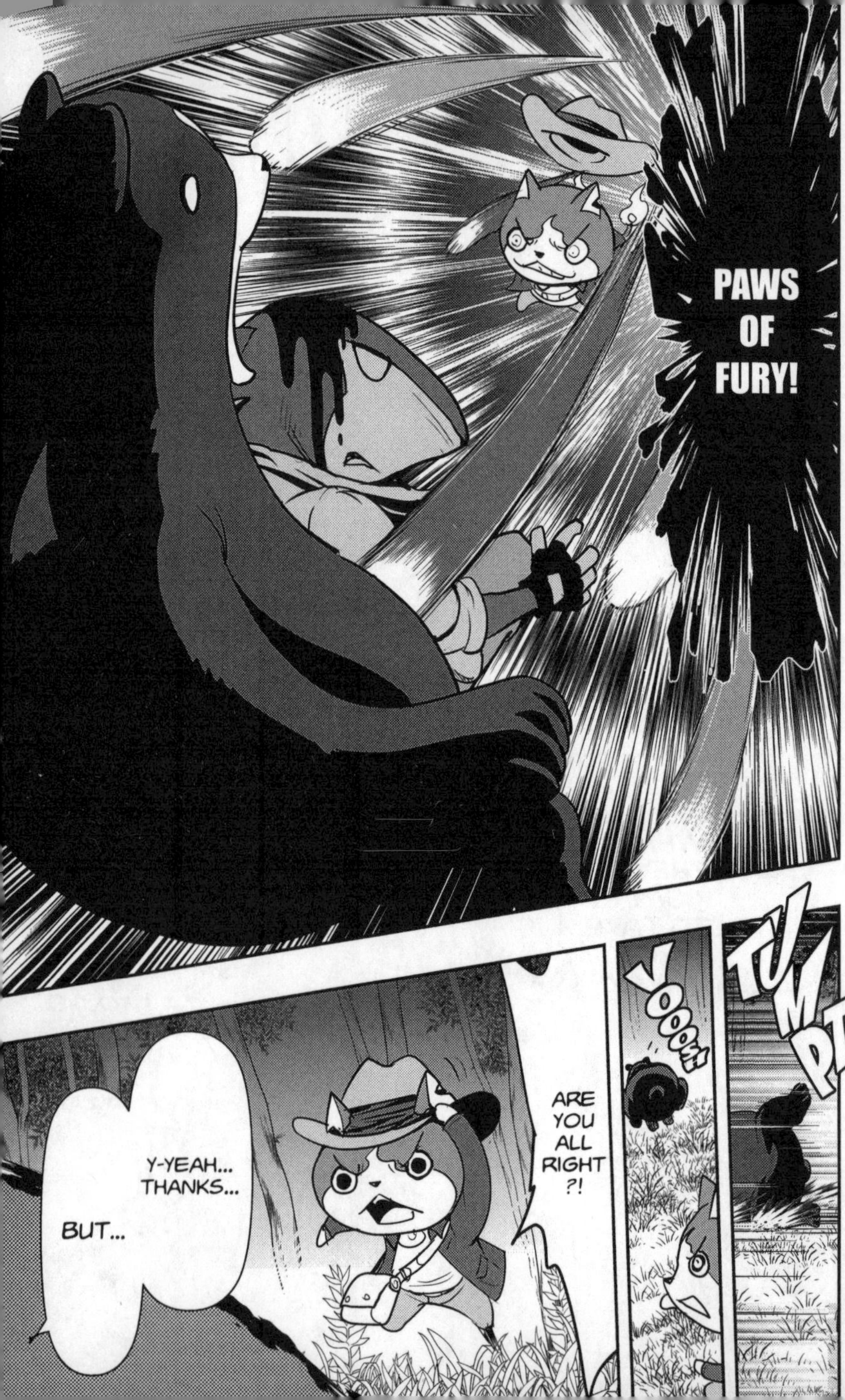
PAWS OF FURY!
TUMPT
VOOOM!
ARE YOU ALL RIGHT ?!
Y-YEAH... THANKS...
BUT...

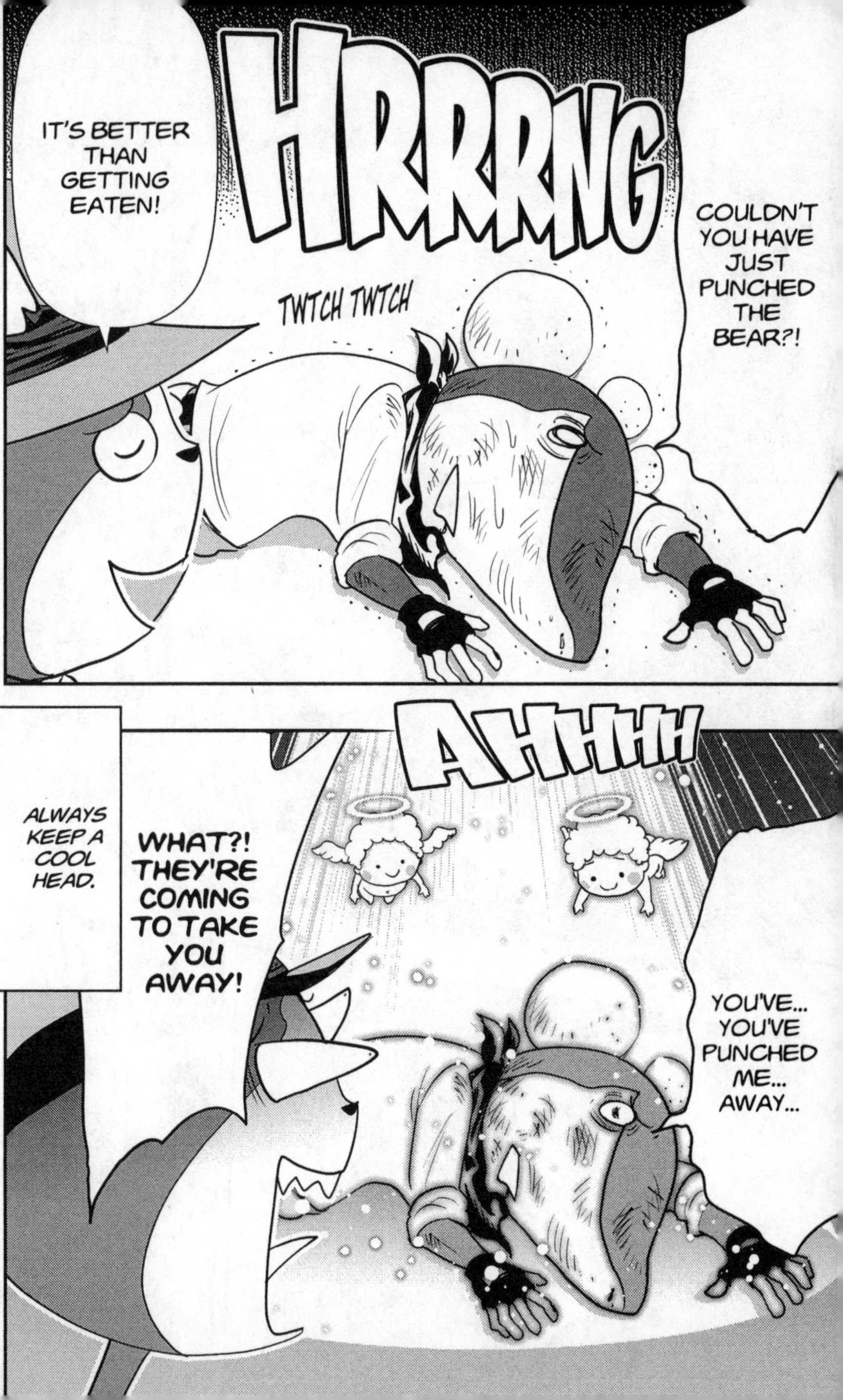
COULDN'T YOU HAVE JUST PUNCHED THE BEAR?!
HRRRNG
TWTCH TWTCH
IT'S BETTER THAN GETTING EATEN!
AHHHHH
YOU'VE... YOU'VE PUNCHED ME... AWAY...
WHAT?! THEY'RE COMING TO TAKE YOU AWAY!
ALWAYS KEEP A COOL HEAD.

CHAPTER 136
YO-KAI WATCH BLASTERS TREASURE RAIDERS ARC: INDIANA JAWS

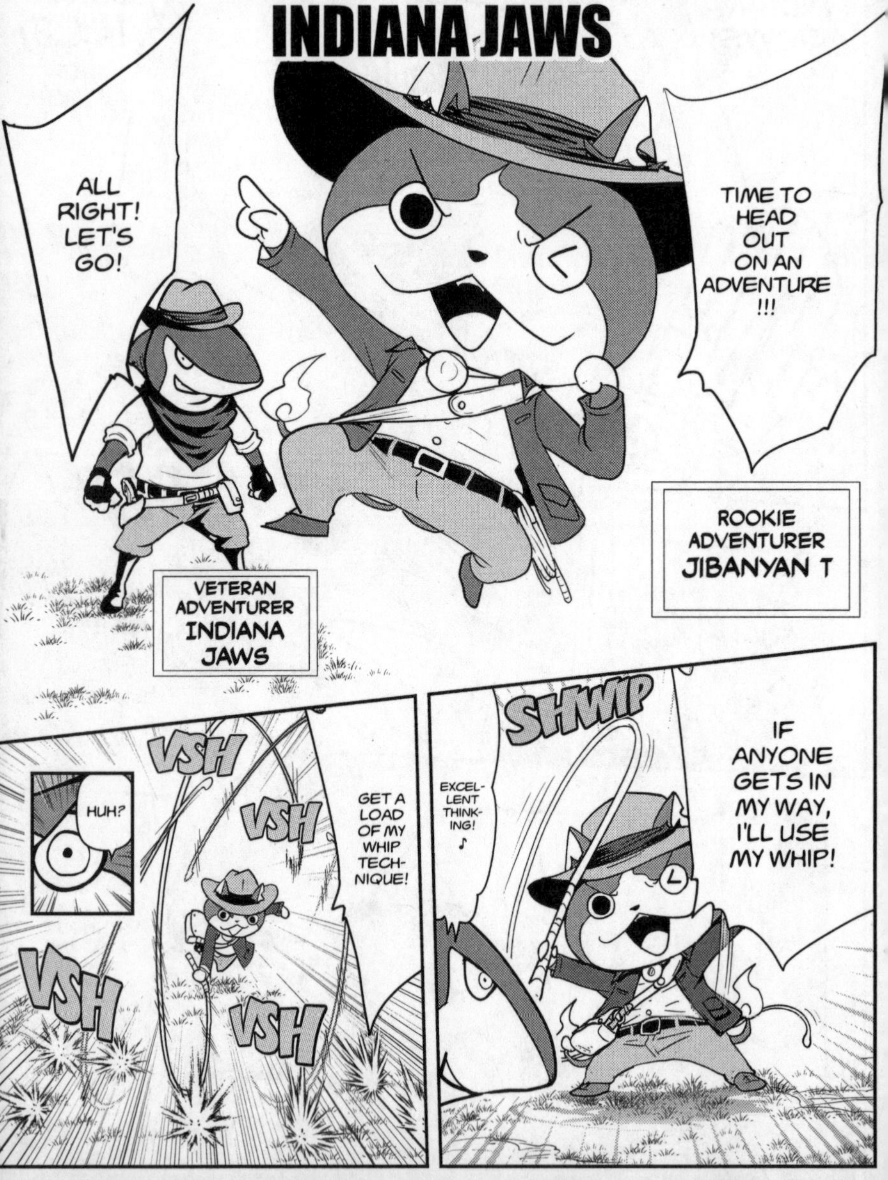
TIME TO HEAD OUT ON AN ADVENTURE!!!
ALL RIGHT! LET'S GO!
ROOKIE ADVENTURER JIBANYAN T
VETERAN ADVENTURER INDIANA JAWS
SHWIP
IF ANYONE GETS IN MY WAY, I'LL USE MY WHIP!
EXCEL-LENT THINK-ING! ♪
GET A LOAD OF MY WHIP TECH-NIQUE!
VSH
VSH
VSH
VSH
HUH?

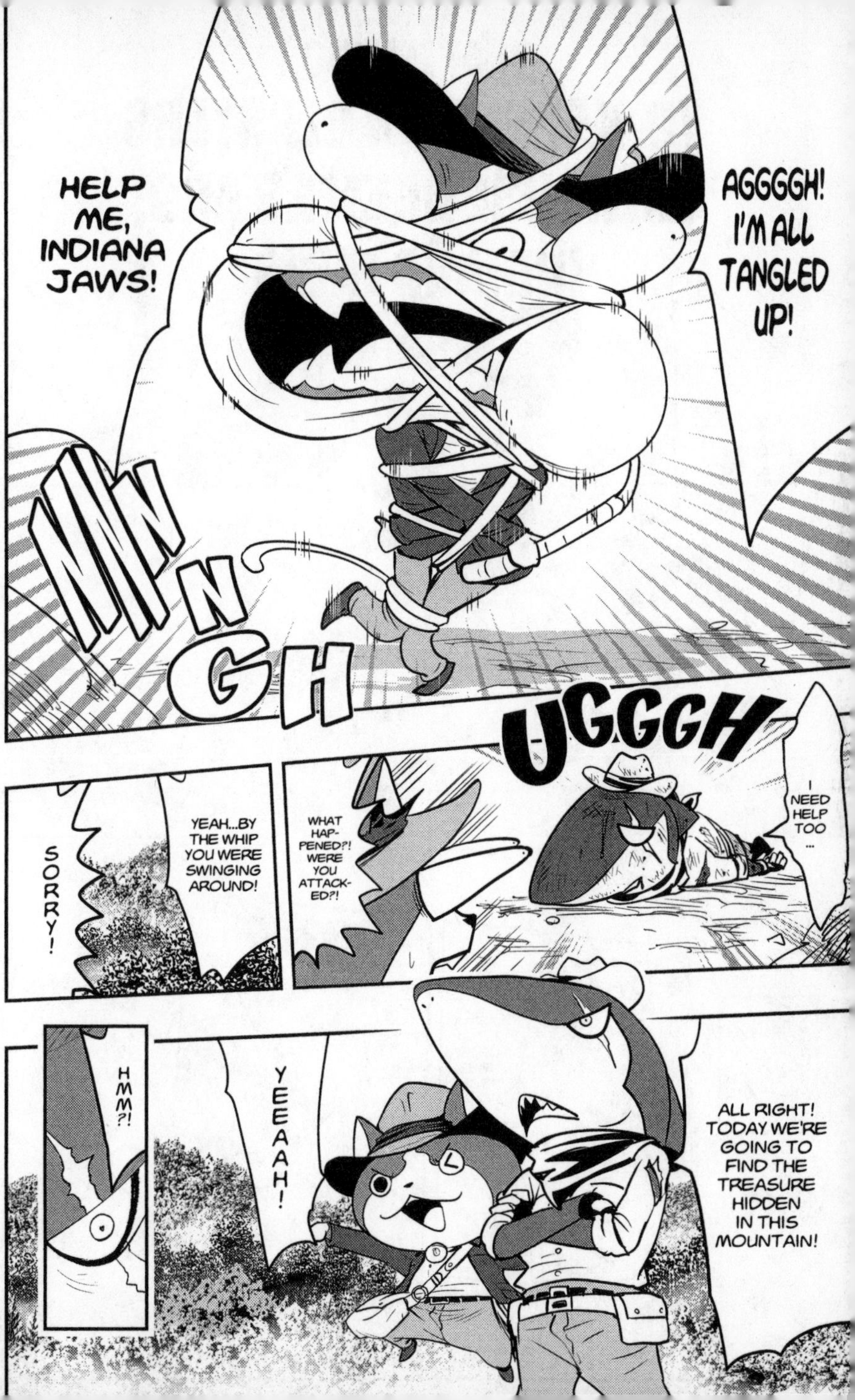
AGGGGH! I'M ALL TANGLED UP!
HELP ME, INDIANA JAWS!
NNNNGH
UGGGH
I NEED HELP TOO ...
WHAT HAP-PENED?! WERE YOU ATTACK-ED?!
YEAH...BY THE WHIP YOU WERE SWINGING AROUND!
SORRY!
ALL RIGHT! TODAY WE'RE GOING TO FIND THE TREASURE HIDDEN IN THIS MOUNTAIN!
YEEAAH!
HMM?!

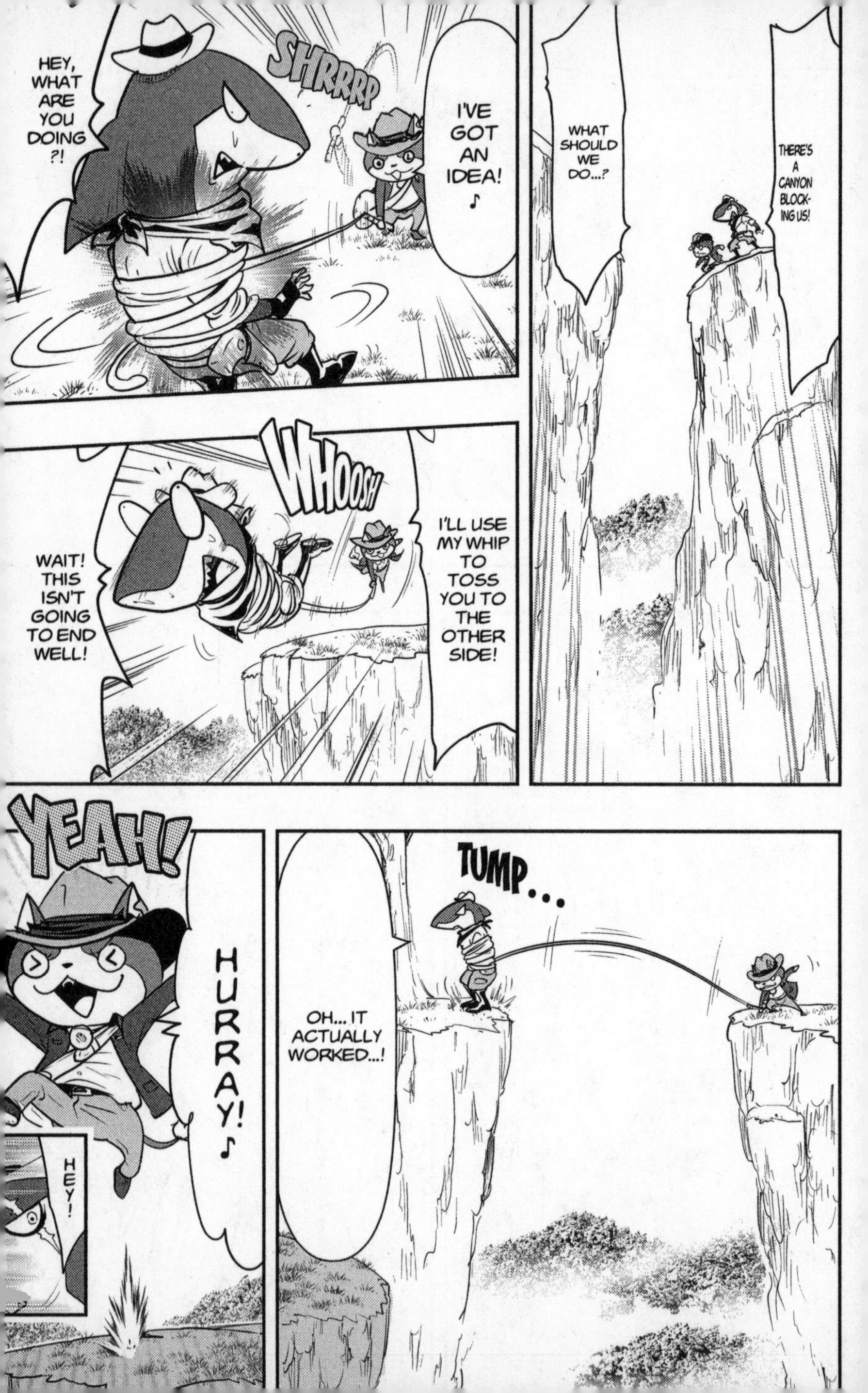
THERE'S A CANYON BLOCKING US!
WHAT SHOULD WE DO...?
SHRRRRP
I'VE GOT AN IDEA! ♪
HEY, WHAT ARE YOU DOING?!
WHOOSH
I'LL USE MY WHIP TO TOSS YOU TO THE OTHER SIDE!
WAIT! THIS ISN'T GOING TO END WELL!
TUMP...
OH... IT ACTUALLY WORKED...!
YEAH!
HURRAY! ♪
HEY!

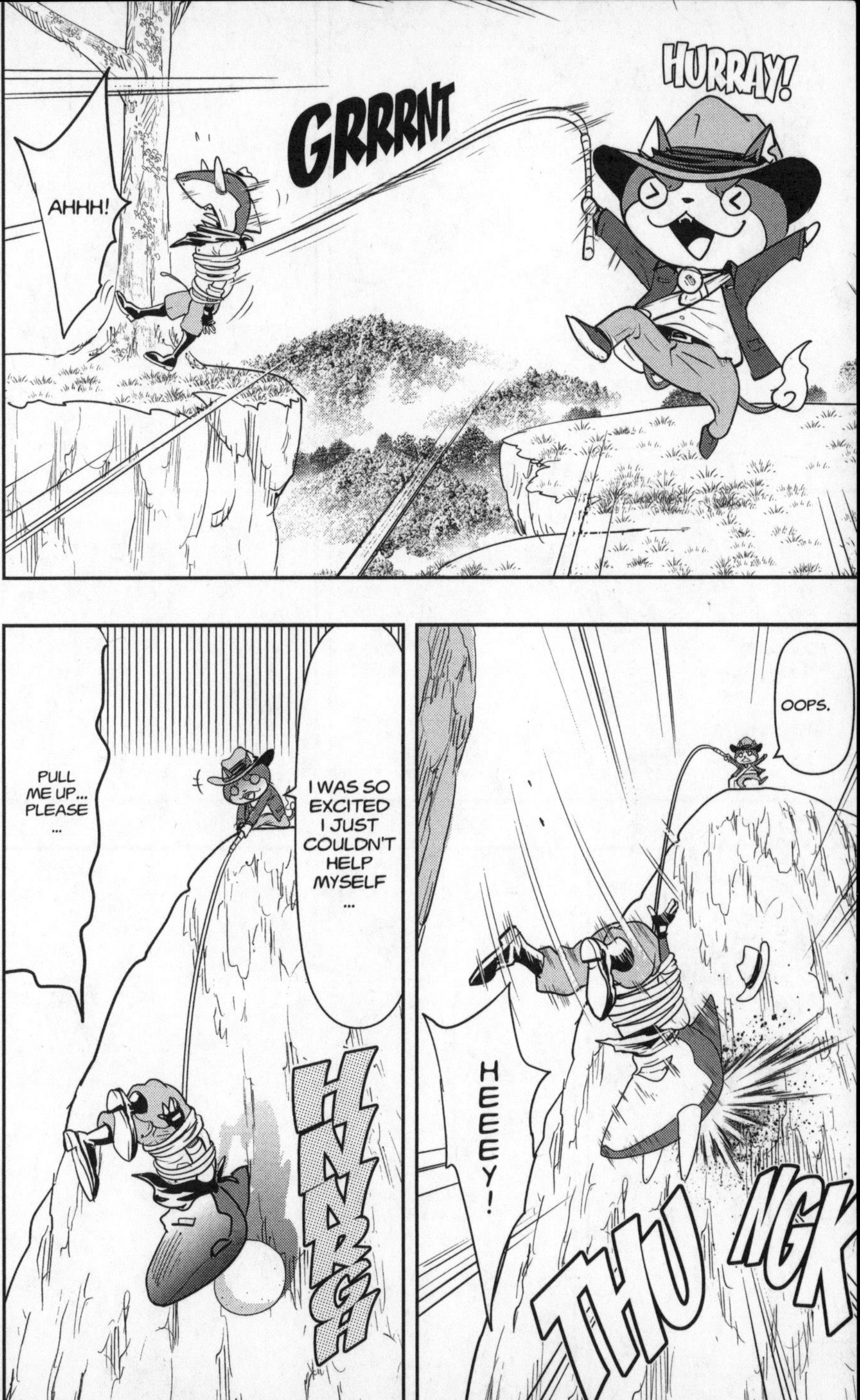

HURRAY!
GRRRNT
AHHH!
OOPS.
HEEEEY!
THUNGK
I WAS SO EXCITED I JUST COULDN'T HELP MYSELF ...
PULL ME UP... PLEASE ...

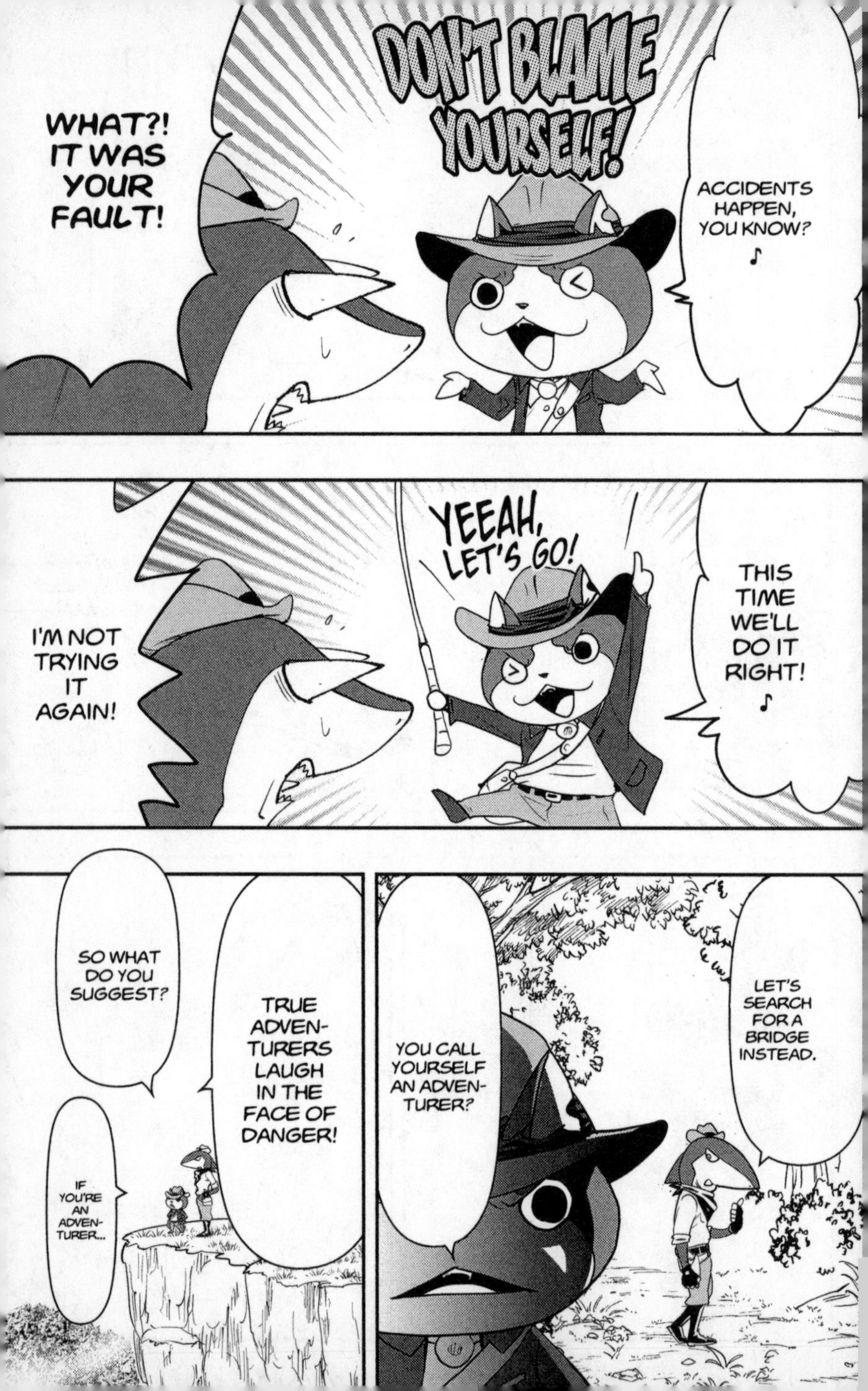
ACCIDENTS HAPPEN, YOU KNOW? ♪
DON'T BLAME YOURSELF!
WHAT?! IT WAS YOUR FAULT!
THIS TIME WE'LL DO IT RIGHT! ♪
YEEAH, LET'S GO!
I'M NOT TRYING IT AGAIN!
LET'S SEARCH FOR A BRIDGE INSTEAD.
YOU CALL YOURSELF AN ADVEN-TURER?
TRUE ADVEN-TURERS LAUGH IN THE FACE OF DANGER!
SO WHAT DO YOU SUGGEST?
IF YOU'RE AN ADVEN-TURER...

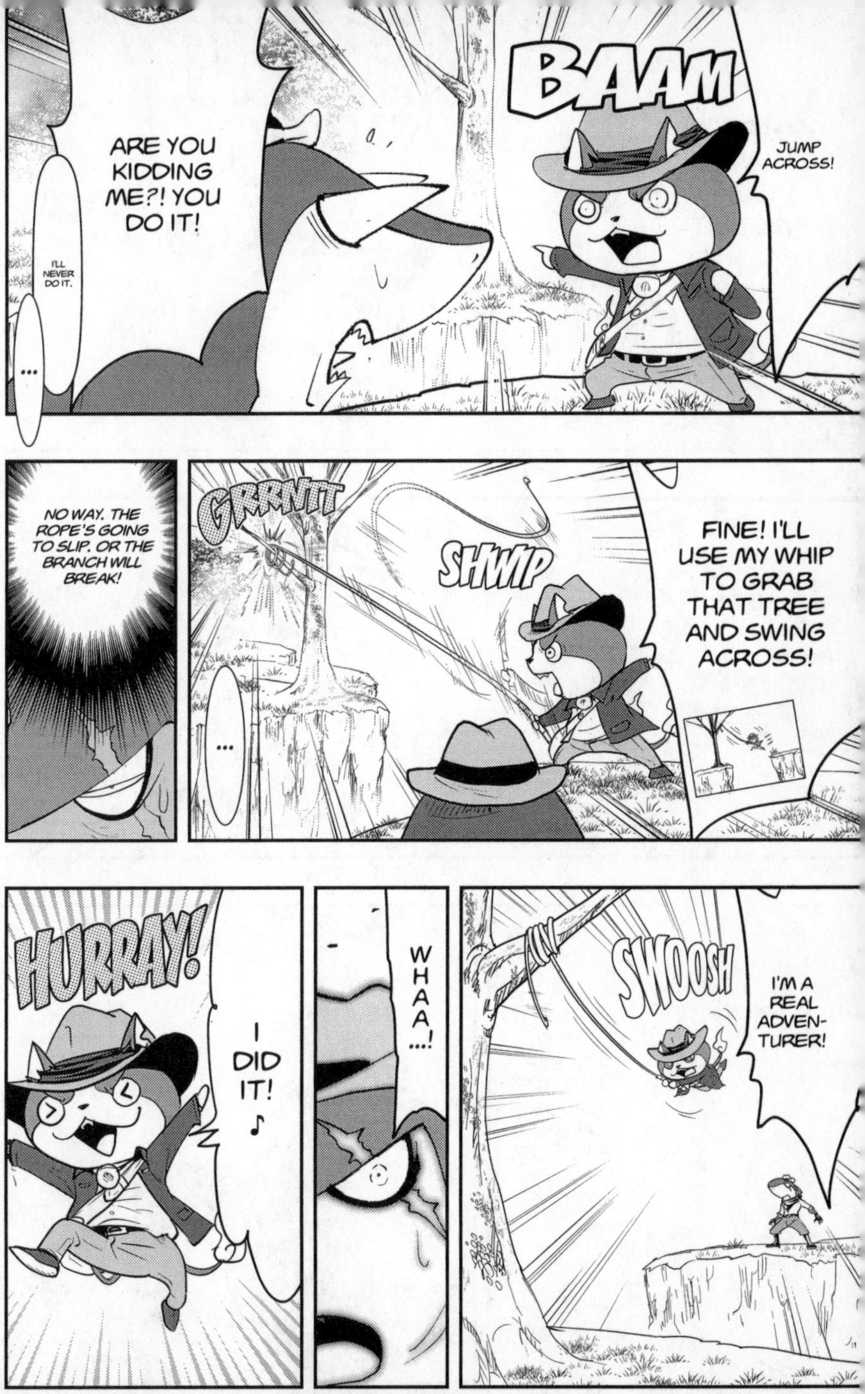
BAAM
JUMP ACROSS!
ARE YOU KIDDING ME?! YOU DO IT!
I'LL NEVER DO IT.
...
GRRNTT
SHWIP
FINE! I'LL USE MY WHIP TO GRAB THAT TREE AND SWING ACROSS!
...
NO WAY. THE ROPE'S GOING TO SLIP. OR THE BRANCH WILL BREAK!
SWOOSH
I'M A REAL ADVEN-TURER!
WHAA...!
HURRAY!
I DID IT! ♪

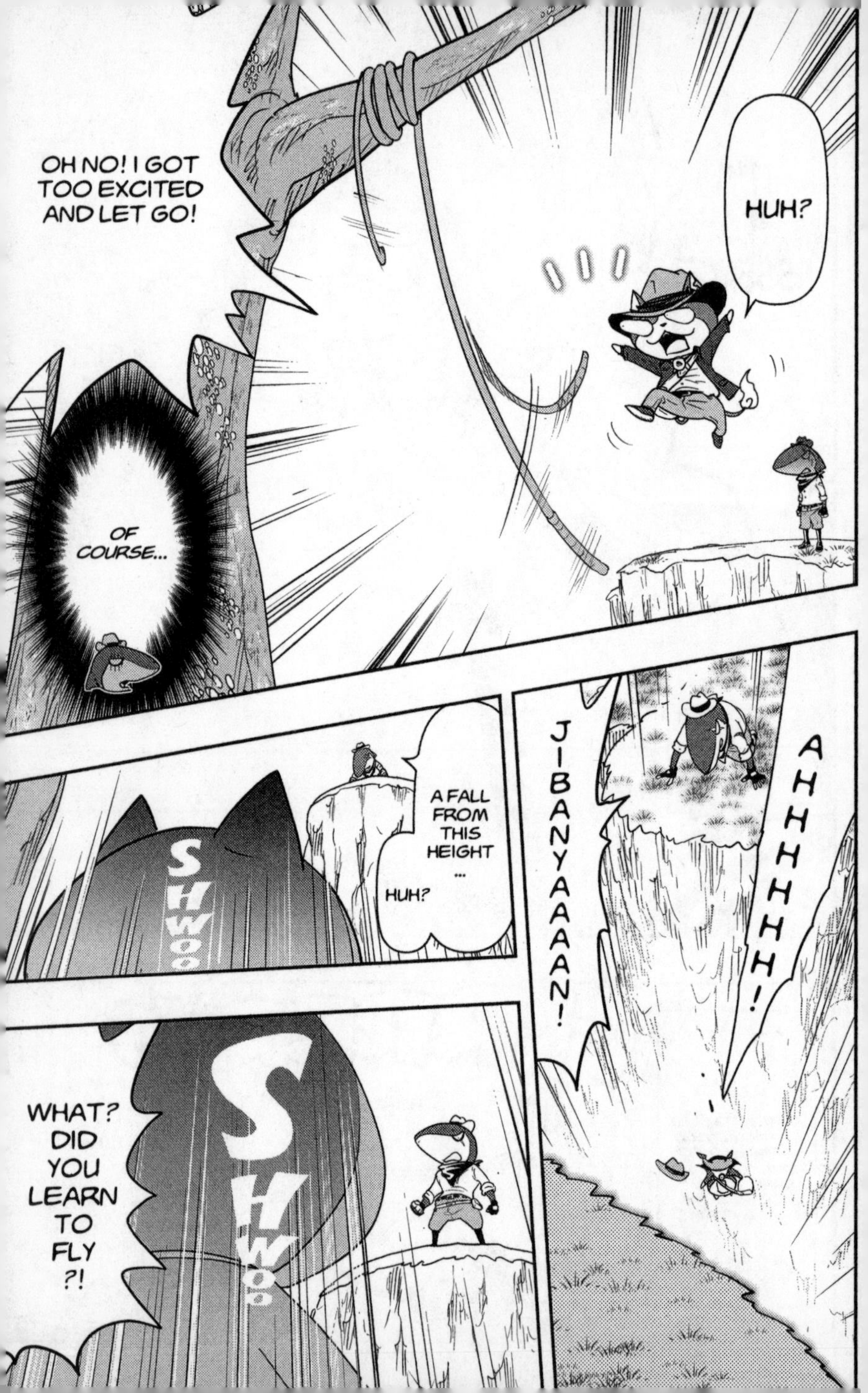
HUH?
OH NO! I GOT TOO EXCITED AND LET GO!
OF COURSE...
AHHHHHHH!
JIBANYAAAAAN!
A FALL FROM THIS HEIGHT ...
HUH?
SHWOO
SHWOO
WHAT? DID YOU LEARN TO FLY ?!

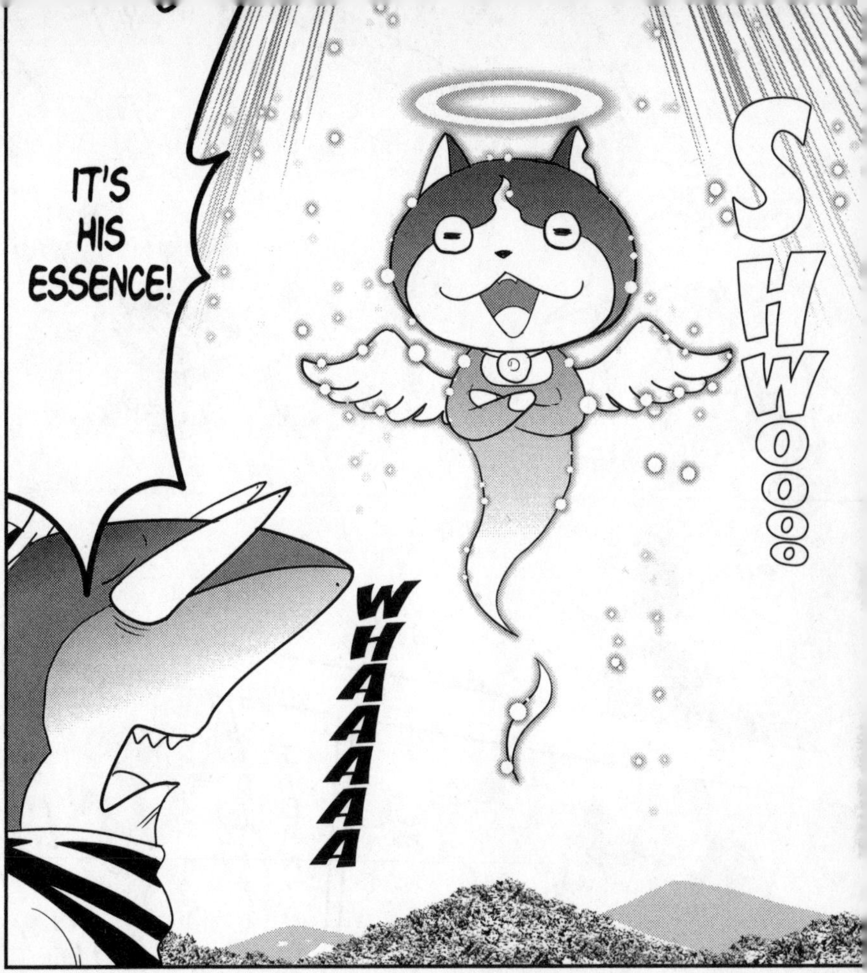
SHWOOOO
IT'S HIS ESSENCE!
WHAAAAAA
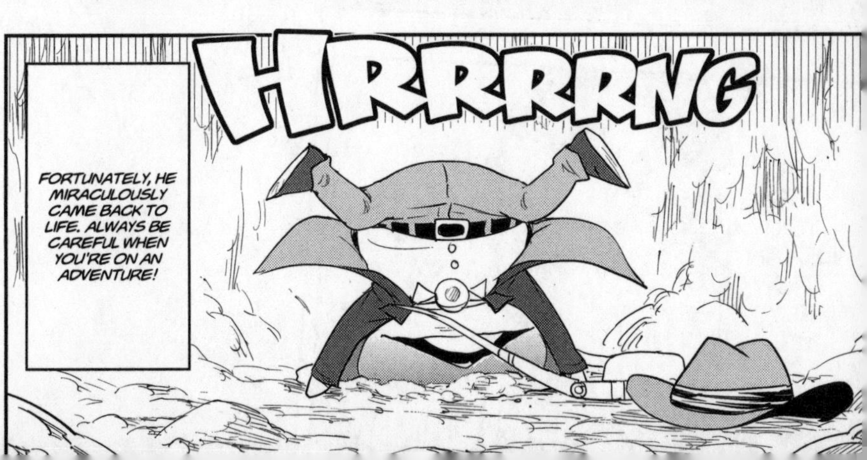
HRRRRRNG
FORTUNATELY, HE MIRACULOUSLY CAME BACK TO LIFE. ALWAYS BE CAREFUL WHEN YOU'RE ON AN ADVENTURE!

CHAPTER 137
YO-KAI WATCH BLASTERS TREASURE RAIDERS ARC: KOMASAN T AND SHOVULCAN

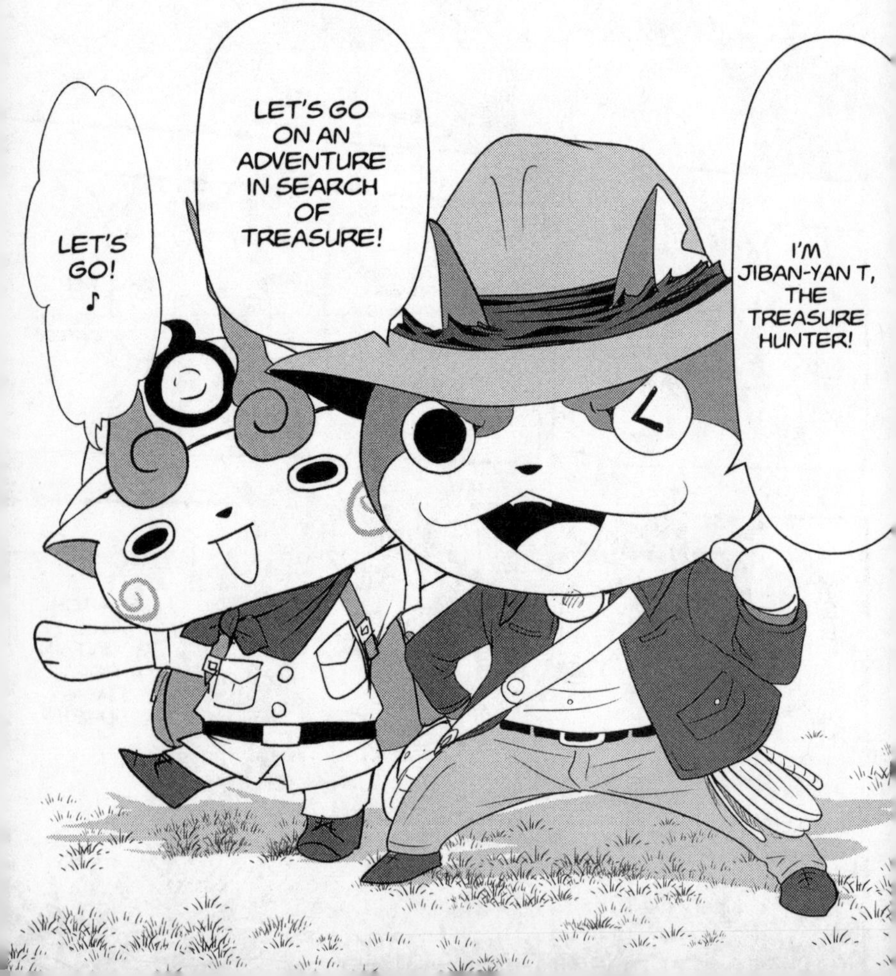
I'M JIBAN-YAN T, THE TREASURE HUNTER!
LET'S GO ON AN ADVENTURE IN SEARCH OF TREASURE!
LET'S GO! ♪

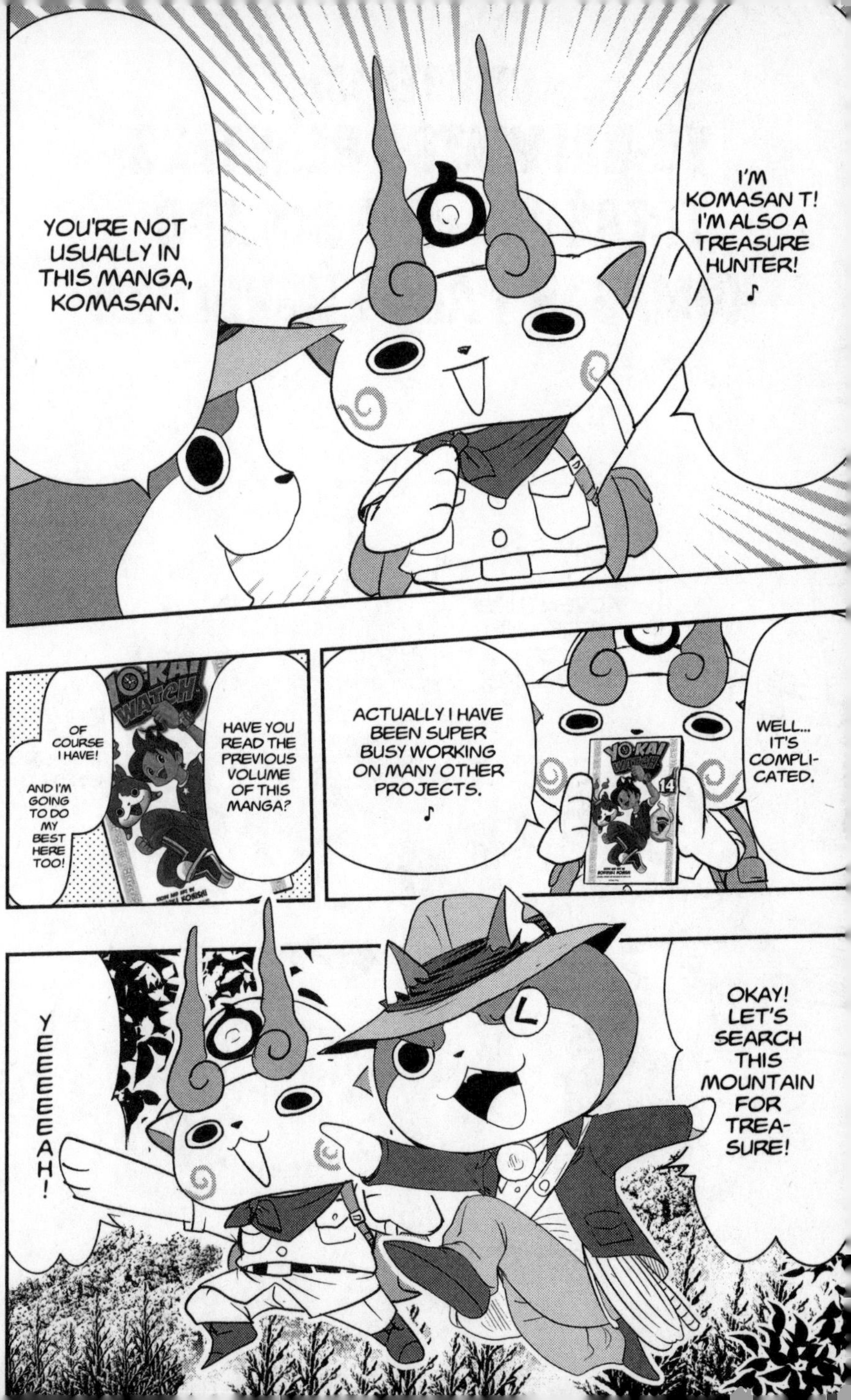
I'M KOMASAN T! I'M ALSO A TREASURE HUNTER! ♪
YOU'RE NOT USUALLY IN THIS MANGA, KOMASAN.
WELL... IT'S COMPLICATED.
YO-KAI WATCH 14
ACTUALLY I HAVE BEEN SUPER BUSY WORKING ON MANY OTHER PROJECTS. ♪
HAVE YOU READ THE PREVIOUS VOLUME OF THIS MANGA?
YO-KAI WATCH
OF COURSE I HAVE!
AND I'M GOING TO DO MY BEST HERE TOO!
OKAY! LET'S SEARCH THIS MOUNTAIN FOR TREASURE!
YEEEEEAH!

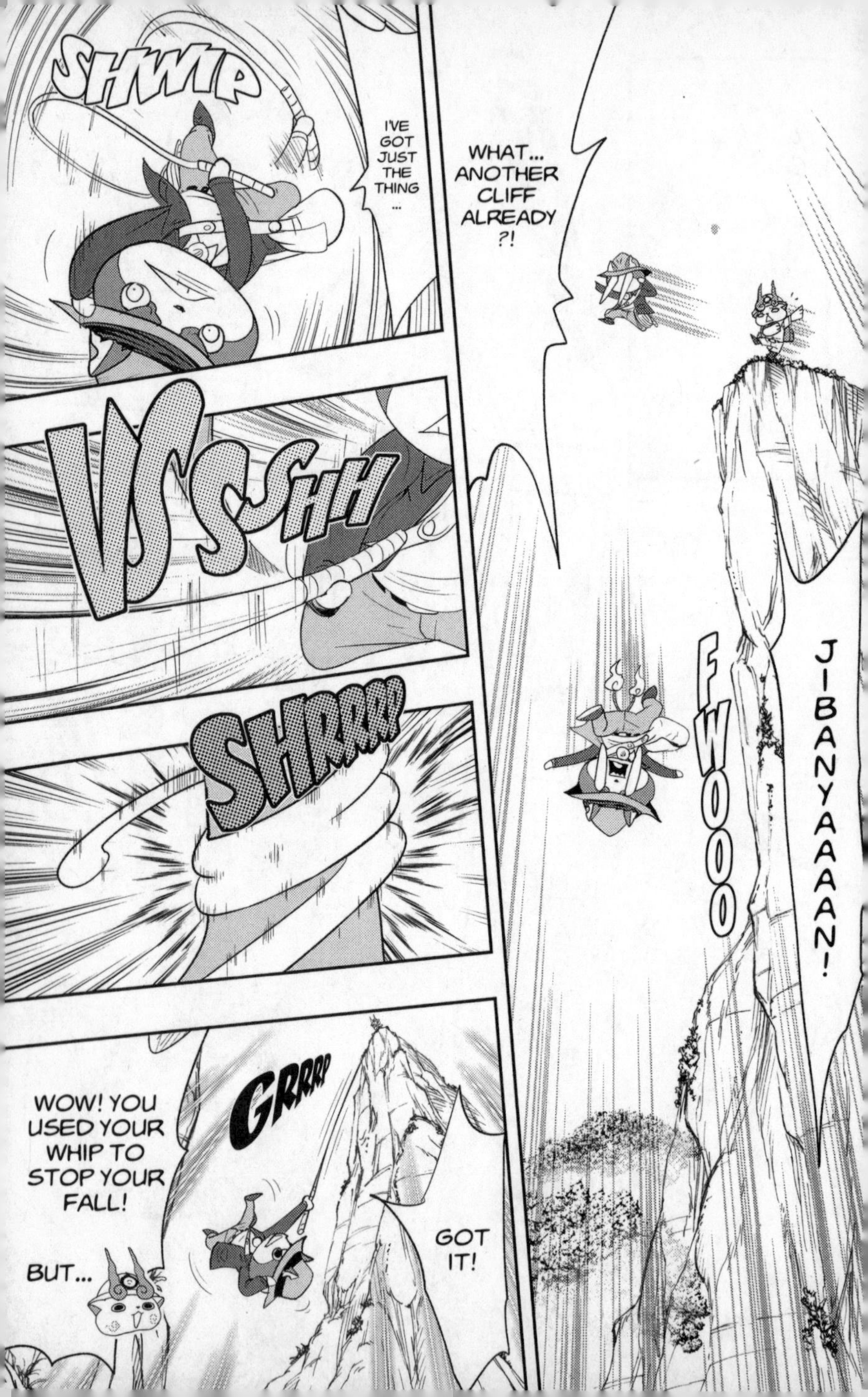
WHAT... ANOTHER CLIFF ALREADY ?!
JIBANYAAAAAN!
FWOOO
I'VE GOT JUST THE THING ...
SHWIP
VSSHH
SHRRRP
GOT IT!
GRRRP
WOW! YOU USED YOUR WHIP TO STOP YOUR FALL!
BUT...

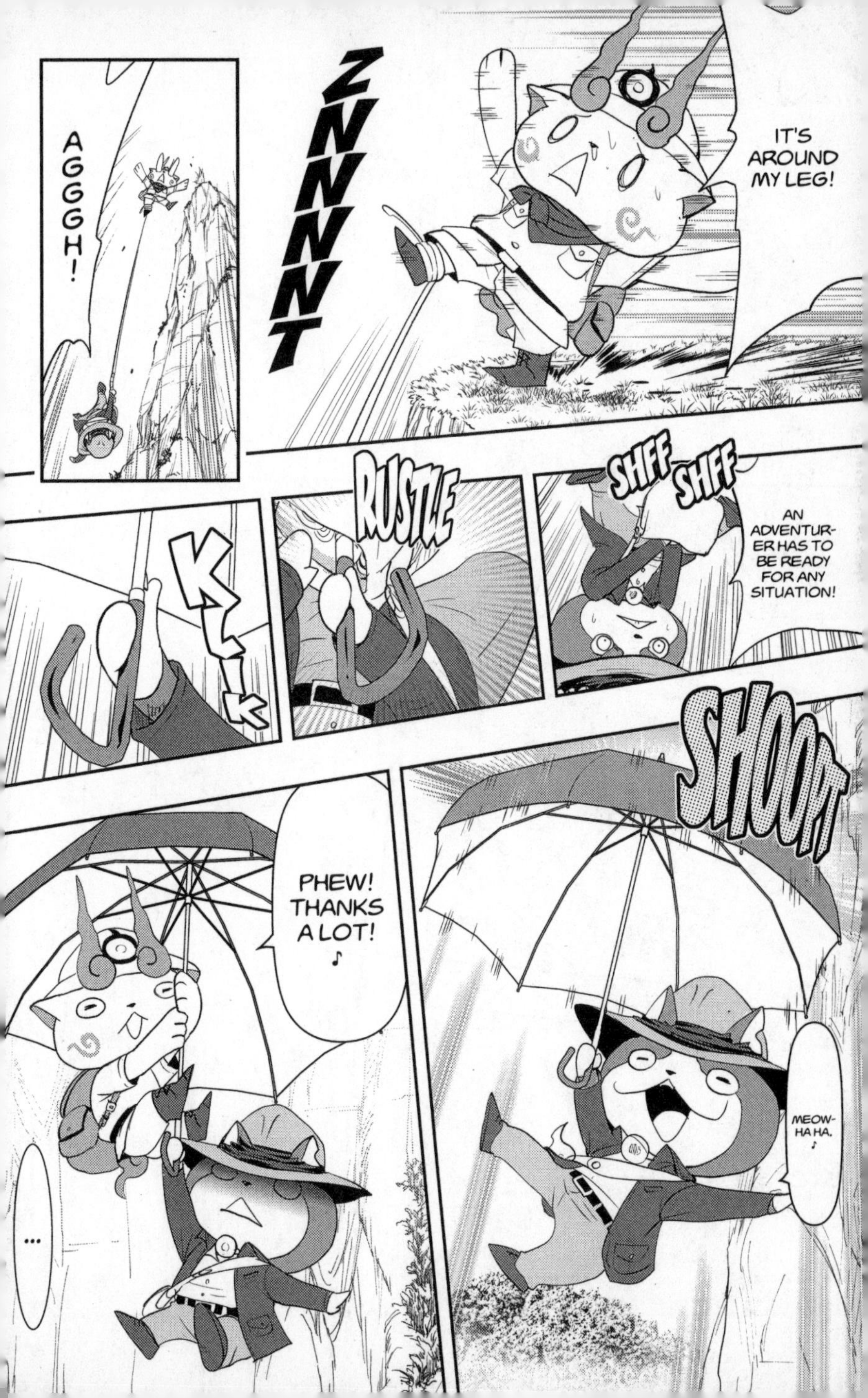
IT'S AROUND MY LEG!
ZNNNNT
AGGGH!
SHFF SHFF
AN ADVENTURER HAS TO BE READY FOR ANY SITUATION!
RUSTLE
KLIK
SHOOPT
MEOW-HA HA. ♪
PHEW! THANKS A LOT! ♪
...

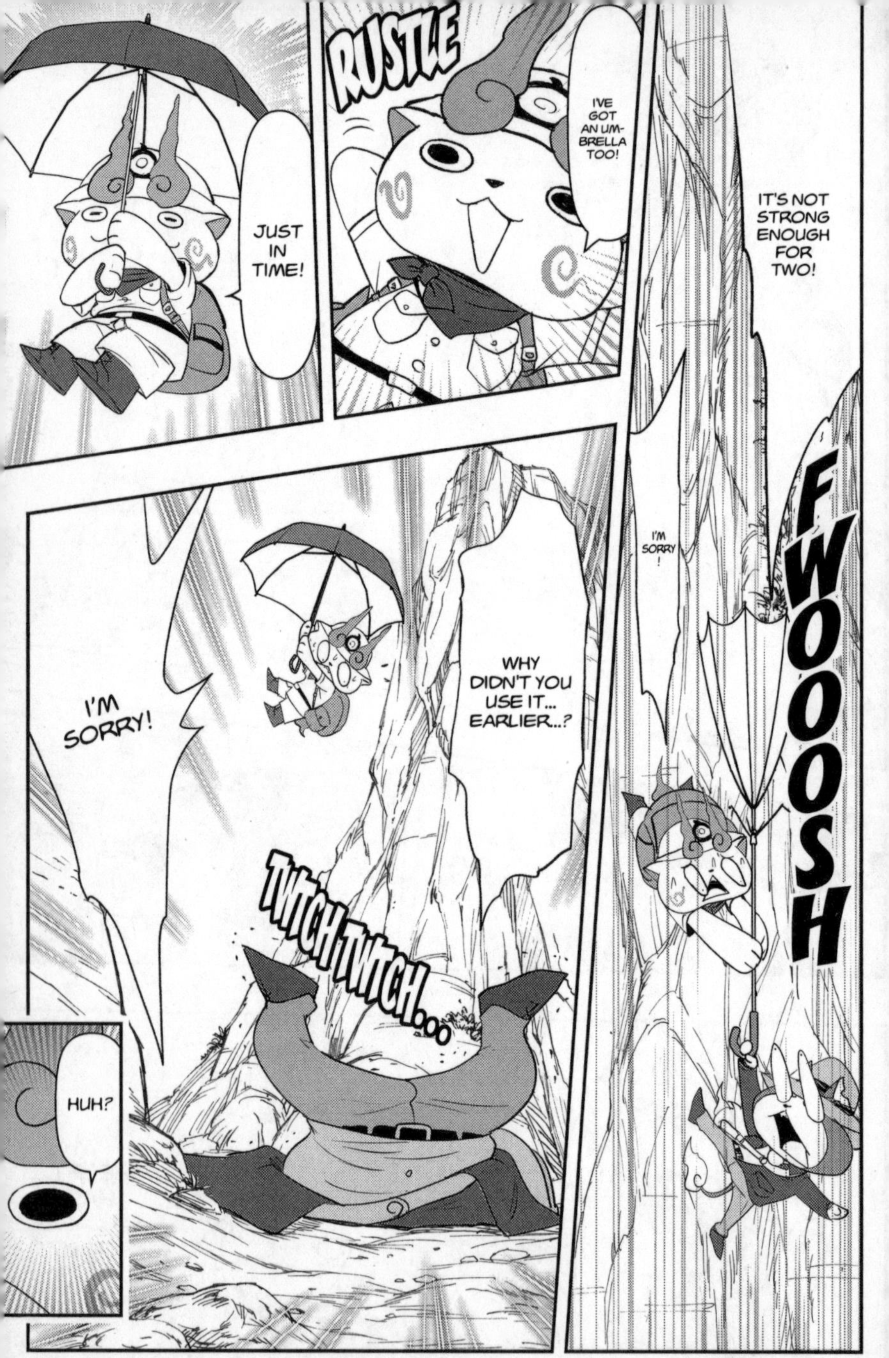
JUST IN TIME!
RUSTLE
I'VE GOT AN UM-BRELLA TOO!
IT'S NOT STRONG ENOUGH FOR TWO!
FWOOOSH
I'M SORRY!
I'M SORRY!
WHY DIDN'T YOU USE IT... EARLIER...?
TWITCH TWITCH...
HUH?

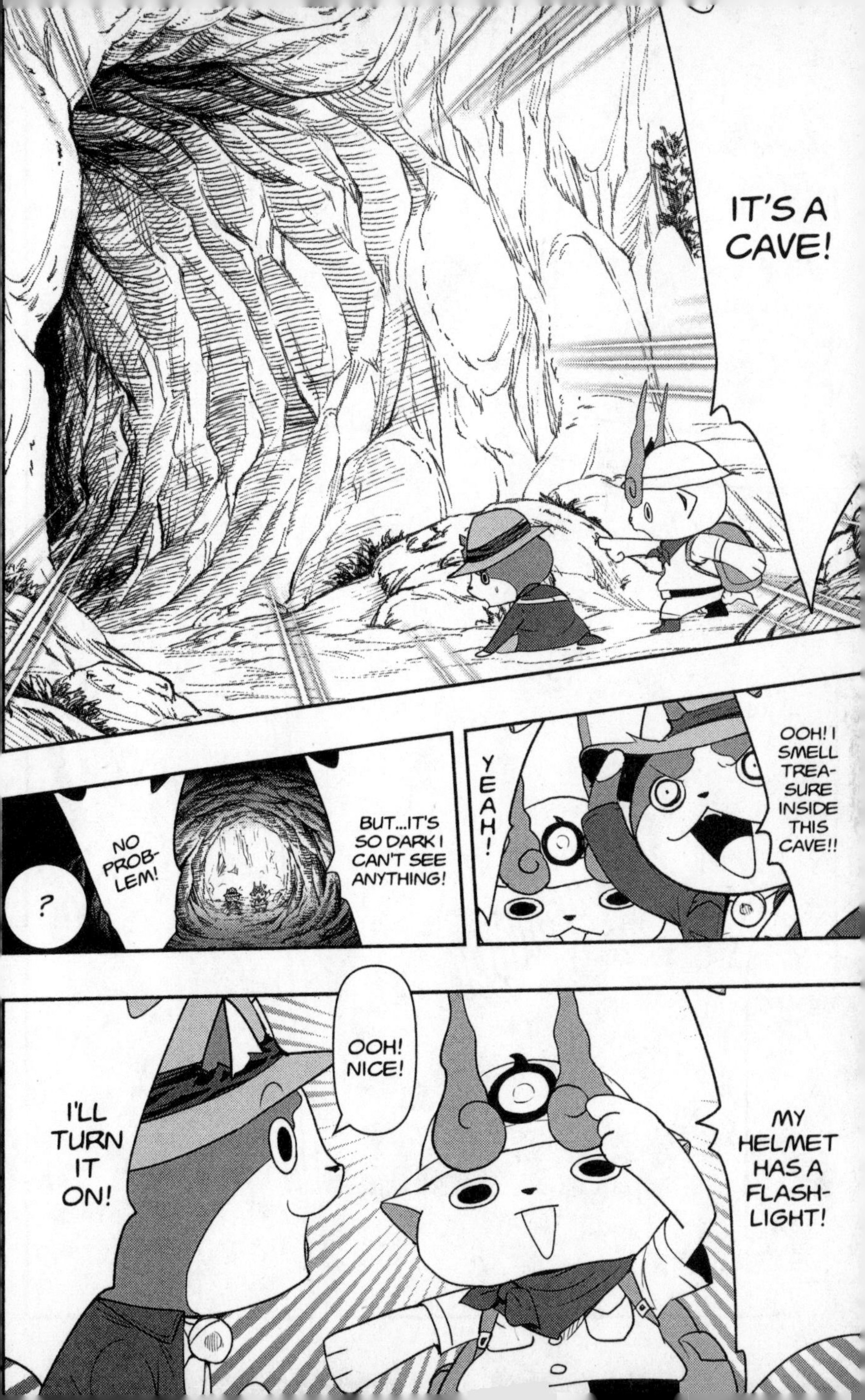
IT'S A CAVE!
OOH! I SMELL TREA-SURE INSIDE THIS CAVE!!
YEAH!
BUT...IT'S SO DARK I CAN'T SEE ANYTHING!
NO PROB-LEM!
?
MY HELMET HAS A FLASH-LIGHT!
OOH! NICE!
I'LL TURN IT ON!

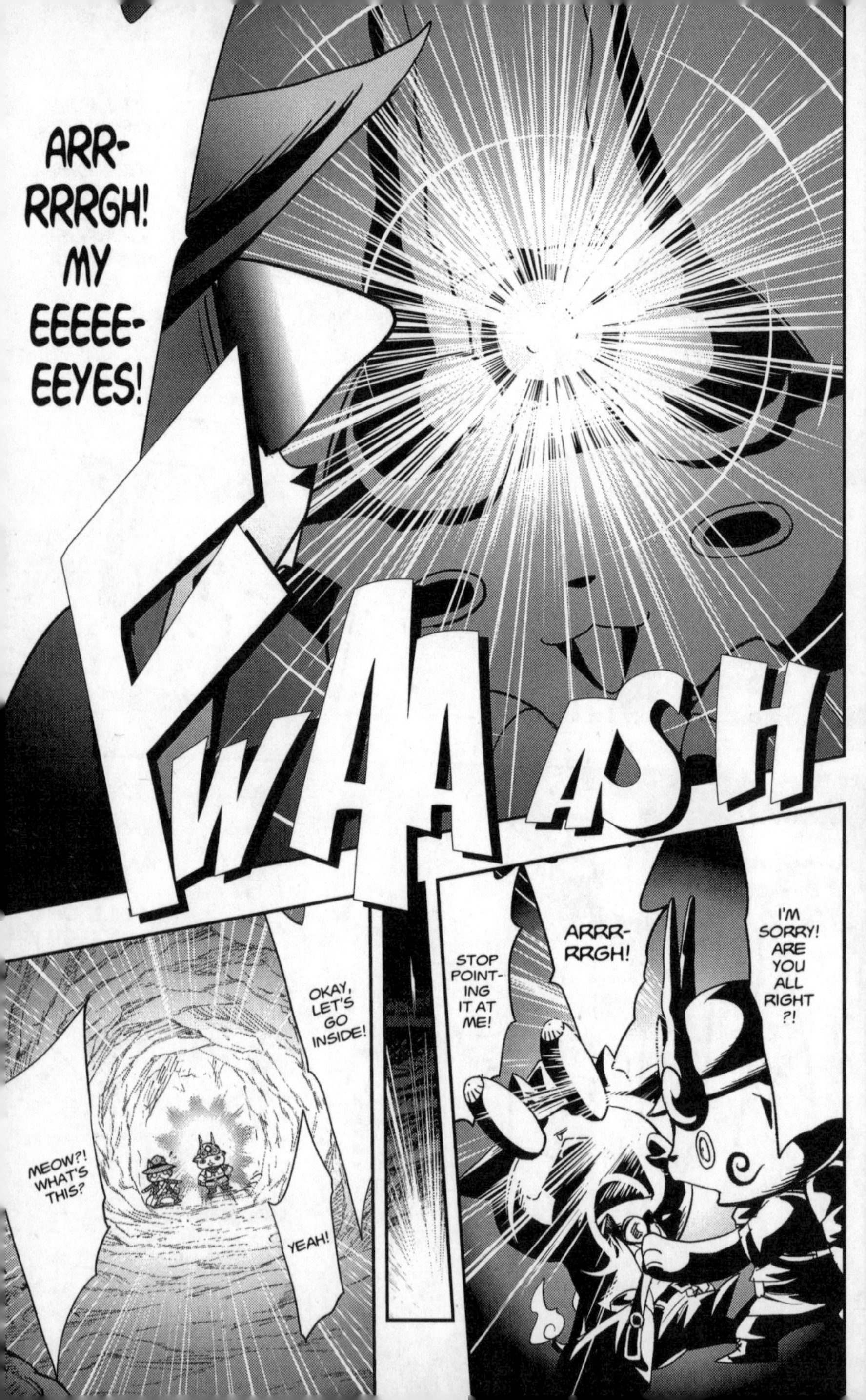
ARR-RRRGH! MY EEEEEE-EEYES!
WAASH
I'M SORRY! ARE YOU ALL RIGHT?!
ARRR-RRGH!
STOP POINT-ING IT AT ME!
OKAY, LET'S GO INSIDE!
YEAH!
MEOW?! WHAT'S THIS?

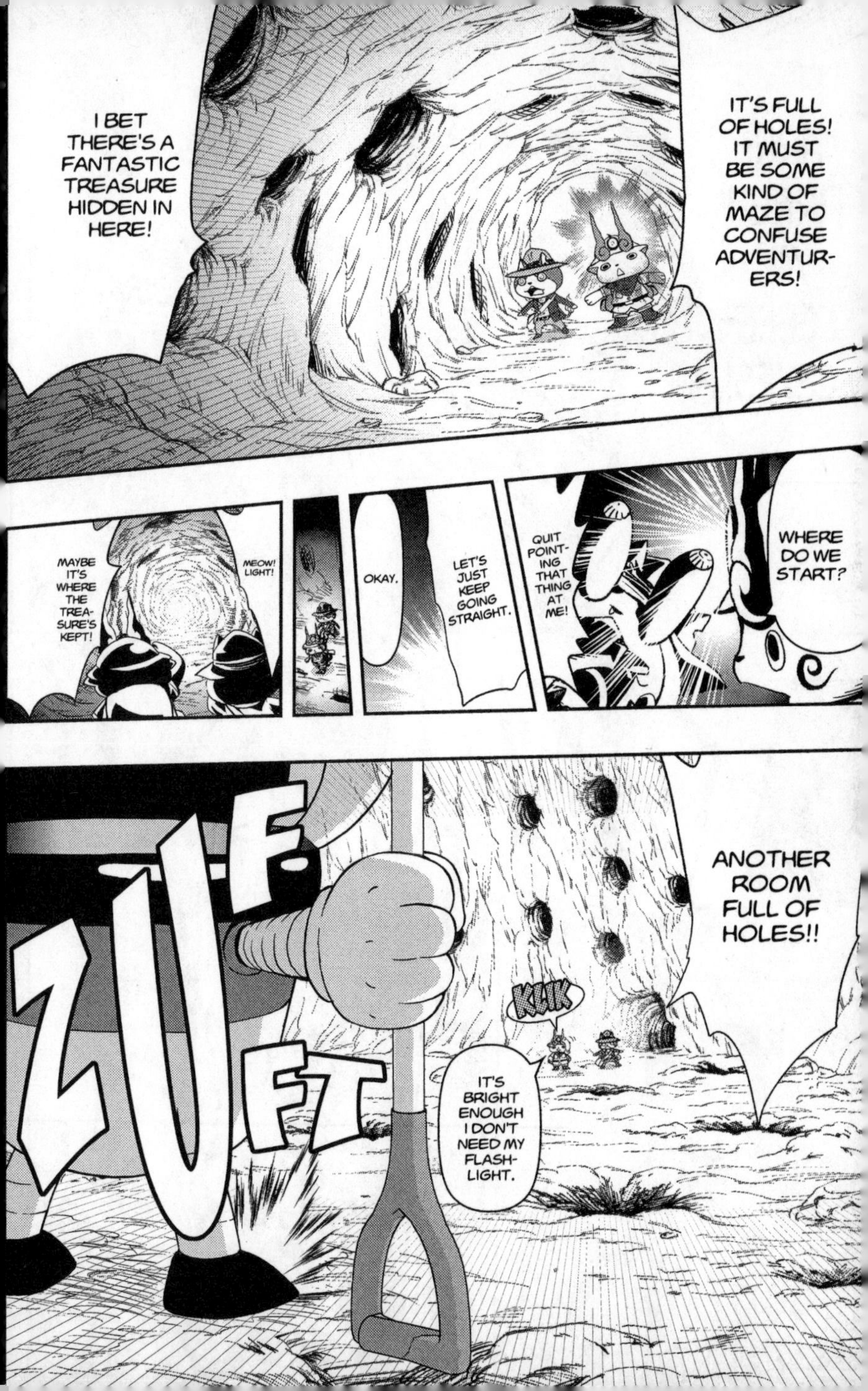
IT'S FULL OF HOLES! IT MUST BE SOME KIND OF MAZE TO CONFUSE ADVENTURERS!
I BET THERE'S A FANTASTIC TREASURE HIDDEN IN HERE!
WHERE DO WE START?
QUIT POINTING THAT THING AT ME!
LET'S JUST KEEP GOING STRAIGHT.
OKAY.
MEOW! LIGHT!
MAYBE IT'S WHERE THE TREASURE'S KEPT!
ANOTHER ROOM FULL OF HOLES!!
KLIK
IT'S BRIGHT ENOUGH I DON'T NEED MY FLASHLIGHT.
ZUFFT

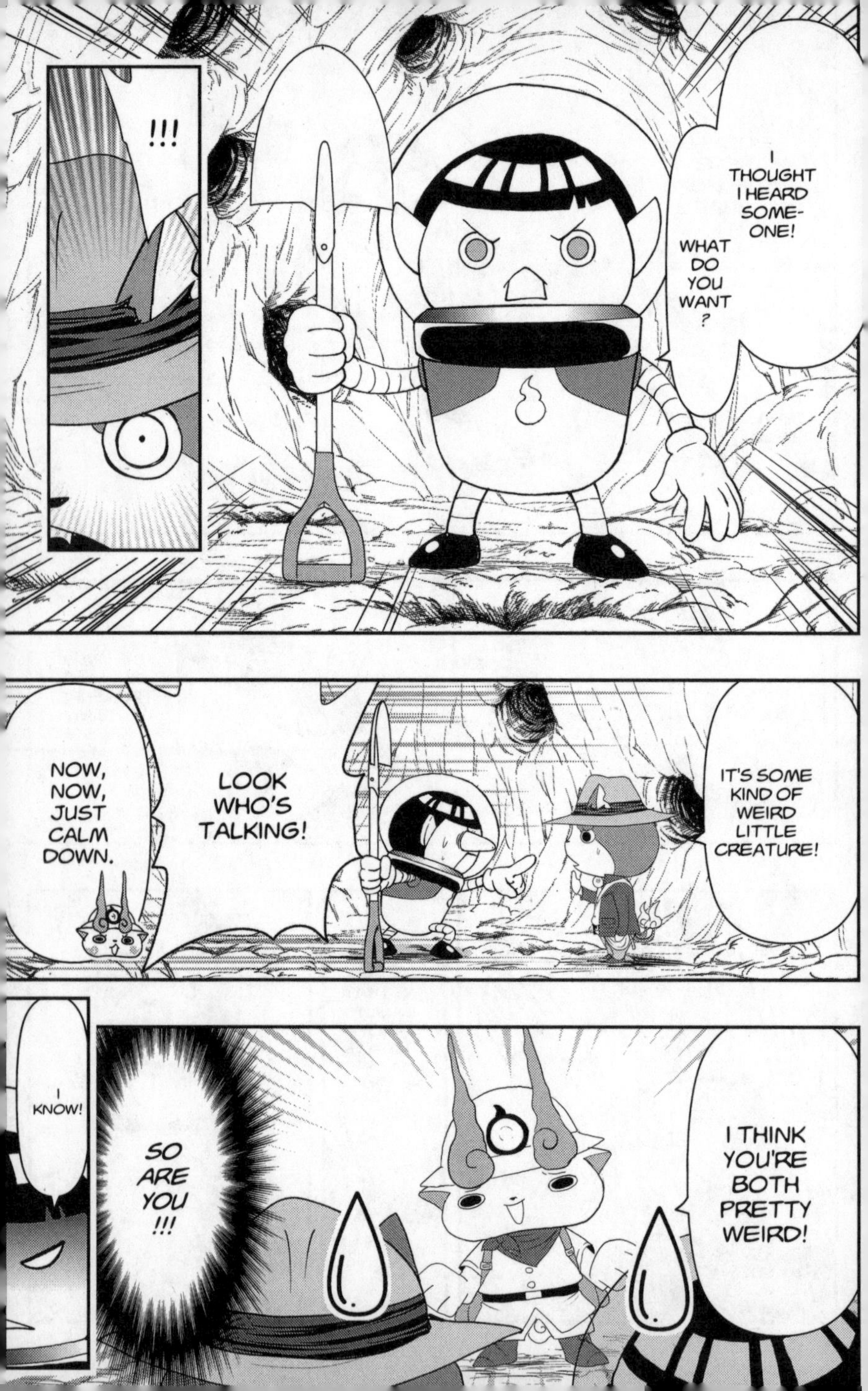
I THOUGHT I HEARD SOME-ONE!
WHAT DO YOU WANT?
!!!
IT'S SOME KIND OF WEIRD LITTLE CREATURE!
LOOK WHO'S TALKING!
NOW, NOW, JUST CALM DOWN.
I THINK YOU'RE BOTH PRETTY WEIRD!
SO ARE YOU!!!
I KNOW!

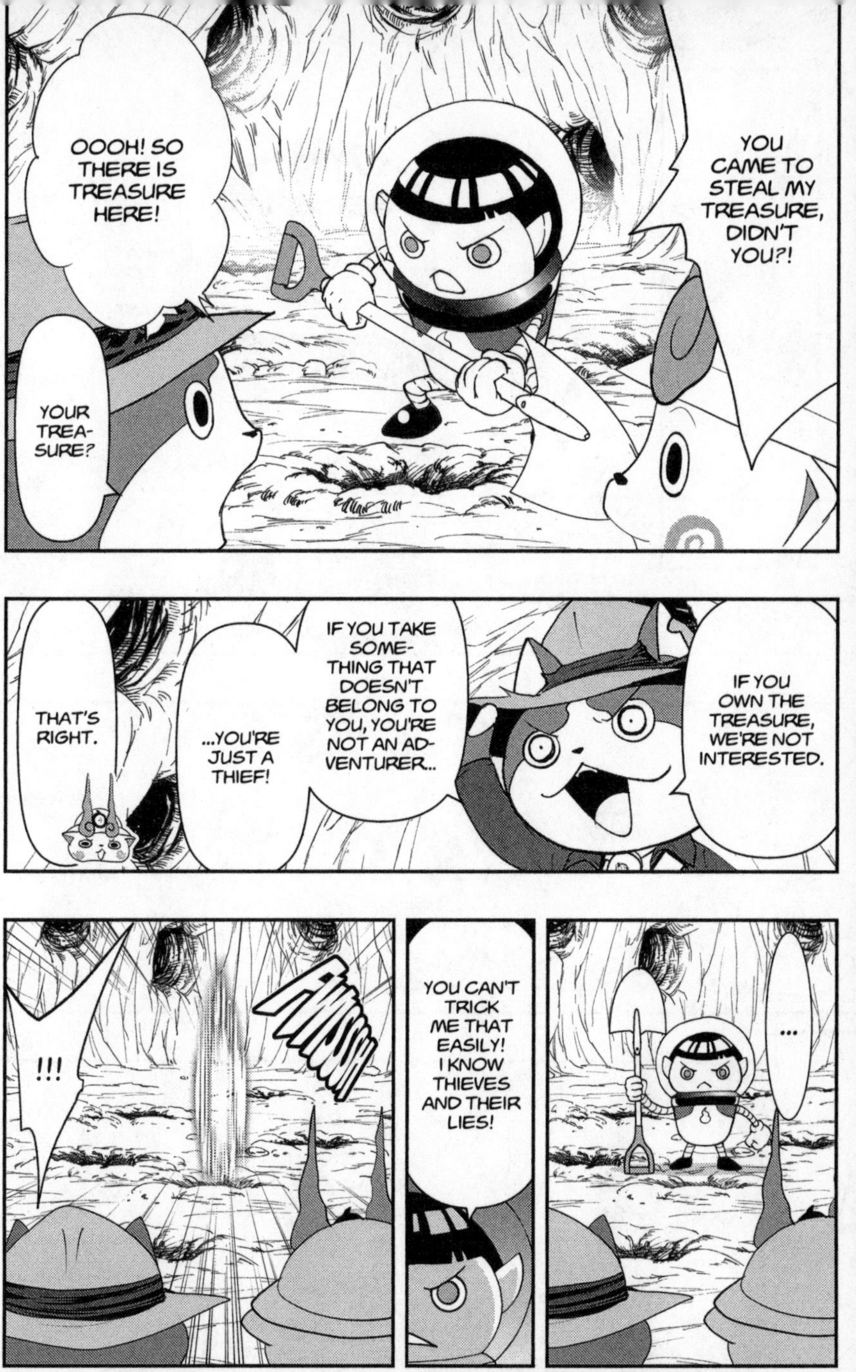
YOU CAME TO STEAL MY TREASURE, DIDN'T YOU?!
OOOH! SO THERE IS TREASURE HERE!
YOUR TREA-SURE?
IF YOU OWN THE TREASURE, WE'RE NOT INTERESTED.
IF YOU TAKE SOME-THING THAT DOESN'T BELONG TO YOU, YOU'RE NOT AN AD-VENTURER...
...YOU'RE JUST A THIEF!
THAT'S RIGHT.
...
YOU CAN'T TRICK ME THAT EASILY! I KNOW THIEVES AND THEIR LIES!
!!!

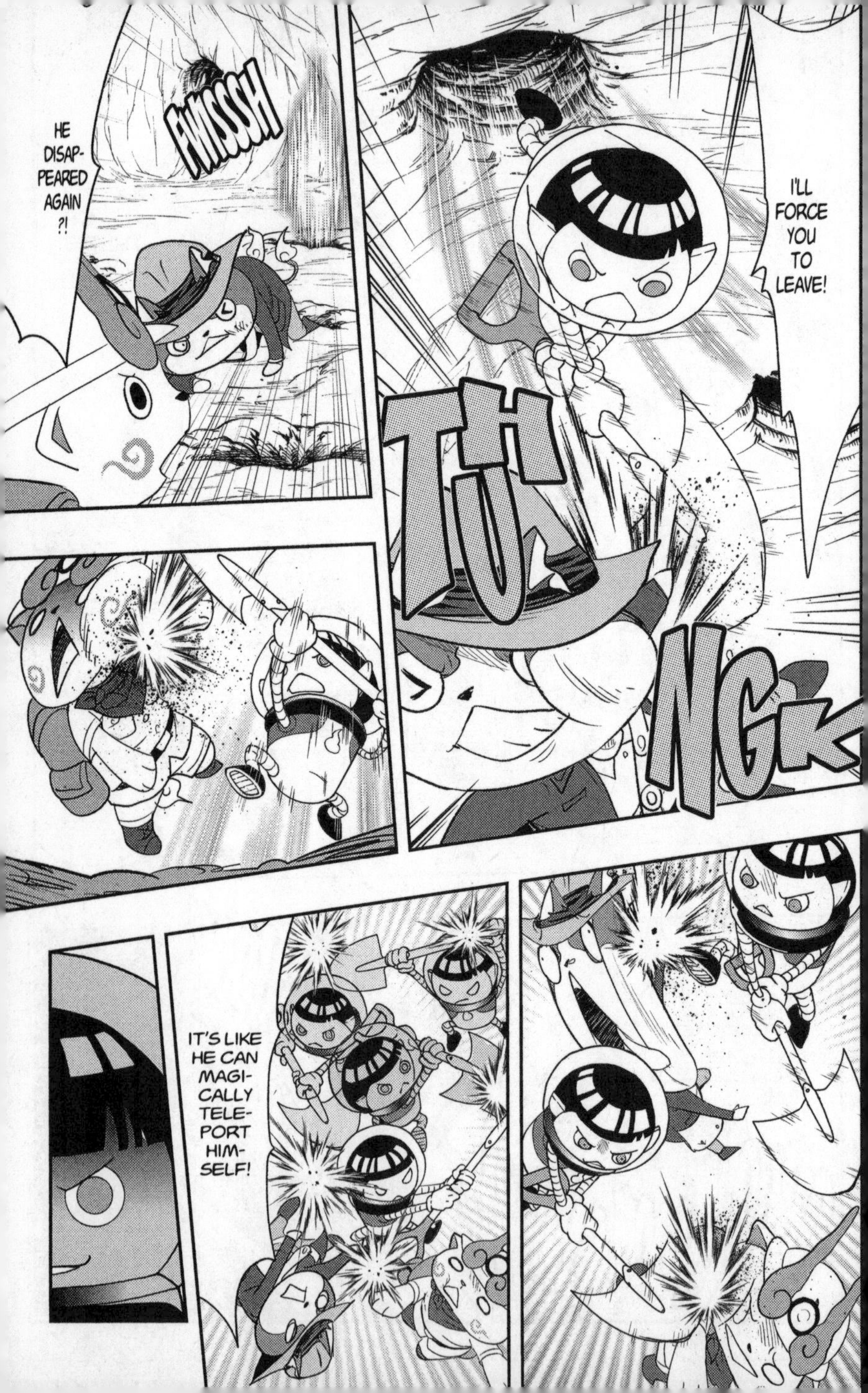
HE DISAP-PEARED AGAIN?!
FWOOSH
I'LL FORCE YOU TO LEAVE!
THUNGK
IT'S LIKE HE CAN MAGI-CALLY TELE-PORT HIM-SELF!

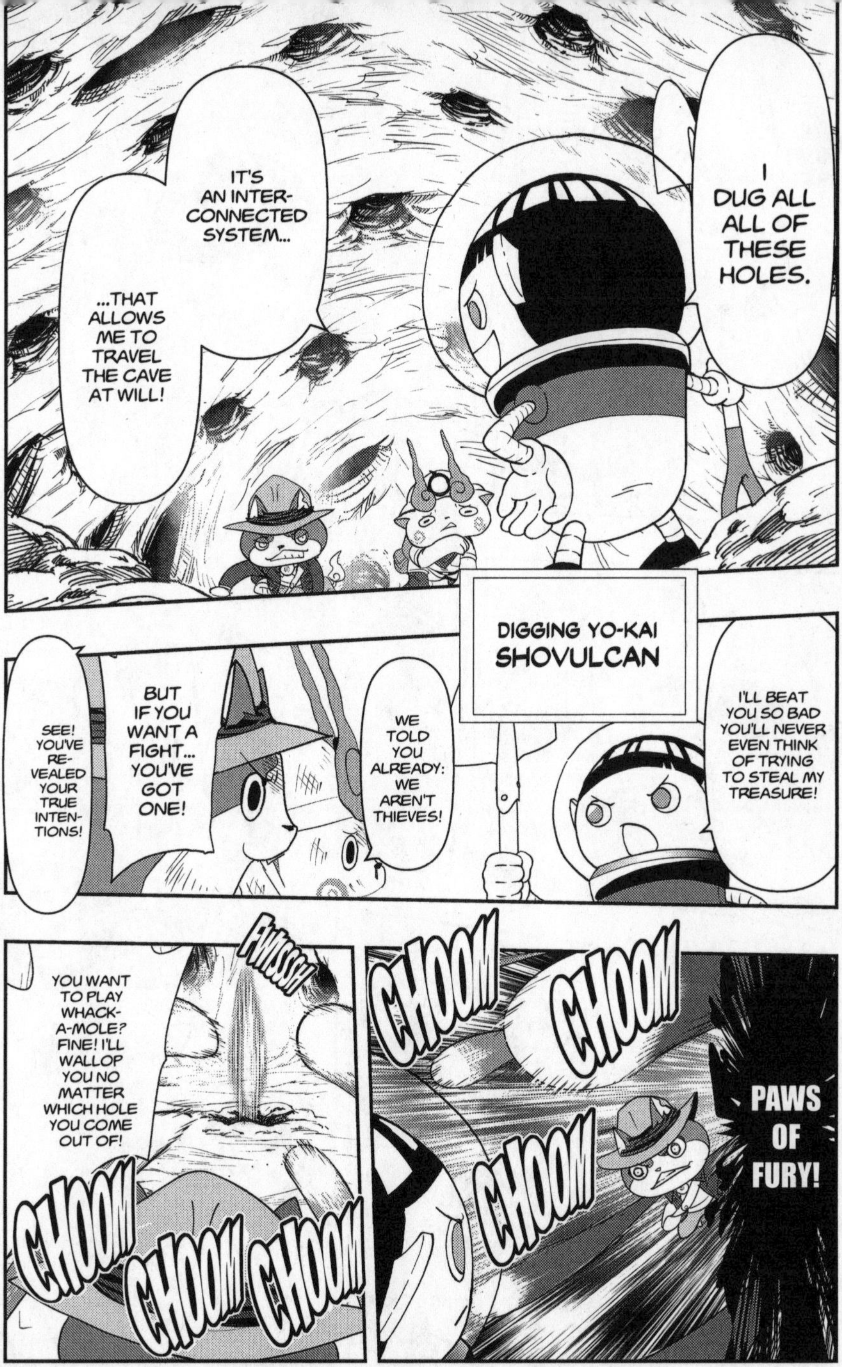
I DUG ALL ALL OF THESE HOLES.
IT'S AN INTER-CONNECTED SYSTEM...
...THAT ALLOWS ME TO TRAVEL THE CAVE AT WILL!
DIGGING YO-KAI SHOVULCAN
I'LL BEAT YOU SO BAD YOU'LL NEVER EVEN THINK OF TRYING TO STEAL MY TREASURE!
WE TOLD YOU ALREADY: WE AREN'T THIEVES!
BUT IF YOU WANT A FIGHT... YOU'VE GOT ONE!
SEE! YOU'VE RE-VEALED YOUR TRUE INTEN-TIONS!
CHOOM
CHOOM
CHOOM
PAWS OF FURY!
FWISSSH
YOU WANT TO PLAY WHACK-A-MOLE? FINE! I'LL WALLOP YOU NO MATTER WHICH HOLE YOU COME OUT OF!
CHOOM
CHOOM
CHOOM

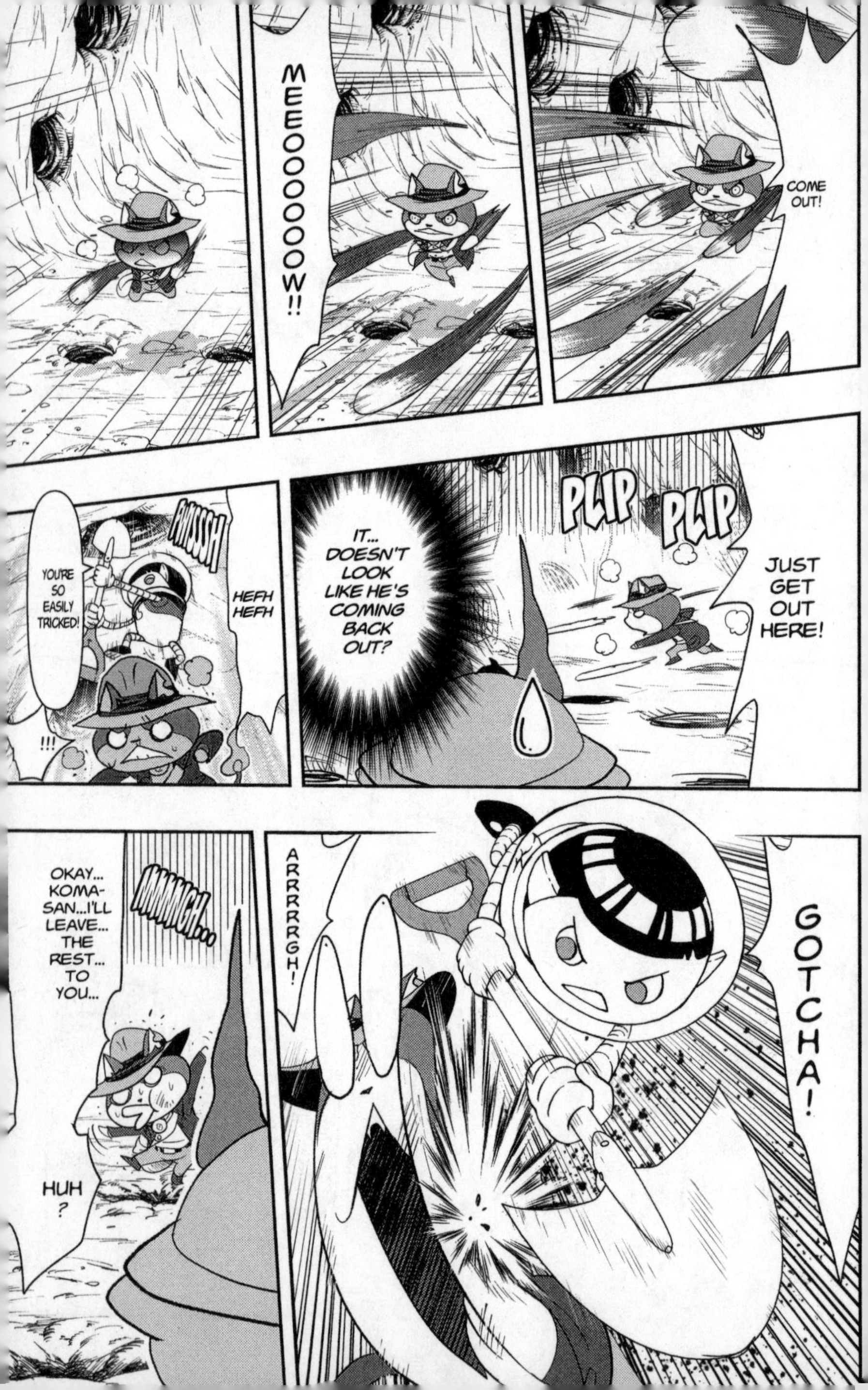
COME OUT!
MEEOOOOOOW!!
PLIP PLIP
JUST GET OUT HERE!
IT... DOESN'T LOOK LIKE HE'S COMING BACK OUT?
FWSSSH
HEFH HEFH
YOU'RE SO EASILY TRICKED!
!!!
GOTCHA!
ARRRRGH!
OKAY... KOMA-SAN...I'LL LEAVE... THE REST... TO YOU...
HUH?

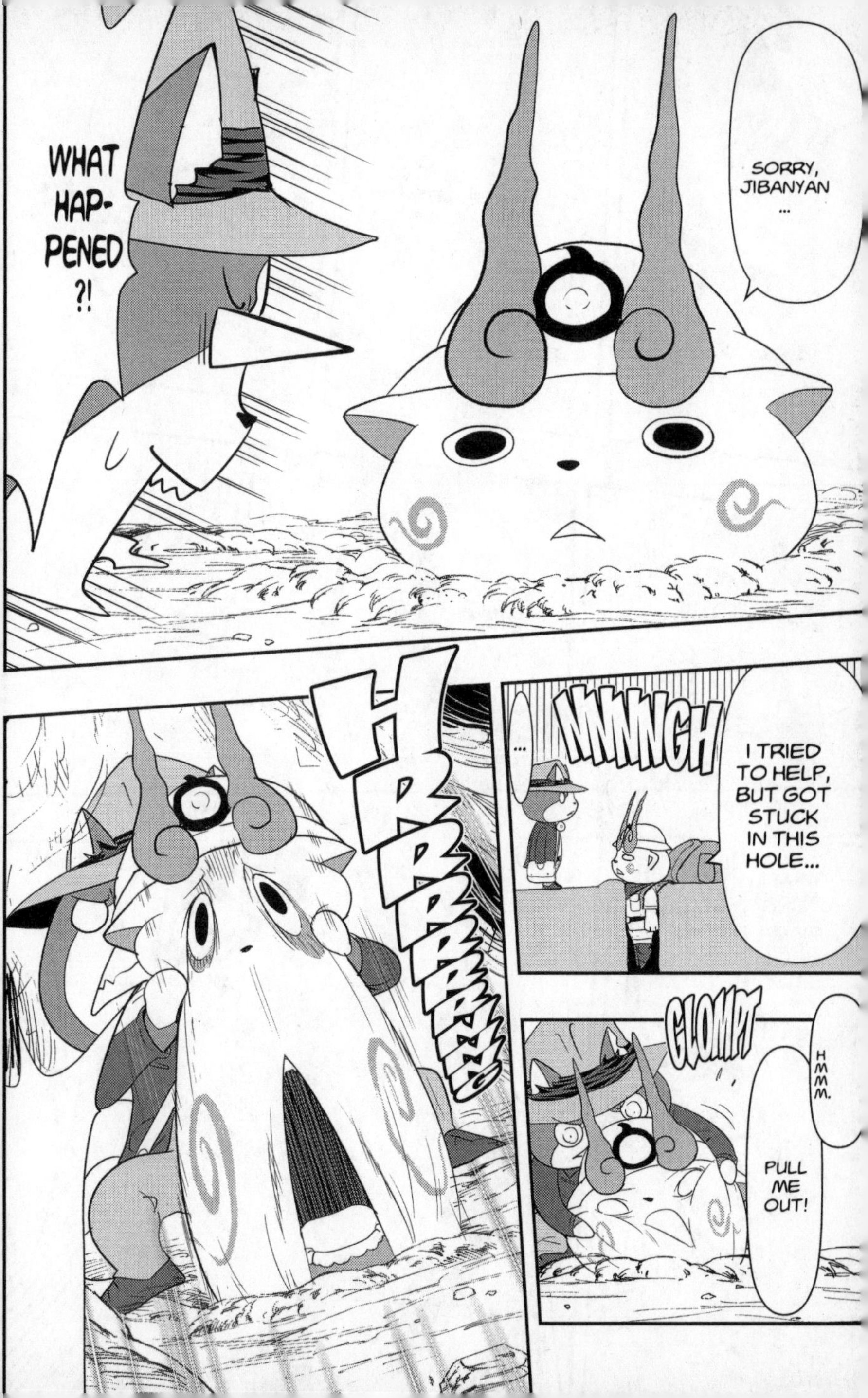
WHAT HAP-PENED ?!
SORRY, JIBANYAN ...
...
NNNNNGH
I TRIED TO HELP, BUT GOT STUCK IN THIS HOLE...
GLOMP
HMMM.
PULL ME OUT!
HRRRRRNNG

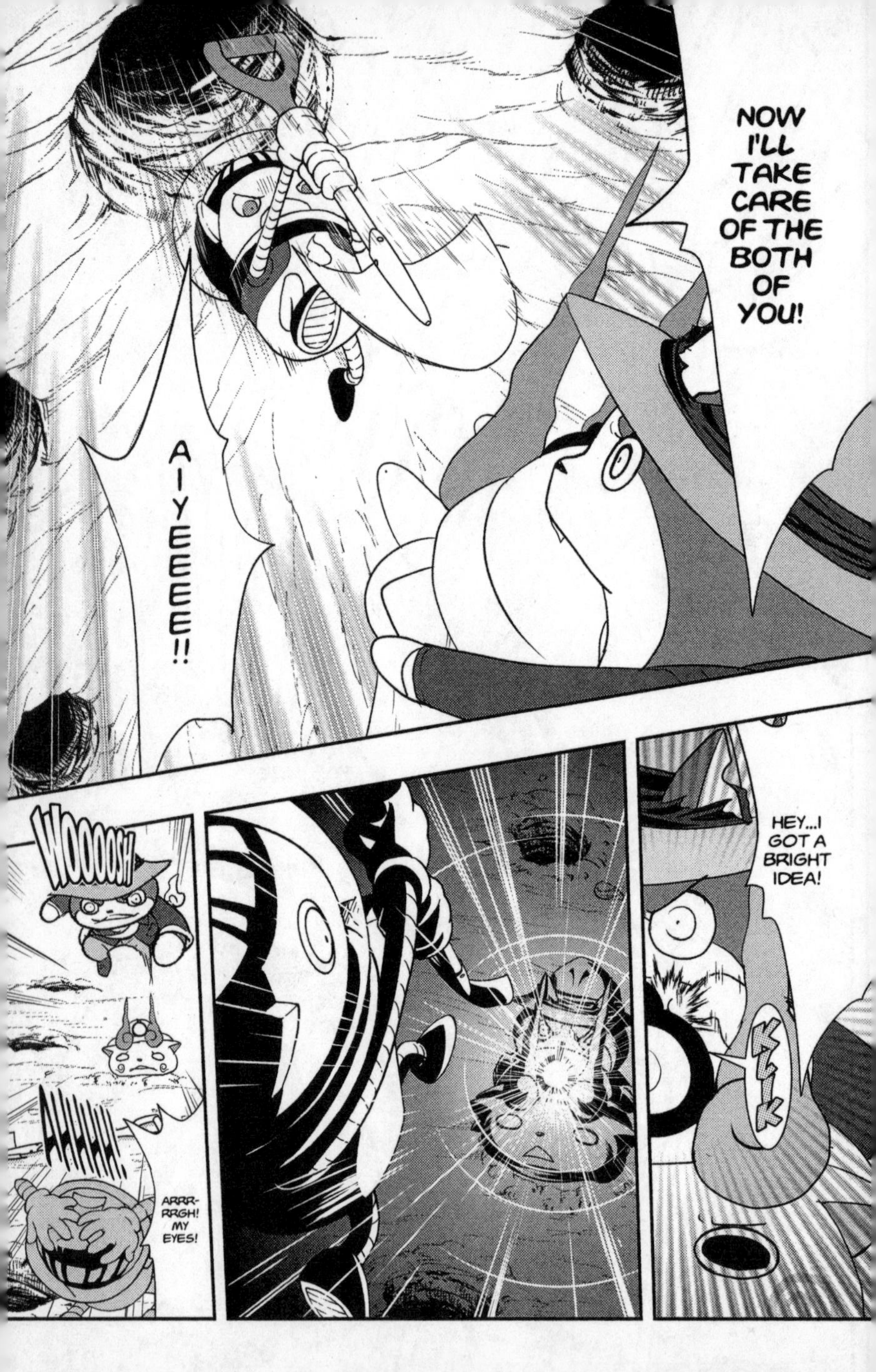
NOW I'LL TAKE CARE OF THE BOTH OF YOU!
AIYEEEEE!!
HEY...I GOT A BRIGHT IDEA!
KLIK
WOOOOSH
AHHHHH!
ARRRRRGH! MY EYES!

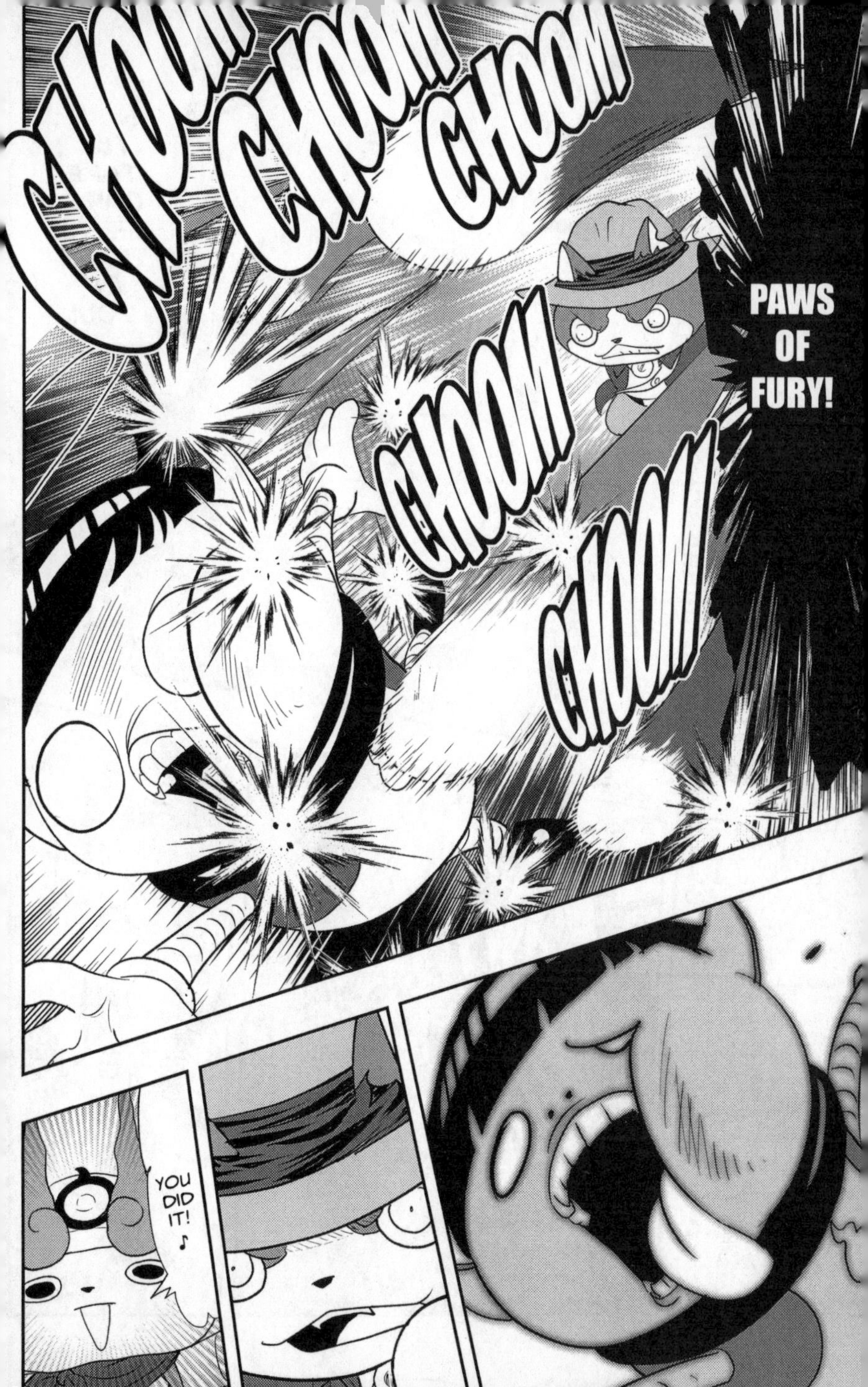
PAWS OF FURY!
CHOOM
CHOOM
CHOOM
CHOOM
CHOOM
YOU DID IT! ♪

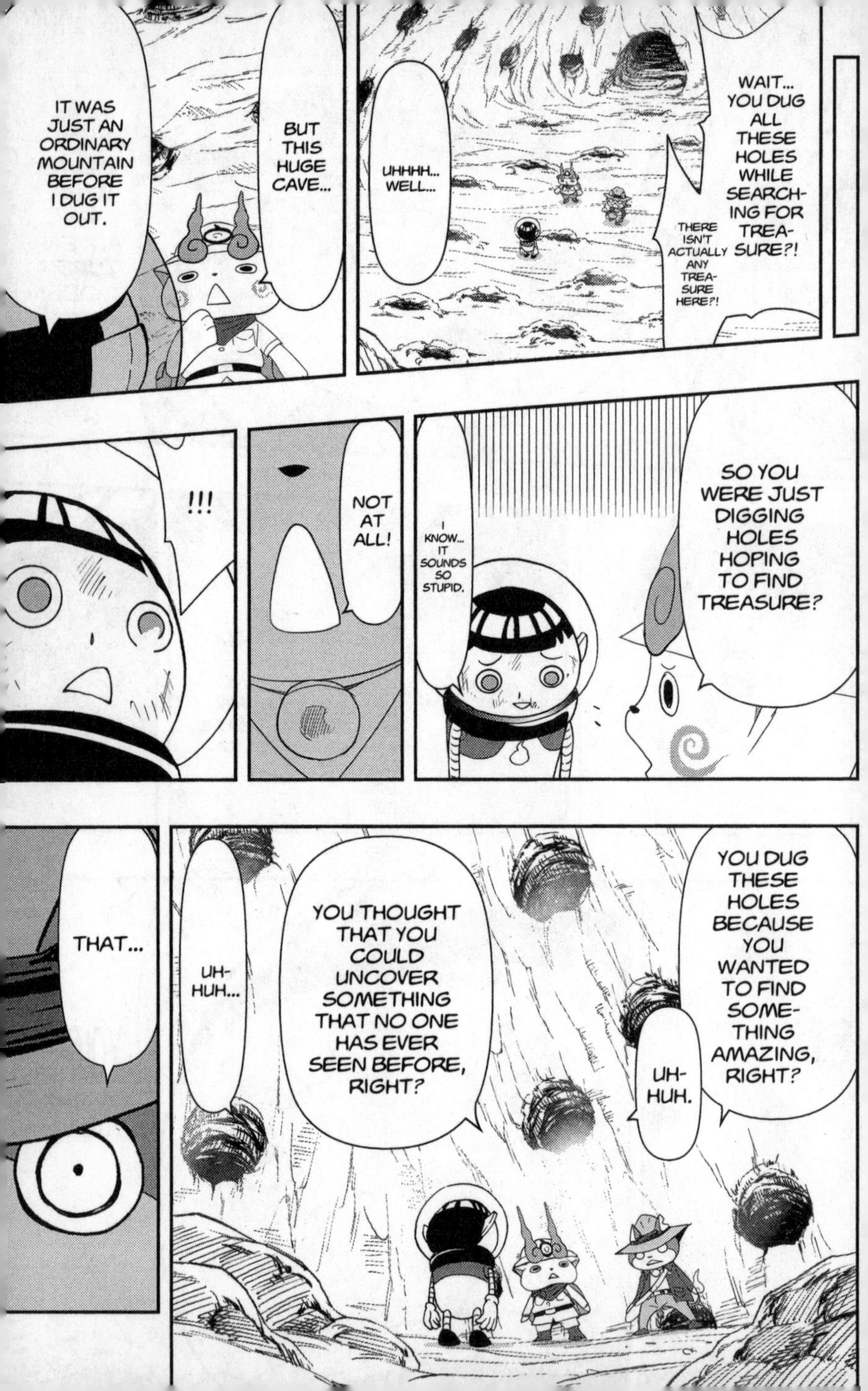
WAIT... YOU DUG ALL THESE HOLES WHILE SEARCHING FOR TREASURE?!
THERE ISN'T ACTUALLY ANY TREASURE HERE?!
UHHHH... WELL...
BUT THIS HUGE CAVE...
IT WAS JUST AN ORDINARY MOUNTAIN BEFORE I DUG IT OUT.
SO YOU WERE JUST DIGGING HOLES HOPING TO FIND TREASURE?
I KNOW... IT SOUNDS SO STUPID.
NOT AT ALL!
!!!
YOU DUG THESE HOLES BECAUSE YOU WANTED TO FIND SOMETHING AMAZING, RIGHT?
UH-HUH.
YOU THOUGHT THAT YOU COULD UNCOVER SOMETHING THAT NO ONE HAS EVER SEEN BEFORE, RIGHT?
UH-HUH...
THAT...

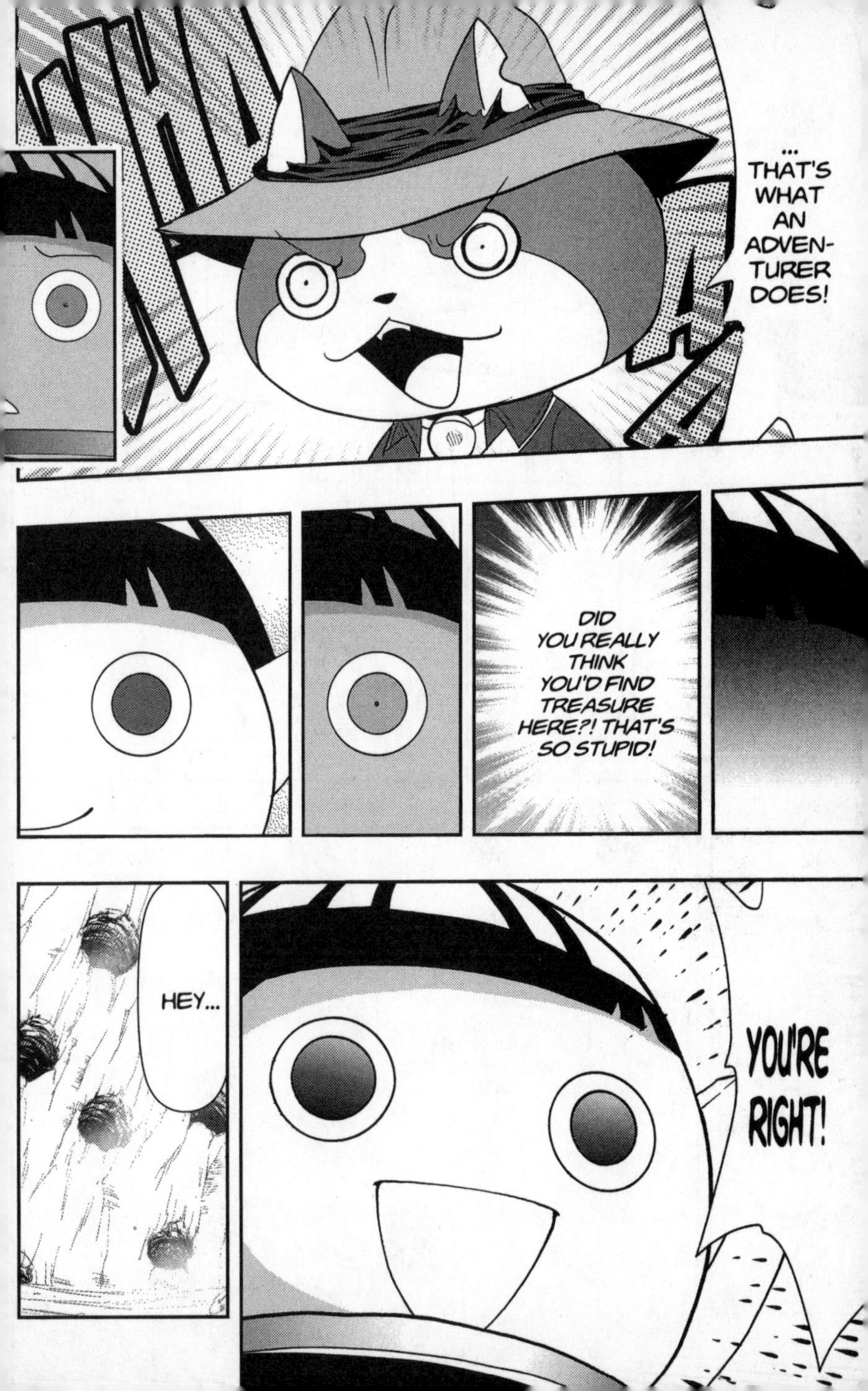
...THAT'S WHAT AN ADVEN-TURER DOES!
DID YOU REALLY THINK YOU'D FIND TREASURE HERE?! THAT'S SO STUPID!
YOU'RE RIGHT!
HEY...

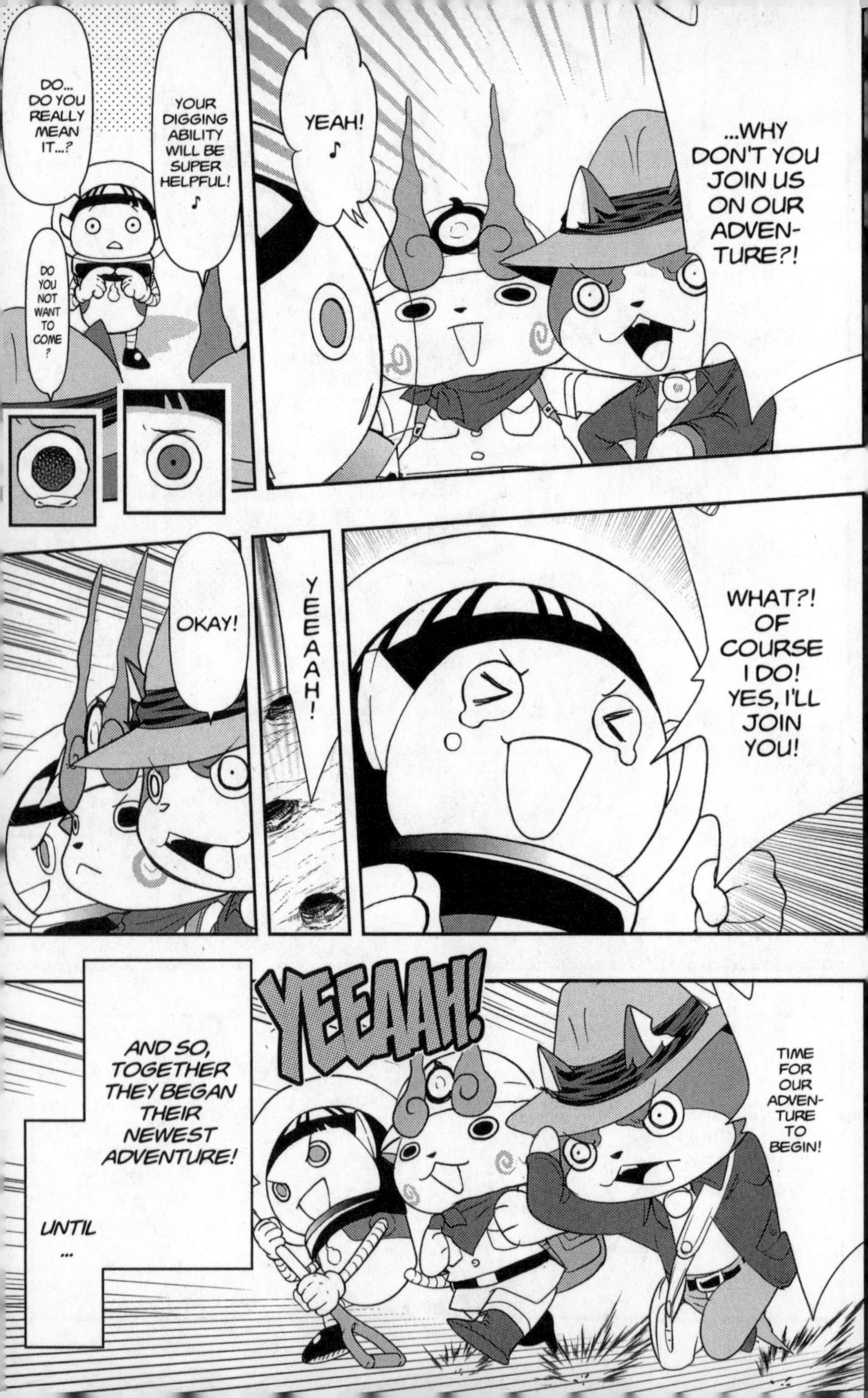
...WHY DON'T YOU JOIN US ON OUR ADVENTURE?!
YEAH! ♪
YOUR DIGGING ABILITY WILL BE SUPER HELPFUL! ♪
DO... DO YOU REALLY MEAN IT...?
DO YOU NOT WANT TO COME?
WHAT?! OF COURSE I DO! YES, I'LL JOIN YOU!
YEEAAH!
OKAY!
YEEAAH!
TIME FOR OUR ADVENTURE TO BEGIN!
AND SO, TOGETHER THEY BEGAN THEIR NEWEST ADVENTURE!
UNTIL ...

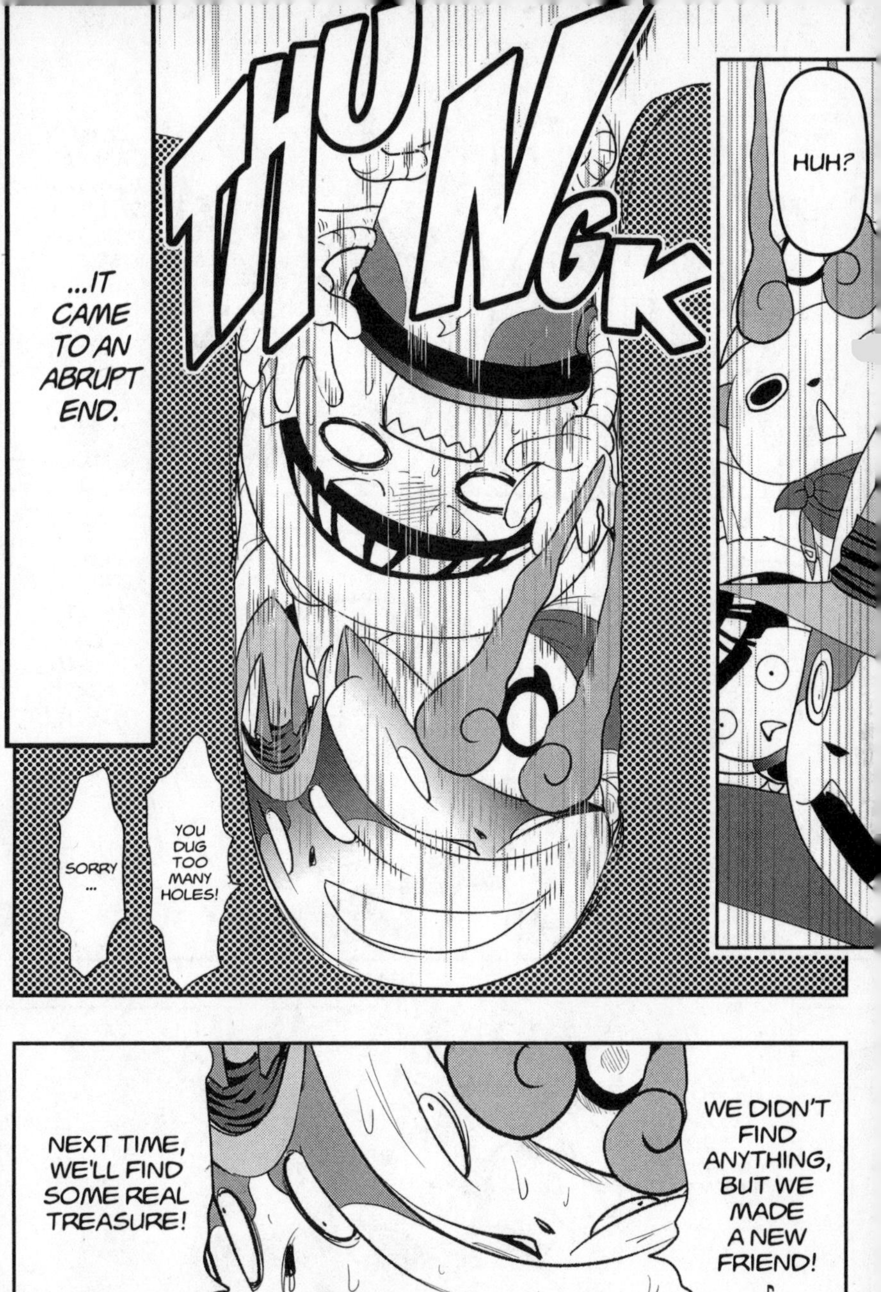
HUH?
THUNGK
...IT CAME TO AN ABRUPT END.
YOU DUG TOO MANY HOLES!
SORRY...
WE DIDN'T FIND ANYTHING, BUT WE MADE A NEW FRIEND! ♪
NEXT TIME, WE'LL FIND SOME REAL TREASURE!

CHAPTER 138
YO-KAI WATCH BLASTERS TREASURE RAIDERS ARC: BOOGIEMUM

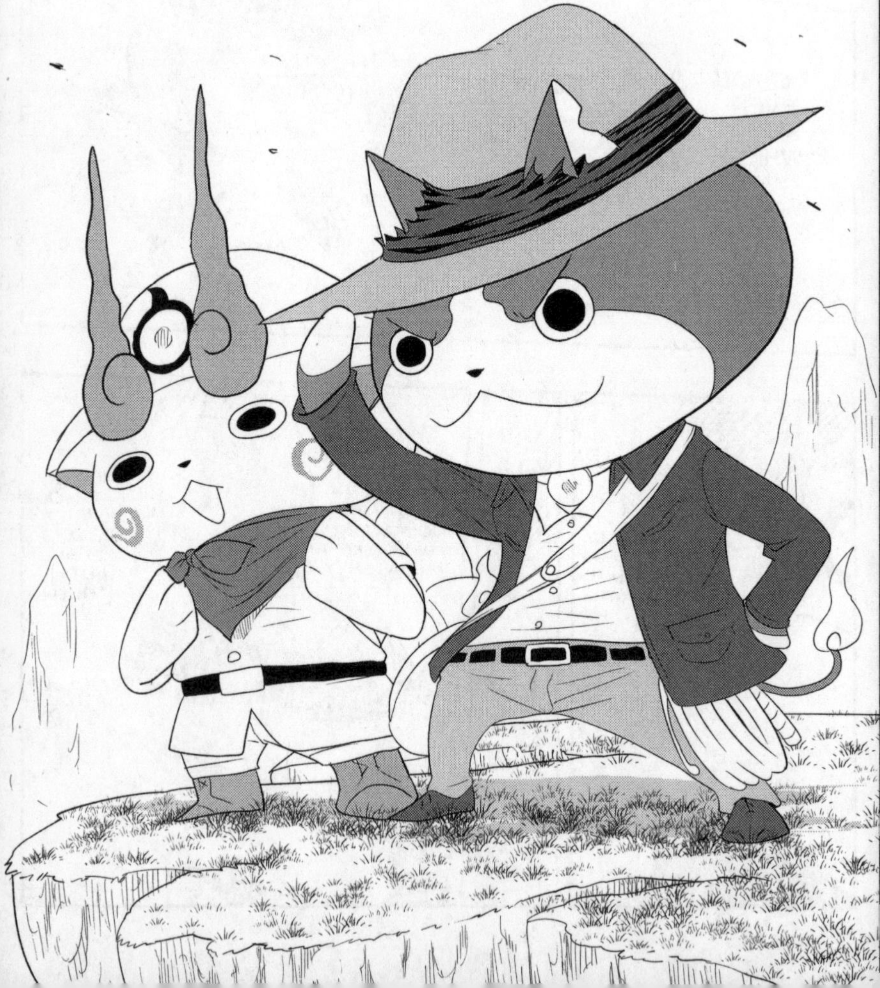

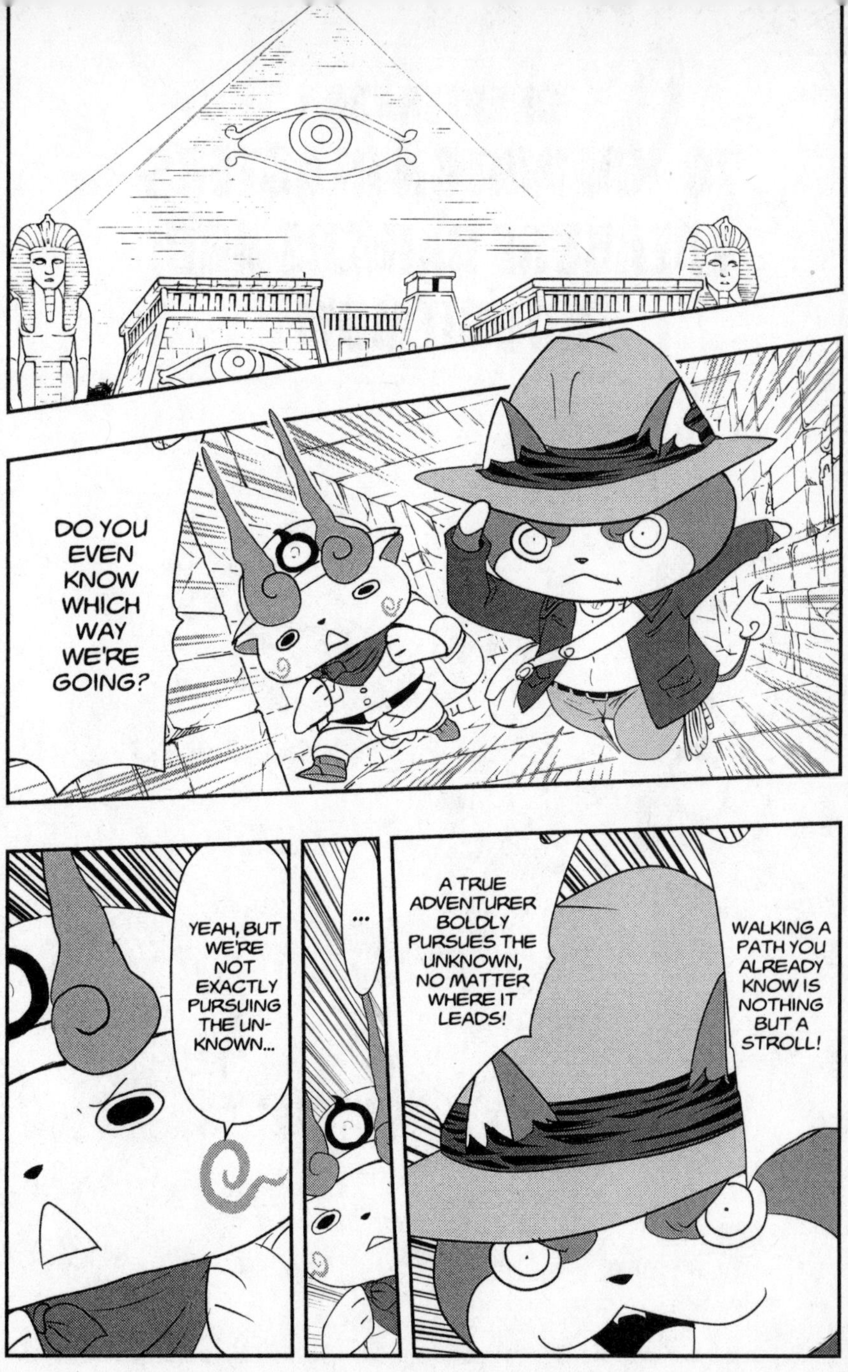
DO YOU EVEN KNOW WHICH WAY WE'RE GOING?
WALKING A PATH YOU ALREADY KNOW IS NOTHING BUT A STROLL!
A TRUE ADVENTURER BOLDLY PURSUES THE UNKNOWN, NO MATTER WHERE IT LEADS!
...
YEAH, BUT WE'RE NOT EXACTLY PURSUING THE UN-KNOWN...

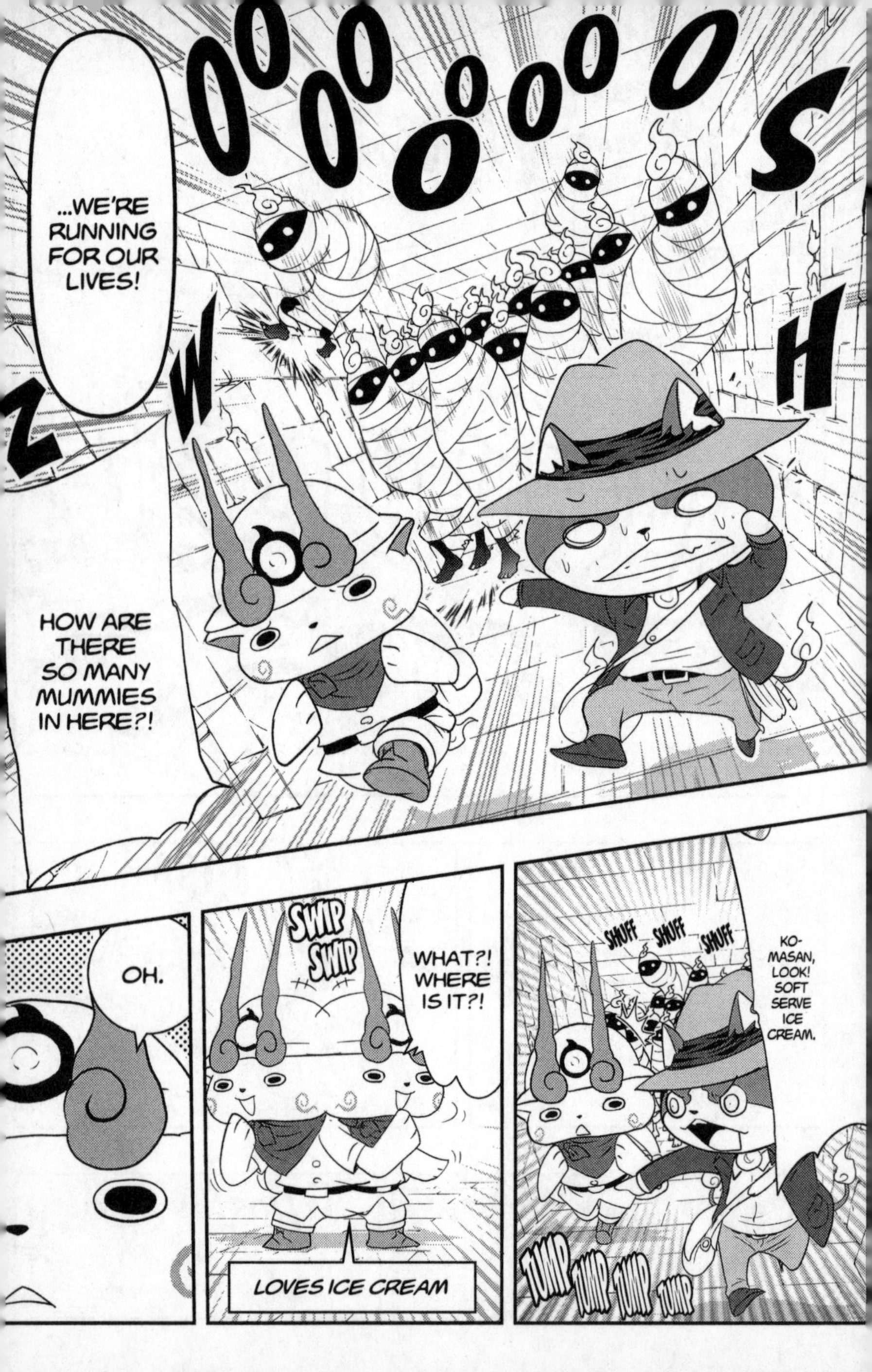
ZWOOOOOOOOOOSH
...WE'RE RUNNING FOR OUR LIVES!
HOW ARE THERE SO MANY MUMMIES IN HERE?!
SHUFF SHUFF SHUFF
KO-MASAN, LOOK! SOFT SERVE ICE CREAM.
TUMP TUMP TUMP TUMP
SWIP SWIP
WHAT?! WHERE IS IT?!
LOVES ICE CREAM
OH.

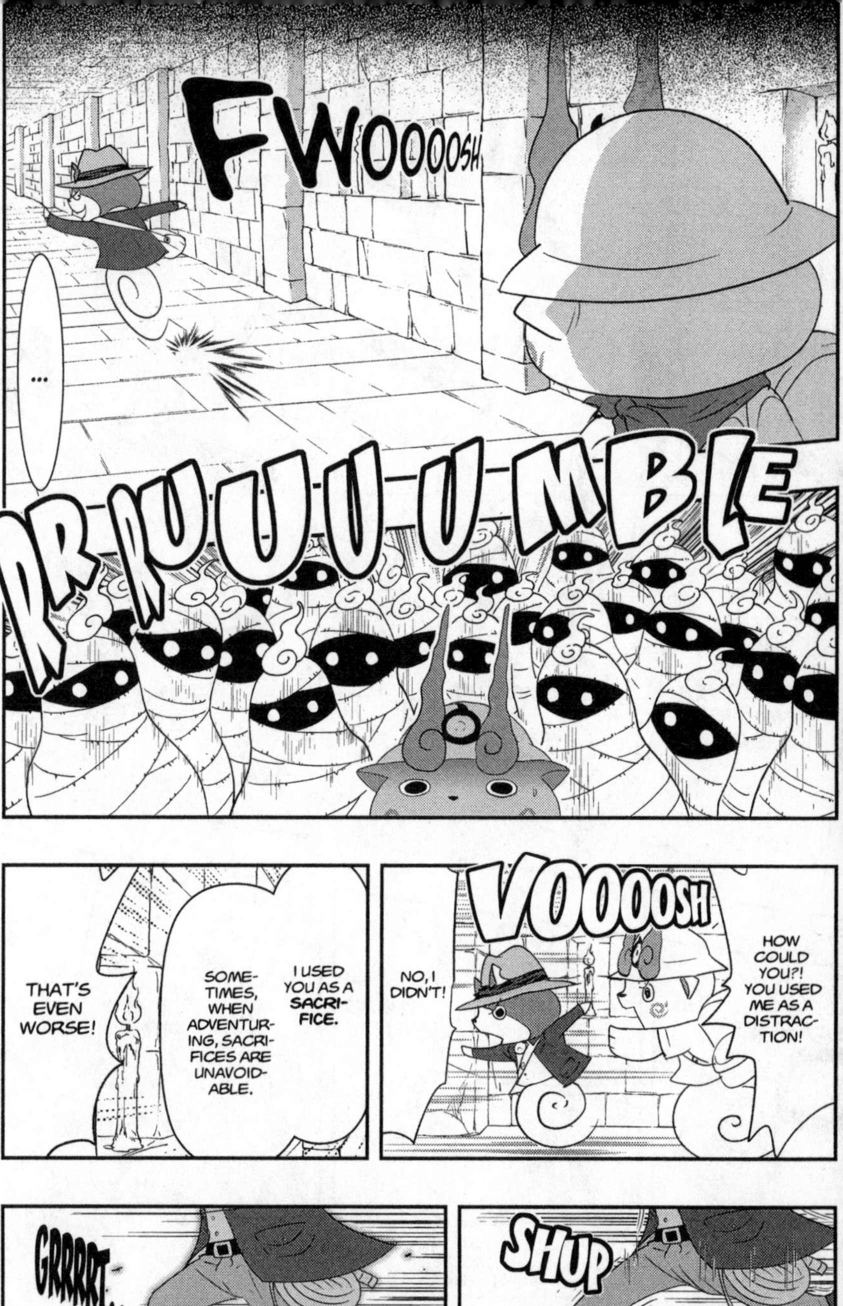
FWOOOOSH
...
RRRUUUUMBLE
VOOOOSH
HOW COULD YOU?! YOU USED ME AS A DISTRACTION!
NO, I DIDN'T!
I USED YOU AS A **SACRIFICE**.
SOMETIMES, WHEN ADVENTURING, SACRIFICES ARE UNAVOIDABLE.
THAT'S EVEN WORSE!
SHUP
GRRRRT...

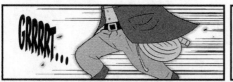

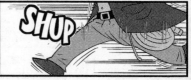

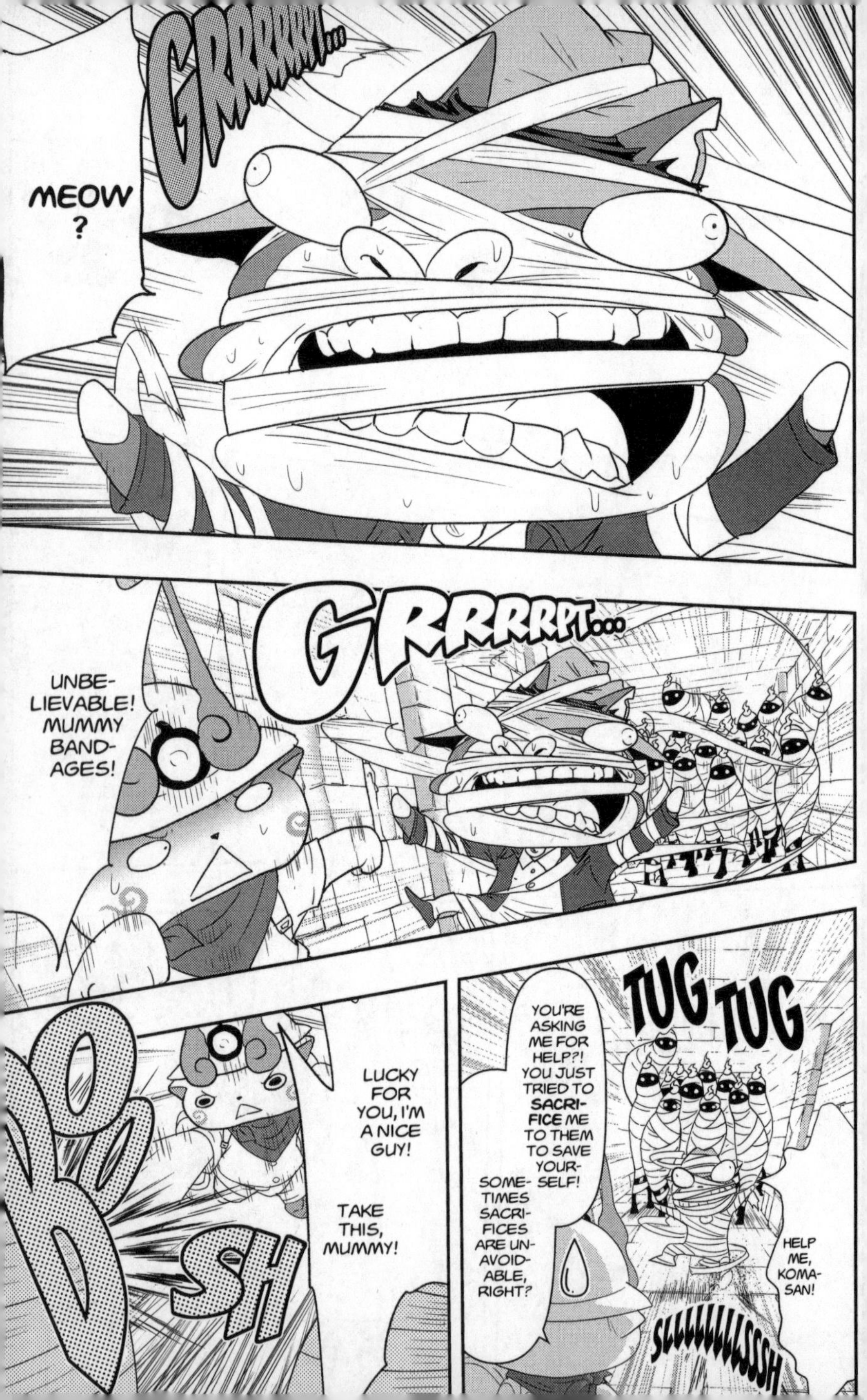
GRRRRRR...
MEOW ?
GRRRRPT...
UNBE-LIEVABLE! MUMMY BAND-AGES!
TUG TUG
HELP ME, KOMA-SAN!
YOU'RE ASKING ME FOR HELP?! YOU JUST TRIED TO SACRI-FICE ME TO THEM TO SAVE YOUR-SELF!
SOME-TIMES SACRI-FICES ARE UN-AVOID-ABLE, RIGHT?
SLLLLLLLLSSSH
LUCKY FOR YOU, I'M A NICE GUY!
TAKE THIS, MUMMY!
BOOSH

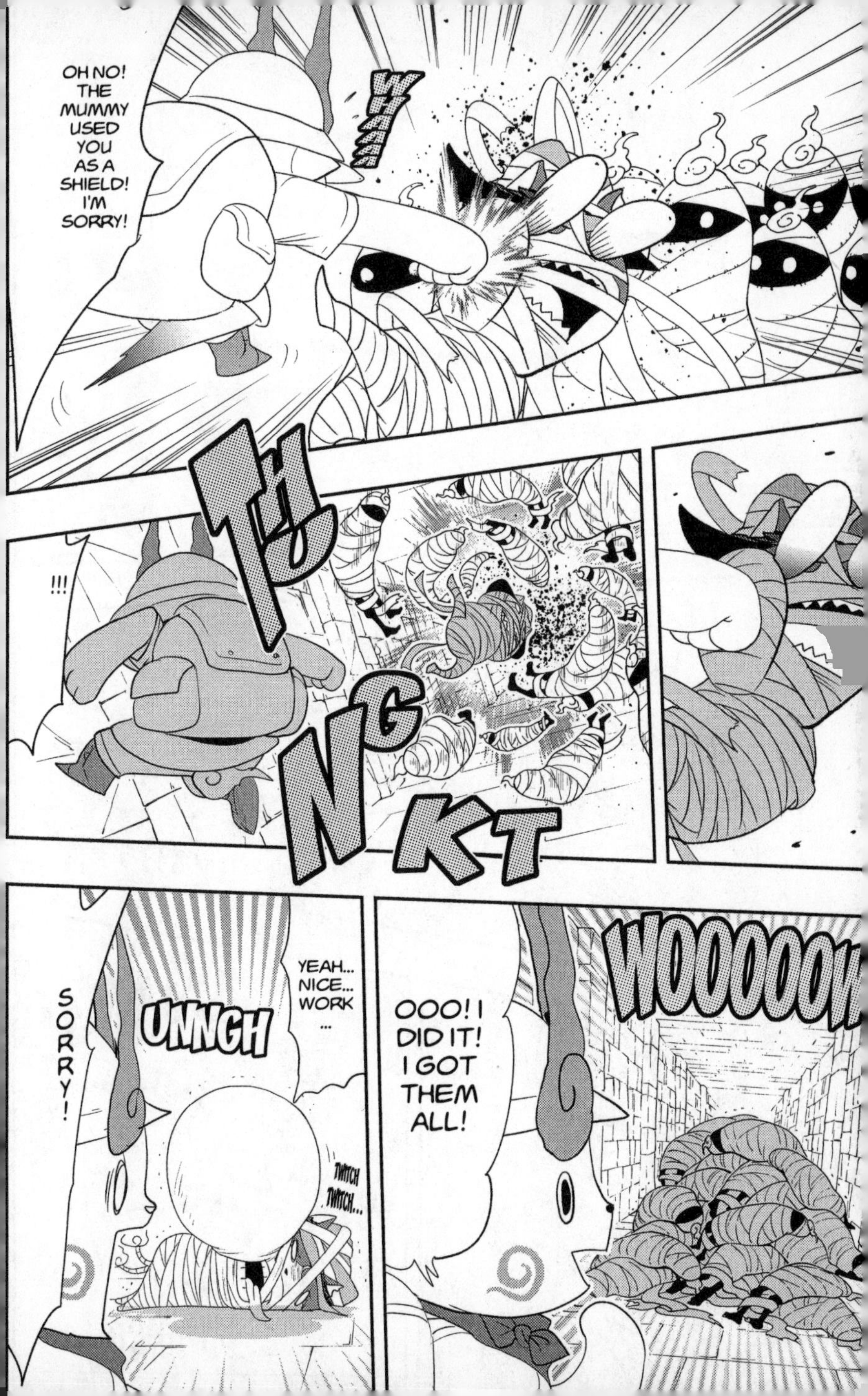
OH NO! THE MUMMY USED YOU AS A SHIELD! I'M SORRY!
!!!
THUNGKT
WOOOOOOW
OOO! I DID IT! I GOT THEM ALL!
YEAH... NICE... WORK ...
UNNGH
TWITCH TWITCH...
SORRY!

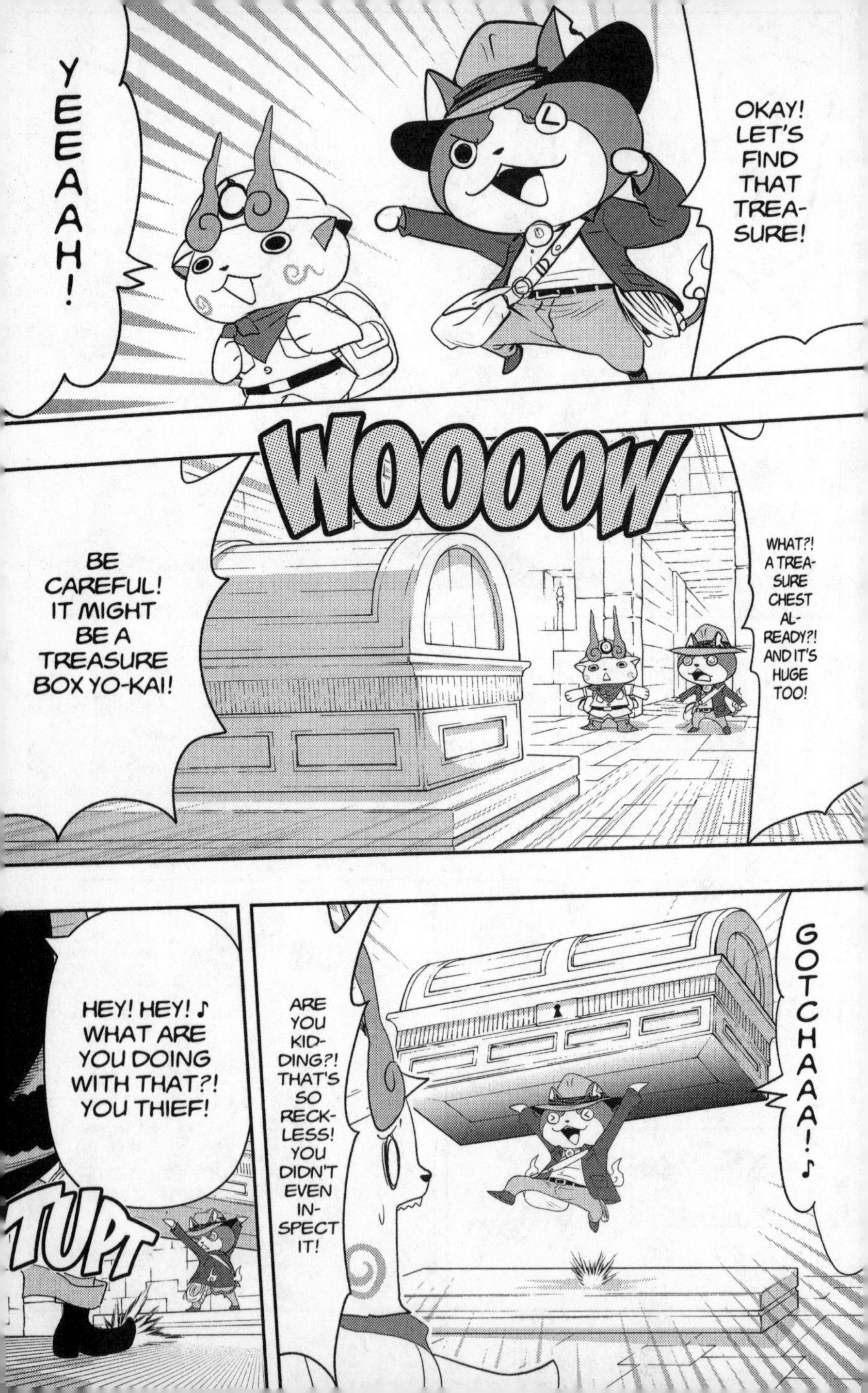
OKAY! LET'S FIND THAT TREASURE!
YEEAAAH!
WOOOOW
WHAT?! A TREASURE CHEST ALREADY?! AND IT'S HUGE TOO!
BE CAREFUL! IT MIGHT BE A TREASURE BOX YO-KAI!
GOTCHAAA!♪
ARE YOU KIDDING?! THAT'S SO RECKLESS! YOU DIDN'T EVEN INSPECT IT!
HEY! HEY! ♪ WHAT ARE YOU DOING WITH THAT?! YOU THIEF!
TUPT

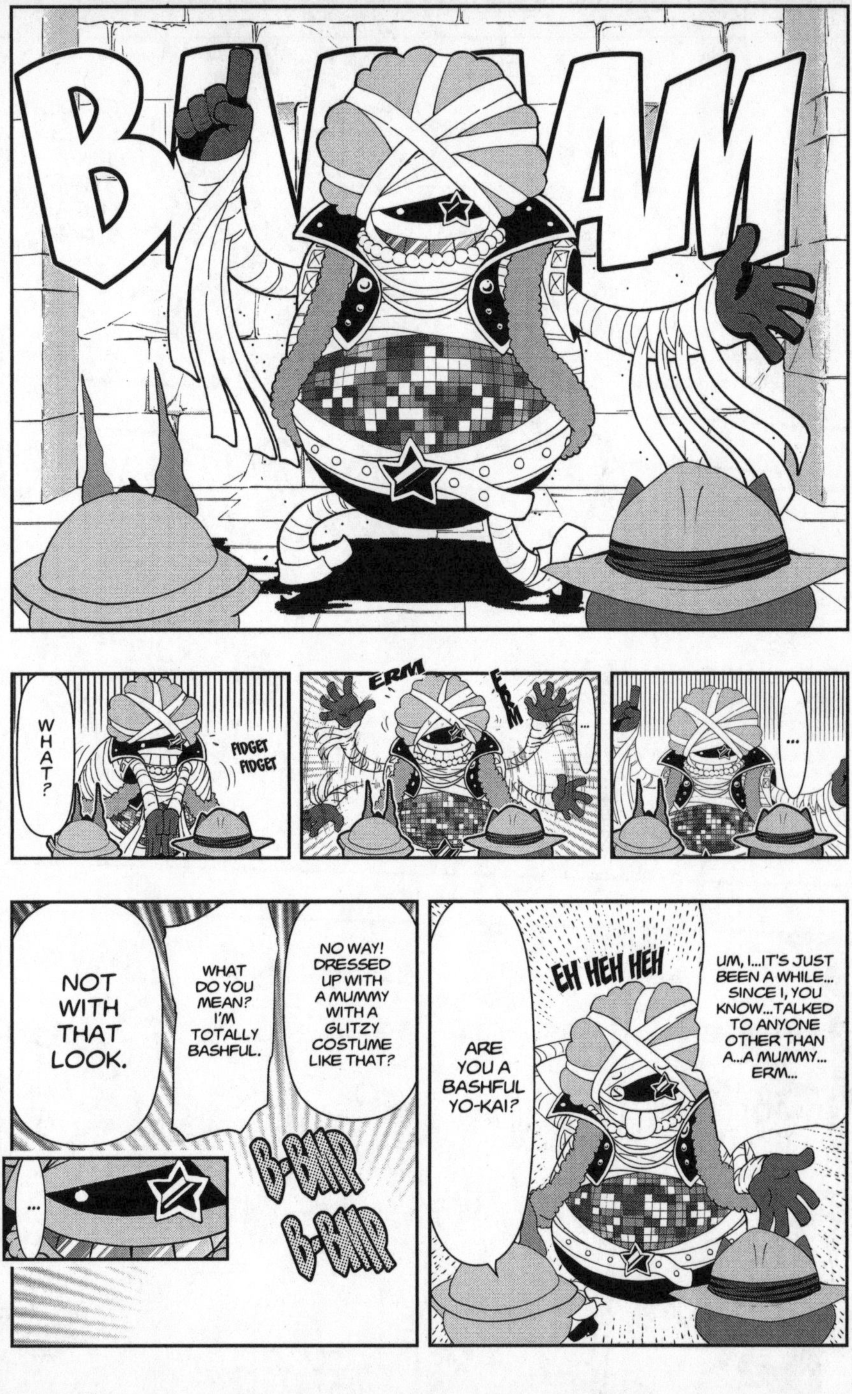
...
ERM
ERM
...
WHAT?
FIDGET FIDGET
UM, I...IT'S JUST BEEN A WHILE... SINCE I, YOU KNOW...TALKED TO ANYONE OTHER THAN A...A MUMMY... ERM...
EH HEH HEH
ARE YOU A BASHFUL YO-KAI?
NO WAY! DRESSED UP WITH A MUMMY WITH A GLITZY COSTUME LIKE THAT?
WHAT DO YOU MEAN? I'M TOTALLY BASHFUL.
NOT WITH THAT LOOK.
B-BHIP
B-BHIP
...

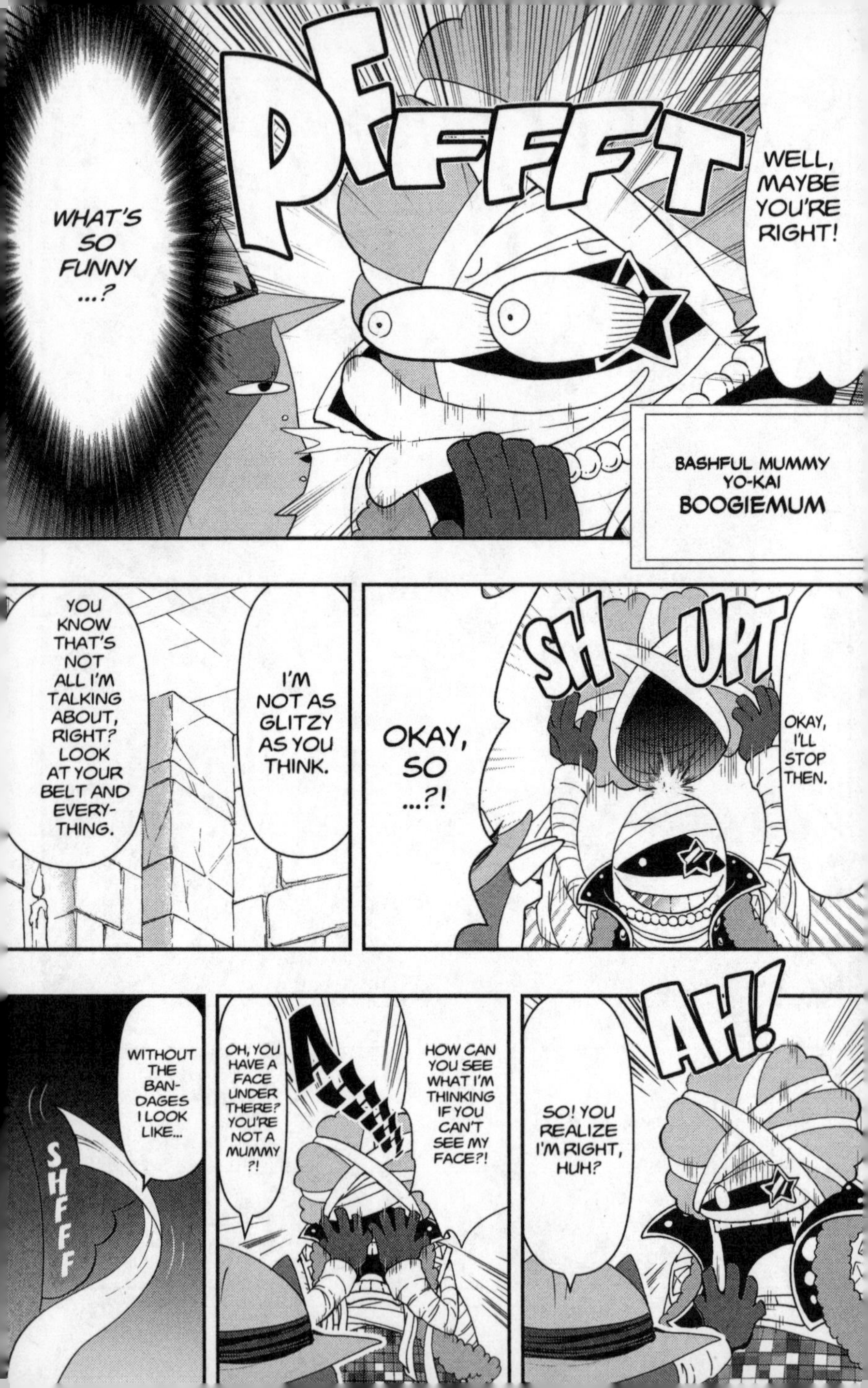
WELL, MAYBE YOU'RE RIGHT!
PFFFFT
BASHFUL MUMMY YO-KAI BOOGIEMUM
WHAT'S SO FUNNY ...?
OKAY, I'LL STOP THEN.
SHUPT
OKAY, SO ...?!
I'M NOT AS GLITZY AS YOU THINK.
YOU KNOW THAT'S NOT ALL I'M TALKING ABOUT, RIGHT? LOOK AT YOUR BELT AND EVERYTHING.
AH!
SO! YOU REALIZE I'M RIGHT, HUH?
HOW CAN YOU SEE WHAT I'M THINKING IF YOU CAN'T SEE MY FACE?!
OH, YOU HAVE A FACE UNDER THERE? YOU'RE NOT A MUMMY?!
WITHOUT THE BAN-DAGES I LOOK LIKE...
SHFFF

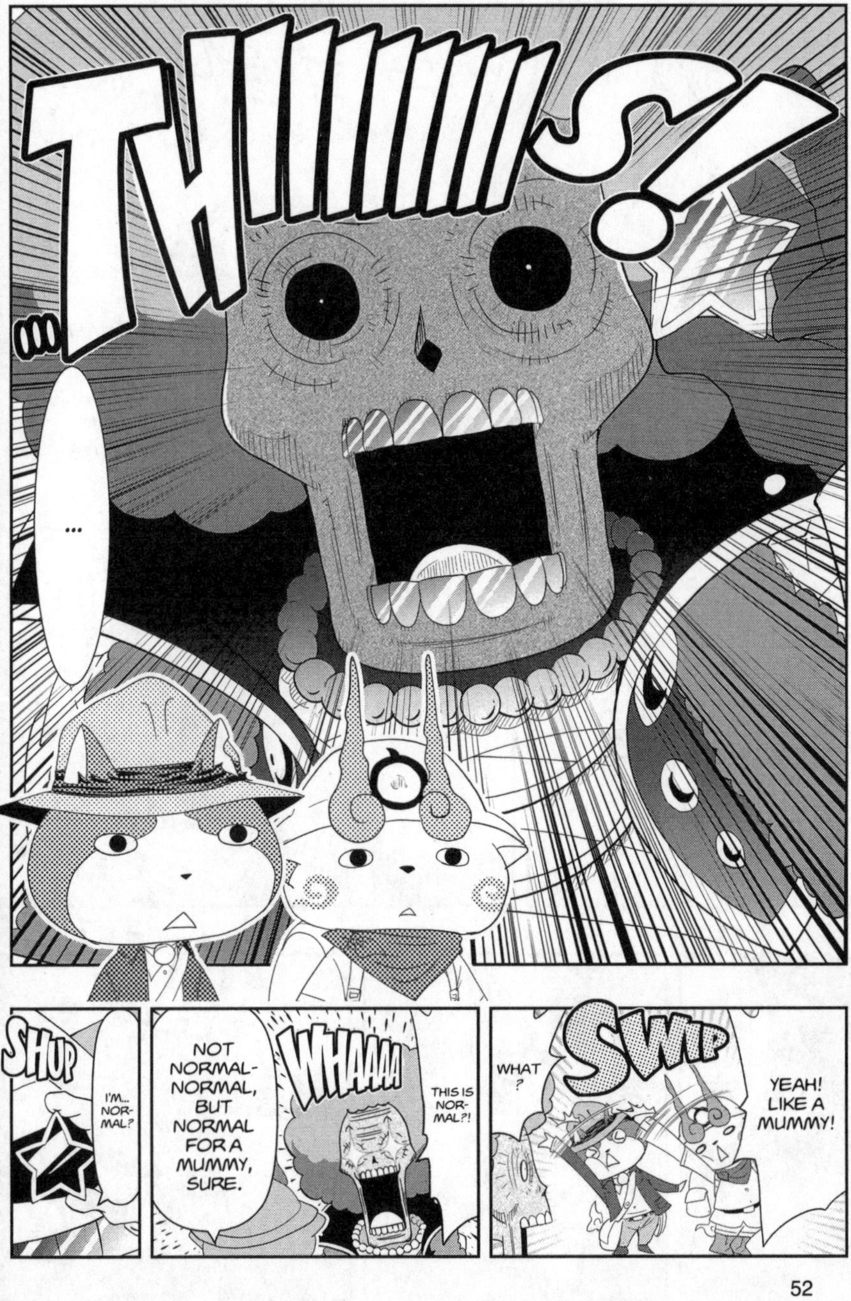
...THIIIIIIIS?!
...
SWIP
YEAH! LIKE A MUMMY!
WHAT?
WHAAAA
THIS IS NORMAL?!
NOT NORMAL-NORMAL, BUT NORMAL FOR A MUMMY, SURE.
SHUP
I'M... NORMAL?

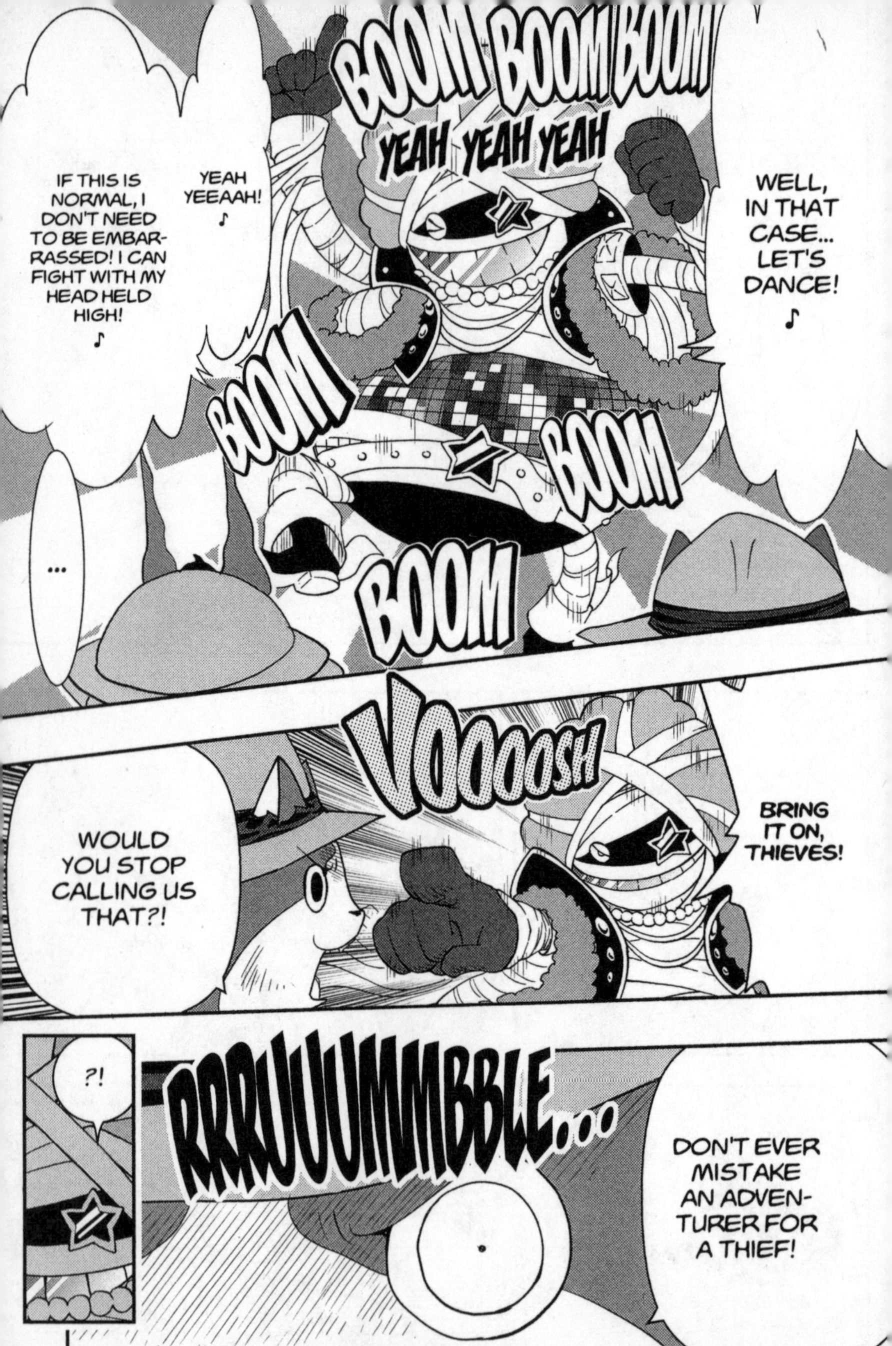

WELL, IN THAT CASE... LET'S DANCE! ♪
BOOM BOOM BOOM
YEAH YEAH YEAH
YEAH YEEAAH! ♪
IF THIS IS NORMAL, I DON'T NEED TO BE EMBARRASSED! I CAN FIGHT WITH MY HEAD HELD HIGH! ♪
BOOM
BOOM
BOOM
...
VOOOOOSH
BRING IT ON, THIEVES!
WOULD YOU STOP CALLING US THAT?!
DON'T EVER MISTAKE AN ADVENTURER FOR A THIEF!
RRRUUUMMBBLE...
?!

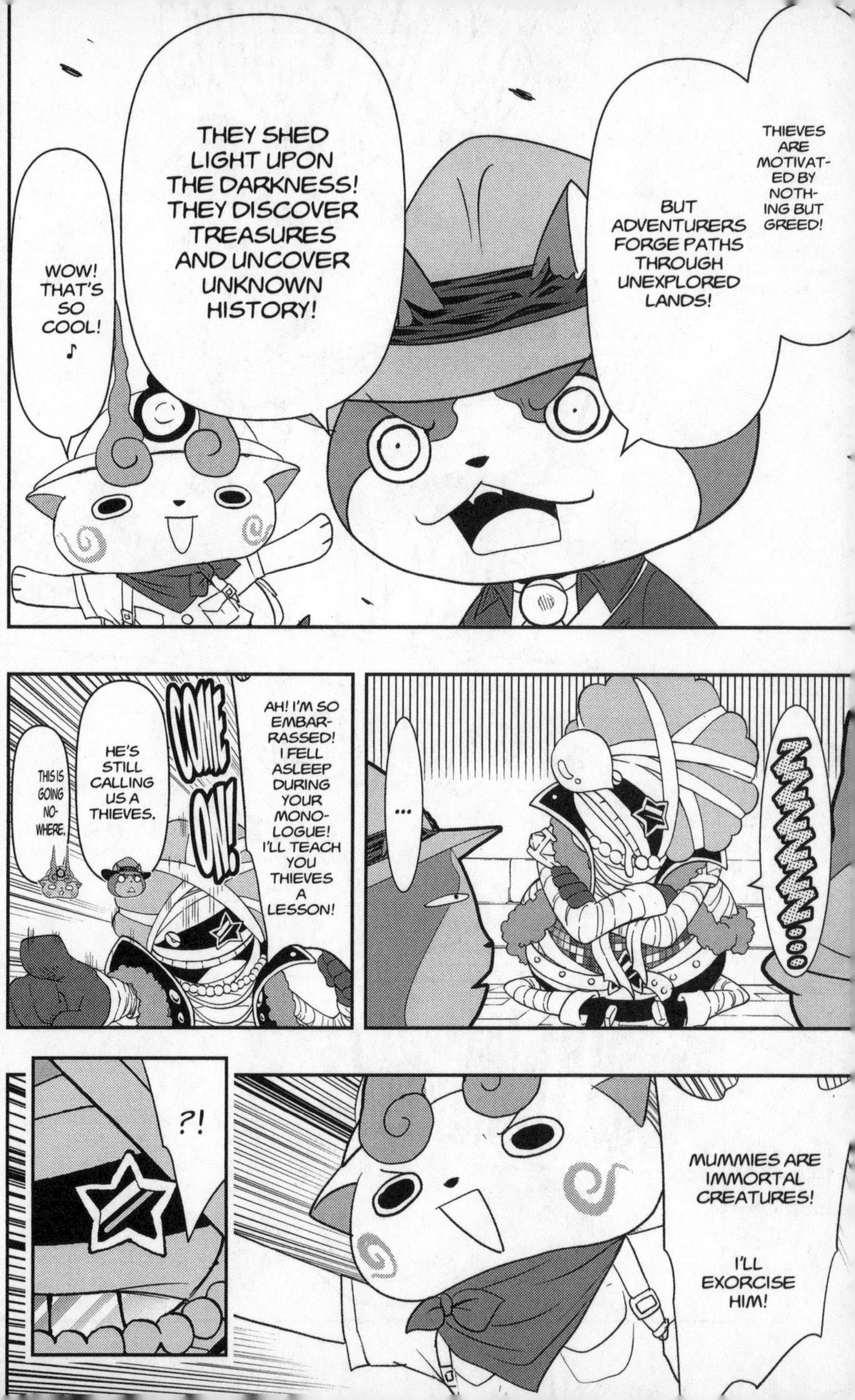
THIEVES ARE MOTIVATED BY NOTHING BUT GREED!
BUT ADVENTURERS FORGE PATHS THROUGH UNEXPLORED LANDS!
THEY SHED LIGHT UPON THE DARKNESS! THEY DISCOVER TREASURES AND UNCOVER UNKNOWN HISTORY!
WOW! THAT'S SO COOL! ♪
NNNNNNNOOO
...
AH! I'M SO EMBARRASSED! I FELL ASLEEP DURING YOUR MONOLOGUE! I'LL TEACH YOU THIEVES A LESSON!
COME ON!
HE'S STILL CALLING US A THIEVES.
THIS IS GOING NOWHERE.
MUMMIES ARE IMMORTAL CREATURES!
I'LL EXORCISE HIM!
?!

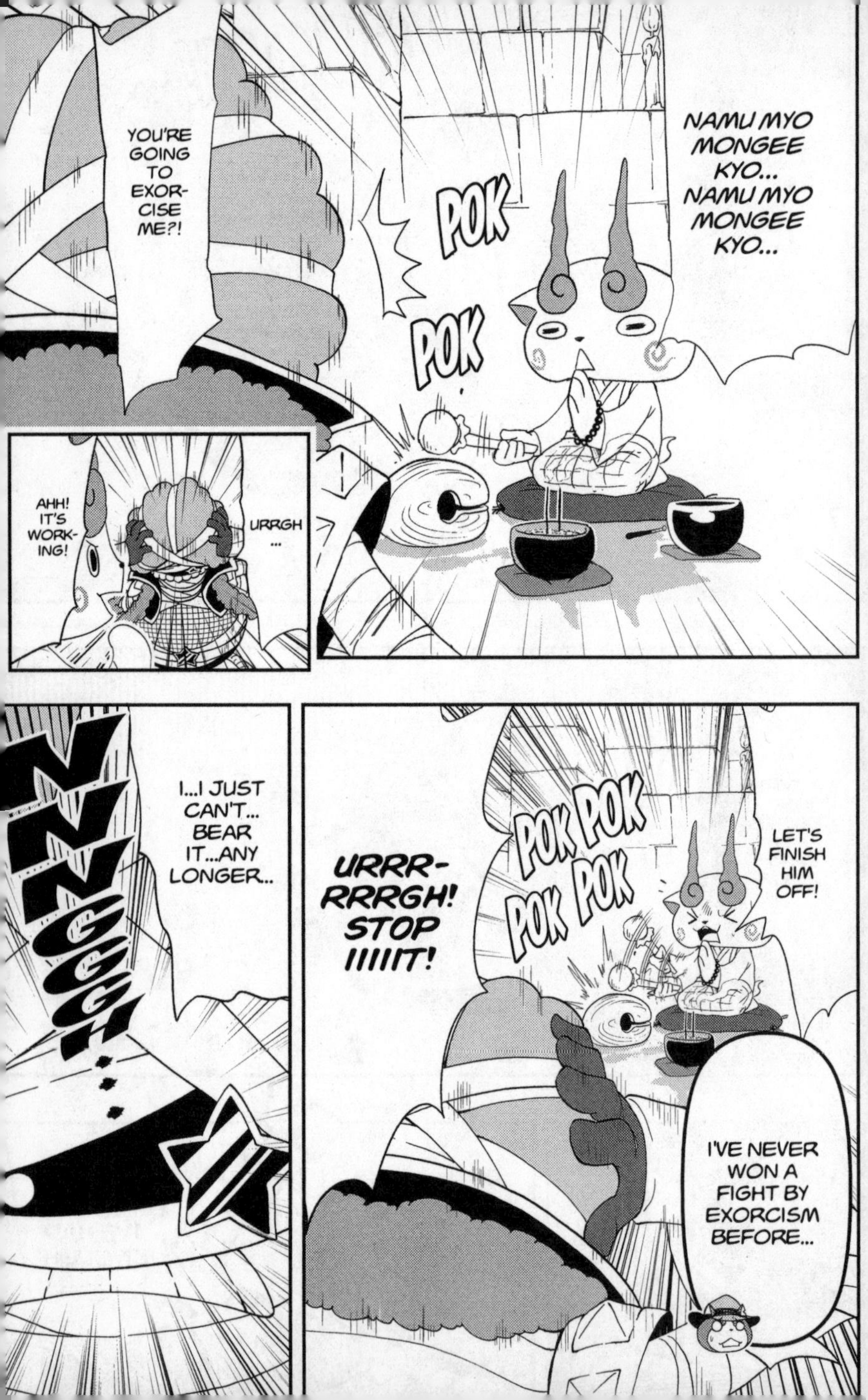
NAMU MYO MONGEE KYO... NAMU MYO MONGEE KYO...
POK
POK
YOU'RE GOING TO EXORCISE ME?!
URRGH...
AHH! IT'S WORKING!
LET'S FINISH HIM OFF!
POK POK POK POK
URRRRRRGH! STOP IIIIIT!
I'VE NEVER WON A FIGHT BY EXORCISM BEFORE...
I...I JUST CAN'T... BEAR IT...ANY LONGER...
NNNGGGH...

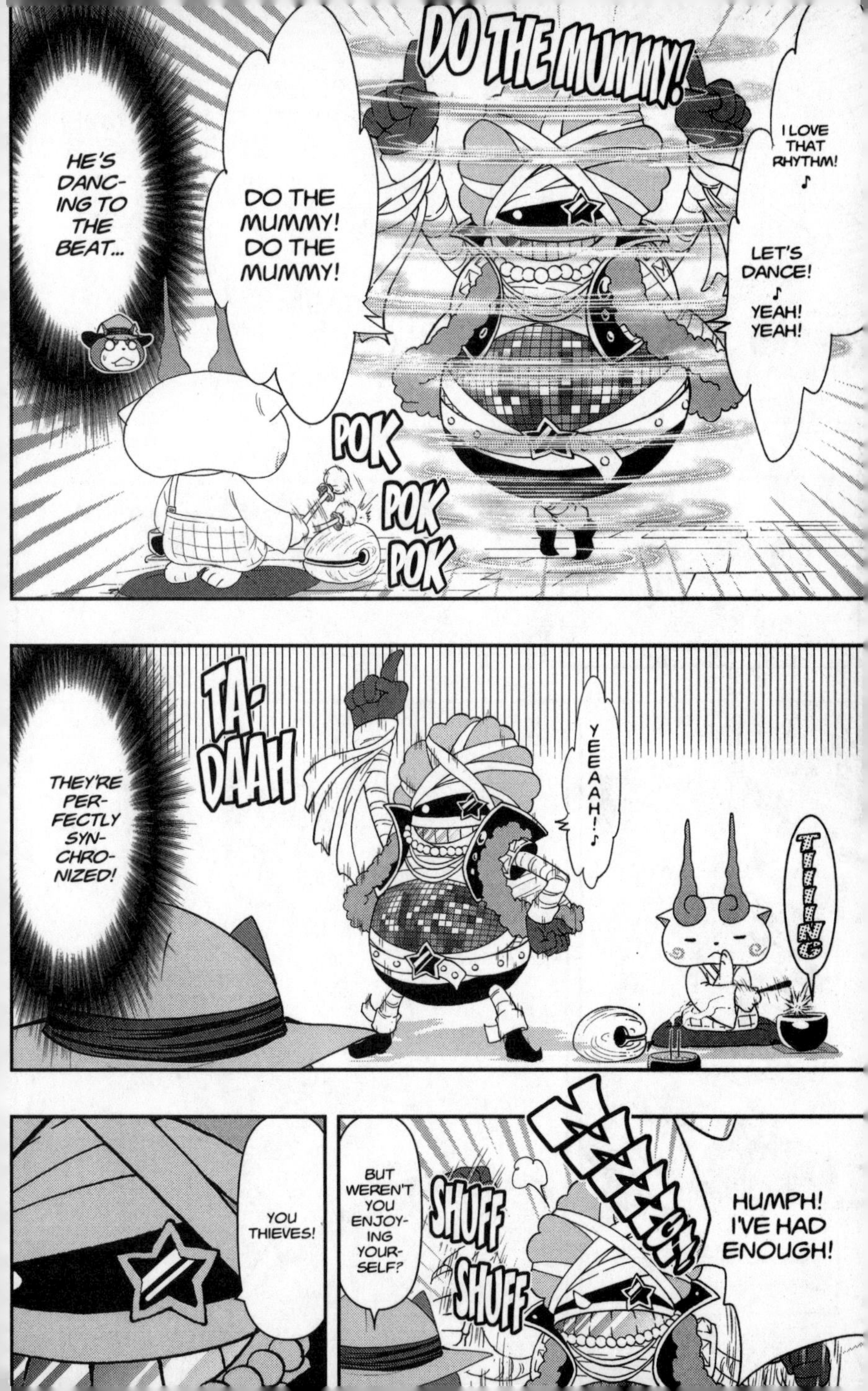
I LOVE THAT RHYTHM! ♪
LET'S DANCE! ♪ YEAH! YEAH!
DO THE MUMMY!
DO THE MUMMY! DO THE MUMMY!
POK POK POK
HE'S DANC-ING TO THE BEAT...
TIIIING
YEEAAH!♪
TA-DAAH
THEY'RE PER-FECTLY SYN-CHRO-NIZED!
HUMPH! I'VE HAD ENOUGH!
NNNNGH!
SHUFF SHUFF
BUT WEREN'T YOU ENJOY-ING YOUR-SELF?
YOU THIEVES!

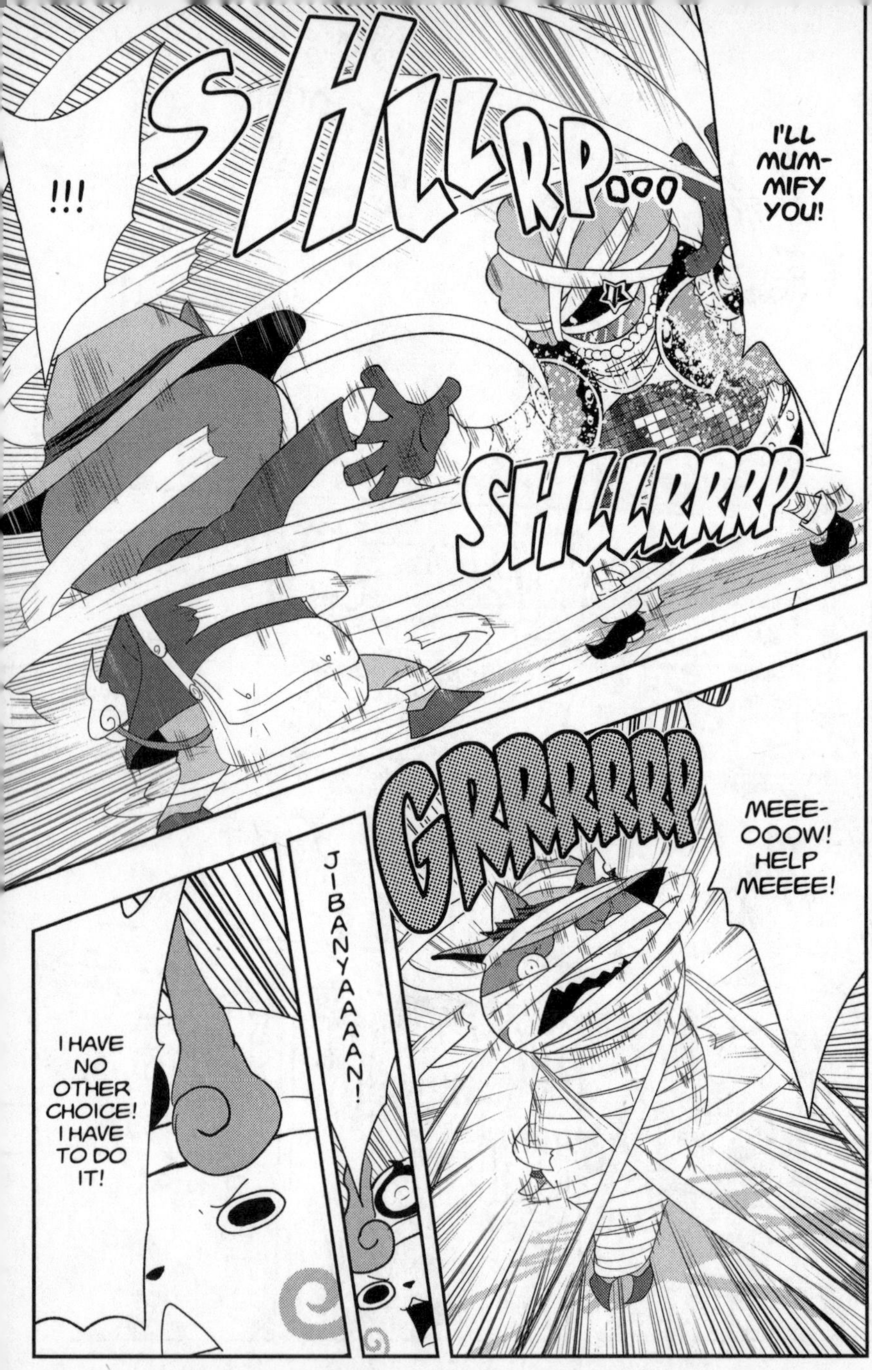
I'LL MUM-MIFY YOU!
SHLLRP...
!!!
SHLLRRRP
MEEE-OOOW! HELP MEEEE!
GRRRRRP
JIBANYAAAAAN!
I HAVE NO OTHER CHOICE! I HAVE TO DO IT!

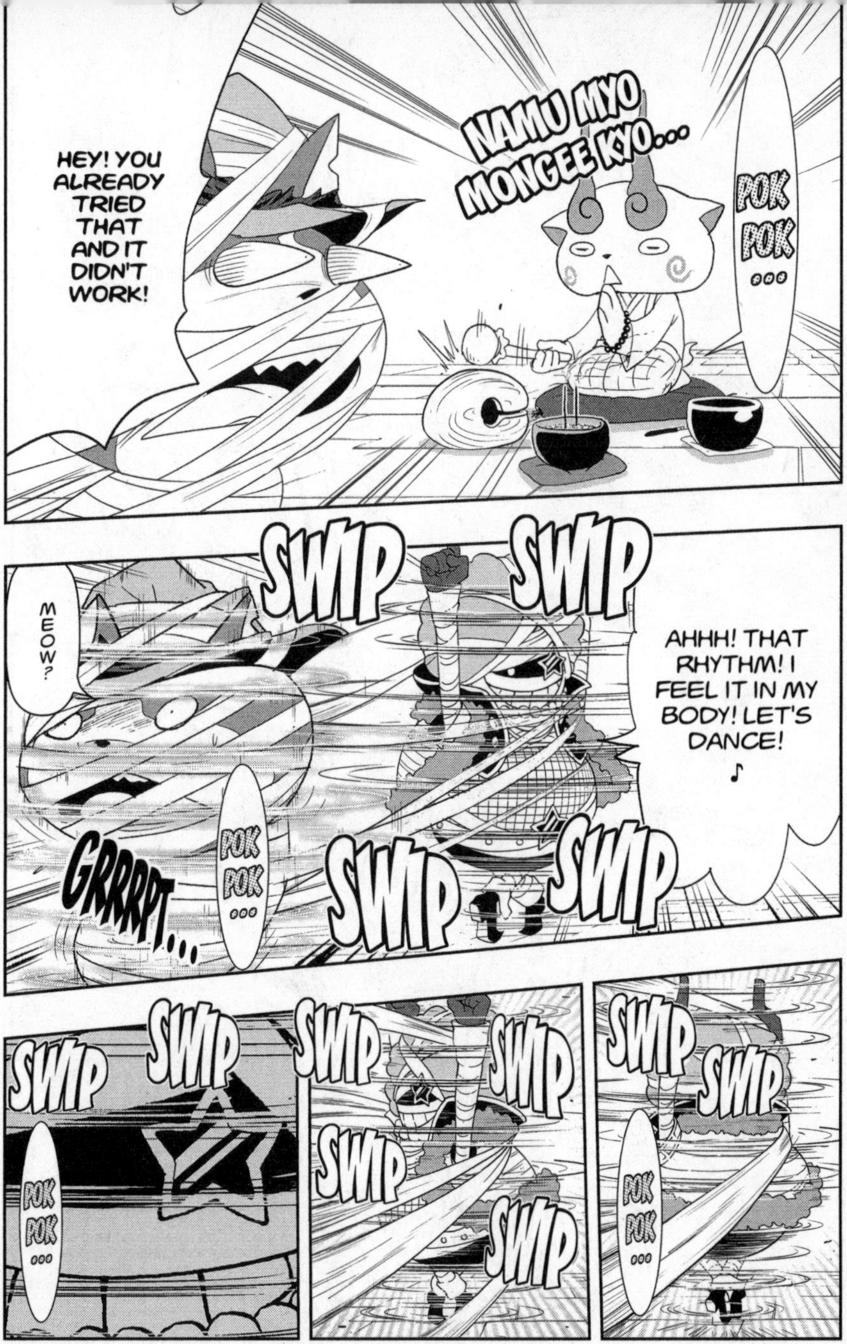
POK POK ...
NAMU MYO MONGEE KYO...
HEY! YOU ALREADY TRIED THAT AND IT DIDN'T WORK!
SWIP
SWIP
AHHH! THAT RHYTHM! I FEEL IT IN MY BODY! LET'S DANCE! ♪
SWIP
SWIP
MEOW?
POK POK ...
GRRRPT...
SWIP
SWIP
POK POK ...
SWIP
SWIP
SWIP
SWIP
SWIP
SWIP
POK POK ...

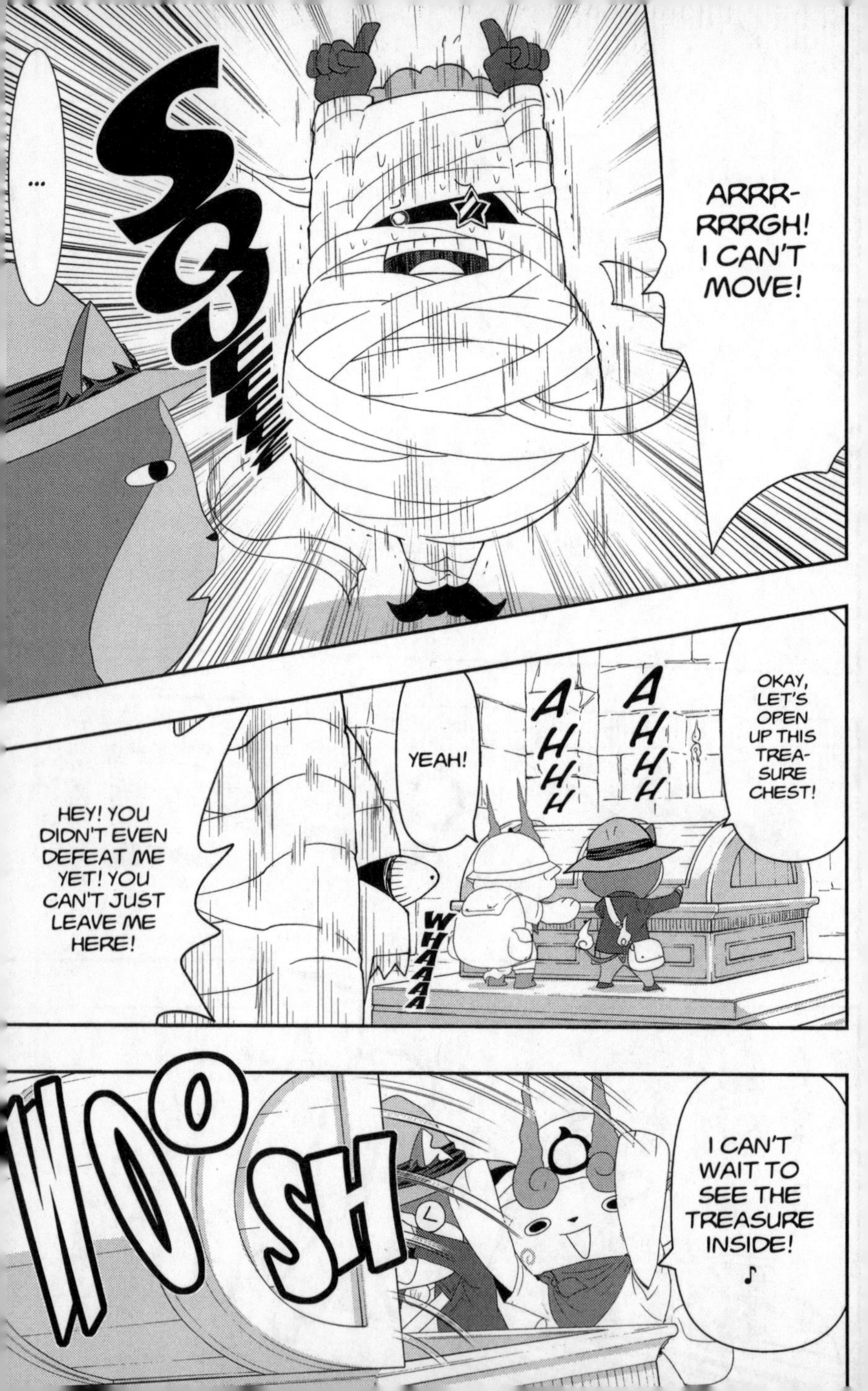
ARRRR-RRRGH! I CAN'T MOVE!
SQUEEE
...
OKAY, LET'S OPEN UP THIS TREA-SURE CHEST!
AHHH
AHHH
YEAH!
HEY! YOU DIDN'T EVEN DEFEAT ME YET! YOU CAN'T JUST LEAVE ME HERE!
WHAAAAA
I CAN'T WAIT TO SEE THE TREASURE INSIDE! ♪
WOOOSH

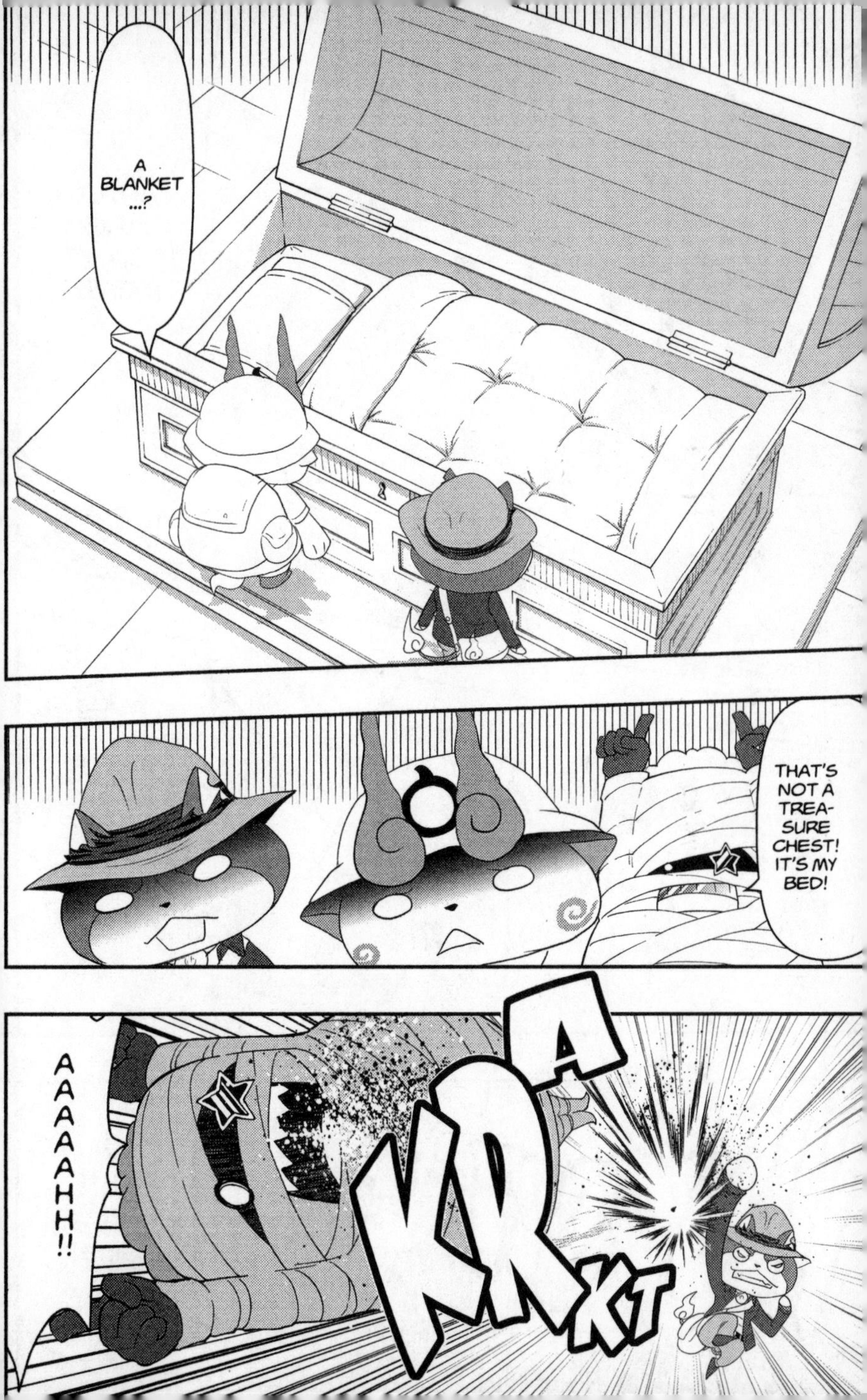
A BLANKET ...?
THAT'S NOT A TREASURE CHEST! IT'S MY BED!
AAAAAAHH!!
KRAKT

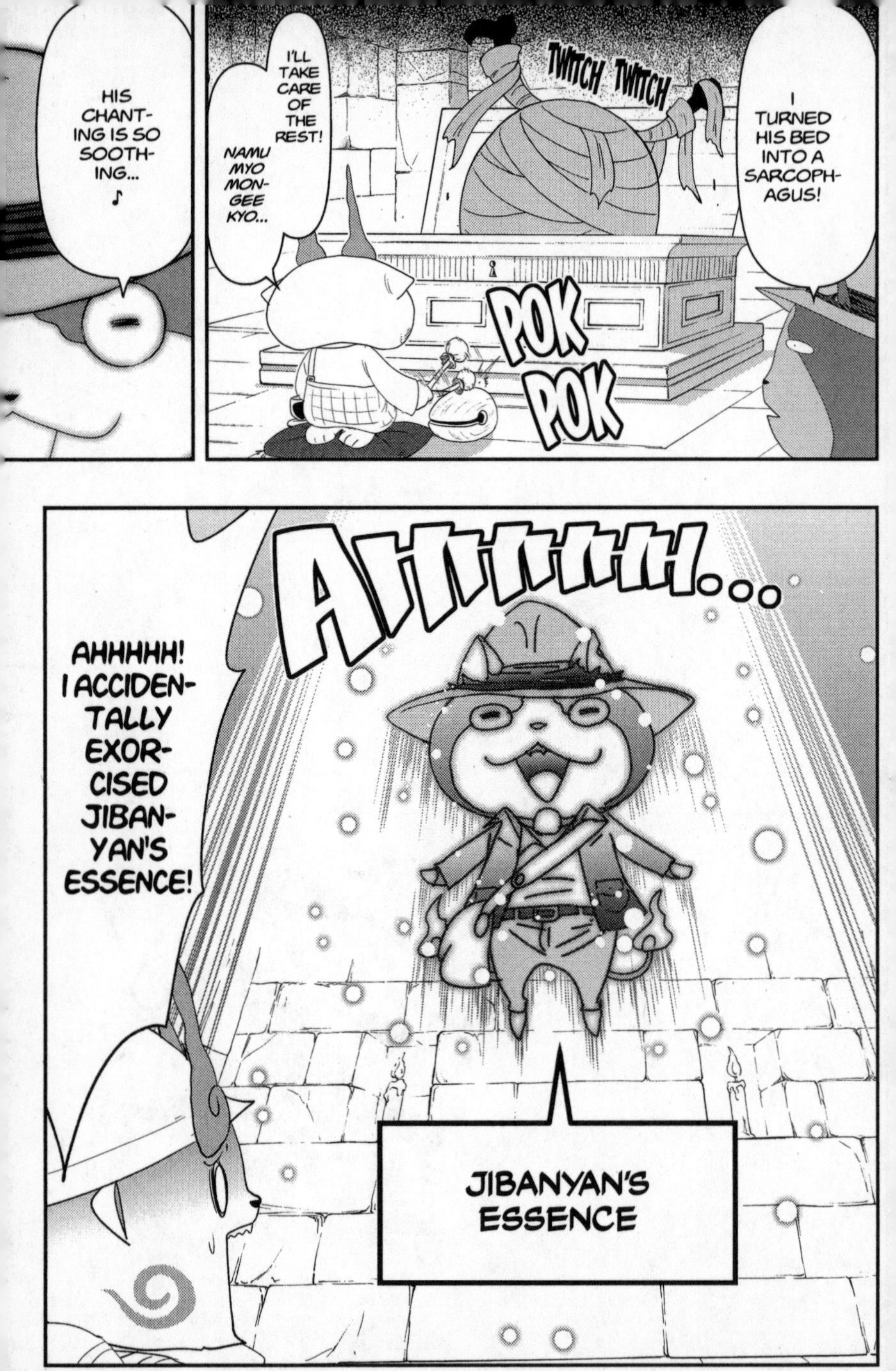
I TURNED HIS BED INTO A SARCOPH-AGUS!
TWITCH TWITCH
I'LL TAKE CARE OF THE REST!
NAMU MYO MON-GEE KYO...
POK POK
HIS CHANT-ING IS SO SOOTH-ING... ♪
AHHHHHH...
AHHHHH! I ACCIDEN-TALLY EXOR-CISED JIBAN-YAN'S ESSENCE!
JIBANYAN'S ESSENCE

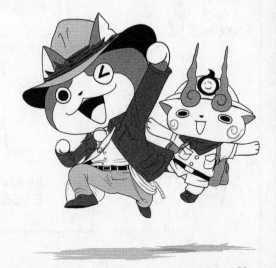

CHAPTER 139
YO-KAI WATCH BLASTERS TREASURE RAIDERS ARC: KOMASAN T ②

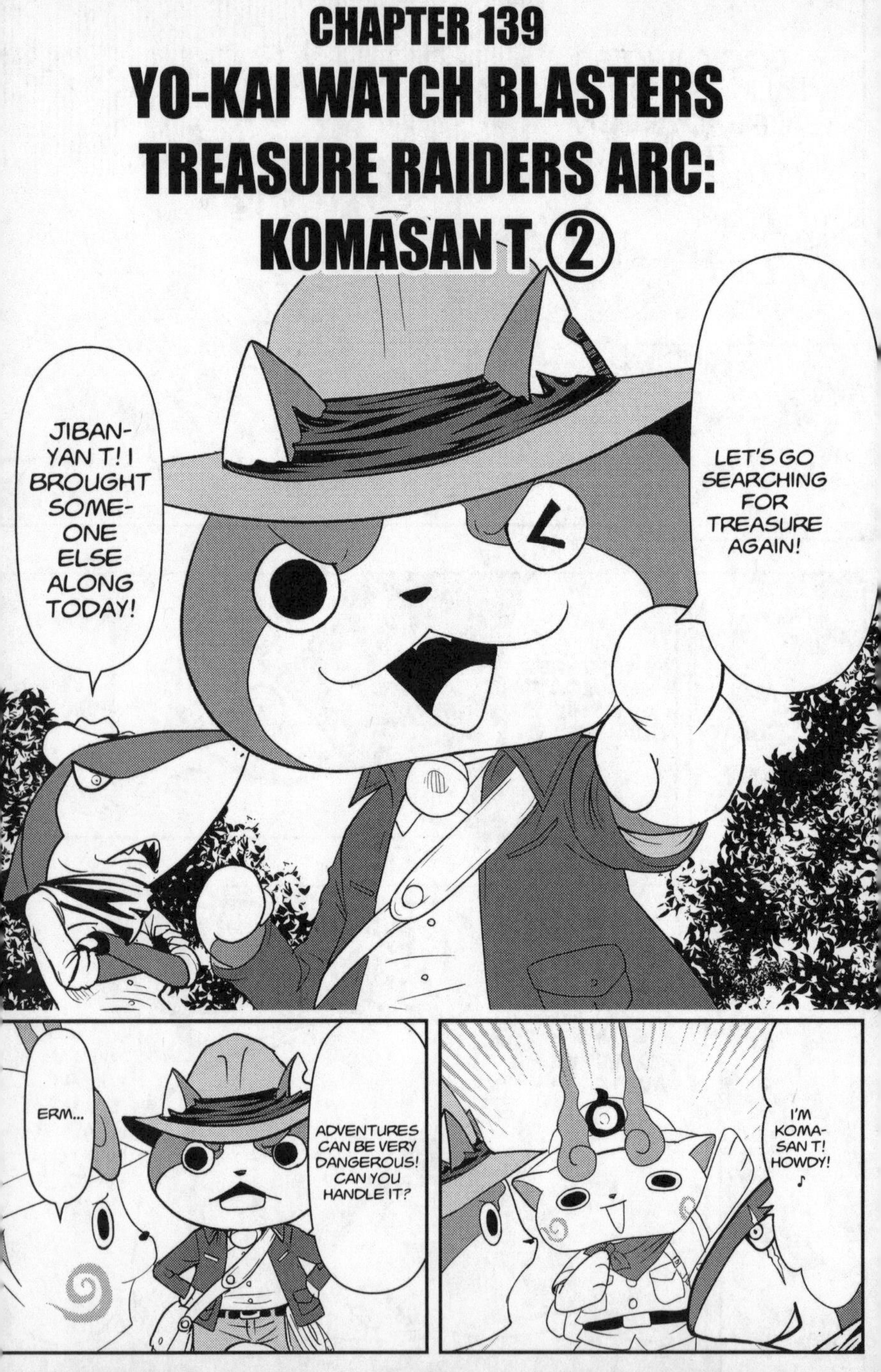
LET'S GO SEARCHING FOR TREASURE AGAIN!
JIBAN-YAN T! I BROUGHT SOME-ONE ELSE ALONG TODAY!
I'M KOMA-SAN T! HOWDY! ♪
ADVENTURES CAN BE VERY DANGEROUS! CAN YOU HANDLE IT?
ERM...

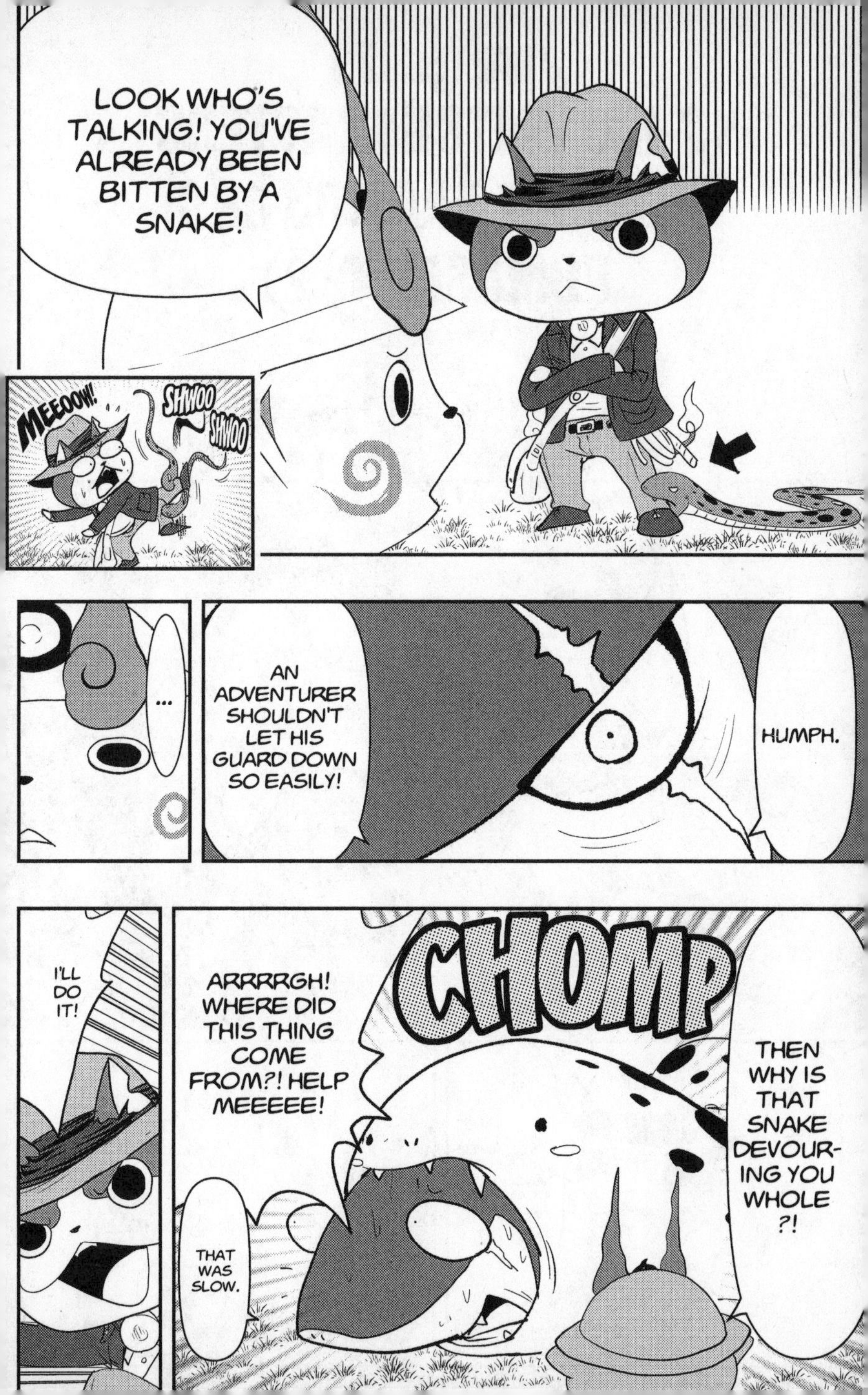
LOOK WHO'S TALKING! YOU'VE ALREADY BEEN BITTEN BY A SNAKE!
SHWOO
SHWOO
MEEEOOW!
HUMPH.
AN ADVENTURER SHOULDN'T LET HIS GUARD DOWN SO EASILY!
...
THEN WHY IS THAT SNAKE DEVOURING YOU WHOLE?!
CHOMP
ARRRRGH! WHERE DID THIS THING COME FROM?! HELP MEEEEEE!
THAT WAS SLOW.
I'LL DO IT!

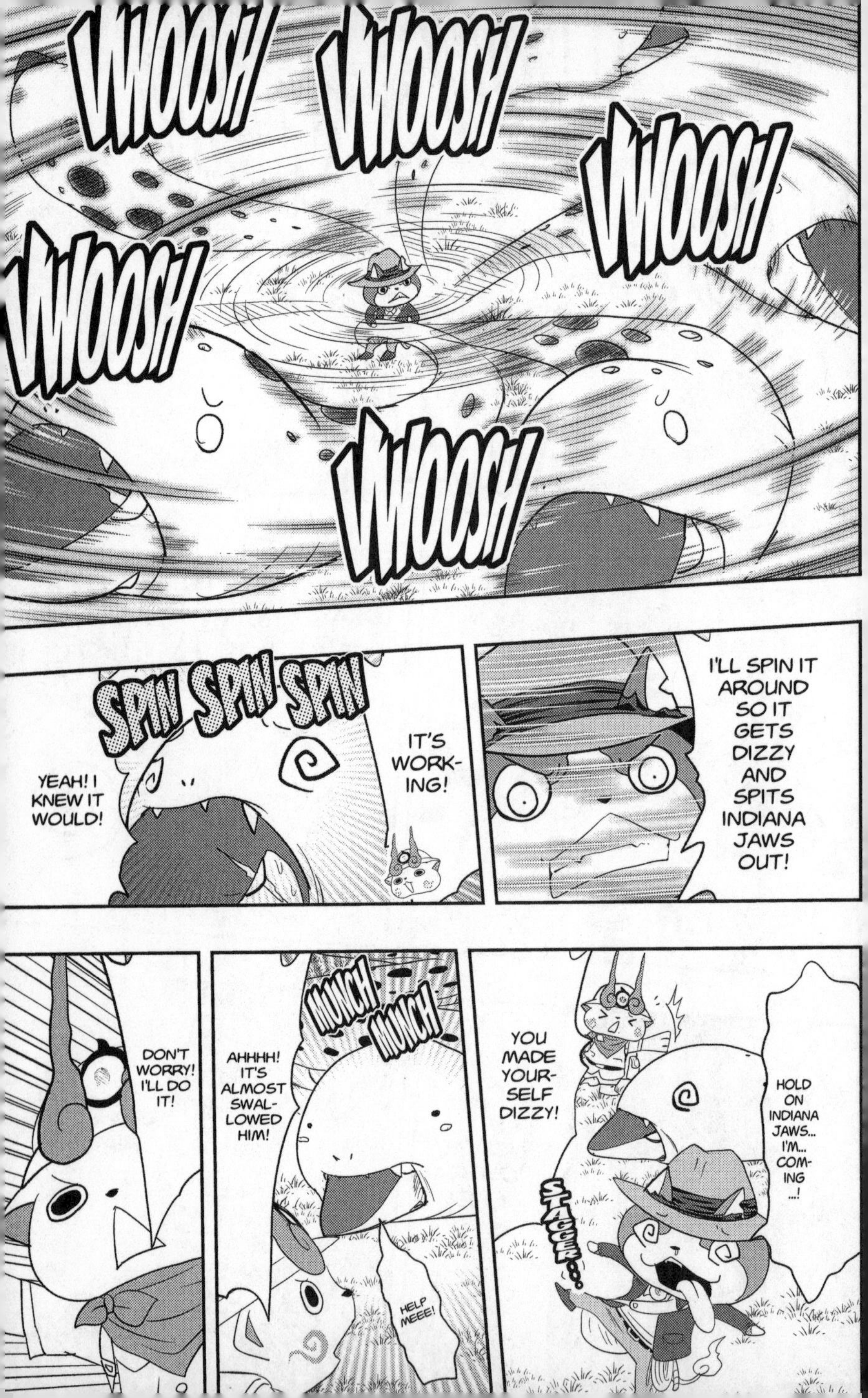

VWOOSH
VWOOSH
VWOOSH
VWOOSH
VWOOSH
I'LL SPIN IT AROUND SO IT GETS DIZZY AND SPITS INDIANA JAWS OUT!
SPIN SPIN SPIN
IT'S WORKING!
YEAH! I KNEW IT WOULD!
HOLD ON INDIANA JAWS... I'M... COMING...!
YOU MADE YOURSELF DIZZY!
STAGGER
MUNCH MUNCH
AHHHH! IT'S ALMOST SWALLOWED HIM!
HELP MEEE!
DON'T WORRY! I'LL DO IT!

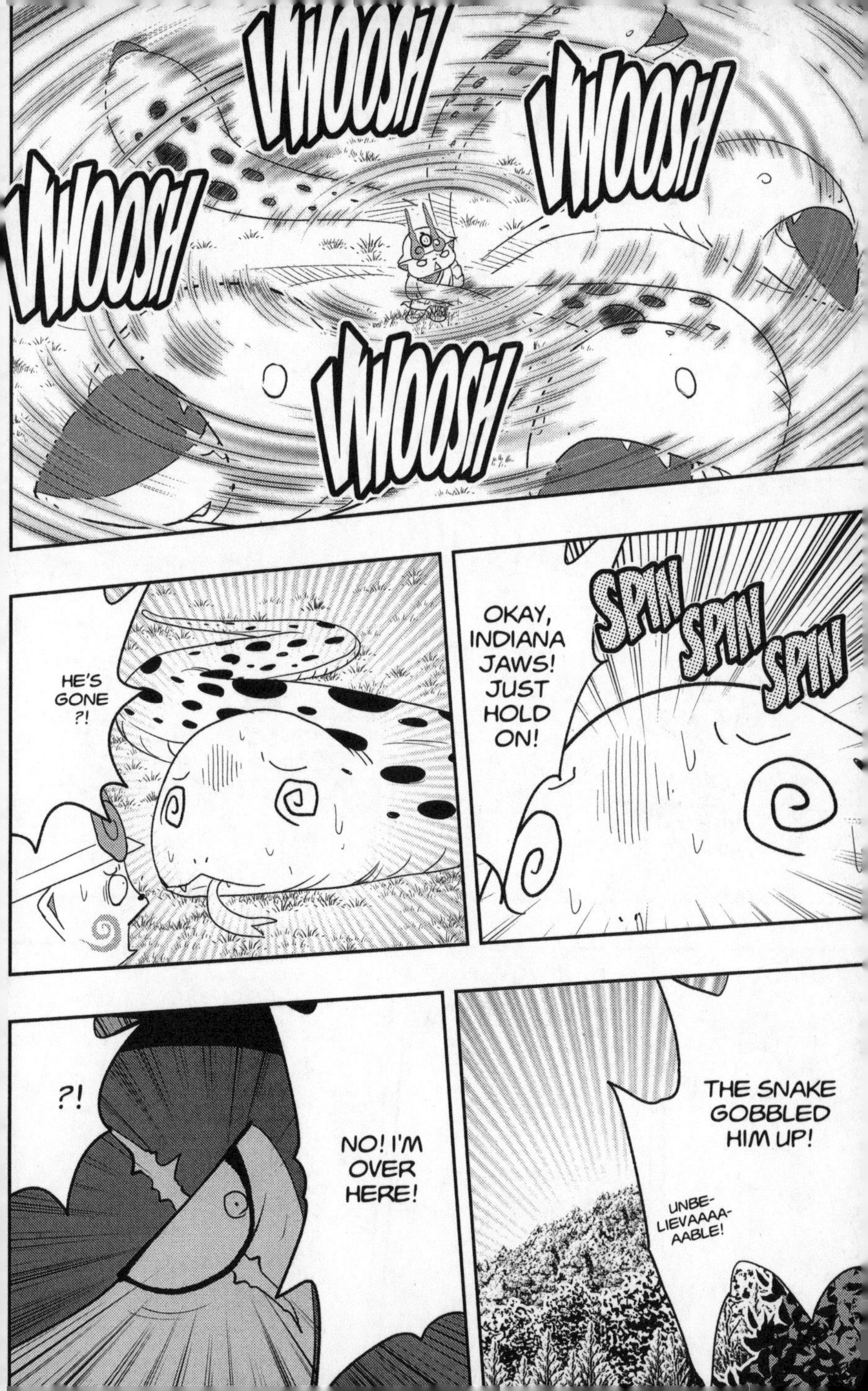
VWOOSH
VWOOSH
VWOOSH
VWOOSH
SPIN SPIN SPIN
OKAY, INDIANA JAWS! JUST HOLD ON!
HE'S GONE ?!
THE SNAKE GOBBLED HIM UP!
UNBE-LIEVAAAA-AABLE!
?!
NO! I'M OVER HERE!

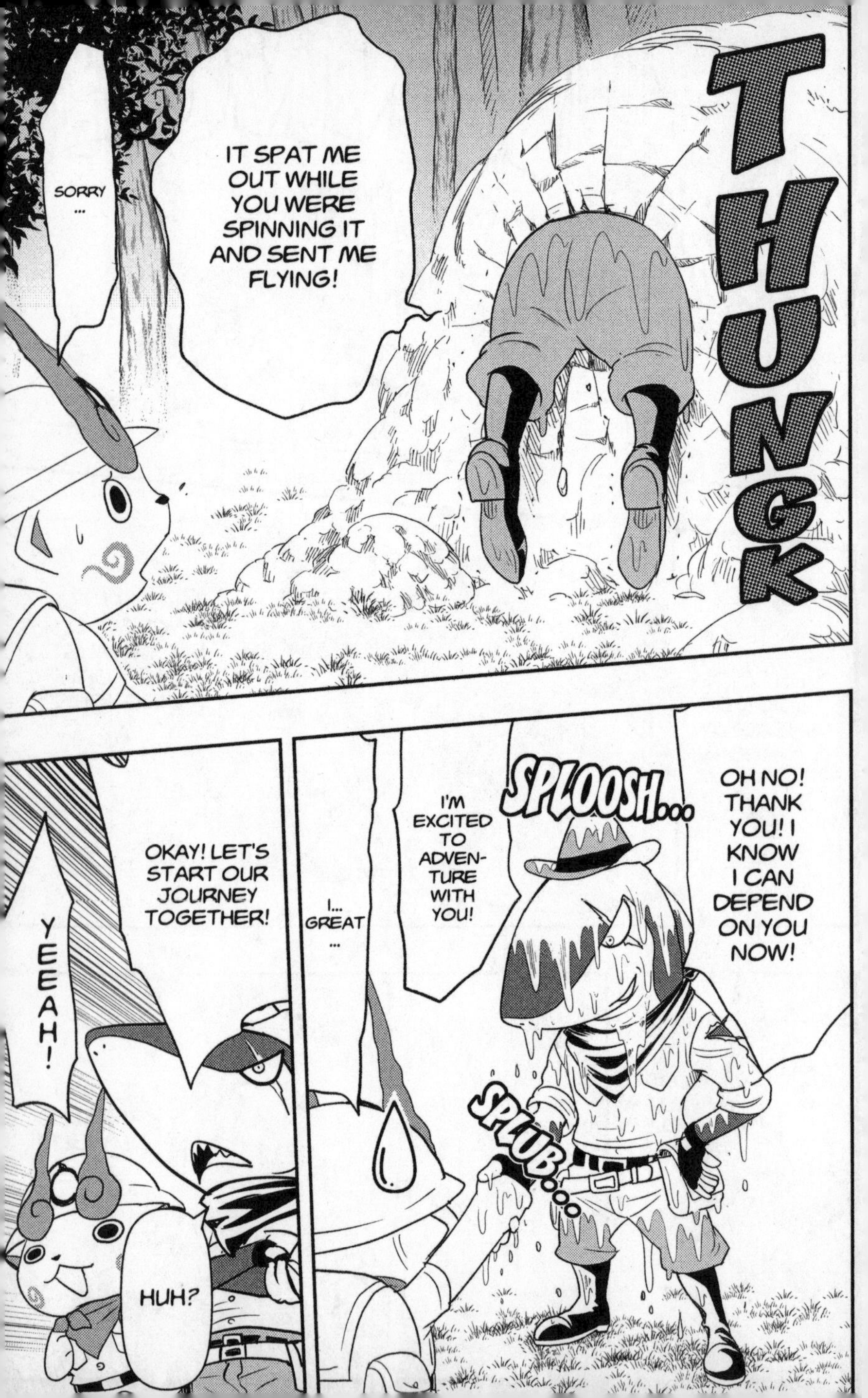
THUNGK
IT SPAT ME OUT WHILE YOU WERE SPINNING IT AND SENT ME FLYING!
SORRY...
OH NO! THANK YOU! I KNOW I CAN DEPEND ON YOU NOW!
SPLOOSH...
I'M EXCITED TO ADVEN-TURE WITH YOU!
I... GREAT...
SPLUB...
OKAY! LET'S START OUR JOURNEY TOGETHER!
YEEEAH!
HUH?

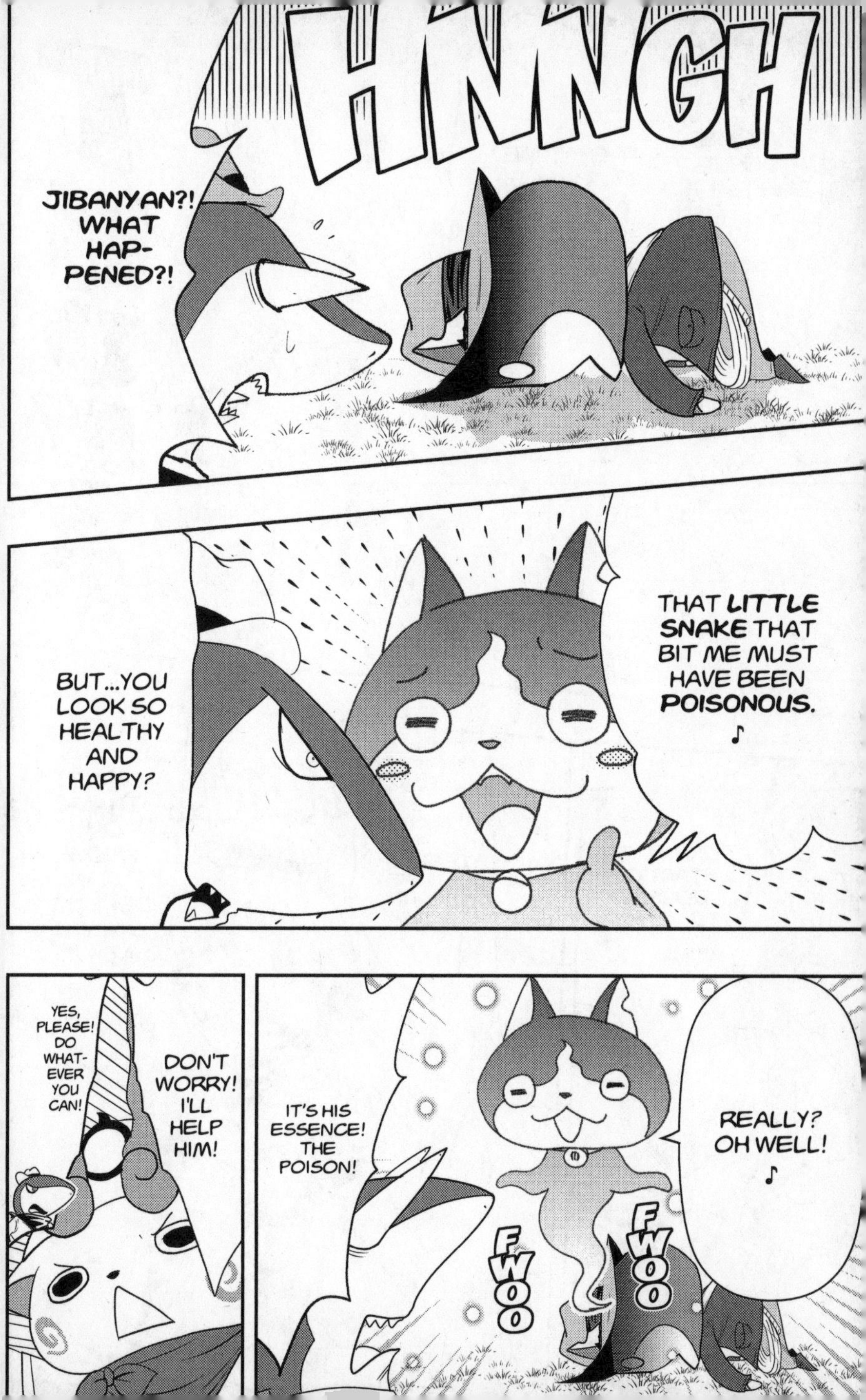
HNNGH
JIBANYAN?! WHAT HAP-PENED?!
THAT LITTLE SNAKE THAT BIT ME MUST HAVE BEEN POISONOUS. ♪
BUT...YOU LOOK SO HEALTHY AND HAPPY?
REALLY? OH WELL! ♪
FWOO
FWOO
IT'S HIS ESSENCE! THE POISON!
DON'T WORRY! I'LL HELP HIM!
YES, PLEASE! DO WHAT-EVER YOU CAN!

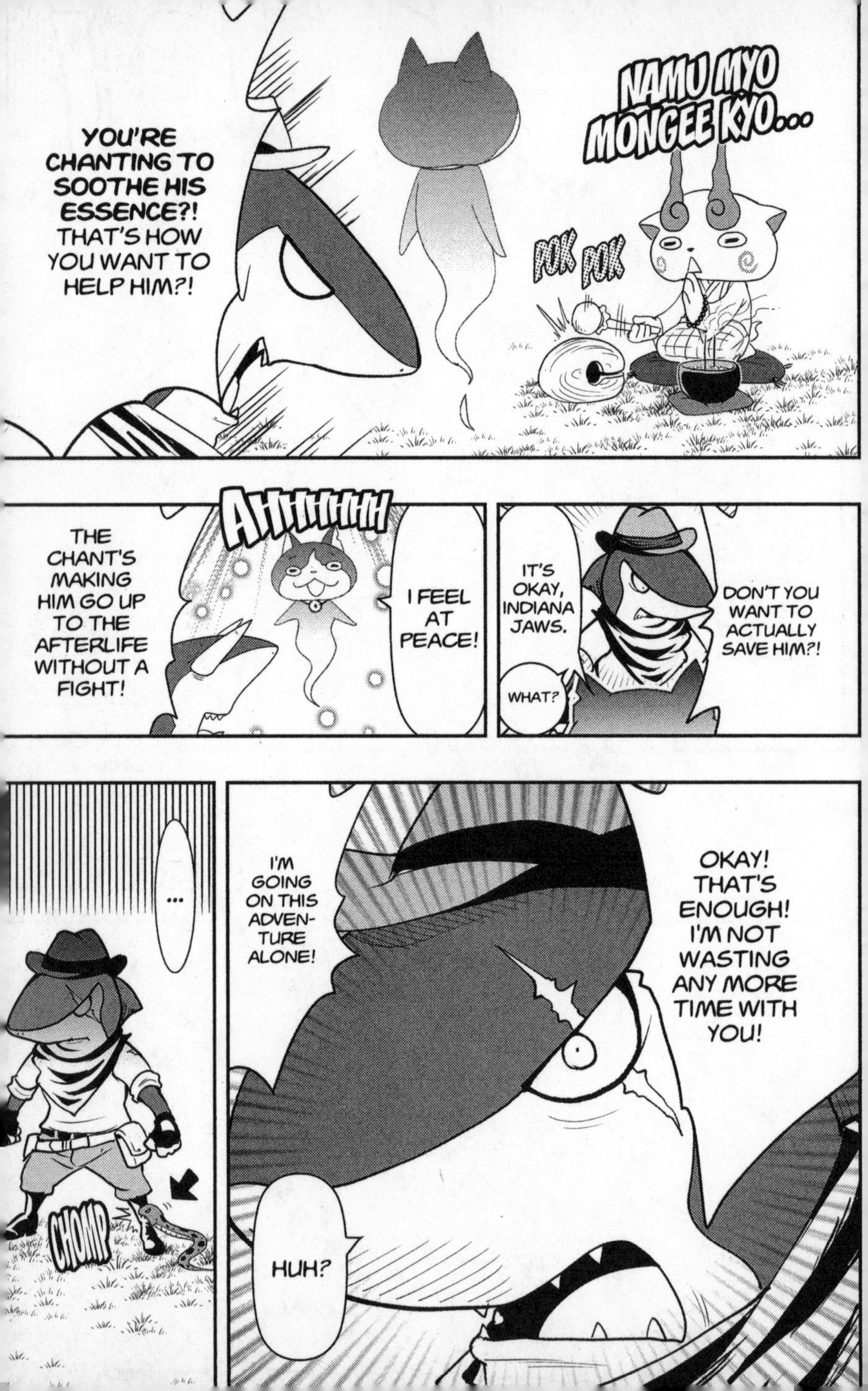
NAMU MYO MONGEE KYO...
POK POK
YOU'RE CHANTING TO SOOTHE HIS ESSENCE?! THAT'S HOW YOU WANT TO HELP HIM?!
DON'T YOU WANT TO ACTUALLY SAVE HIM?!
IT'S OKAY, INDIANA JAWS.
WHAT?
AHHHHHHHH
I FEEL AT PEACE!
THE CHANT'S MAKING HIM GO UP TO THE AFTERLIFE WITHOUT A FIGHT!
OKAY! THAT'S ENOUGH! I'M NOT WASTING ANY MORE TIME WITH YOU!
I'M GOING ON THIS ADVEN-TURE ALONE!
HUH?
...
CHOMP

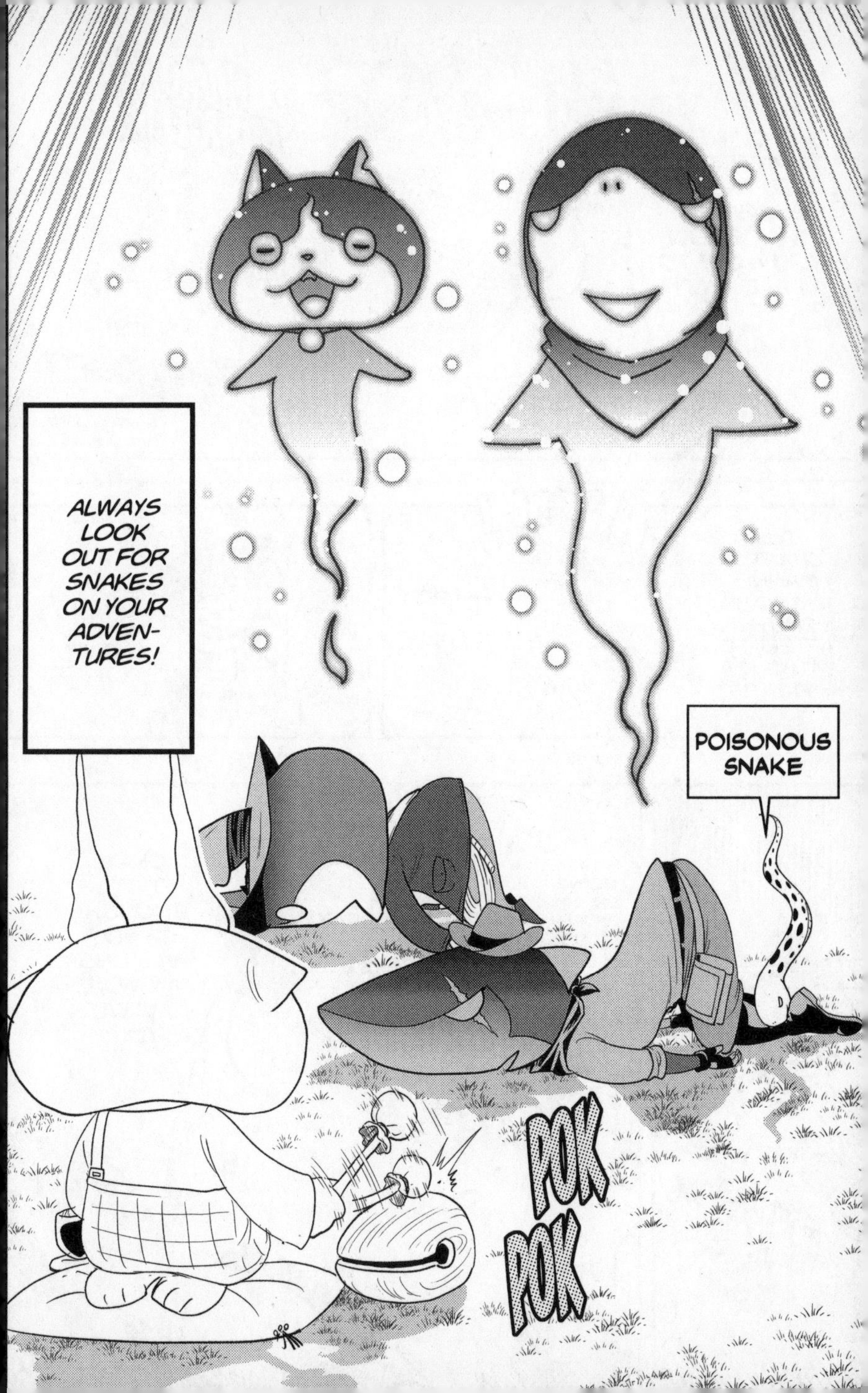
ALWAYS LOOK OUT FOR SNAKES ON YOUR ADVEN-TURES!
POISONOUS SNAKE
POK POK

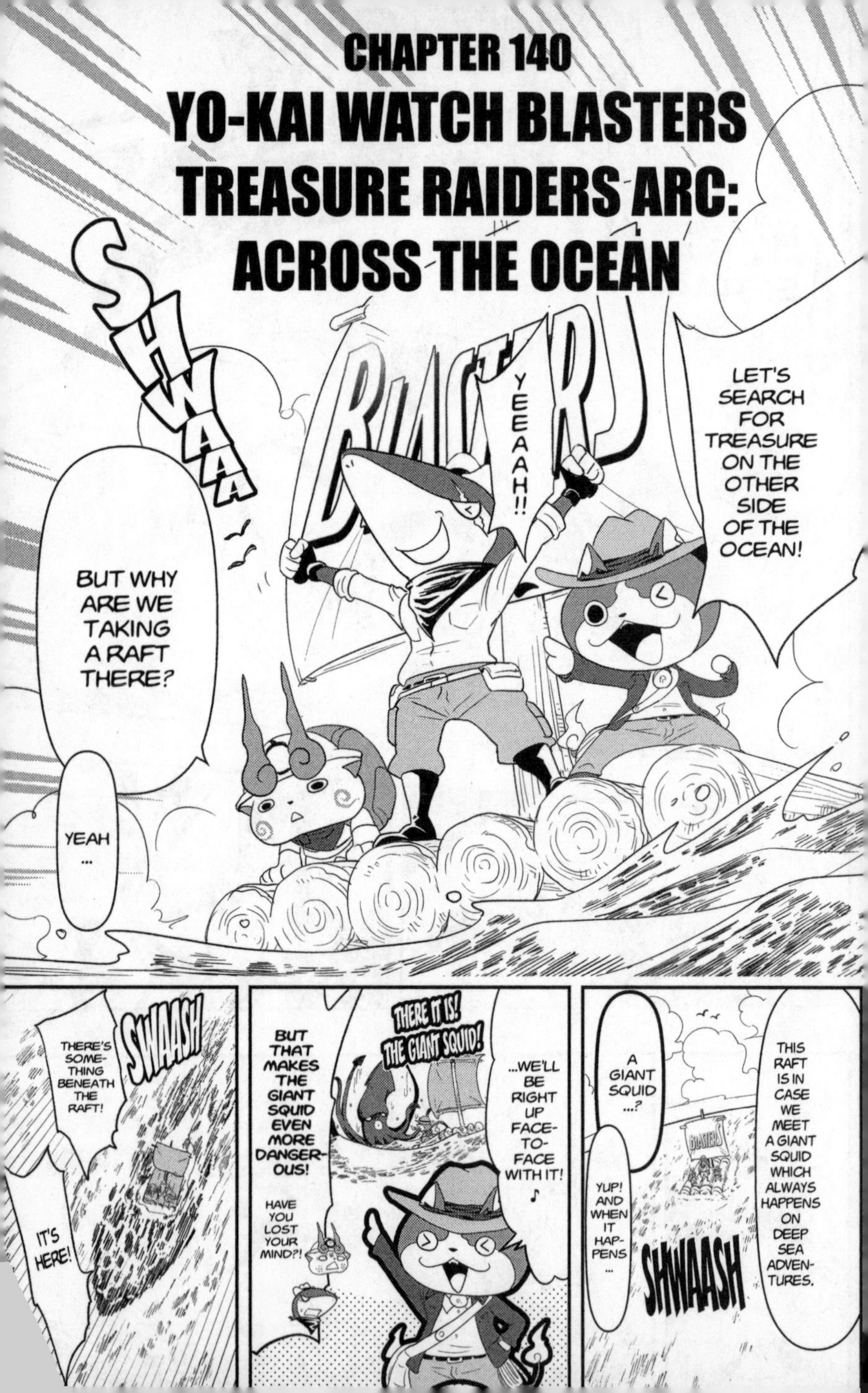
CHAPTER 140
YO-KAI WATCH BLASTERS TREASURE RAIDERS ARC: ACROSS THE OCEAN
LET'S SEARCH FOR TREASURE ON THE OTHER SIDE OF THE OCEAN!
YEEAAAH!!
BLASTERS
SHWAAA
BUT WHY ARE WE TAKING A RAFT THERE?
YEAH ...
THIS RAFT IS IN CASE WE MEET A GIANT SQUID WHICH ALWAYS HAPPENS ON DEEP SEA ADVENTURES.
A GIANT SQUID ...?
YUP! AND WHEN IT HAPPENS ...
SHWAASH
...WE'LL BE RIGHT UP FACE-TO-FACE WITH IT! ♪
THERE IT IS! THE GIANT SQUID!
BUT THAT MAKES THE GIANT SQUID EVEN MORE DANGEROUS!
HAVE YOU LOST YOUR MIND?!
SWAASH
THERE'S SOMETHING BENEATH THE RAFT!
IT'S HERE!

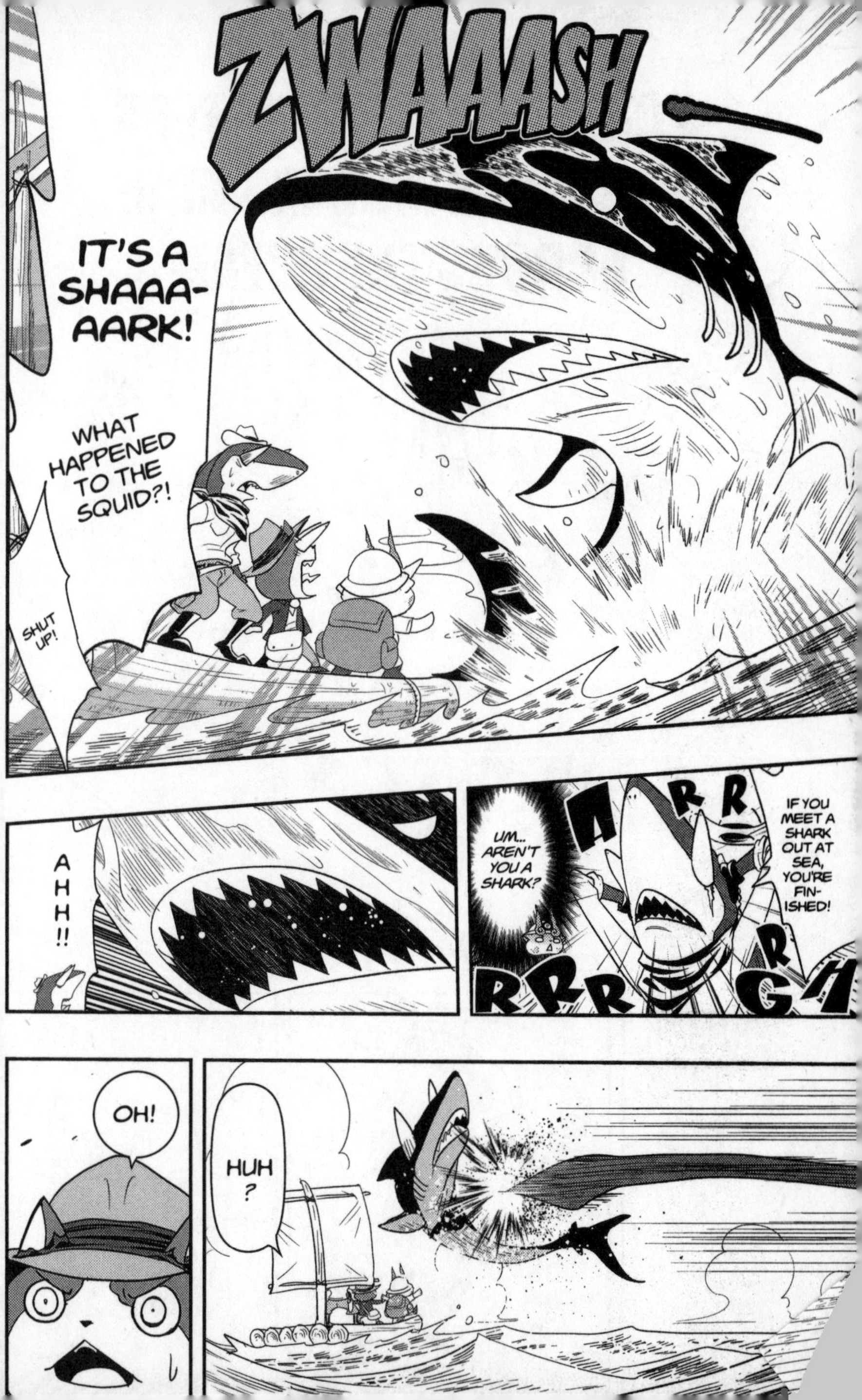
ZWAAASH
IT'S A SHAAAA-AARK!
WHAT HAPPENED TO THE SQUID?!
SHUT UP!
IF YOU MEET A SHARK OUT AT SEA, YOU'RE FIN-ISHED!
UM... AREN'T YOU A SHARK?
ARRRRRRGH
AHHH!!
HUH?
OH!

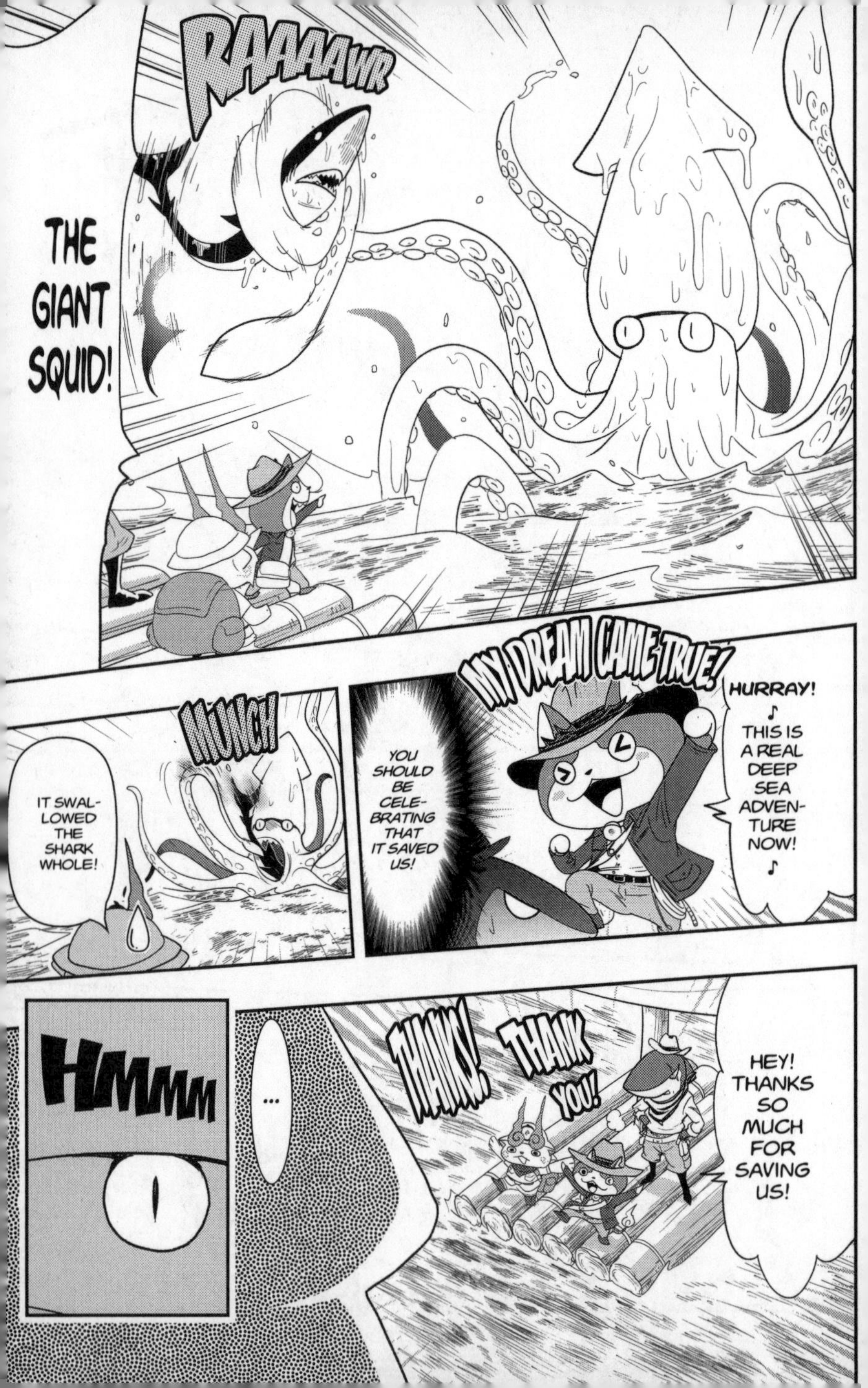
RAAAAWR
THE GIANT SQUID!
MY DREAM CAME TRUE!
HURRAY! ♪ THIS IS A REAL DEEP SEA ADVENTURE NOW! ♪
YOU SHOULD BE CELEBRATING THAT IT SAVED US!
MUNCH!
IT SWALLOWED THE SHARK WHOLE!
HEY! THANKS SO MUCH FOR SAVING US!
THANK YOU!
THANKS!
...
HMMMM

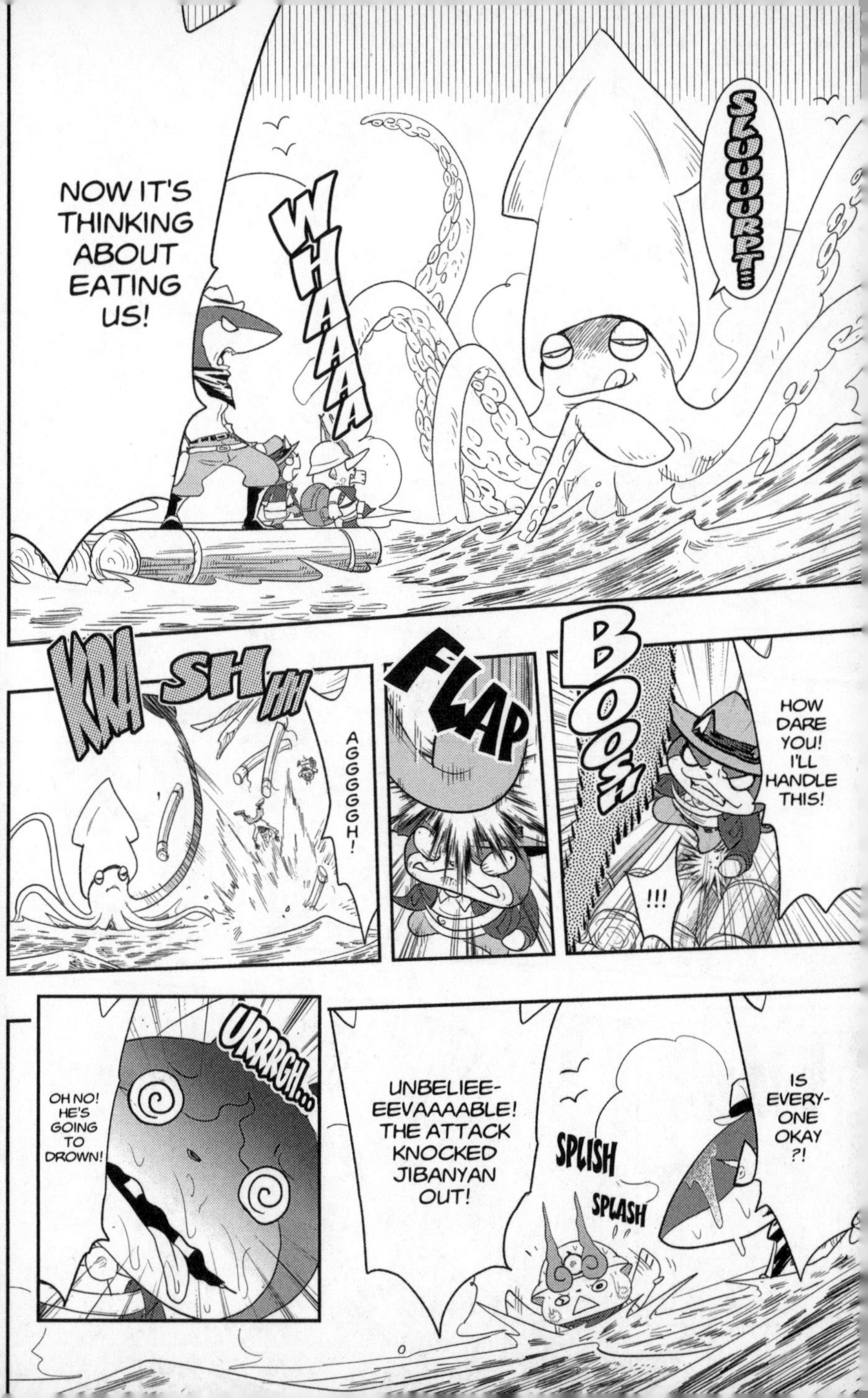
SLUUUURPT!!
WHAAAAA
NOW IT'S THINKING ABOUT EATING US!
BOOM
HOW DARE YOU! I'LL HANDLE THIS!
!!!
FLAP
KRASHHH
AGGGGGH!
IS EVERYONE OKAY?!
SPLISH
SPLASH
UNBELIEEEVAAAABLE! THE ATTACK KNOCKED JIBANYAN OUT!
URRRGH...
OH NO! HE'S GOING TO DROWN!

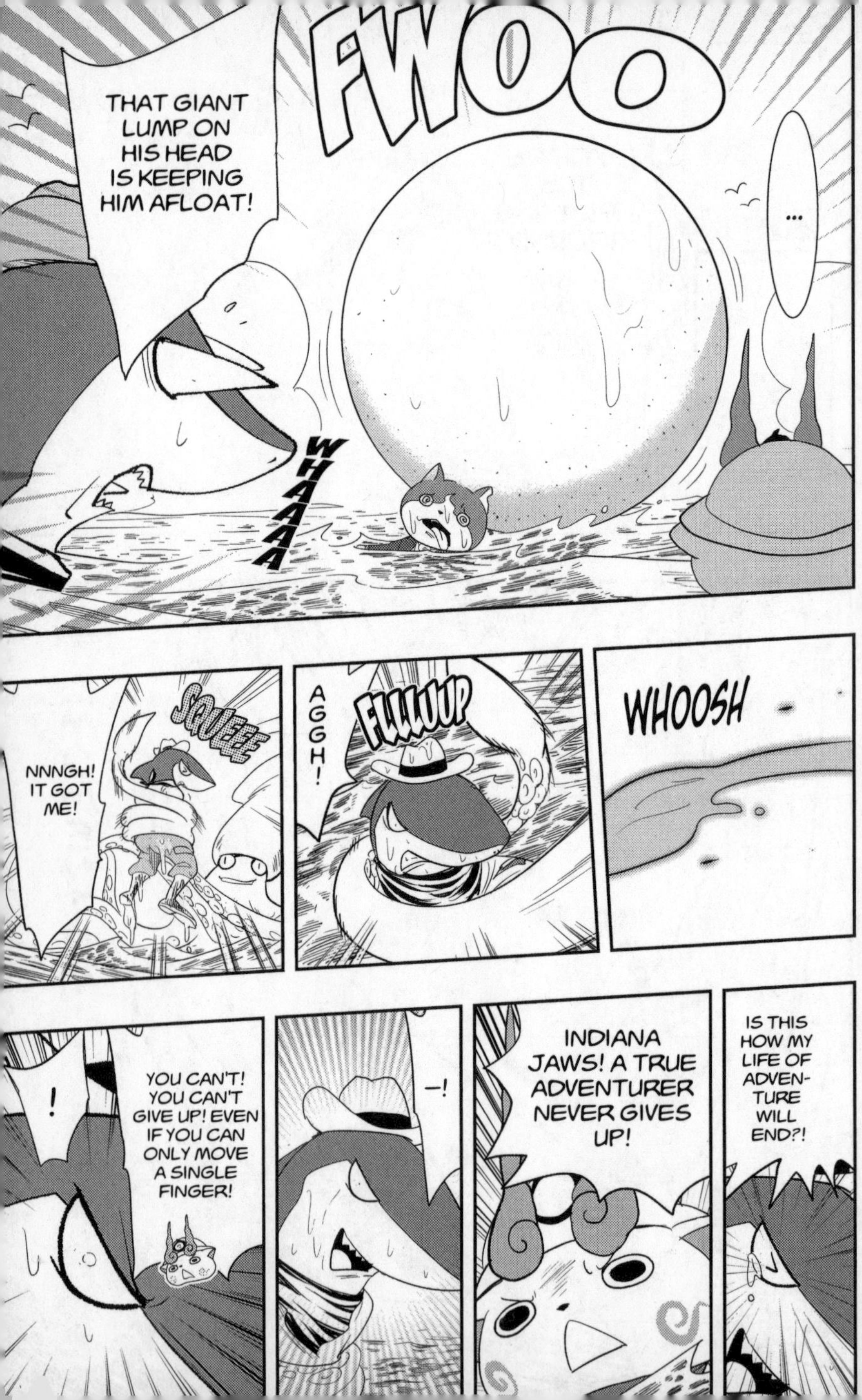
FWOO
...
THAT GIANT LUMP ON HIS HEAD IS KEEPING HIM AFLOAT!
WHAAAAA
WHOOSH
FLLLUUP
AGGH!
SQUEEEE
NNNGH! IT GOT ME!
IS THIS HOW MY LIFE OF ADVEN-TURE WILL END?!
INDIANA JAWS! A TRUE ADVENTURER NEVER GIVES UP!
—!
YOU CAN'T! YOU CAN'T GIVE UP! EVEN IF YOU CAN ONLY MOVE A SINGLE FINGER!
!

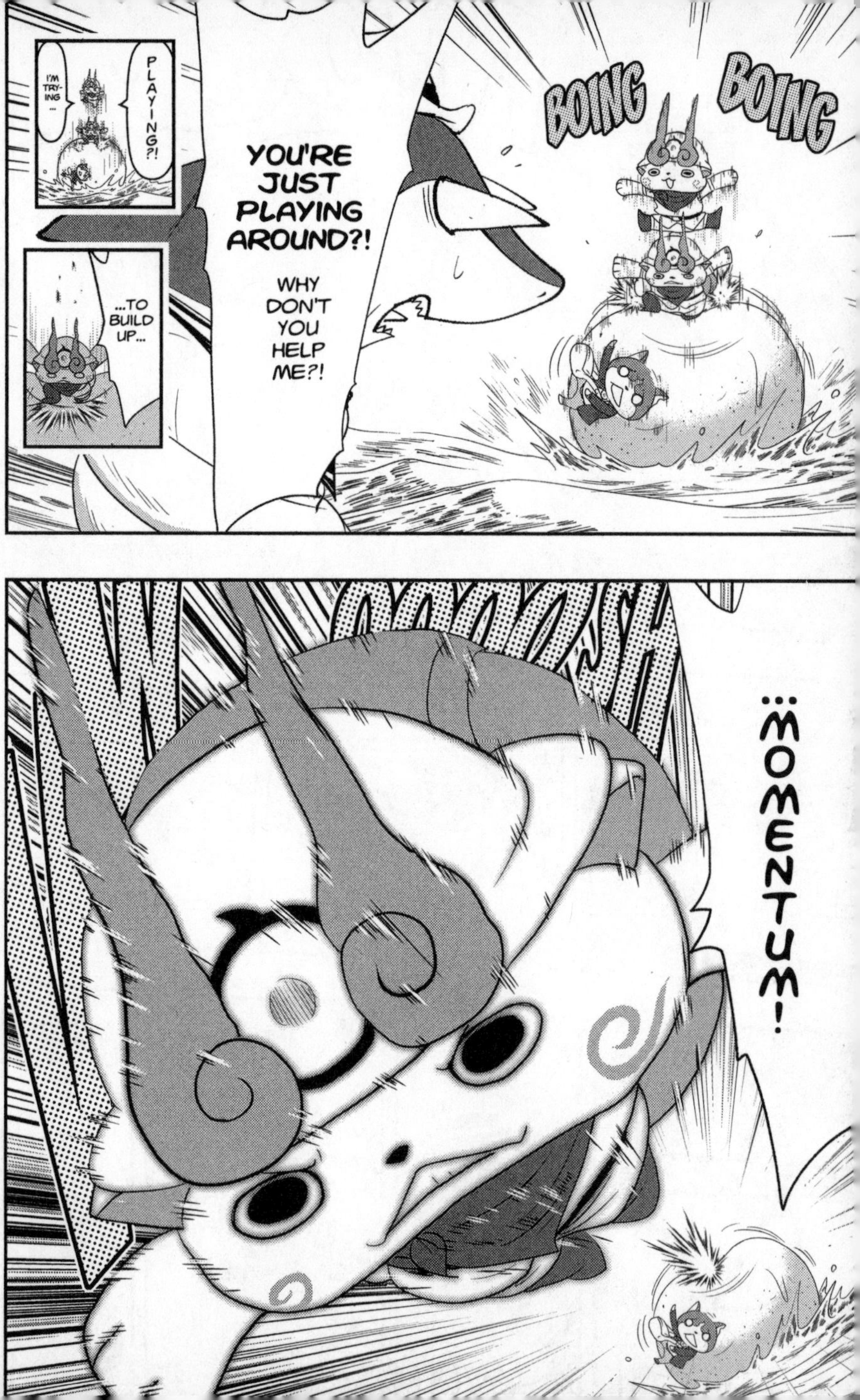
BOING BOING
YOU'RE JUST PLAYING AROUND?!
WHY DON'T YOU HELP ME?!
PLAYING?!
I'M TRYING...
...TO BUILD UP...
...MOMENTUM!

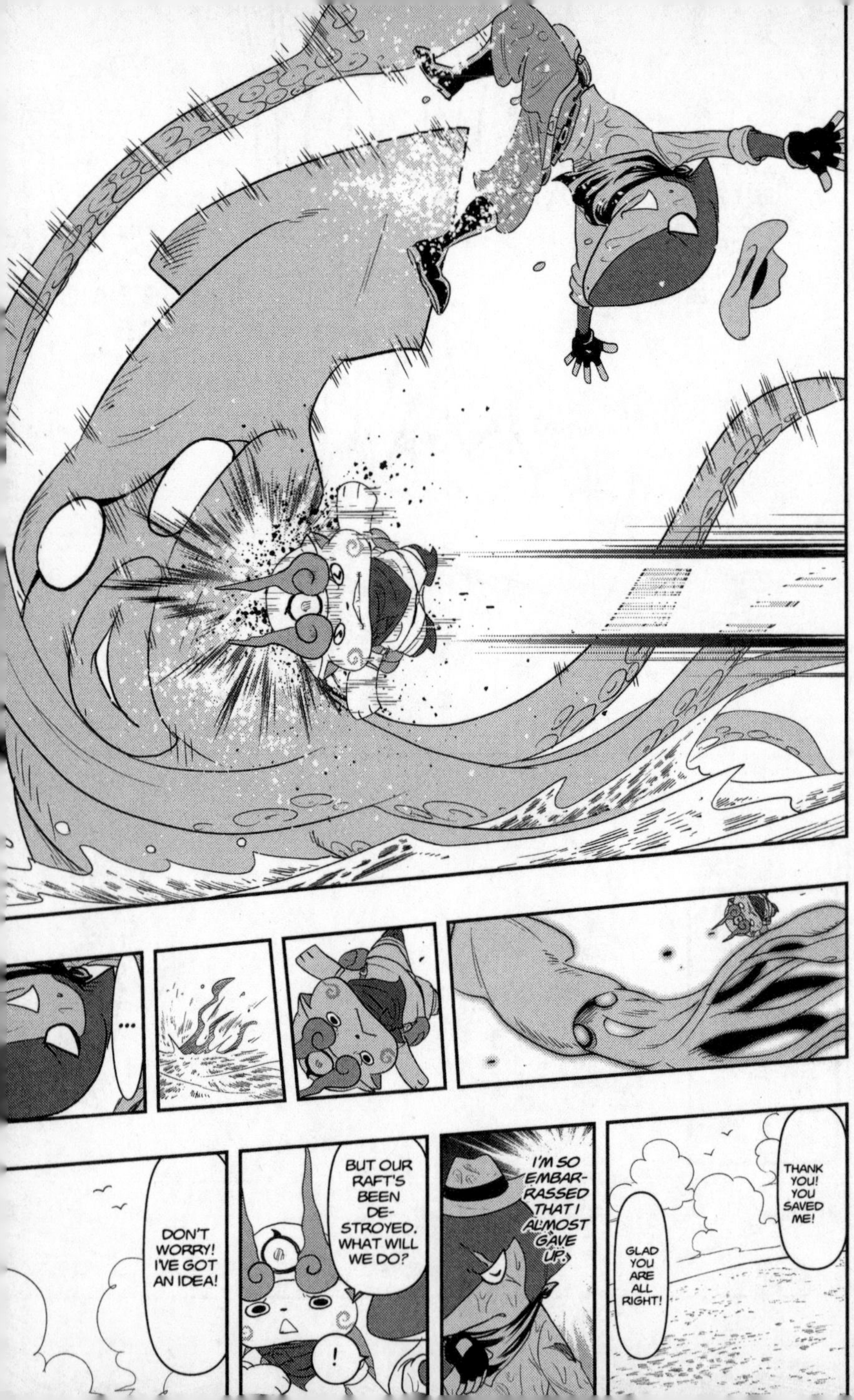
...
THANK YOU! YOU SAVED ME!
GLAD YOU ARE ALL RIGHT!
I'M SO EMBARRASSED THAT I ALMOST GAVE UP.
BUT OUR RAFT'S BEEN DESTROYED. WHAT WILL WE DO?
!
DON'T WORRY! I'VE GOT AN IDEA!

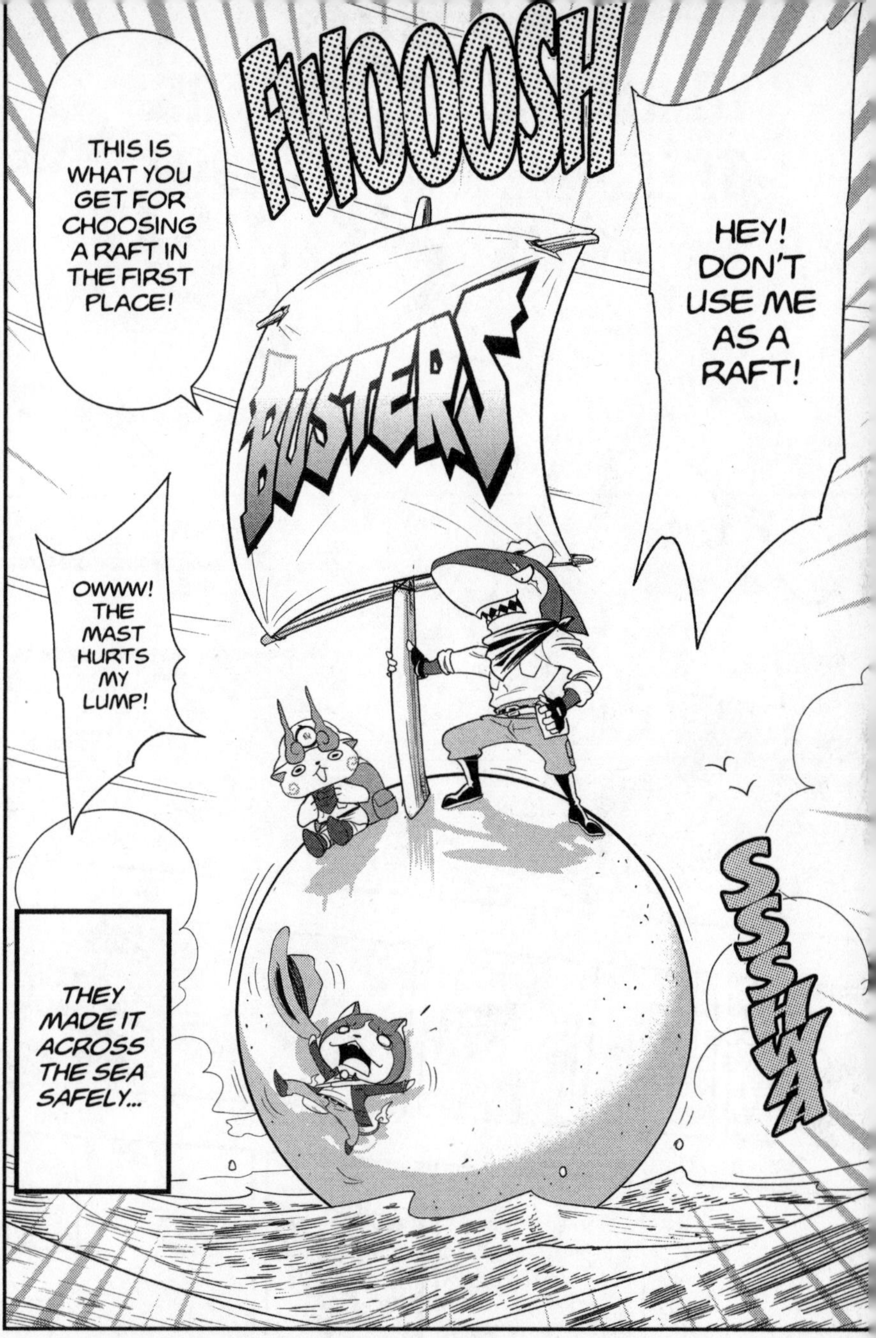
HEY! DON'T USE ME AS A RAFT!
FWOOOSH
THIS IS WHAT YOU GET FOR CHOOSING A RAFT IN THE FIRST PLACE!
BUSTERS
OWWW! THE MAST HURTS MY LUMP!
SSSHAA
THEY MADE IT ACROSS THE SEA SAFELY...

CHAPTER 141
YO-KAI WATCH BLASTERS TREASURE RAIDERS ARC: TREASURE PEST

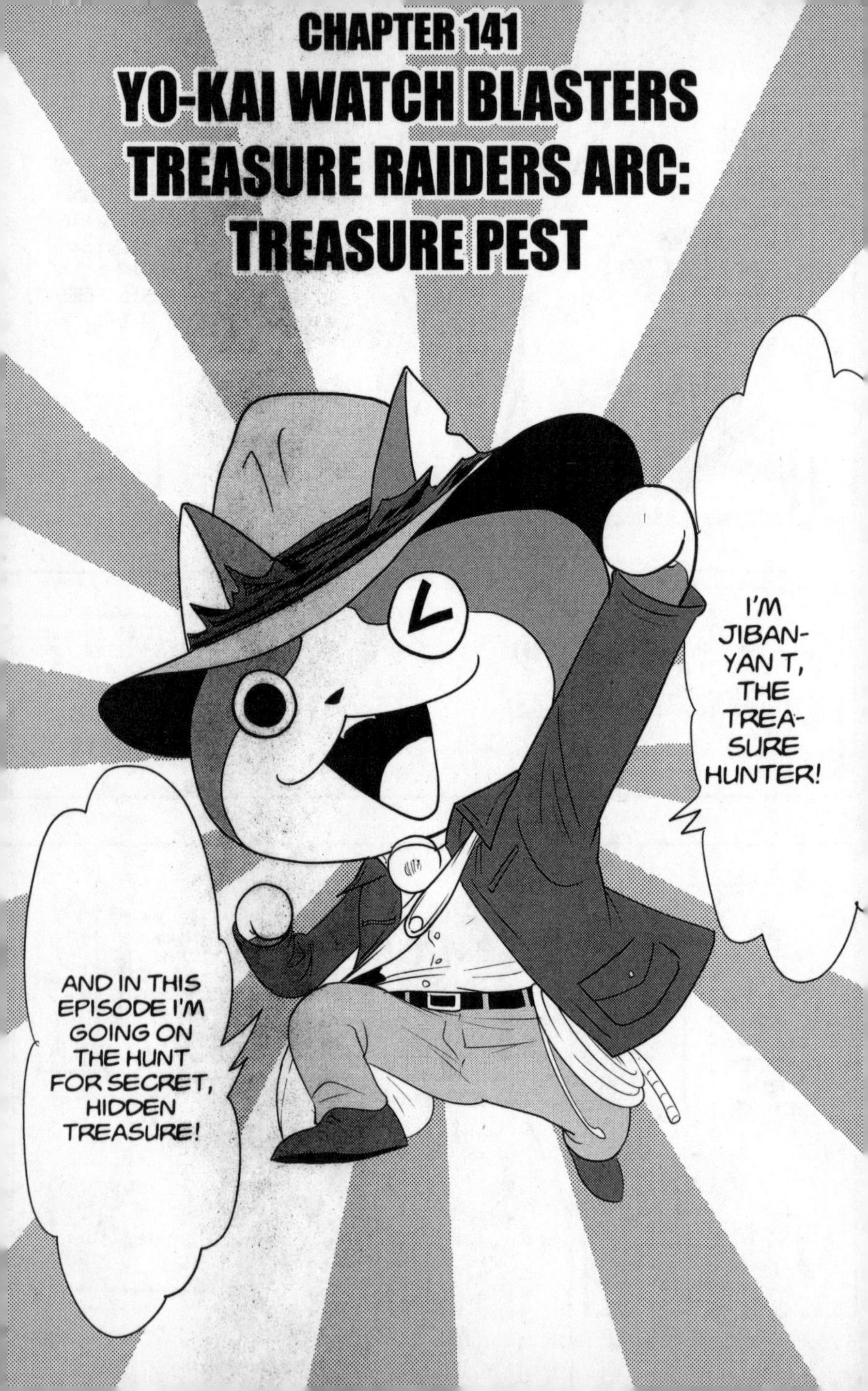
I'M JIBAN-YAN T, THE TREA-SURE HUNTER!
AND IN THIS EPISODE I'M GOING ON THE HUNT FOR SECRET, HIDDEN TREASURE!

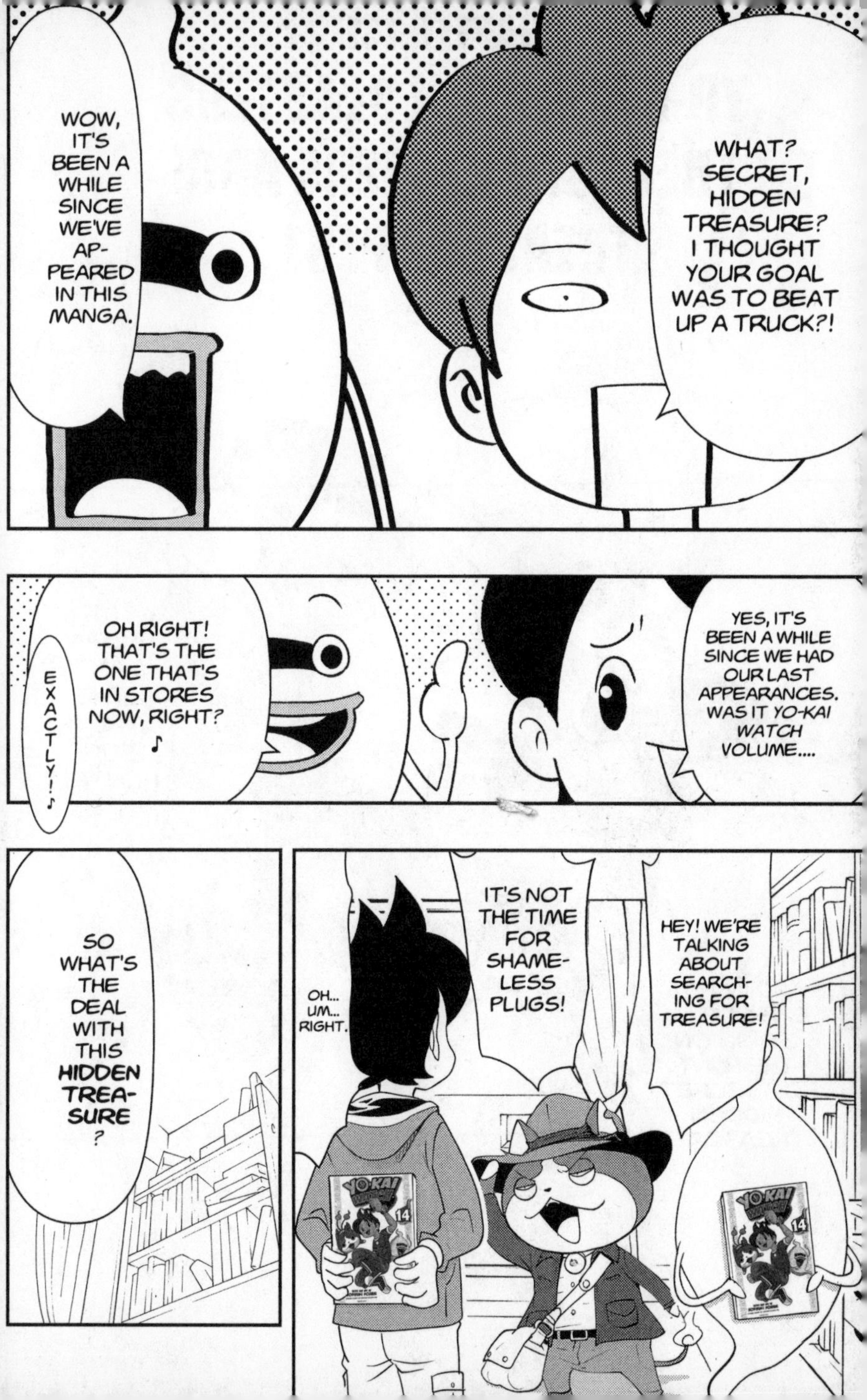
WHAT? SECRET, HIDDEN TREASURE? I THOUGHT YOUR GOAL WAS TO BEAT UP A TRUCK?!
WOW, IT'S BEEN A WHILE SINCE WE'VE AP-PEARED IN THIS MANGA.
YES, IT'S BEEN A WHILE SINCE WE HAD OUR LAST APPEARANCES. WAS IT *YO-KAI WATCH* VOLUME....
OH RIGHT! THAT'S THE ONE THAT'S IN STORES NOW, RIGHT? ♪
EXACTLY!♪
HEY! WE'RE TALKING ABOUT SEARCH-ING FOR TREASURE!
IT'S NOT THE TIME FOR SHAME-LESS PLUGS!
OH... UM... RIGHT.
YO-KAI WATCH 14
YO-KAI WATCH 14
SO WHAT'S THE DEAL WITH THIS **HIDDEN TREA-SURE**?

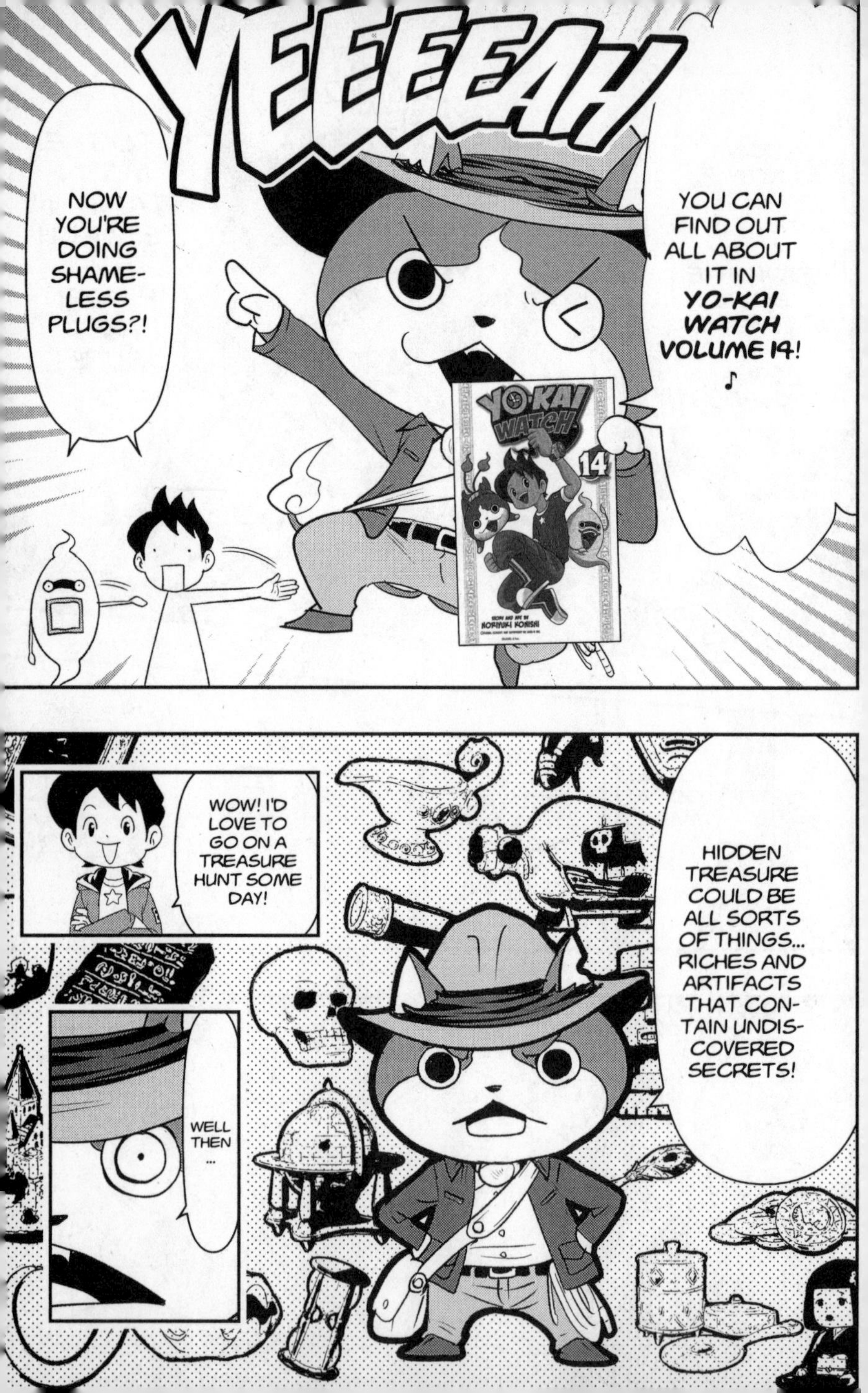
YEEEEAH
YOU CAN FIND OUT ALL ABOUT IT IN *YO-KAI WATCH* VOLUME 14! ♪
NOW YOU'RE DOING SHAME-LESS PLUGS?!
HIDDEN TREASURE COULD BE ALL SORTS OF THINGS... RICHES AND ARTIFACTS THAT CON-TAIN UNDIS-COVERED SECRETS!
WOW! I'D LOVE TO GO ON A TREASURE HUNT SOME DAY!
WELL THEN ...

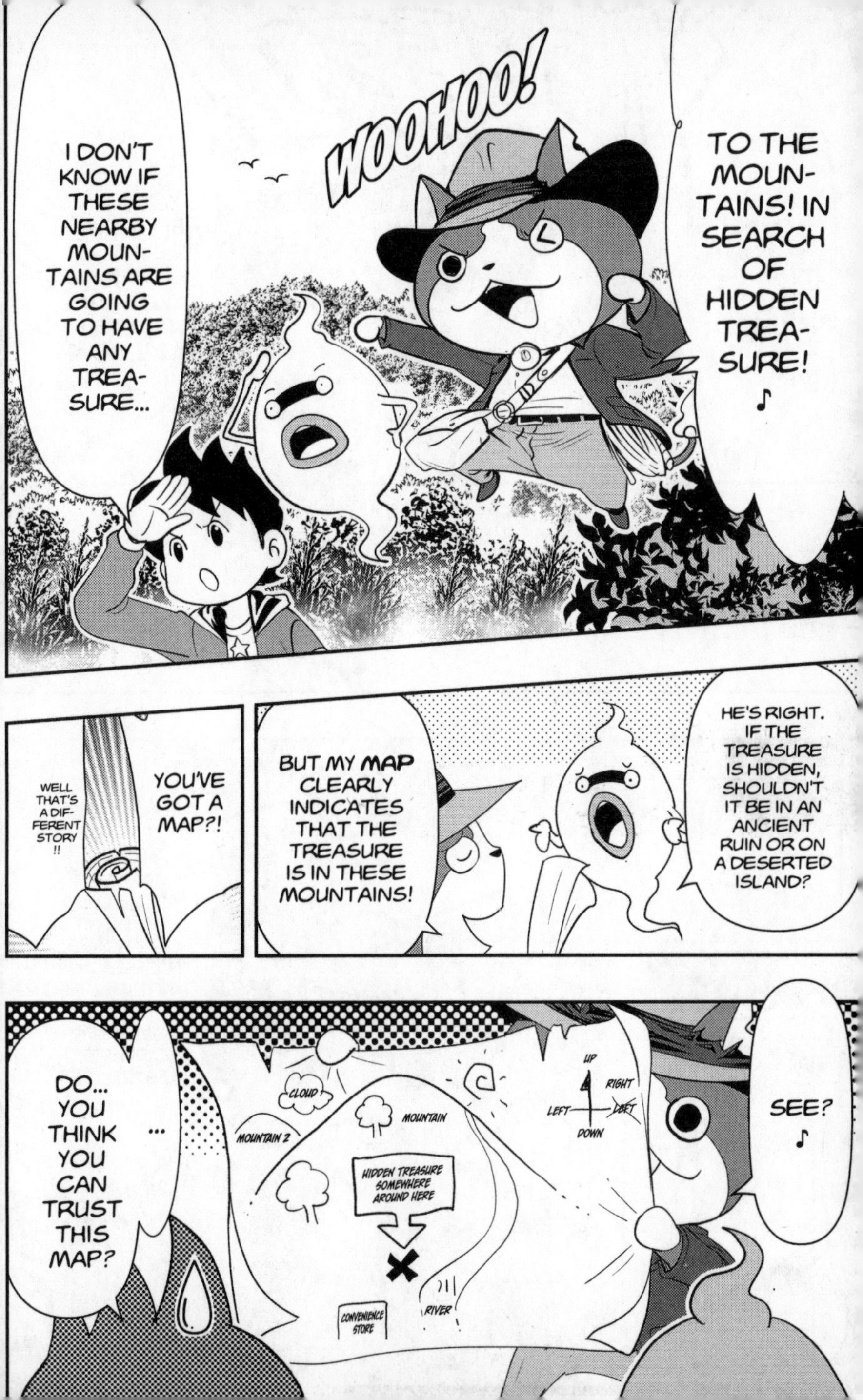
TO THE MOUNTAINS! IN SEARCH OF HIDDEN TREASURE! ♪
WOOHOO!
I DON'T KNOW IF THESE NEARBY MOUNTAINS ARE GOING TO HAVE ANY TREASURE...
HE'S RIGHT. IF THE TREASURE IS HIDDEN, SHOULDN'T IT BE IN AN ANCIENT RUIN OR ON A DESERTED ISLAND?
BUT MY MAP CLEARLY INDICATES THAT THE TREASURE IS IN THESE MOUNTAINS!
YOU'VE GOT A MAP?!
WELL THAT'S A DIFFERENT STORY !!
SEE? ♪
UP
RIGHT
LEFT
LEFT
DOWN
MOUNTAIN
CLOUD
MOUNTAIN 2
HIDDEN TREASURE SOMEWHERE AROUND HERE
RIVER
CONVENIENCE STORE
...
DO... YOU THINK YOU CAN TRUST THIS MAP?

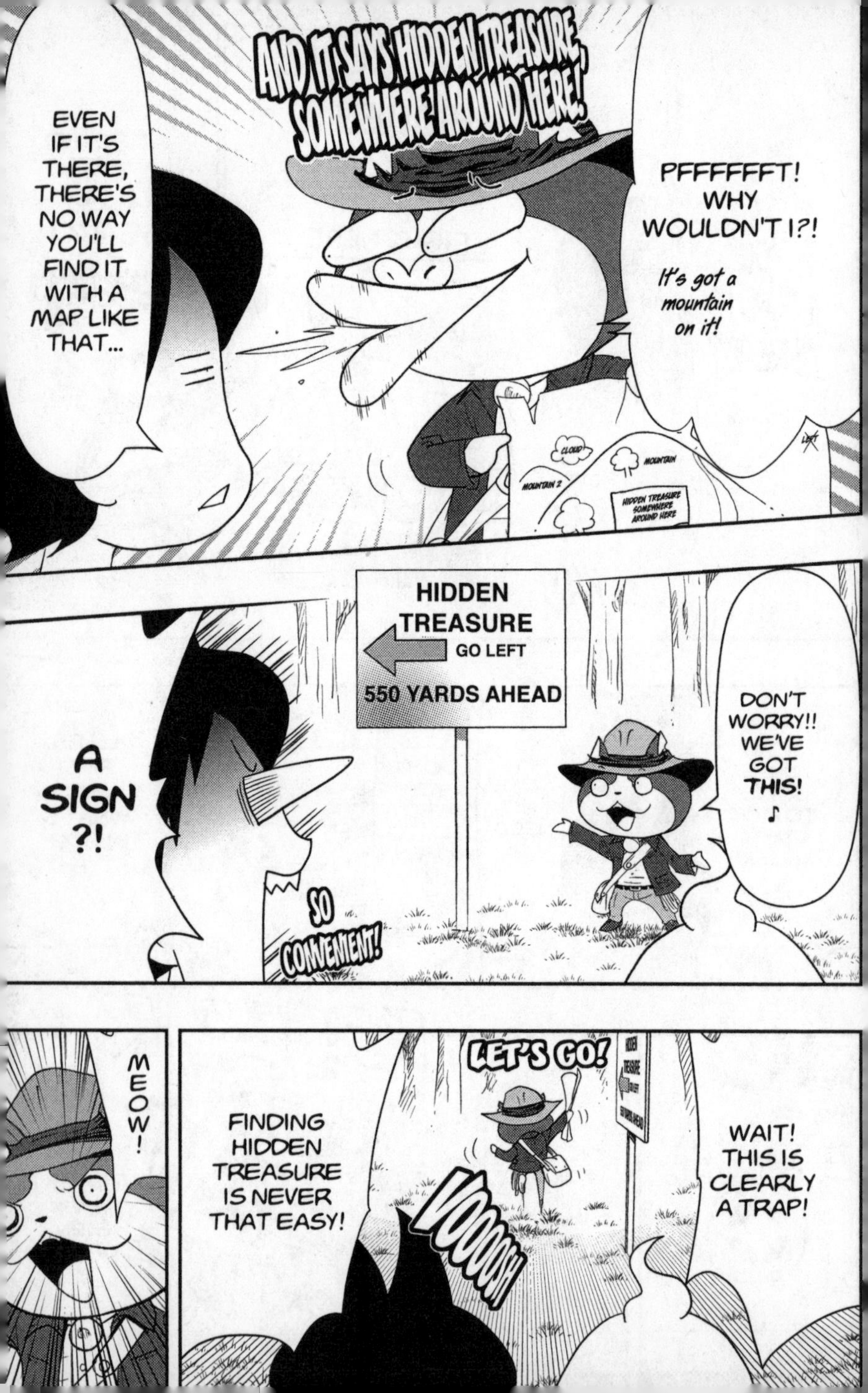
AND IT SAYS HIDDEN TREASURE, SOMEWHERE AROUND HERE!
PFFFFFFT! WHY WOULDN'T I?!
It's got a mountain on it!
EVEN IF IT'S THERE, THERE'S NO WAY YOU'LL FIND IT WITH A MAP LIKE THAT...
LEFT
CLOUD
MOUNTAIN
MOUNTAIN 2
HIDDEN TREASURE SOMEWHERE AROUND HERE
DON'T WORRY!! WE'VE GOT THIS! ♪
HIDDEN TREASURE
GO LEFT
550 YARDS AHEAD
A SIGN?!
SO CONVENIENT!
WAIT! THIS IS CLEARLY A TRAP!
LET'S GO!
FINDING HIDDEN TREASURE IS NEVER THAT EASY!
VOOOOSH
MEOW!

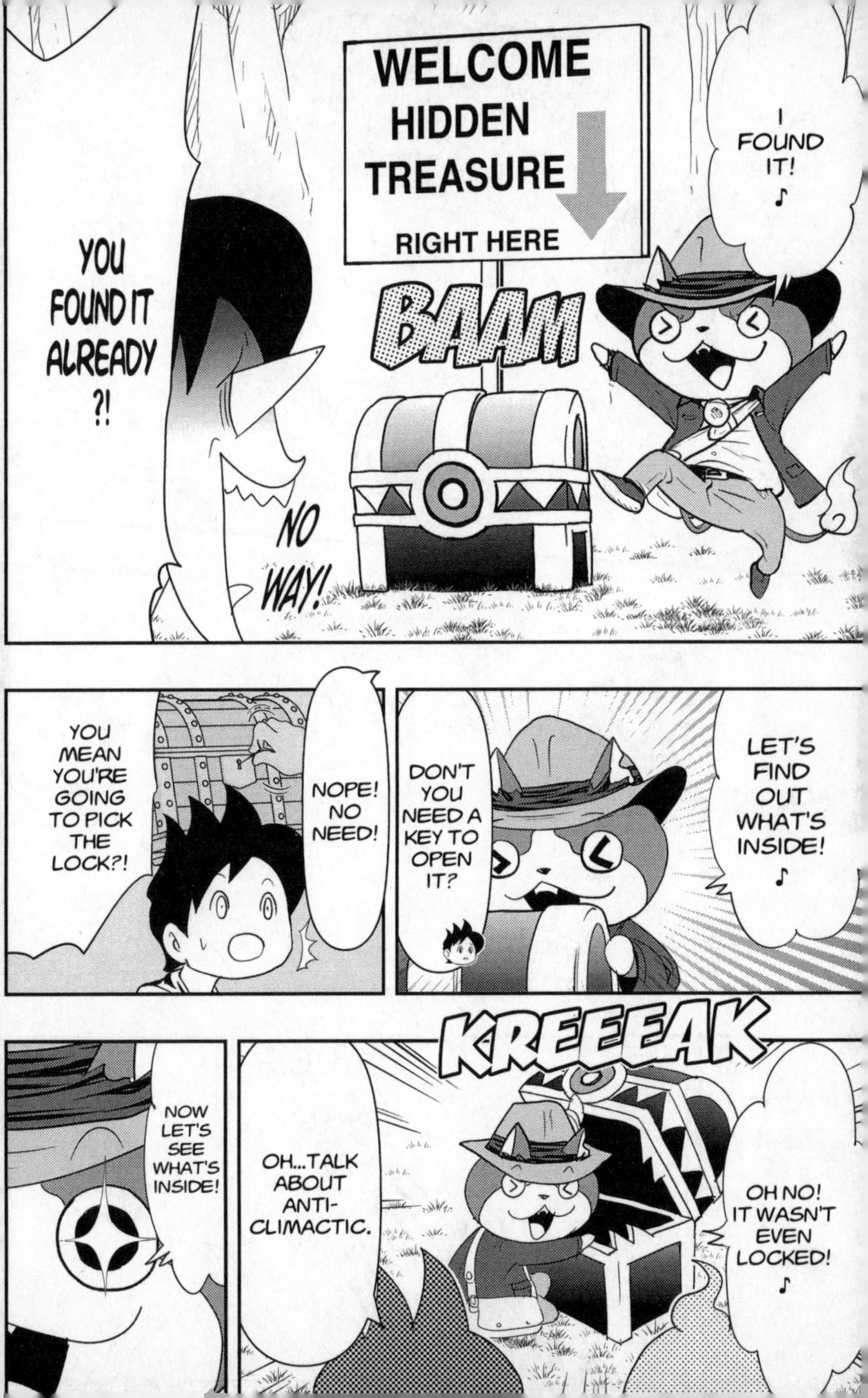
I FOUND IT! ♪
WELCOME HIDDEN TREASURE RIGHT HERE
BAAM
YOU FOUND IT ALREADY?!
NO WAY!
LET'S FIND OUT WHAT'S INSIDE! ♪
DON'T YOU NEED A KEY TO OPEN IT?
NOPE! NO NEED!
YOU MEAN YOU'RE GOING TO PICK THE LOCK?!
KREEEAK
OH NO! IT WASN'T EVEN LOCKED! ♪
OH...TALK ABOUT ANTI-CLIMACTIC.
NOW LET'S SEE WHAT'S INSIDE!

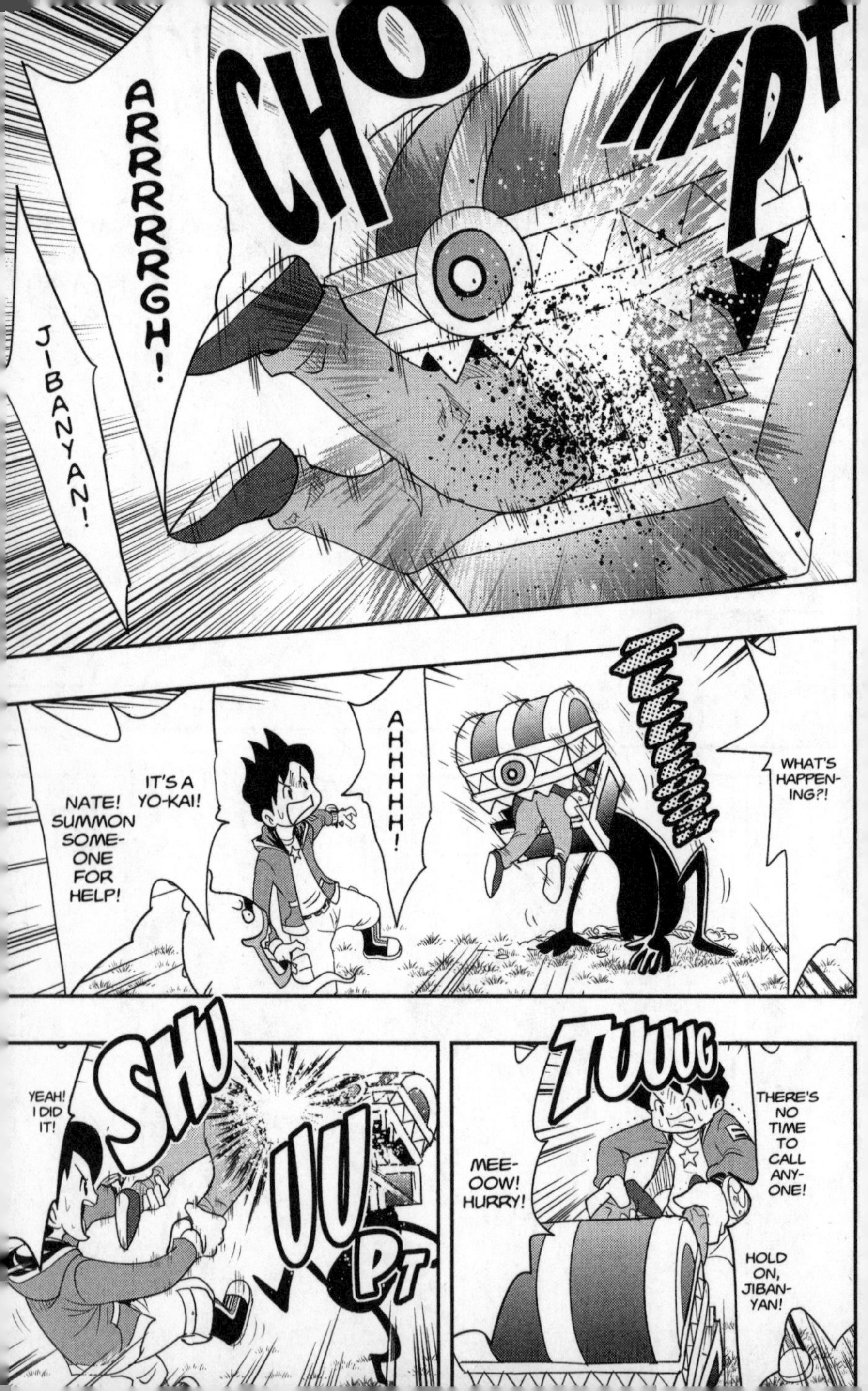
CHOMPT
ARRRRRGH!
JIBANYAN!
WHAT'S HAPPEN-ING?!
AHHHHH!
IT'S A YO-KAI!
NATE! SUMMON SOME-ONE FOR HELP!
TUUUG
THERE'S NO TIME TO CALL ANY-ONE!
MEE-OOW! HURRY!
HOLD ON, JIBAN-YAN!
SHUUUPT
YEAH! I DID IT!

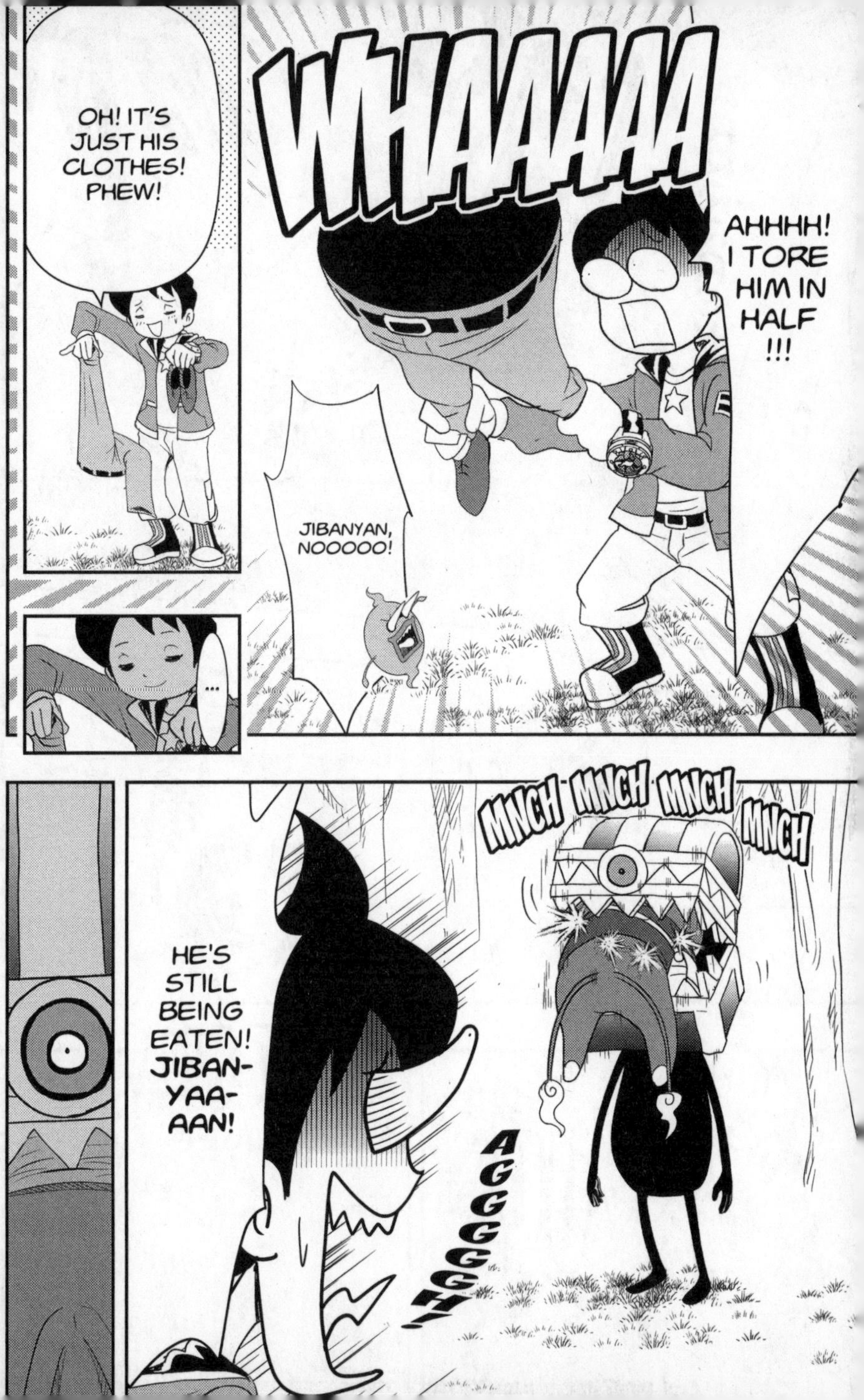
WHAAAAAA
AHHHH! I TORE HIM IN HALF!!!
JIBANYAN, NOOOOO!
OH! IT'S JUST HIS CLOTHES! PHEW!
...
MNCH MNCH MNCH MNCH
HE'S STILL BEING EATEN! JIBAN-YAA-AAN!
AGGGGGH!

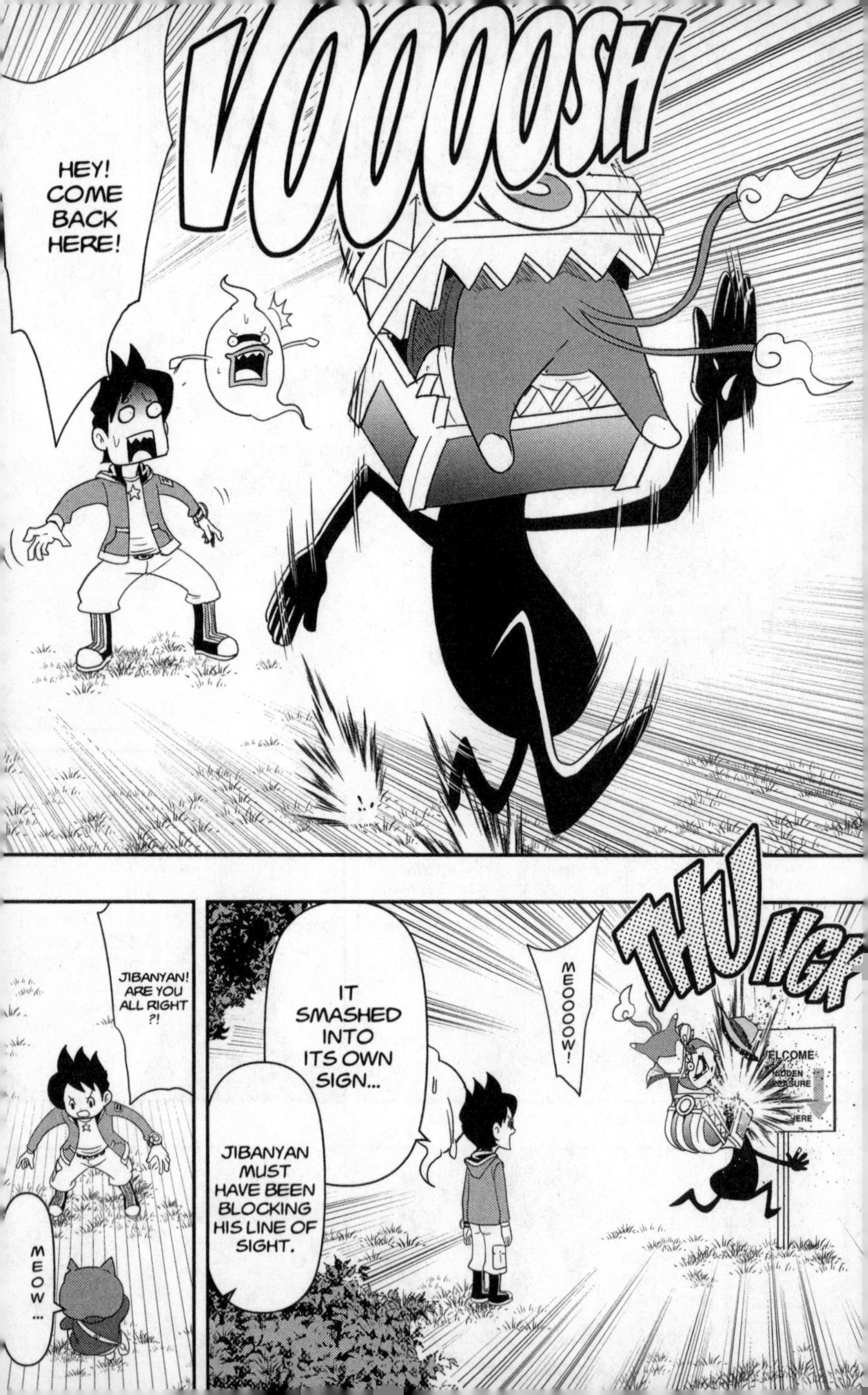
VOOOOSH
HEY! COME BACK HERE!
THUNCK
MEOOOOW!
IT SMASHED INTO ITS OWN SIGN...
JIBANYAN MUST HAVE BEEN BLOCKING HIS LINE OF SIGHT.
JIBANYAN! ARE YOU ALL RIGHT?!
MEOW...

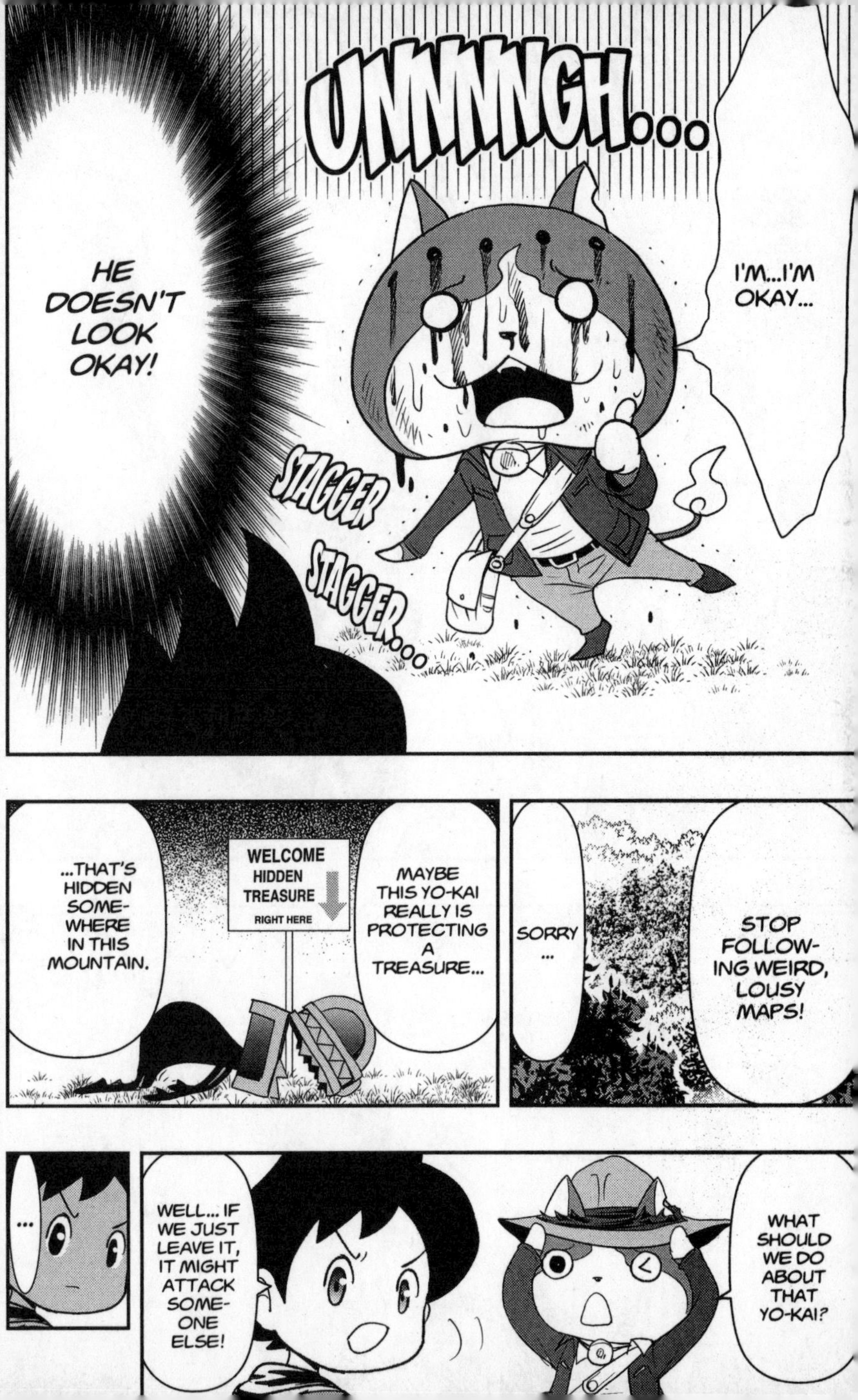
UNNNNGH...
I'M...I'M OKAY...
HE DOESN'T LOOK OKAY!
STAGGER
STAGGER...
STOP FOLLOWING WEIRD, LOUSY MAPS!
SORRY...
MAYBE THIS YO-KAI REALLY IS PROTECTING A TREASURE...
WELCOME HIDDEN TREASURE RIGHT HERE
...THAT'S HIDDEN SOMEWHERE IN THIS MOUNTAIN.
WHAT SHOULD WE DO ABOUT THAT YO-KAI?
WELL... IF WE JUST LEAVE IT, IT MIGHT ATTACK SOMEONE ELSE!
...

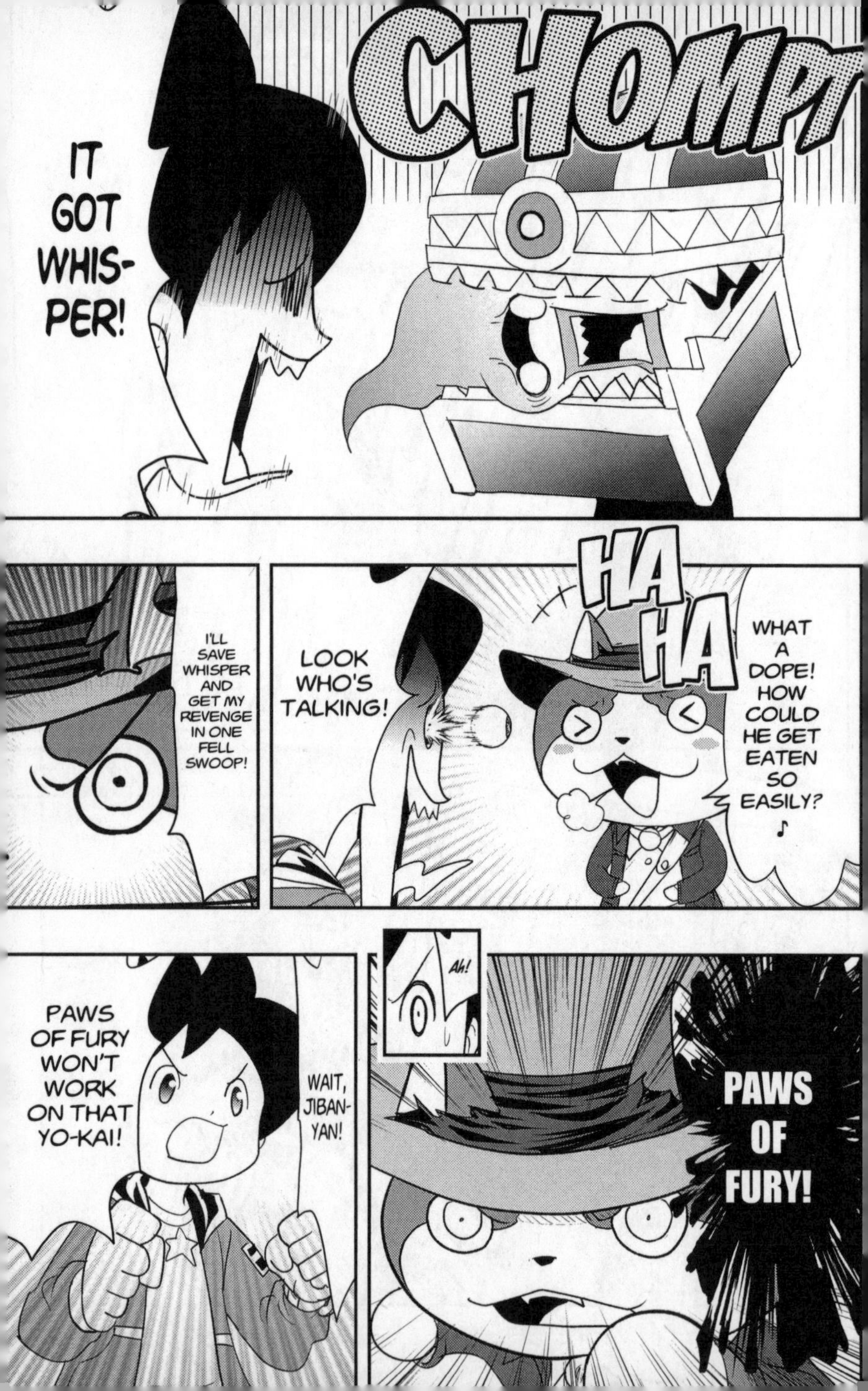
CHOMP!
IT GOT WHISPER!
HA HA
WHAT A DOPE! HOW COULD HE GET EATEN SO EASILY? ♪
LOOK WHO'S TALKING!
I'LL SAVE WHISPER AND GET MY REVENGE IN ONE FELL SWOOP!
PAWS OF FURY!
Ah!
WAIT, JIBANYAN!
PAWS OF FURY WON'T WORK ON THAT YO-KAI!

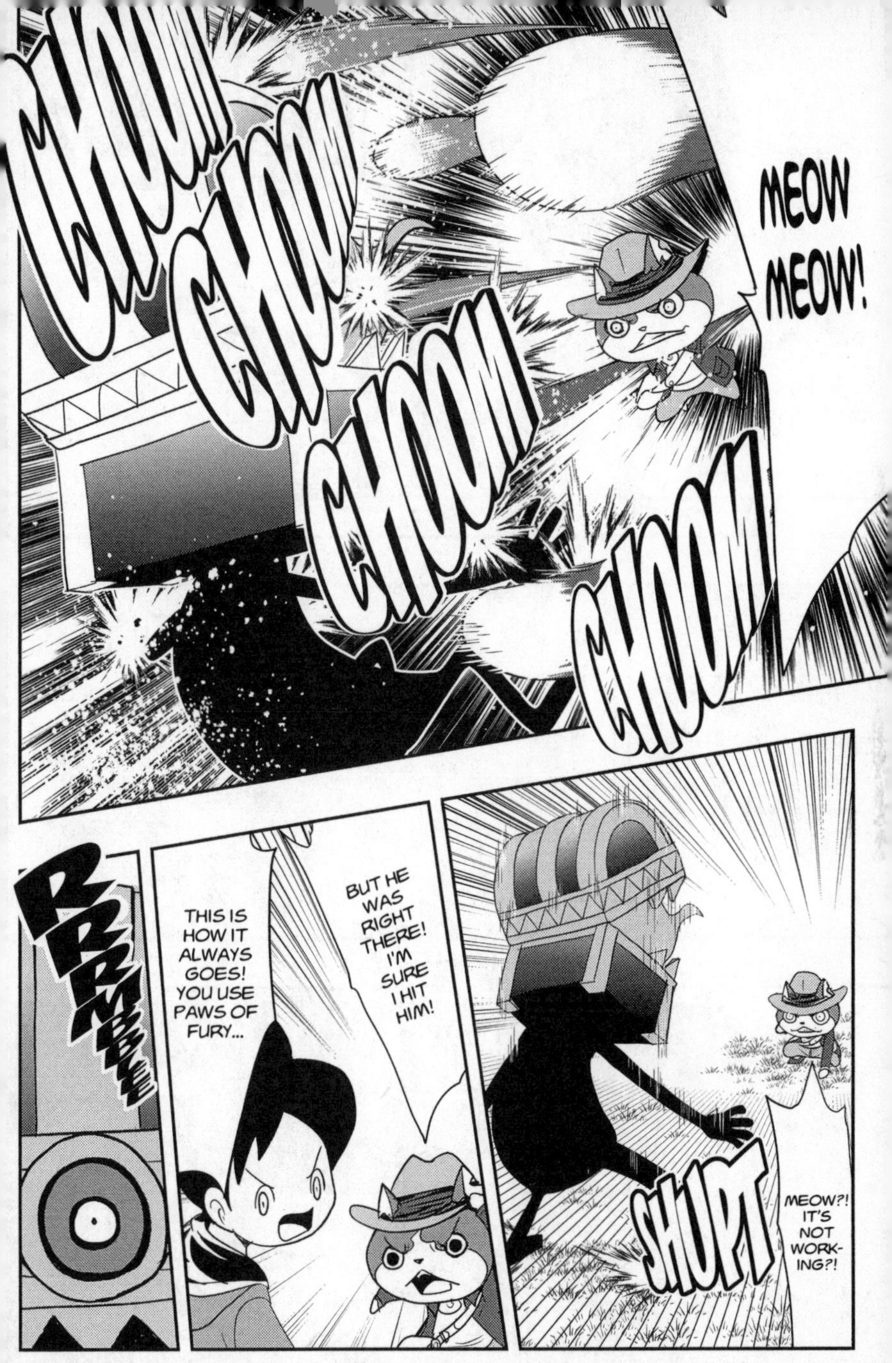
MEOW MEOW!
CHOOM
CHOOM
CHOOM
CHOOM
CHOOM
MEOW?! IT'S NOT WORKING?!
SHOPT
BUT HE WAS RIGHT THERE! I'M SURE I HIT HIM!
THIS IS HOW IT ALWAYS GOES! YOU USE PAWS OF FURY...
RRRUMBLE

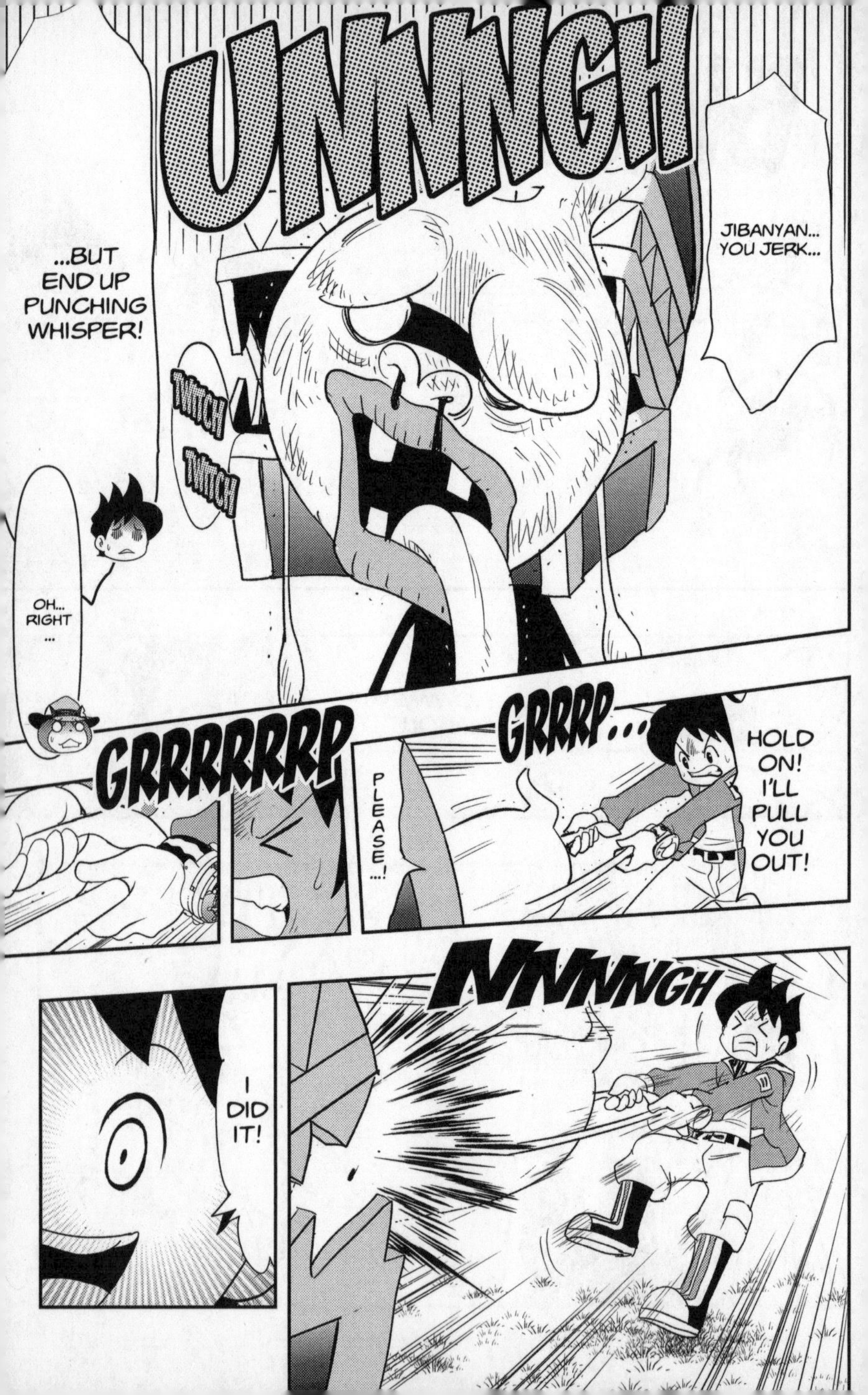
JIBANYAN... YOU JERK...
UNNNGH
...BUT END UP PUNCHING WHISPER!
TWITCH
TWITCH
OH... RIGHT ...
HOLD ON! I'LL PULL YOU OUT!
GRRRP...
PLEASE...!
GRRRRRRP
NNNNGH
I DID IT!

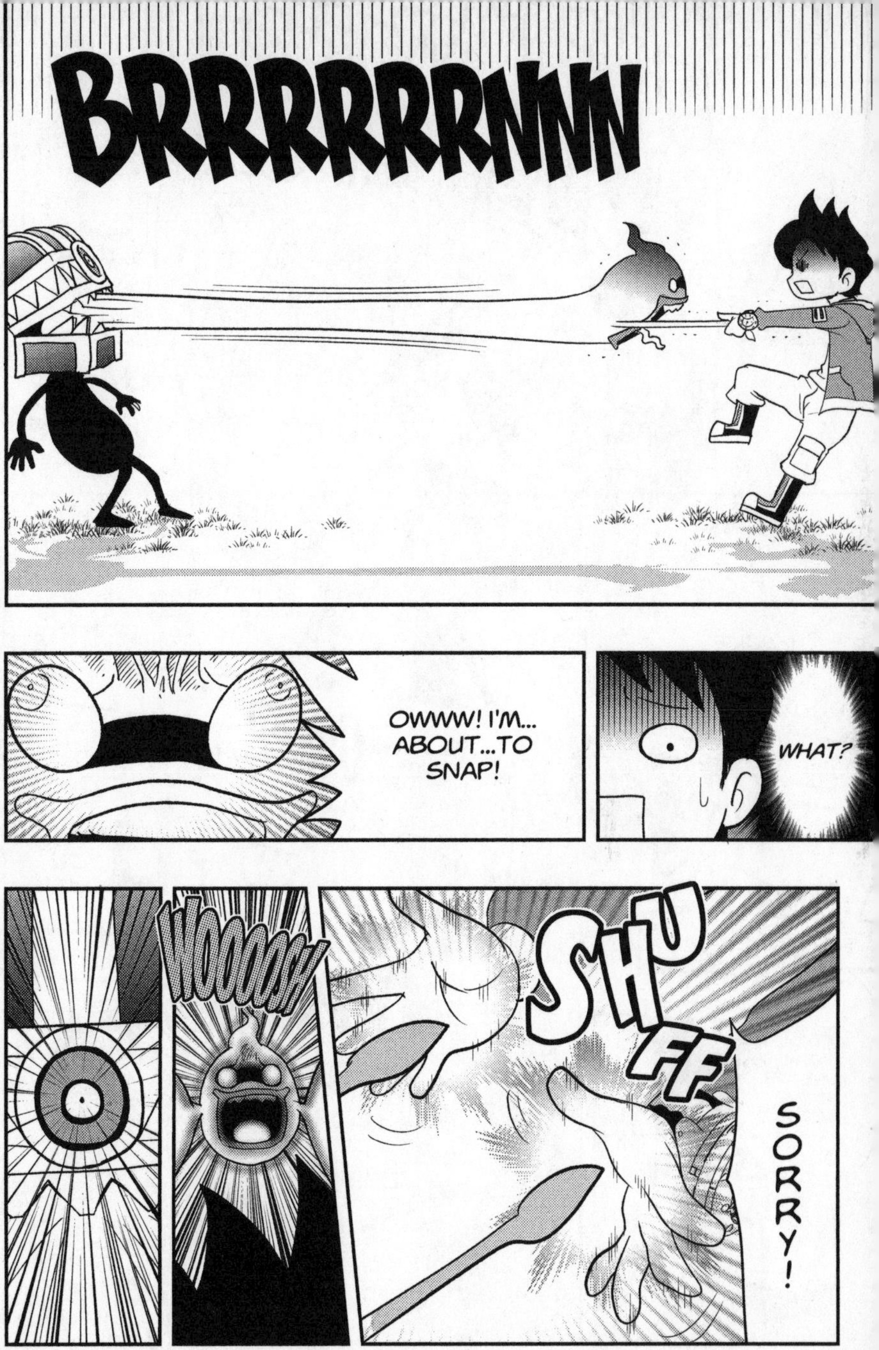
BRRRRRRRNNN
WHAT?
OWWW! I'M... ABOUT...TO SNAP!
SORRY!
SHUFF
WHOOOSH

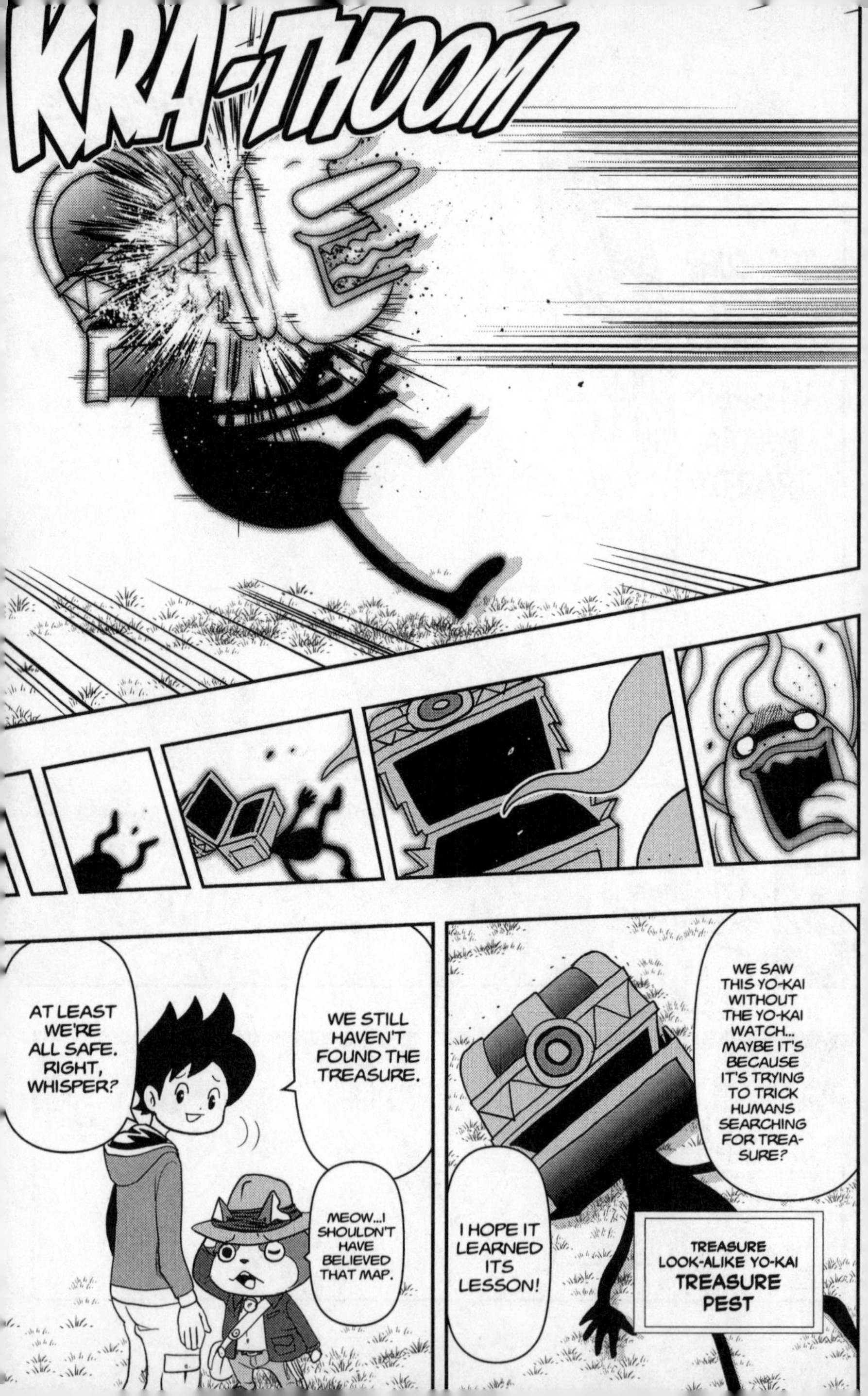
KRA-THOOM
WE SAW THIS YO-KAI WITHOUT THE YO-KAI WATCH... MAYBE IT'S BECAUSE IT'S TRYING TO TRICK HUMANS SEARCHING FOR TREA-SURE?
I HOPE IT LEARNED ITS LESSON!
TREASURE LOOK-ALIKE YO-KAI TREASURE PEST
WE STILL HAVEN'T FOUND THE TREASURE.
AT LEAST WE'RE ALL SAFE. RIGHT, WHISPER?
MEOW...I SHOULDN'T HAVE BELIEVED THAT MAP.

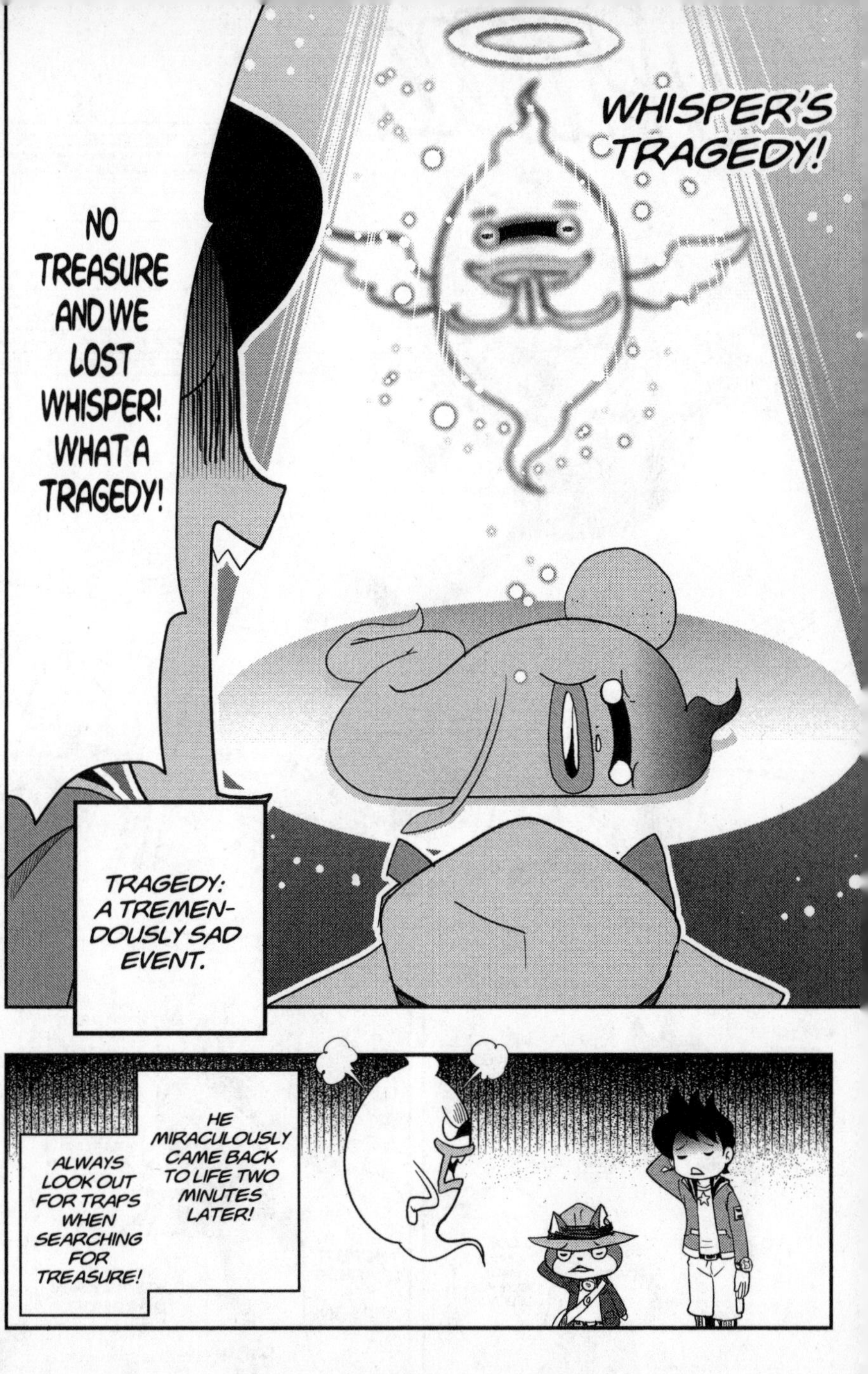
WHISPER'S TRAGEDY!
NO TREASURE AND WE LOST WHISPER! WHAT A TRAGEDY!
TRAGEDY: A TREMEN-DOUSLY SAD EVENT.
HE MIRACULOUSLY CAME BACK TO LIFE TWO MINUTES LATER!
ALWAYS LOOK OUT FOR TRAPS WHEN SEARCHING FOR TREASURE!

CHAPTER 142
USAPYON VERSUS JIBANYAN

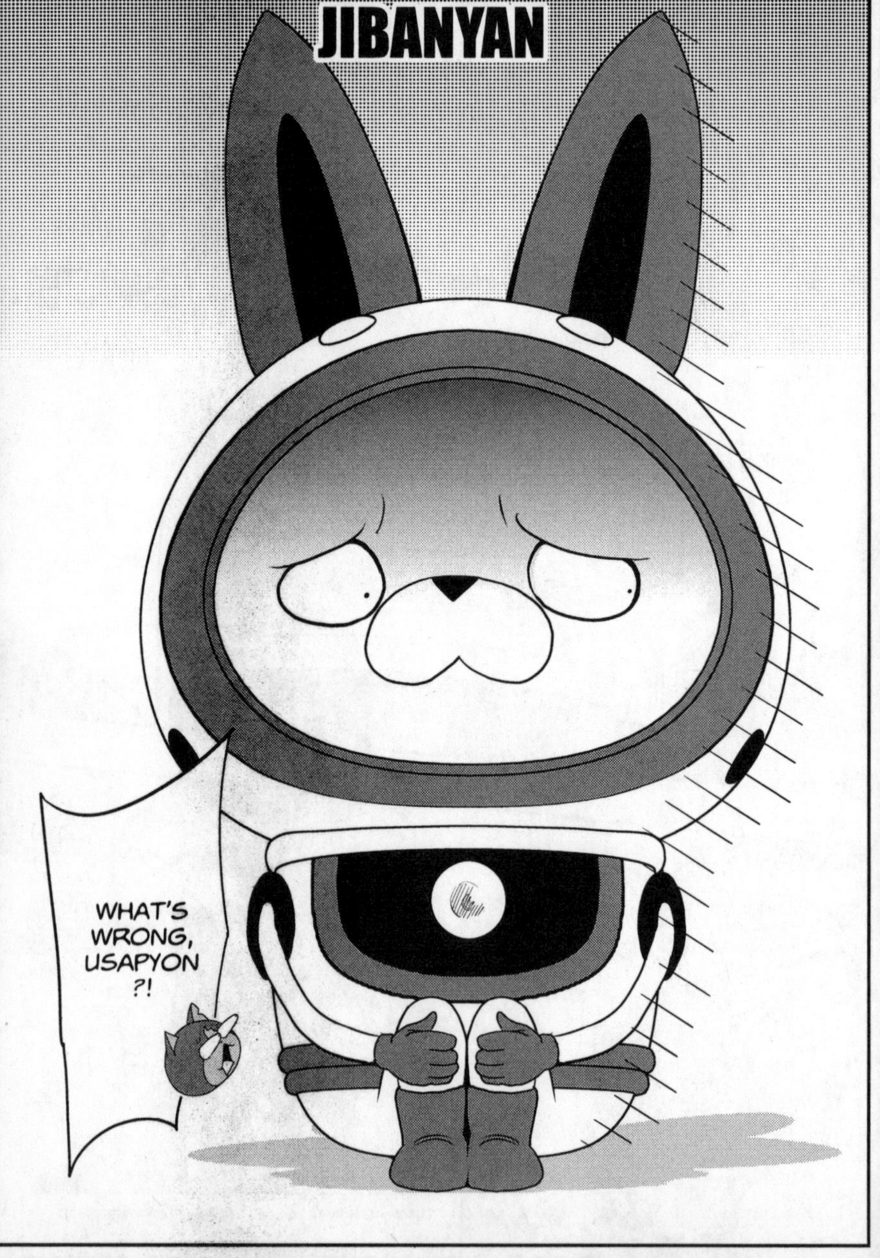
WHAT'S WRONG, USAPYON ?!

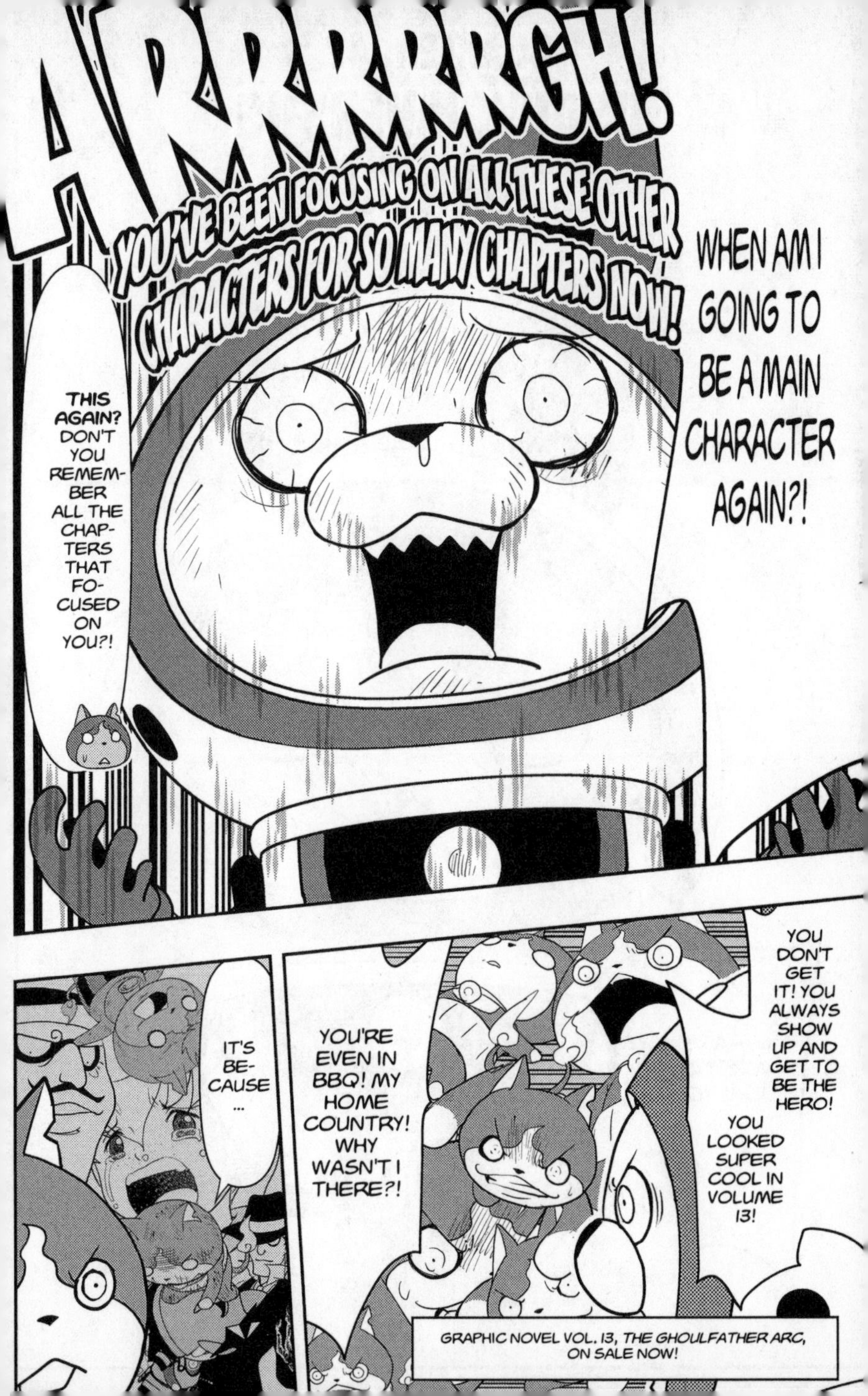
ARRRRRGH!
YOU'VE BEEN FOCUSING ON ALL THESE OTHER CHARACTERS FOR SO MANY CHAPTERS NOW!
WHEN AM I GOING TO BE A MAIN CHARACTER AGAIN?!
THIS AGAIN? DON'T YOU REMEMBER ALL THE CHAPTERS THAT FOCUSED ON YOU?!
YOU DON'T GET IT! YOU ALWAYS SHOW UP AND GET TO BE THE HERO!
YOU LOOKED SUPER COOL IN VOLUME 13!
YOU'RE EVEN IN BBQ! MY HOME COUNTRY! WHY WASN'T I THERE?!
IT'S BECAUSE ...
GRAPHIC NOVEL VOL. 13, THE GHOULFATHER ARC, ON SALE NOW!

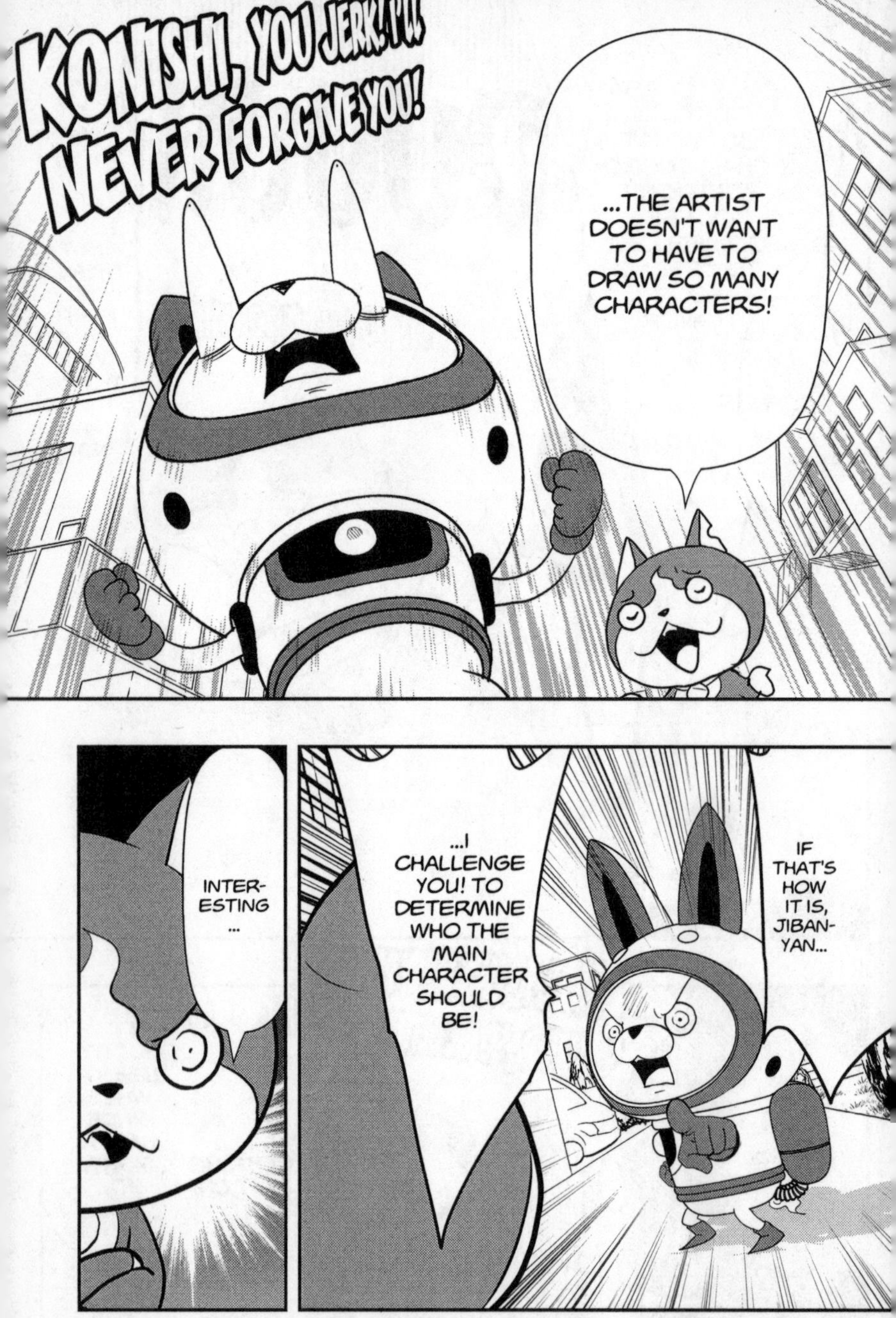
...THE ARTIST DOESN'T WANT TO HAVE TO DRAW SO MANY CHARACTERS!
KONISHI, YOU JERK! I'LL NEVER FORGIVE YOU!
IF THAT'S HOW IT IS, JIBAN-YAN...
...I CHALLENGE YOU! TO DETERMINE WHO THE MAIN CHARACTER SHOULD BE!
INTER-ESTING ...

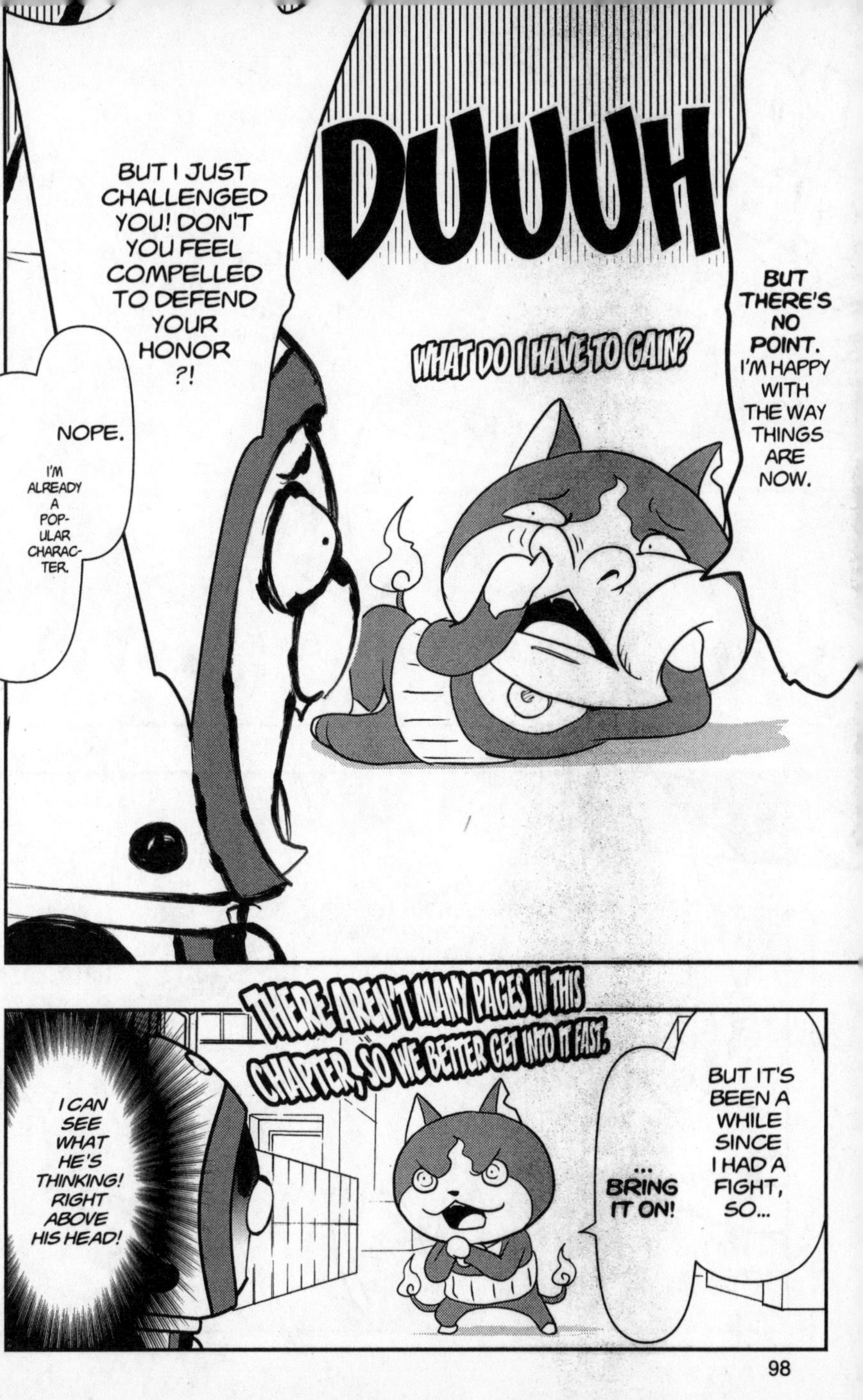
DUUUH
BUT THERE'S NO POINT. I'M HAPPY WITH THE WAY THINGS ARE NOW.
WHAT DO I HAVE TO GAIN?
BUT I JUST CHALLENGED YOU! DON'T YOU FEEL COMPELLED TO DEFEND YOUR HONOR ?!
NOPE.
I'M ALREADY A POP-ULAR CHARAC-TER.
THERE AREN'T MANY PAGES IN THIS CHAPTER, SO WE BETTER GET INTO IT FAST.
BUT IT'S BEEN A WHILE SINCE I HAD A FIGHT, SO...
... BRING IT ON!
I CAN SEE WHAT HE'S THINKING! RIGHT ABOVE HIS HEAD!

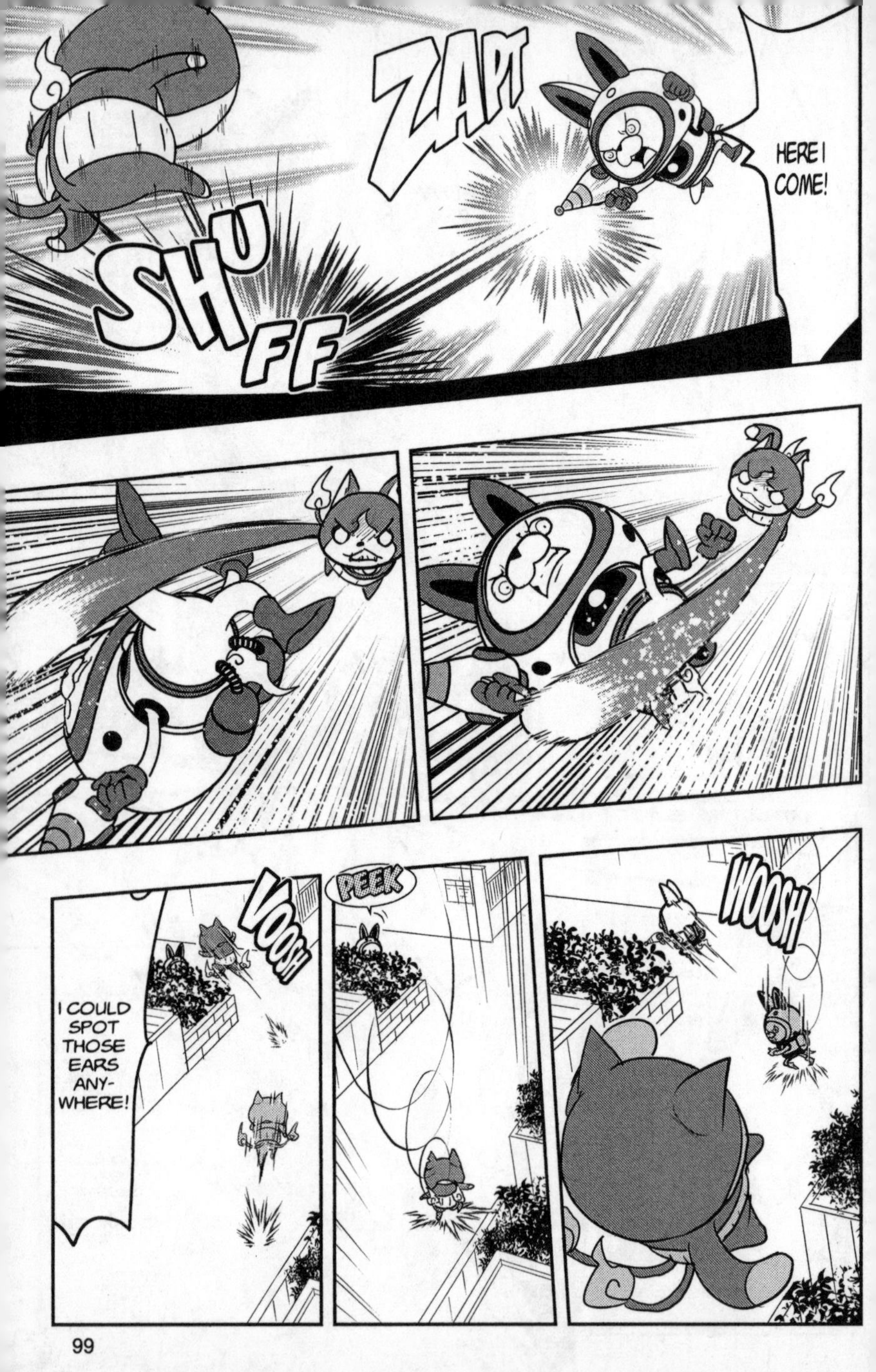
HERE I COME!
ZAP!
SHUFF
WOOSH
PEEK
VOOSH
I COULD SPOT THOSE EARS ANYWHERE!

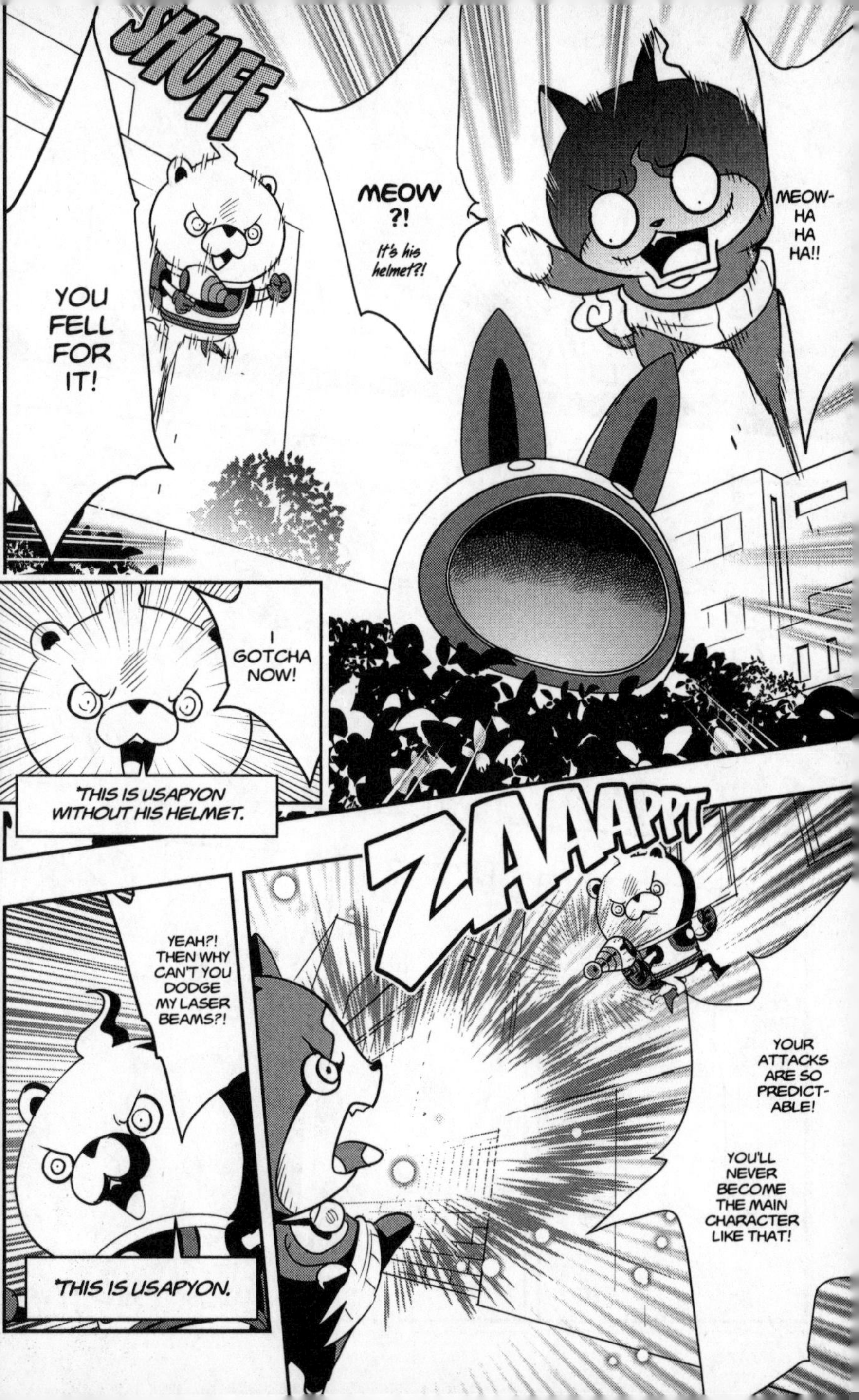
MEOW-HA HA HA!!
MEOW?!
It's his helmet?!
SHUFF
YOU FELL FOR IT!
I GOTCHA NOW!
*THIS IS USAPYON WITHOUT HIS HELMET.
ZAAAPPT
YOUR ATTACKS ARE SO PREDICT-ABLE!
YOU'LL NEVER BECOME THE MAIN CHARACTER LIKE THAT!
YEAH?! THEN WHY CAN'T YOU DODGE MY LASER BEAMS?!
*THIS IS USAPYON.

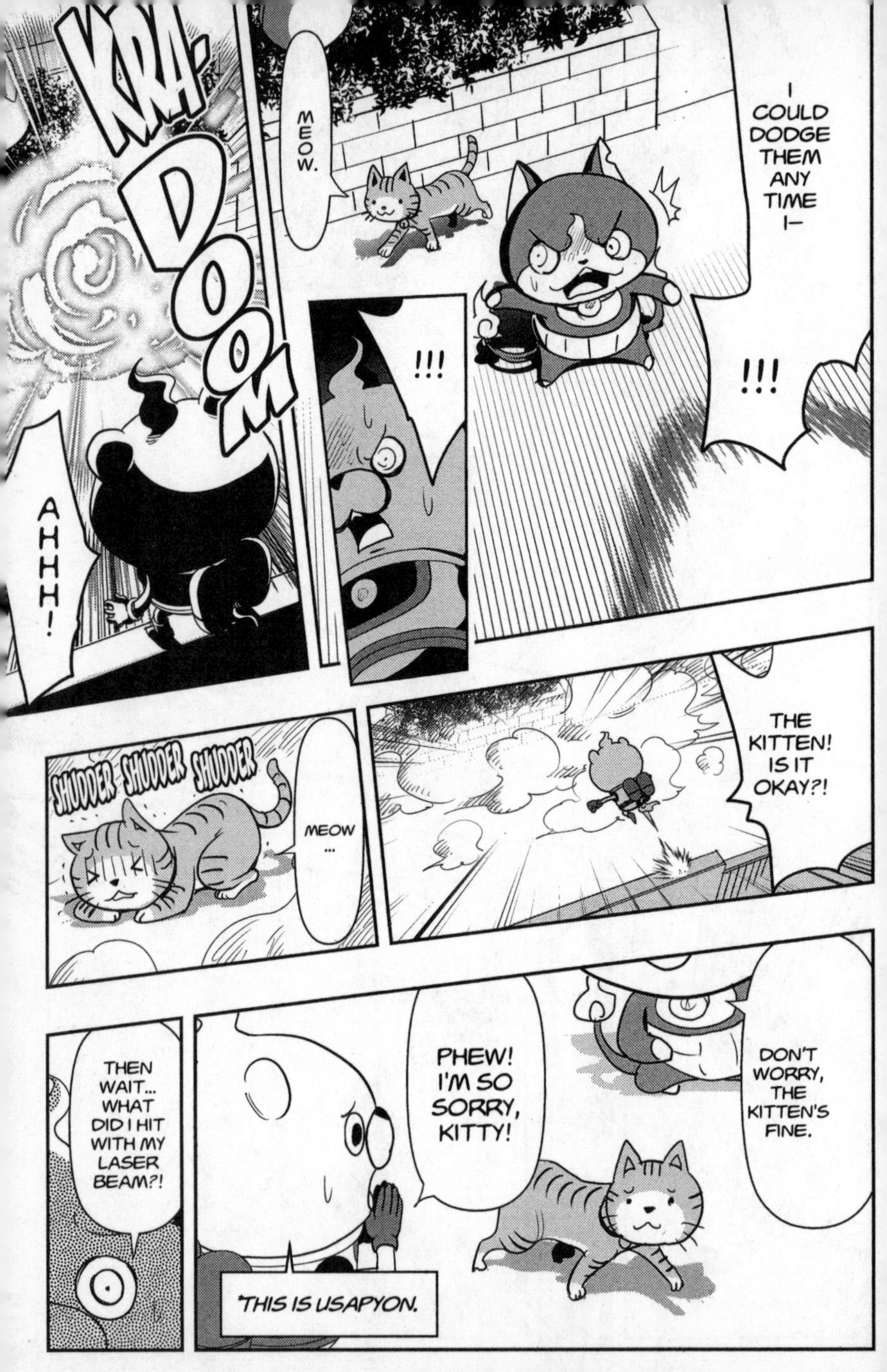
I COULD DODGE THEM ANY TIME I—
MEOW.
!!!
!!!
KRA-DOOOM
AHHHH!
THE KITTEN! IS IT OKAY?!
SHUDDER SHUDDER SHUDDER
MEOW ...
DON'T WORRY, THE KITTEN'S FINE.
PHEW! I'M SO SORRY, KITTY!
*THIS IS USAPYON.
THEN WAIT... WHAT DID I HIT WITH MY LASER BEAM?!

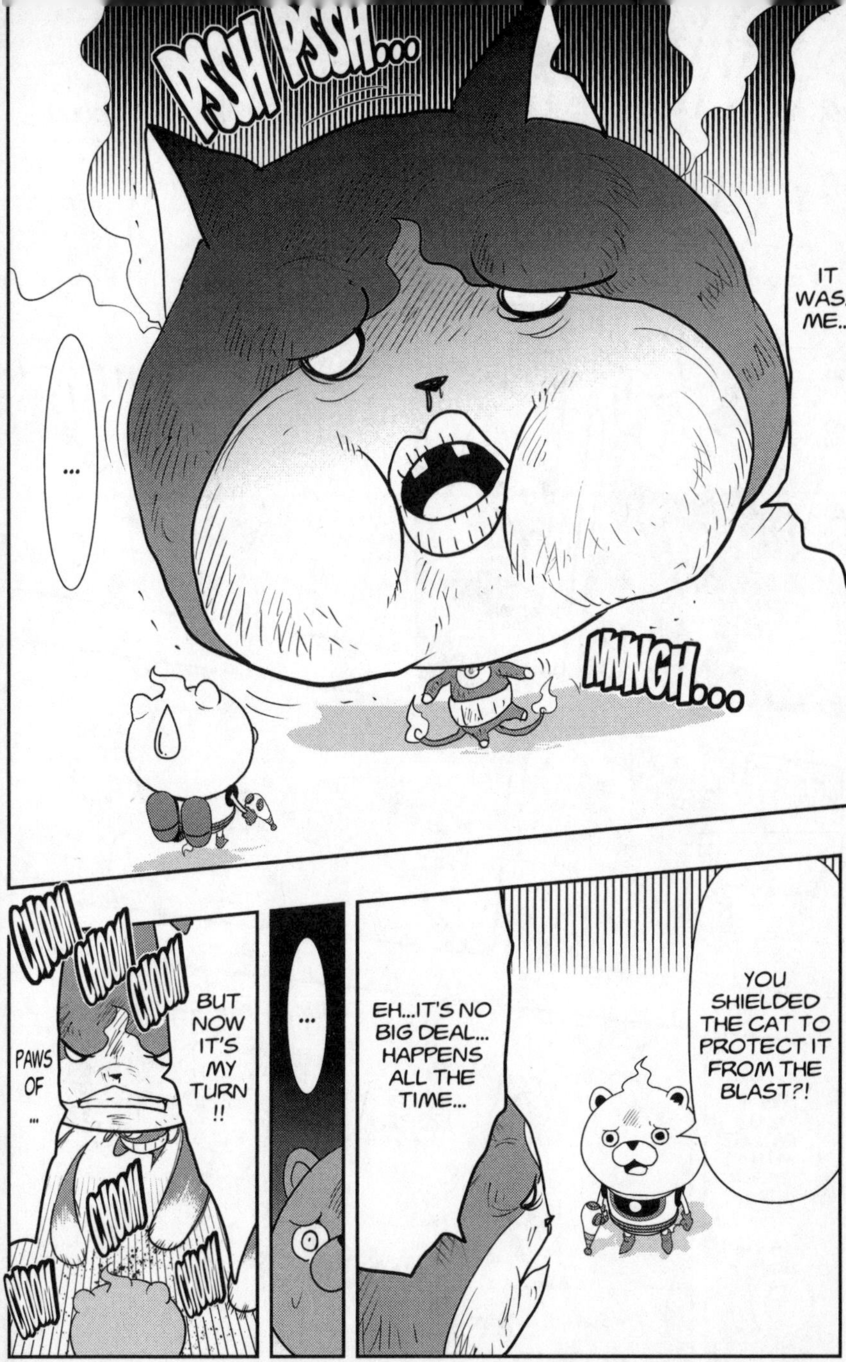
PSSH PSSH...
IT WAS... ME...
...
NNNGH...
YOU SHIELDED THE CAT TO PROTECT IT FROM THE BLAST?!
EH...IT'S NO BIG DEAL... HAPPENS ALL THE TIME...
...
CHOOM CHOOM CHOOM
BUT NOW IT'S MY TURN!!
PAWS OF ...
CHOOM
CHOOM
CHOOM

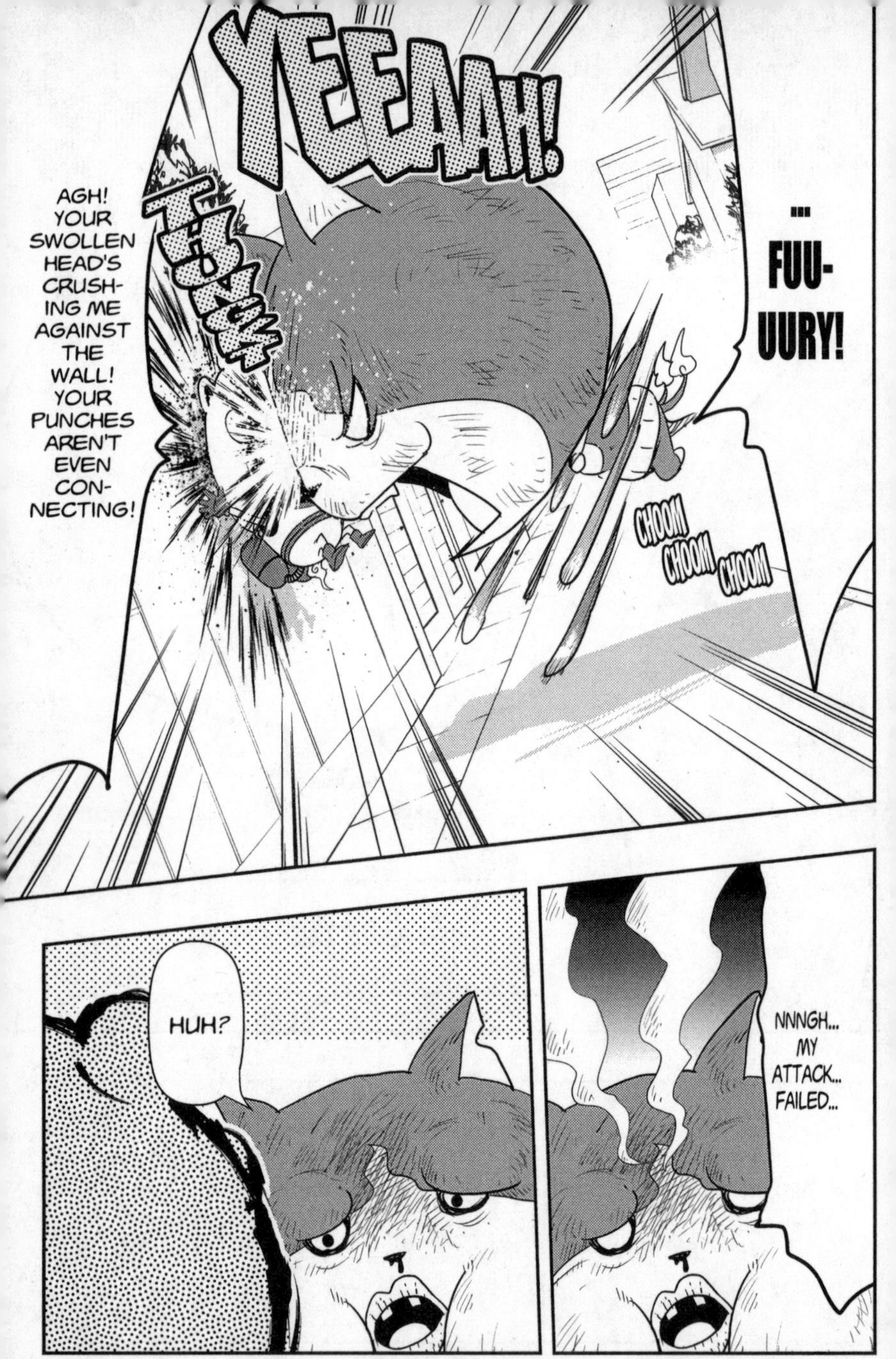
... FUU-UURY!
YEEAAH!
THWACK
CHOOM CHOOM CHOOM
AGH! YOUR SWOLLEN HEAD'S CRUSHING ME AGAINST THE WALL! YOUR PUNCHES AREN'T EVEN CONNECTING!
NNNGH... MY ATTACK... FAILED...
HUH?

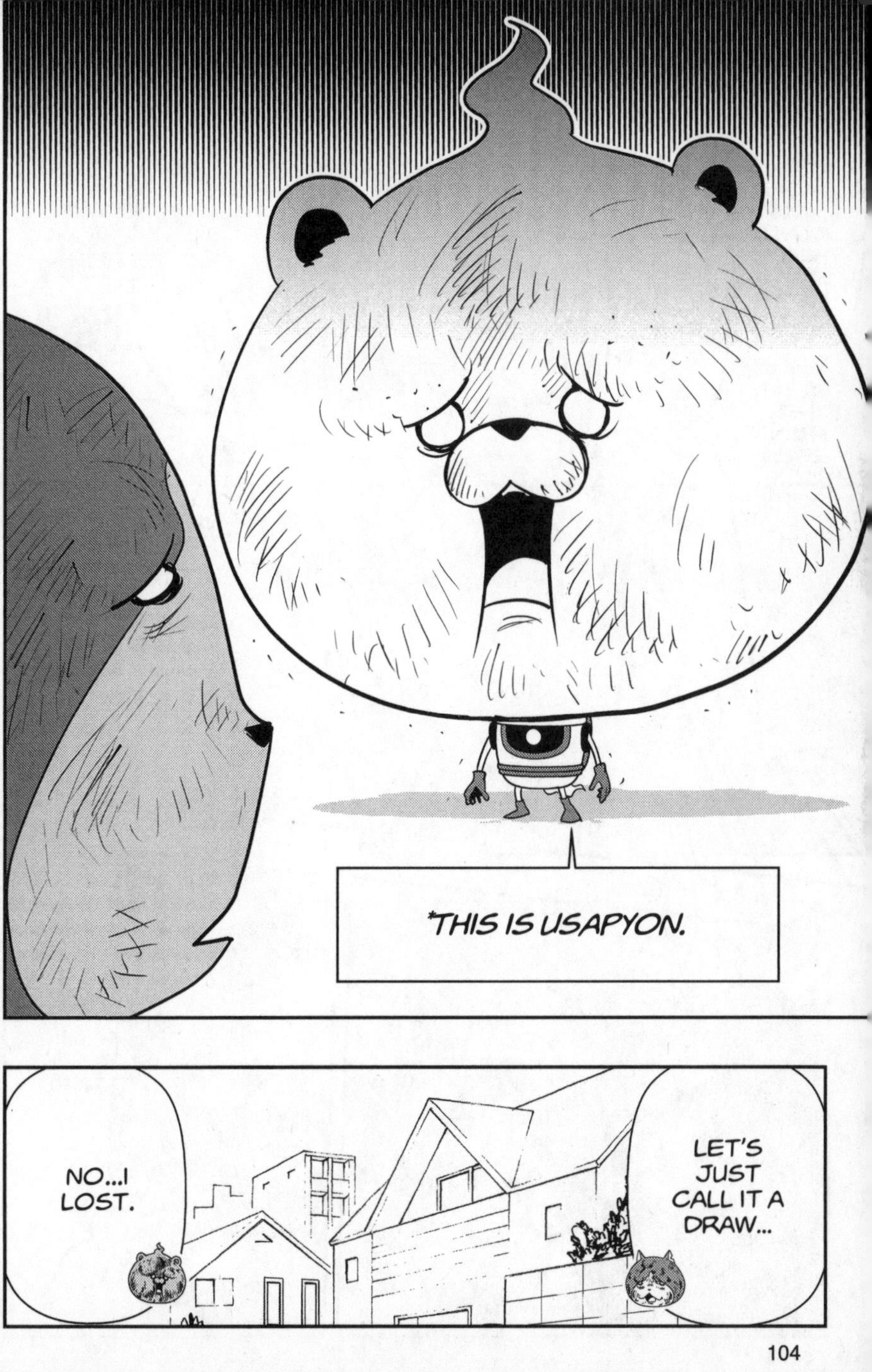
*THIS IS USAPYON.
LET'S JUST CALL IT A DRAW...
NO...I LOST.

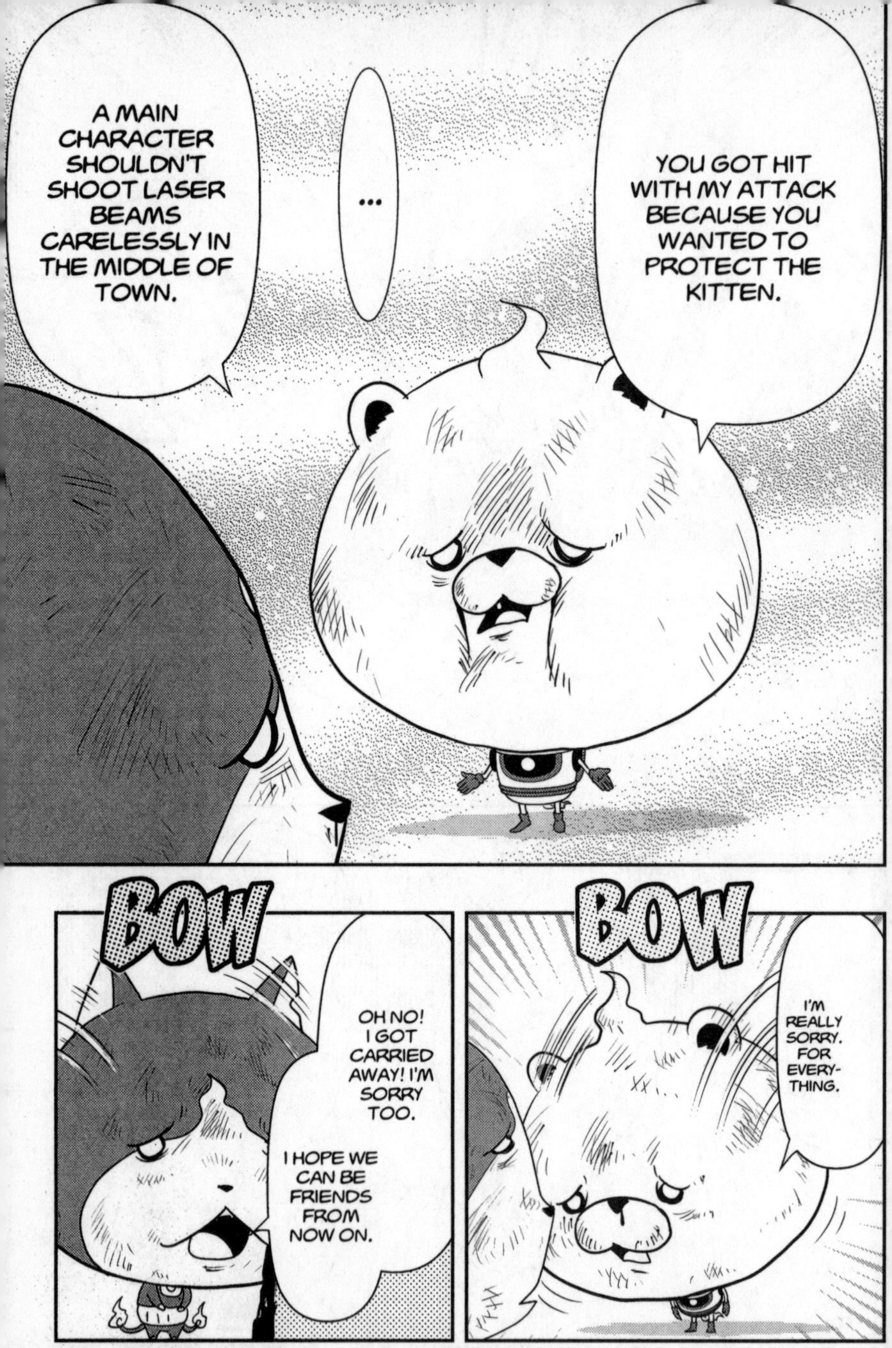
YOU GOT HIT WITH MY ATTACK BECAUSE YOU WANTED TO PROTECT THE KITTEN.
...
A MAIN CHARACTER SHOULDN'T SHOOT LASER BEAMS CARELESSLY IN THE MIDDLE OF TOWN.
BOW
I'M REALLY SORRY. FOR EVERYTHING.
BOW
OH NO! I GOT CARRIED AWAY! I'M SORRY TOO.
I HOPE WE CAN BE FRIENDS FROM NOW ON.

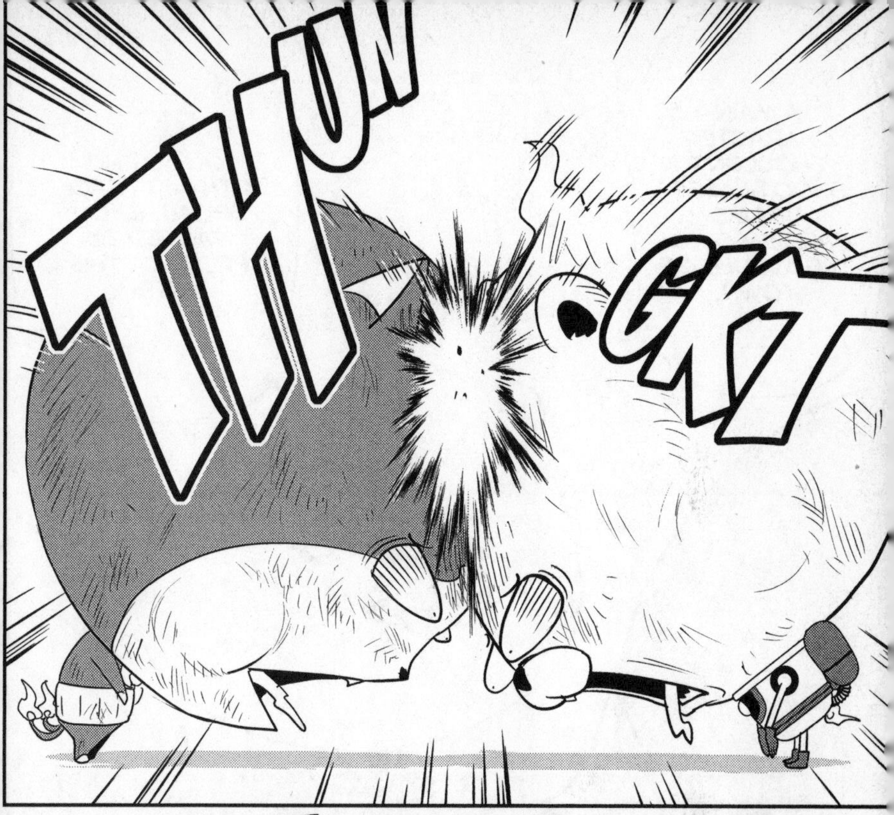
THUN
GKT
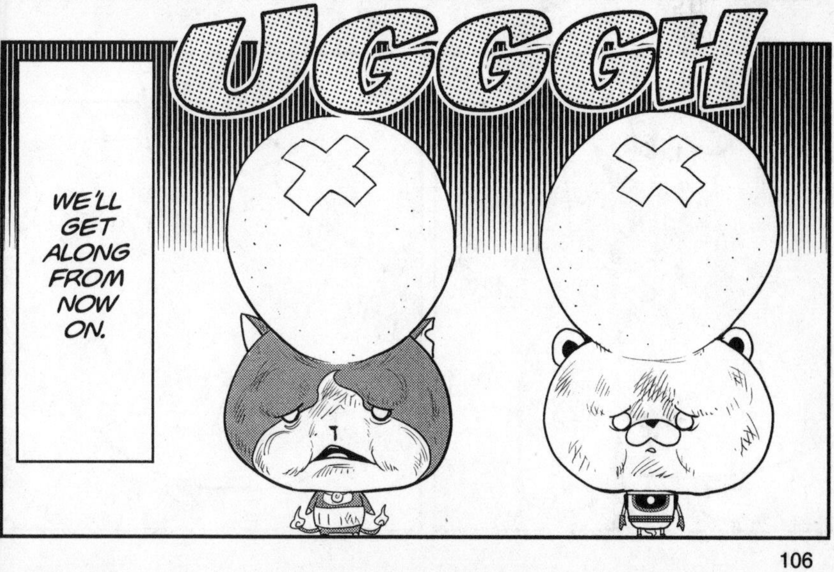
UGGGH
WE'LL GET ALONG FROM NOW ON.

CHAPTER 143
TRIVIA YO-KAI POOFESSOR

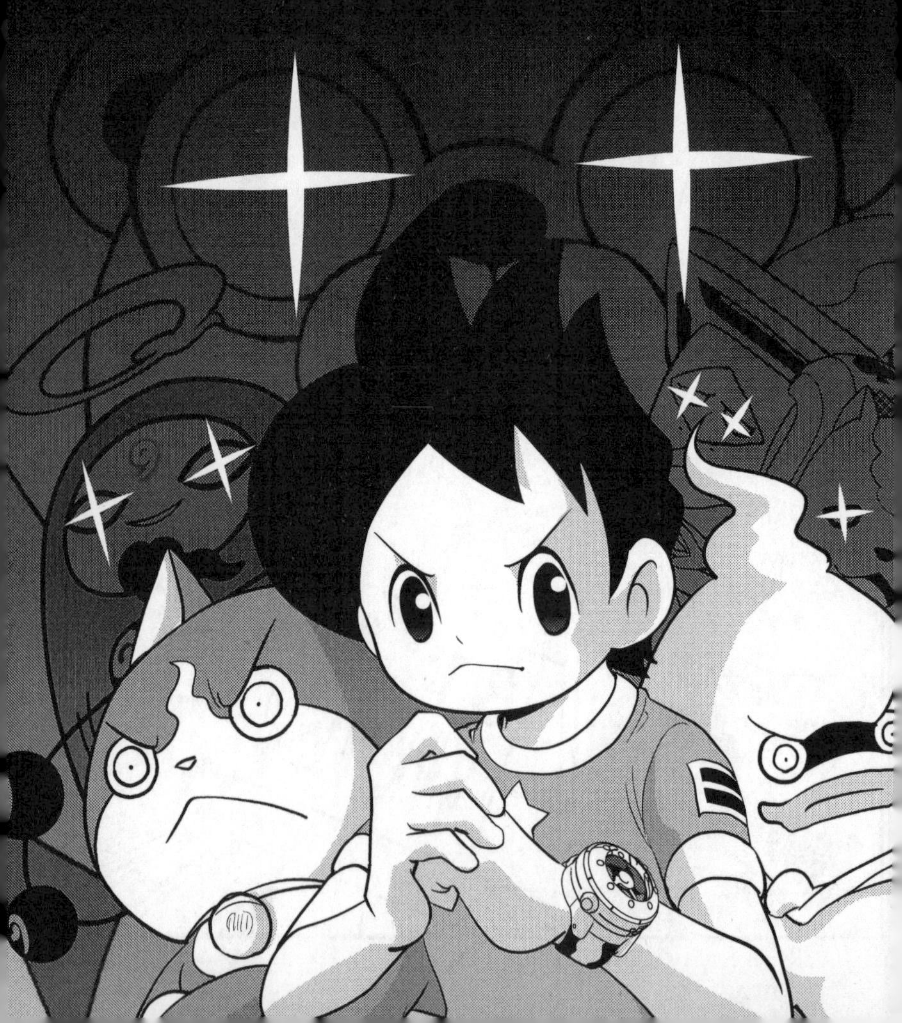

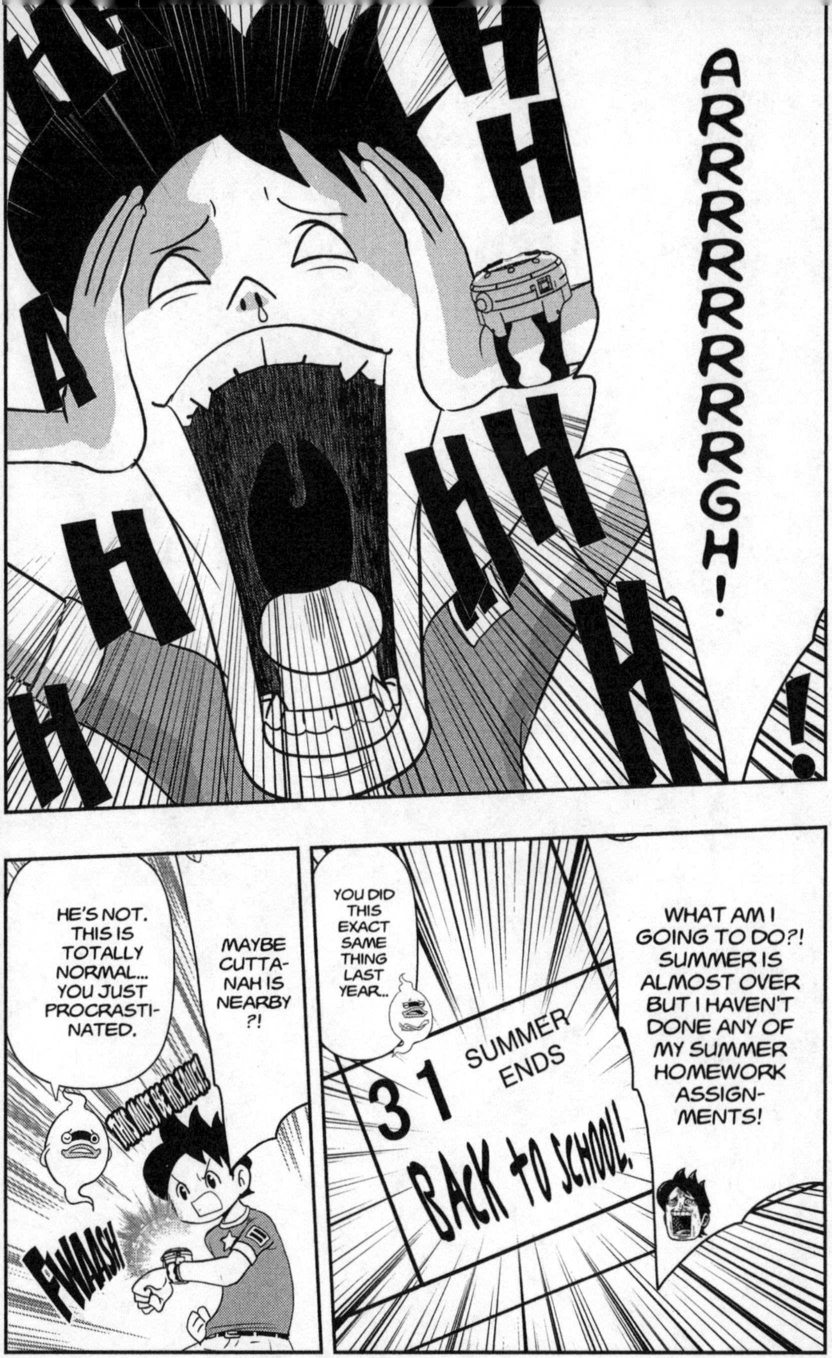
AAAAHHHHHHHHH!
ARRRRRRRRGH!
WHAT AM I GOING TO DO?! SUMMER IS ALMOST OVER BUT I HAVEN'T DONE ANY OF MY SUMMER HOMEWORK ASSIGN-MENTS!
YOU DID THIS EXACT SAME THING LAST YEAR...
31 SUMMER ENDS
BACK TO SCHOOL!
MAYBE CUTTA-NAH IS NEARBY ?!
THIS MUST BE HIS FAULT!
FWAASH
HE'S NOT. THIS IS TOTALLY NORMAL... YOU JUST PROCRASTI-NATED.

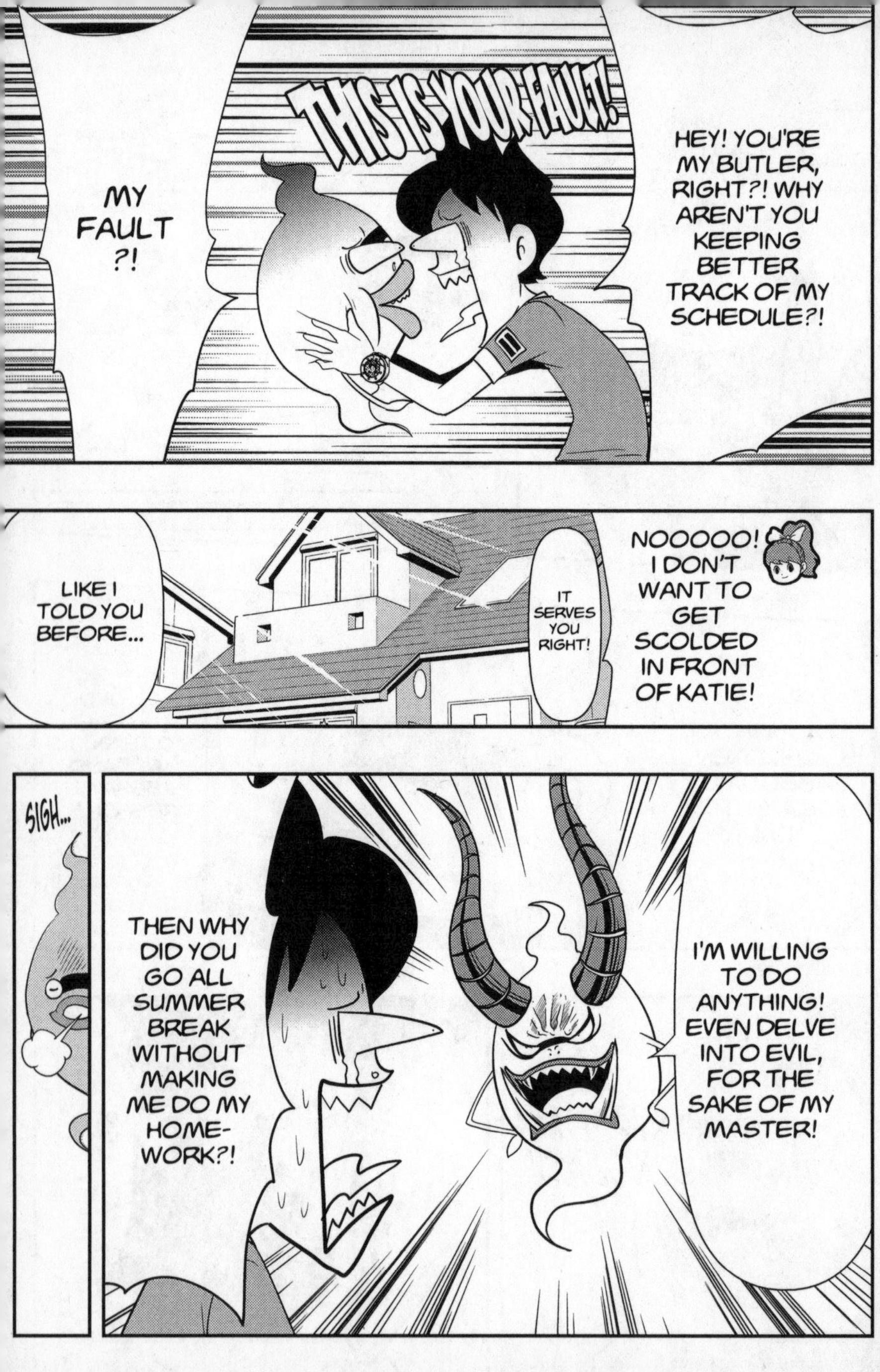
THIS IS YOUR FAULT!
HEY! YOU'RE MY BUTLER, RIGHT?! WHY AREN'T YOU KEEPING BETTER TRACK OF MY SCHEDULE?!
MY FAULT?!
NOOOOO! I DON'T WANT TO GET SCOLDED IN FRONT OF KATIE!
IT SERVES YOU RIGHT!
LIKE I TOLD YOU BEFORE...
I'M WILLING TO DO ANYTHING! EVEN DELVE INTO EVIL, FOR THE SAKE OF MY MASTER!
THEN WHY DID YOU GO ALL SUMMER BREAK WITHOUT MAKING ME DO MY HOME-WORK?!
SIGH...

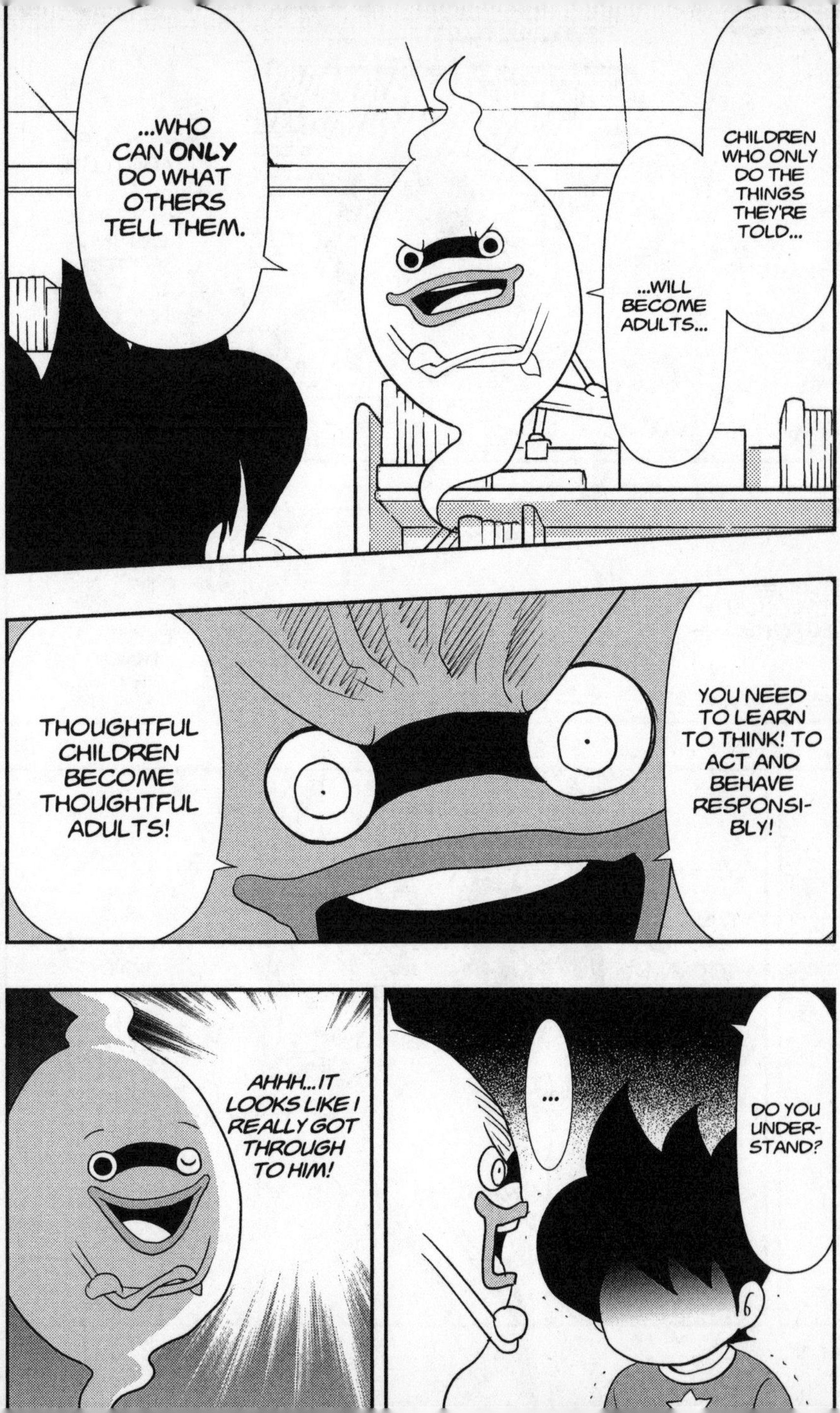
CHILDREN WHO ONLY DO THE THINGS THEY'RE TOLD...
...WILL BECOME ADULTS...
...WHO CAN ONLY DO WHAT OTHERS TELL THEM.
YOU NEED TO LEARN TO THINK! TO ACT AND BEHAVE RESPONSIBLY!
THOUGHTFUL CHILDREN BECOME THOUGHTFUL ADULTS!
DO YOU UNDERSTAND?
...
AHHH...IT LOOKS LIKE I REALLY GOT THROUGH TO HIM!

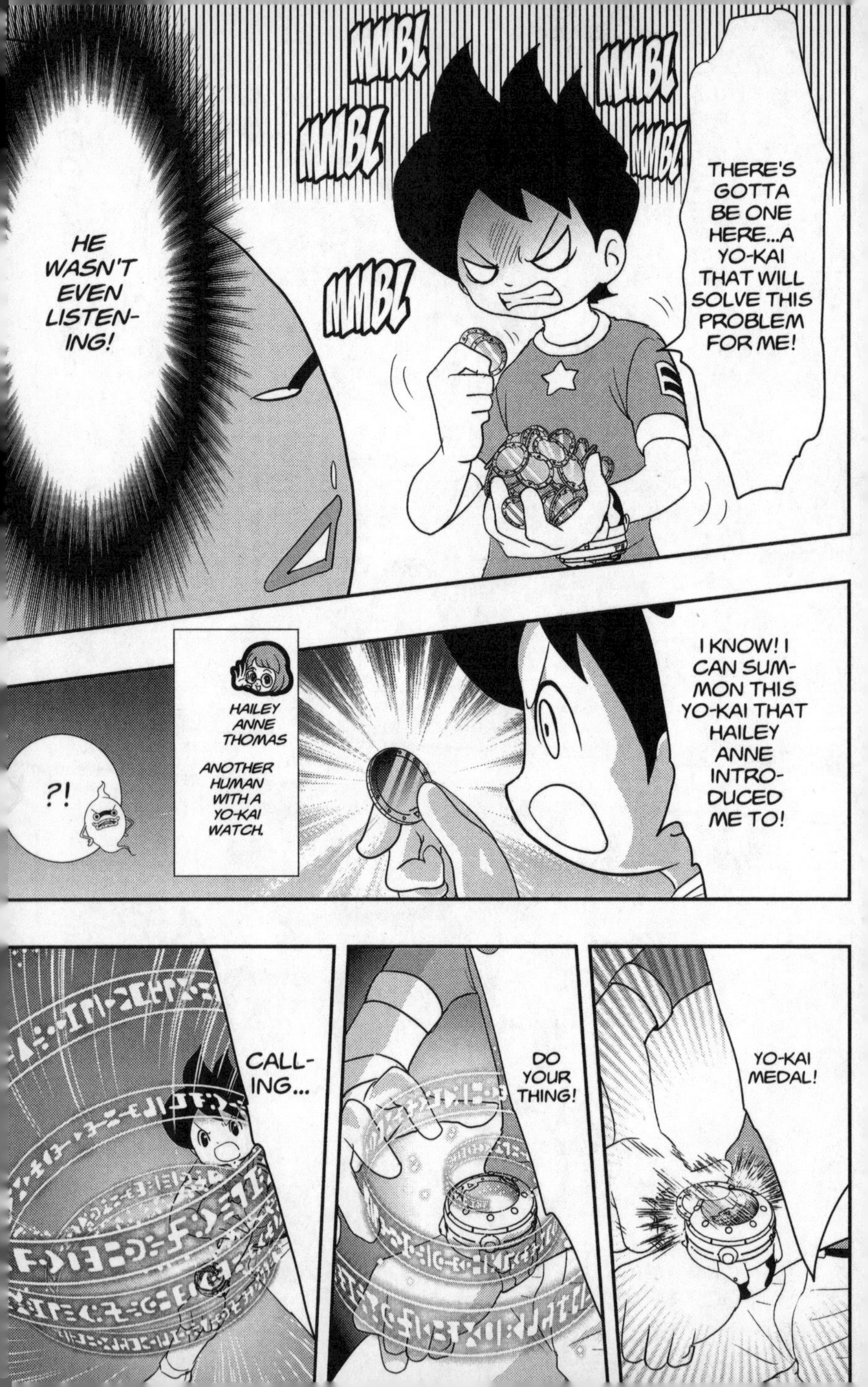
MMBL MMBL
MMBL MMBL
THERE'S GOTTA BE ONE HERE...A YO-KAI THAT WILL SOLVE THIS PROBLEM FOR ME!
MMBL
HE WASN'T EVEN LISTEN-ING!
I KNOW! I CAN SUM-MON THIS YO-KAI THAT HAILEY ANNE INTRO-DUCED ME TO!
HAILEY ANNE THOMAS
ANOTHER HUMAN WITH A YO-KAI WATCH.
?!
YO-KAI MEDAL!
DO YOUR THING!
CALL-ING...

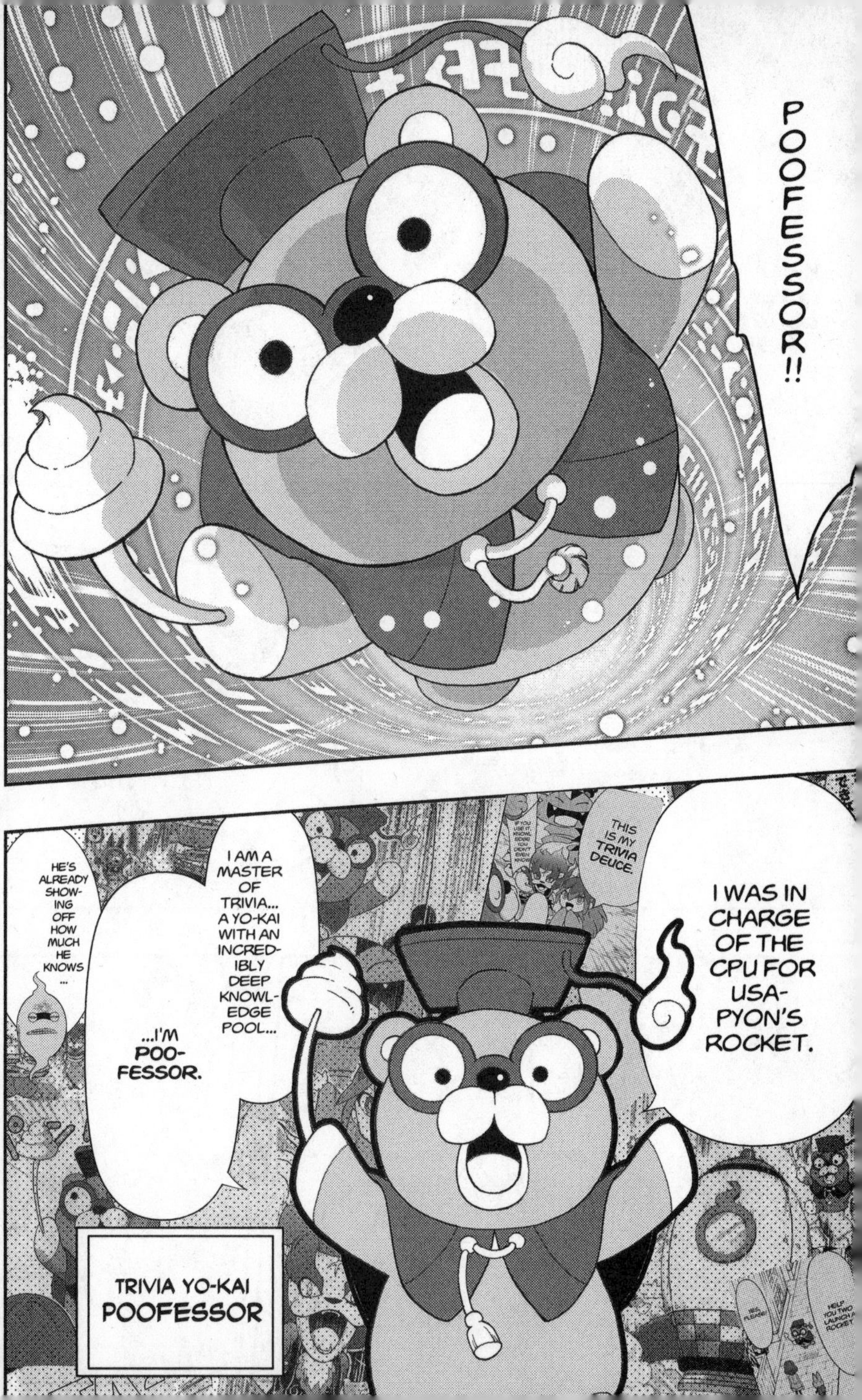
POOFESSOR!!
I WAS IN CHARGE OF THE CPU FOR USA-PYON'S ROCKET.
THIS IS MY TRIVIA DEUCE.
IF YOU USE IT, KNOWL-EDGE YOU DIDN'T EVEN KNOW...
I AM A MASTER OF TRIVIA... A YO-KAI WITH AN INCRED-IBLY DEEP KNOWL-EDGE POOL...
...I'M POO-FESSOR.
HE'S ALREADY SHOW-ING OFF HOW MUCH HE KNOWS...
HELP YOU TWO LAUNCH A ROCKET
YES, PLEASE!
TRIVIA YO-KAI POOFESSOR

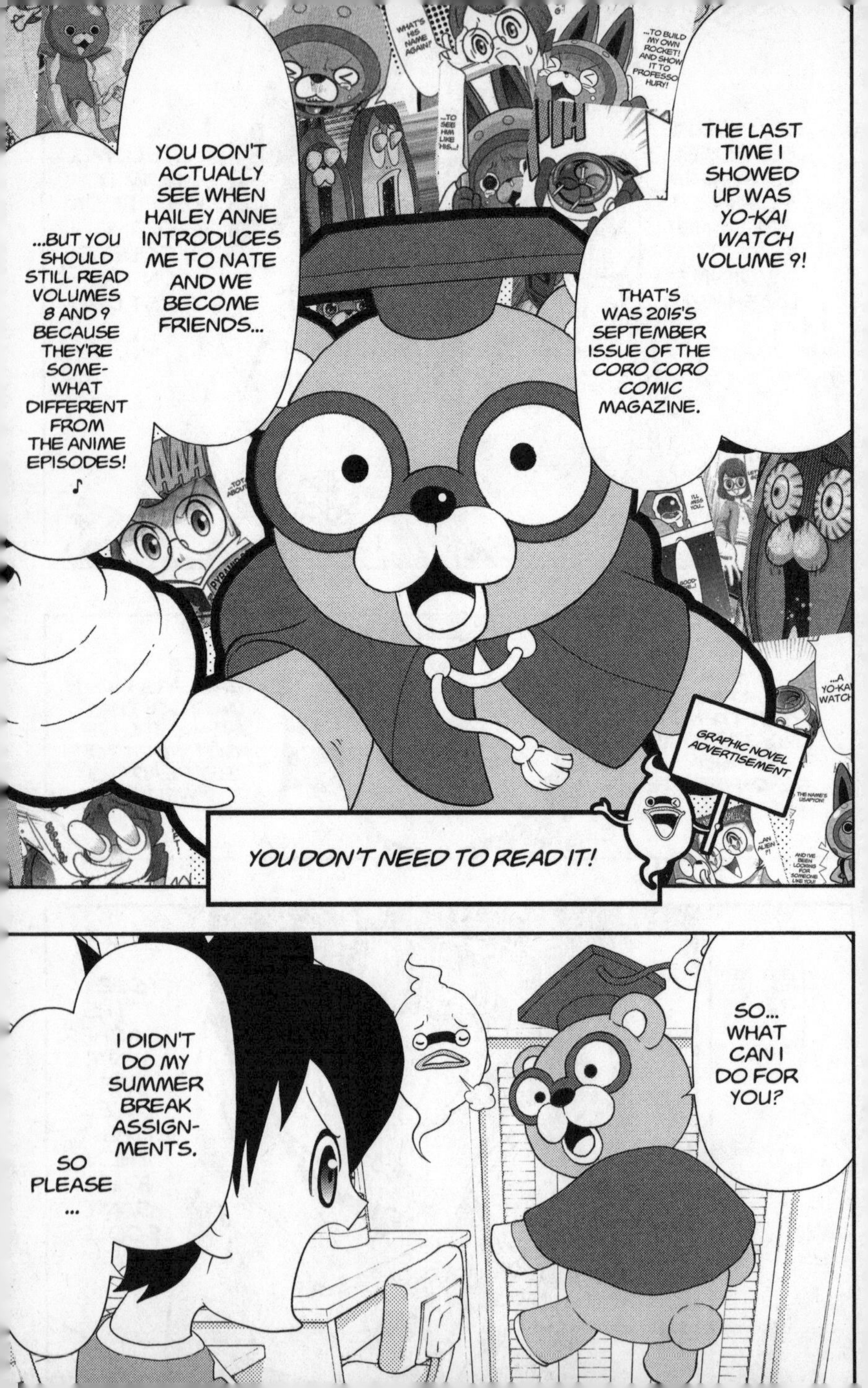
THE LAST TIME I SHOWED UP WAS YO-KAI WATCH VOLUME 9!
THAT'S WAS 2015'S SEPTEMBER ISSUE OF THE CORO CORO COMIC MAGAZINE.
YOU DON'T ACTUALLY SEE WHEN HAILEY ANNE INTRODUCES ME TO NATE AND WE BECOME FRIENDS...
...BUT YOU SHOULD STILL READ VOLUMES 8 AND 9 BECAUSE THEY'RE SOME-WHAT DIFFERENT FROM THE ANIME EPISODES! ♪
GRAPHIC NOVEL ADVERTISEMENT
YOU DON'T NEED TO READ IT!
SO... WHAT CAN I DO FOR YOU?
I DIDN'T DO MY SUMMER BREAK ASSIGN-MENTS.
SO PLEASE ...

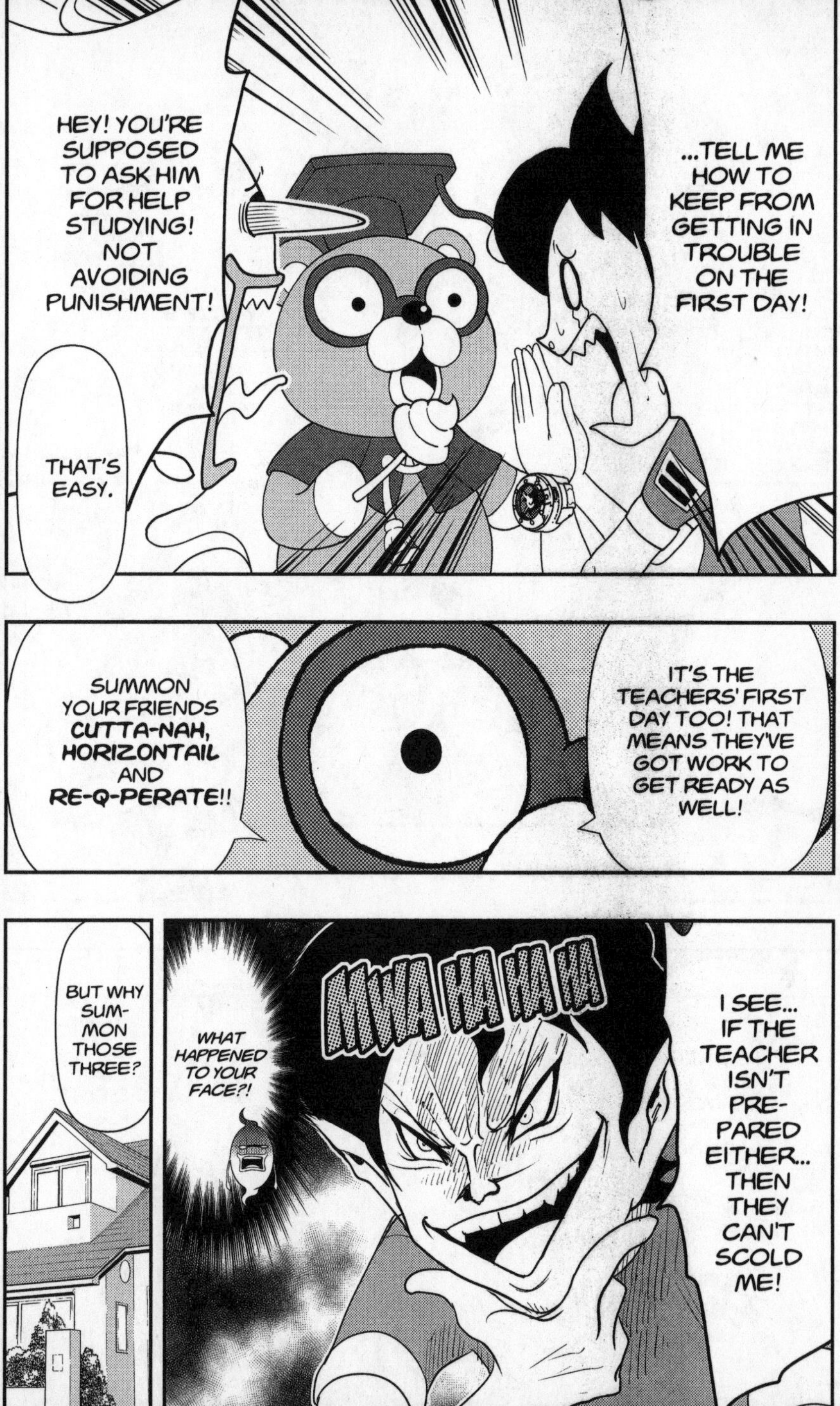
...TELL ME HOW TO KEEP FROM GETTING IN TROUBLE ON THE FIRST DAY!
HEY! YOU'RE SUPPOSED TO ASK HIM FOR HELP STUDYING! NOT AVOIDING PUNISHMENT!
THAT'S EASY.
IT'S THE TEACHERS' FIRST DAY TOO! THAT MEANS THEY'VE GOT WORK TO GET READY AS WELL!
SUMMON YOUR FRIENDS **CUTTA-NAH, HORIZONTAIL** AND **RE-Q-PERATE**!!
I SEE... IF THE TEACHER ISN'T PRE-PARED EITHER... THEN THEY CAN'T SCOLD ME!
MWA HA HA HA
WHAT HAPPENED TO YOUR FACE?!
BUT WHY SUM-MON THOSE THREE?

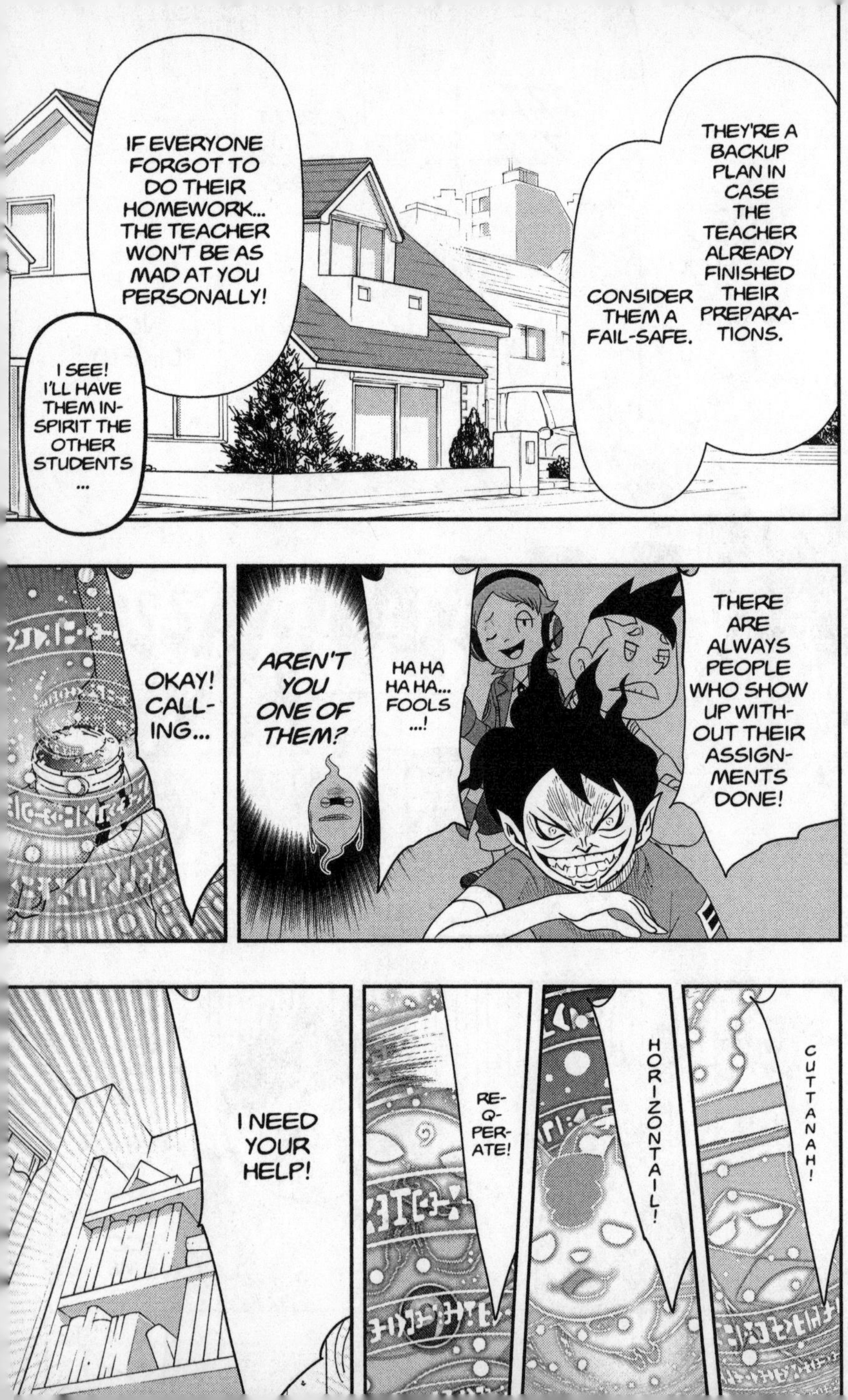
THEY'RE A BACKUP PLAN IN CASE THE TEACHER ALREADY FINISHED THEIR PREPARATIONS.
CONSIDER THEM A FAIL-SAFE.
IF EVERYONE FORGOT TO DO THEIR HOMEWORK... THE TEACHER WON'T BE AS MAD AT YOU PERSONALLY!
I SEE! I'LL HAVE THEM IN-SPIRIT THE OTHER STUDENTS...
THERE ARE ALWAYS PEOPLE WHO SHOW UP WITHOUT THEIR ASSIGNMENTS DONE!
HA HA HA HA... FOOLS...!
AREN'T YOU ONE OF THEM?
OKAY! CALLING...
CUTTANAH!
HORIZONTAIL!
REQPERATE!
I NEED YOUR HELP!

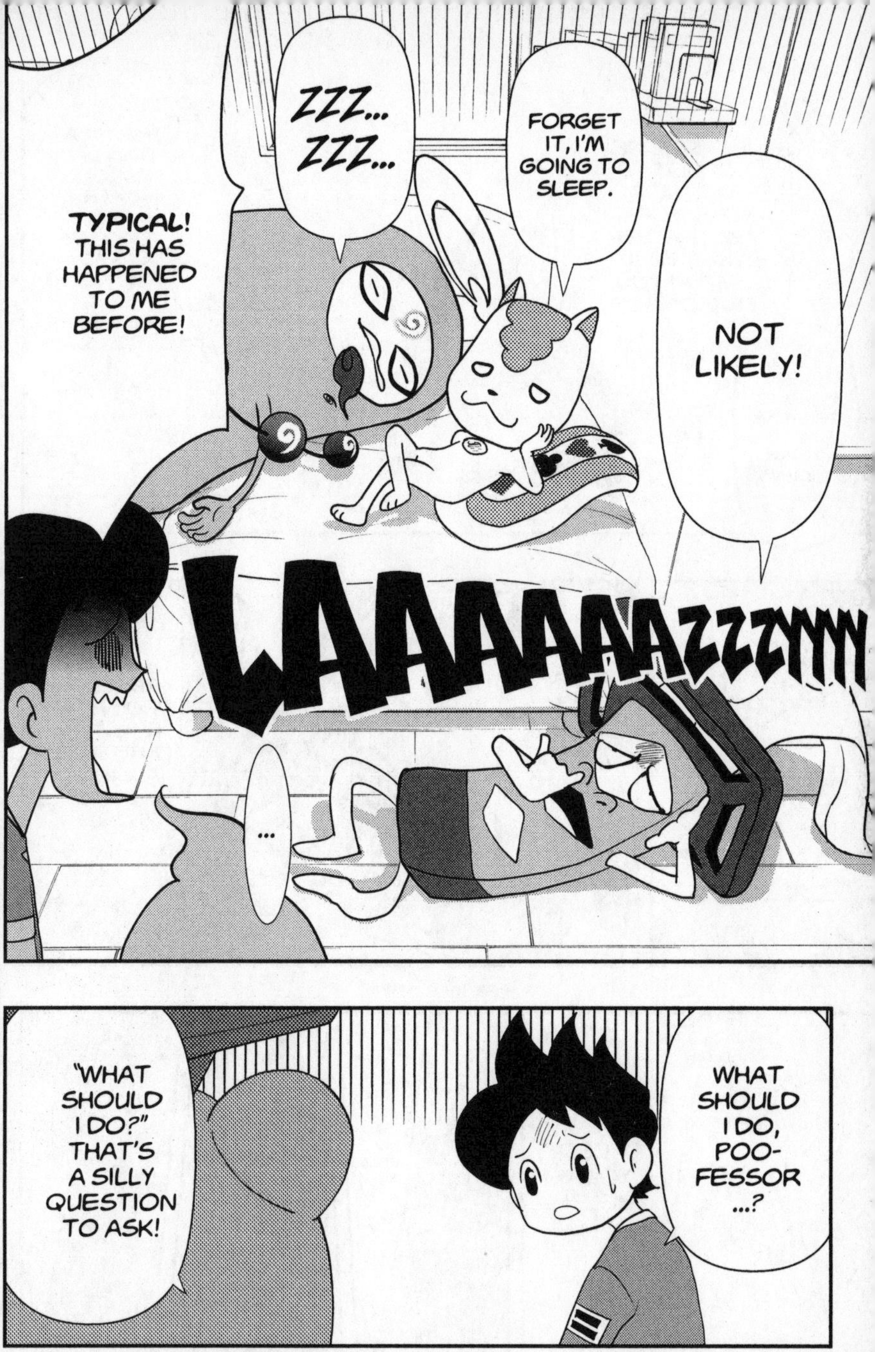
FORGET IT, I'M GOING TO SLEEP.
ZZZ... ZZZ...
NOT LIKELY!
TYPICAL! THIS HAS HAPPENED TO ME BEFORE!
LAAAAAAZZZYYYY
...
WHAT SHOULD I DO, POO-FESSOR...?
"WHAT SHOULD I DO?" THAT'S A SILLY QUESTION TO ASK!

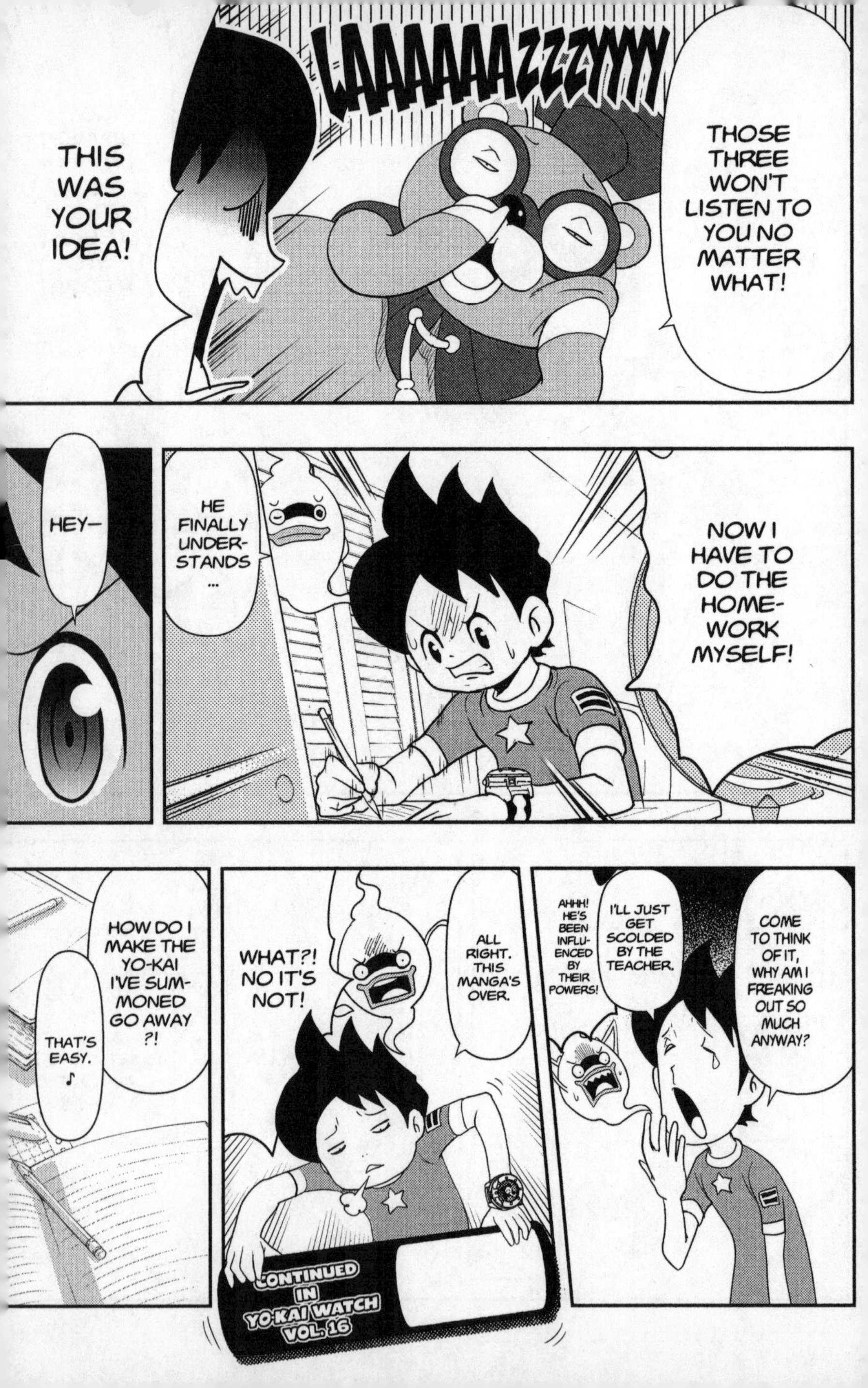
LAAAAAAZZZYYYY
THOSE THREE WON'T LISTEN TO YOU NO MATTER WHAT!
THIS WAS YOUR IDEA!
NOW I HAVE TO DO THE HOME-WORK MYSELF!
HE FINALLY UNDER-STANDS...
HEY—
COME TO THINK OF IT, WHY AM I FREAKING OUT SO MUCH ANYWAY?
I'LL JUST GET SCOLDED BY THE TEACHER.
AHHH! HE'S BEEN INFLU-ENCED BY THEIR POWERS!
ALL RIGHT. THIS MANGA'S OVER.
WHAT?! NO IT'S NOT!
CONTINUED IN YO-KAI WATCH VOL. 16
HOW DO I MAKE THE YO-KAI I'VE SUM-MONED GO AWAY?!
THAT'S EASY. ♪

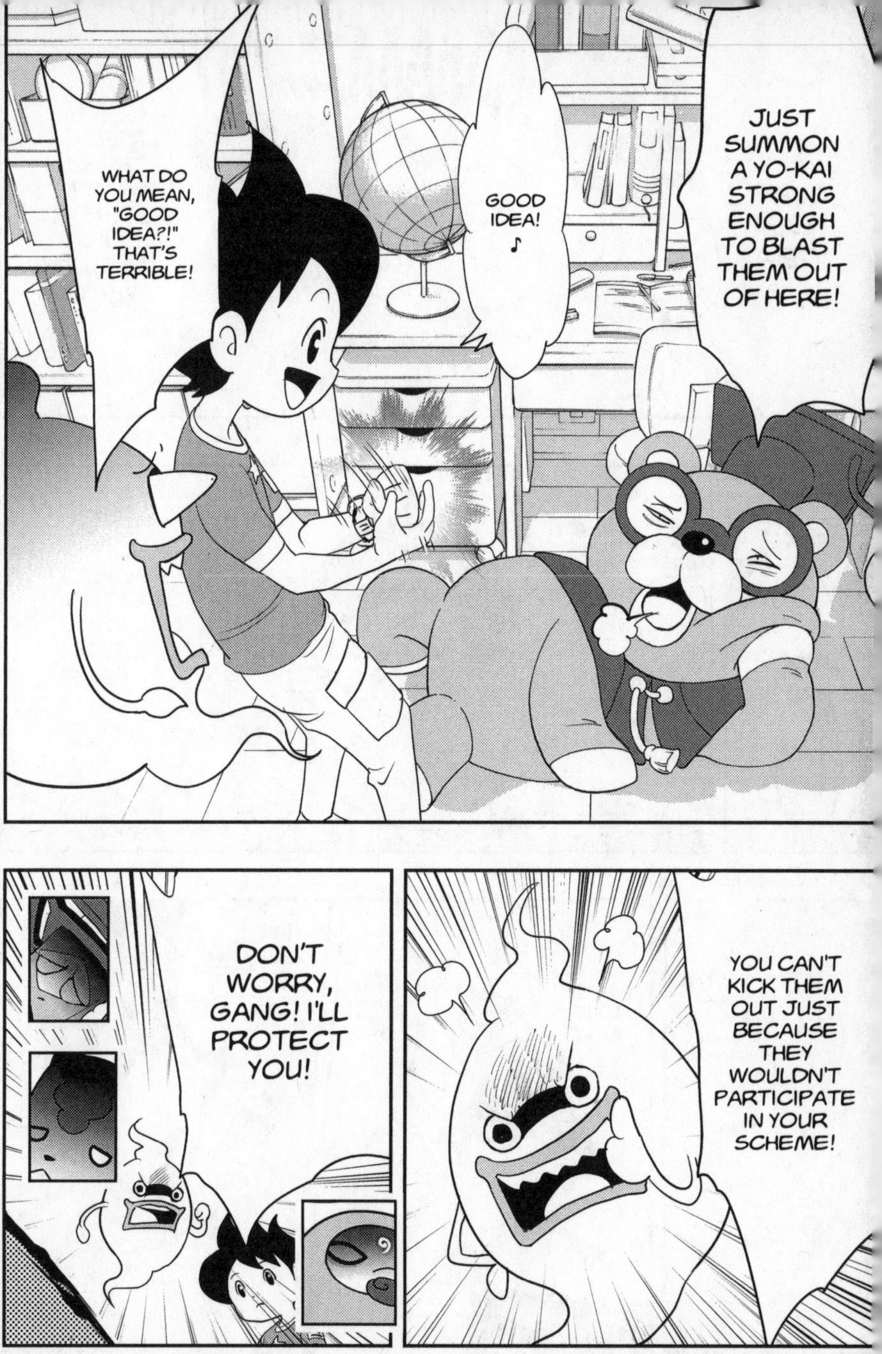
JUST SUMMON A YO-KAI STRONG ENOUGH TO BLAST THEM OUT OF HERE!
GOOD IDEA! ♪
WHAT DO YOU MEAN, "GOOD IDEA?!" THAT'S TERRIBLE!
YOU CAN'T KICK THEM OUT JUST BECAUSE THEY WOULDN'T PARTICIPATE IN YOUR SCHEME!
DON'T WORRY, GANG! I'LL PROTECT YOU!

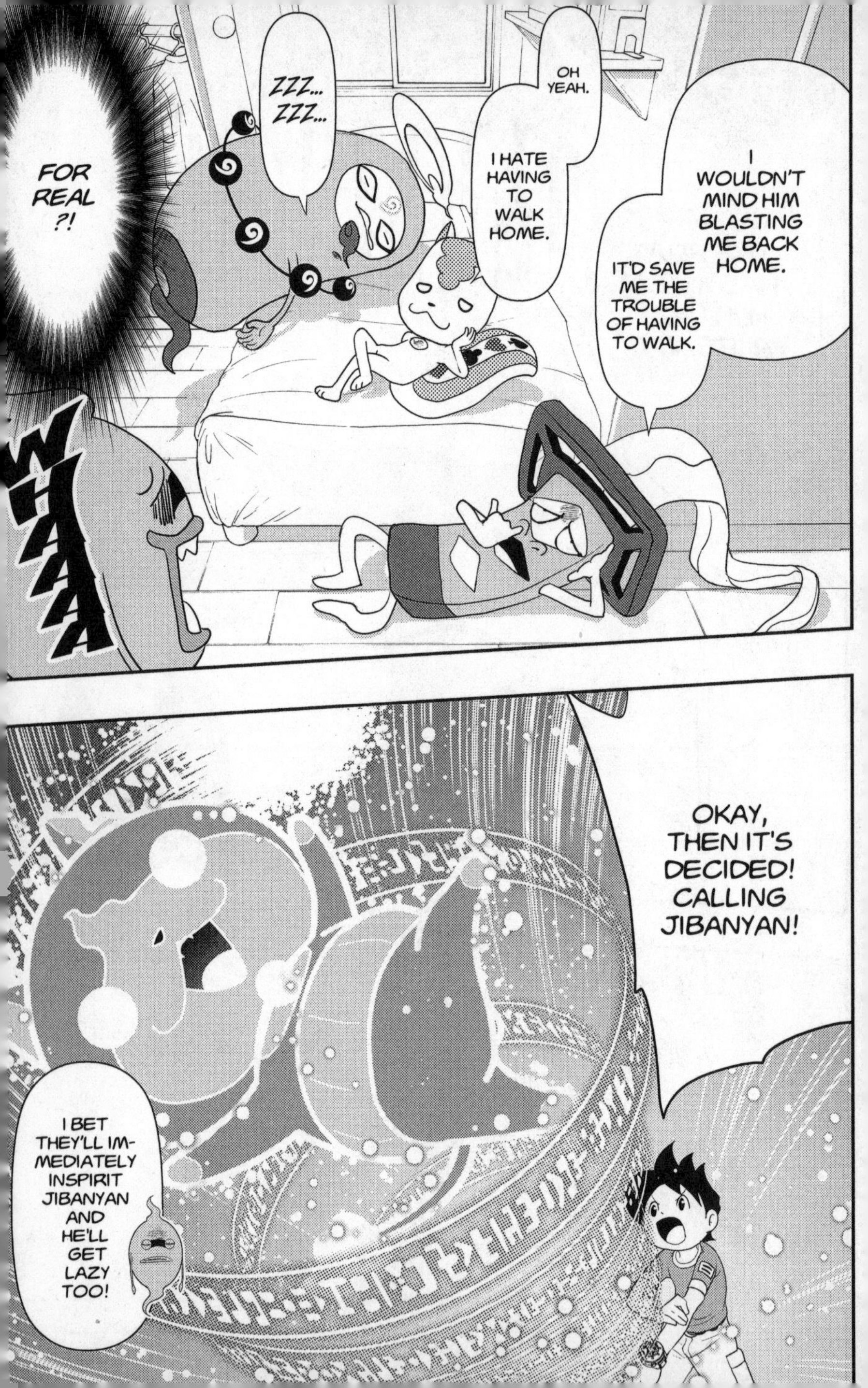
I WOULDN'T MIND HIM BLASTING ME BACK HOME.
IT'D SAVE ME THE TROUBLE OF HAVING TO WALK.
OH YEAH.
I HATE HAVING TO WALK HOME.
ZZZ... ZZZ...
FOR REAL ?!
WHAAAA
OKAY, THEN IT'S DECIDED! CALLING JIBANYAN!
I BET THEY'LL IM-MEDIATELY INSPIRIT JIBANYAN AND HE'LL GET LAZY TOO!

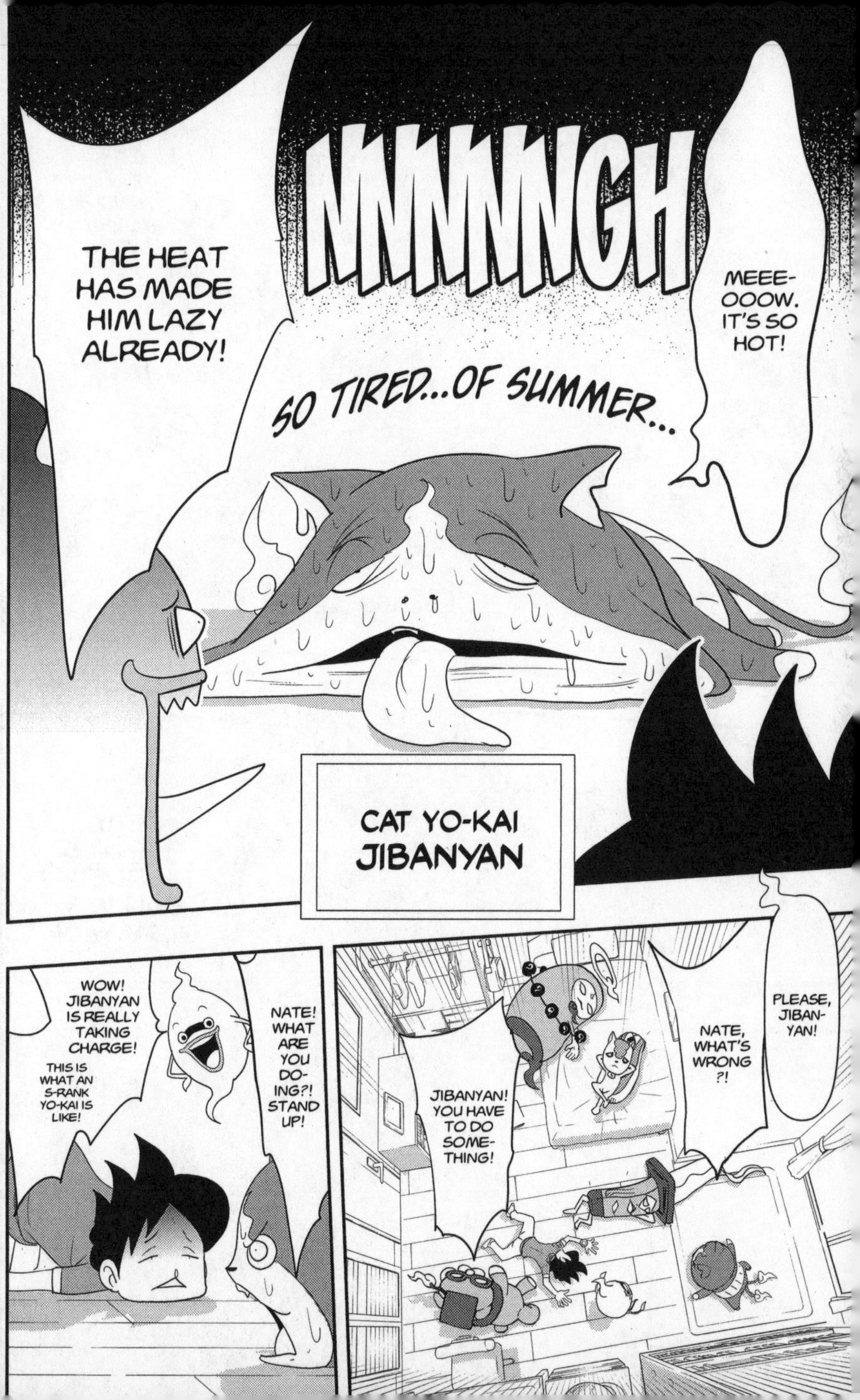
MEEE-OOOW. IT'S SO HOT!
NNNNNNGH
THE HEAT HAS MADE HIM LAZY ALREADY!
SO TIRED...OF SUMMER...
CAT YO-KAI JIBANYAN
PLEASE, JIBAN-YAN!
NATE, WHAT'S WRONG?!
JIBANYAN! YOU HAVE TO DO SOME-THING!
NATE! WHAT ARE YOU DO-ING?! STAND UP!
WOW! JIBANYAN IS REALLY TAKING CHARGE!
THIS IS WHAT AN S-RANK YO-KAI IS LIKE!

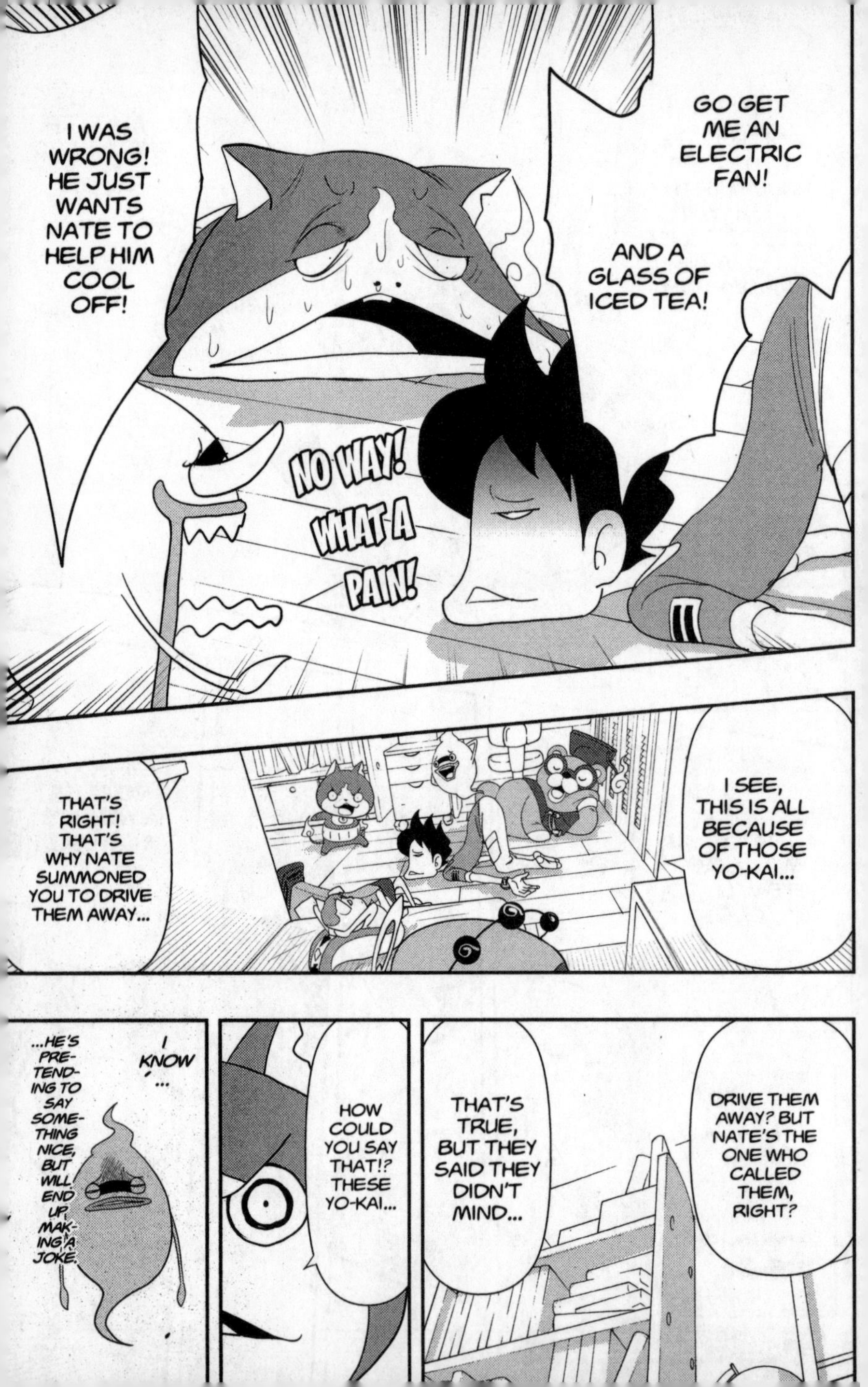
GO GET ME AN ELECTRIC FAN!
AND A GLASS OF ICED TEA!
NO WAY! WHAT A PAIN!
I WAS WRONG! HE JUST WANTS NATE TO HELP HIM COOL OFF!
I SEE, THIS IS ALL BECAUSE OF THOSE YO-KAI...
THAT'S RIGHT! THAT'S WHY NATE SUMMONED YOU TO DRIVE THEM AWAY...
DRIVE THEM AWAY? BUT NATE'S THE ONE WHO CALLED THEM, RIGHT?
THAT'S TRUE, BUT THEY SAID THEY DIDN'T MIND...
HOW COULD YOU SAY THAT!? THESE YO-KAI...
I KNOW...
...HE'S PRETENDING TO SAY SOMETHING NICE, BUT WILL END UP MAKING A JOKE.

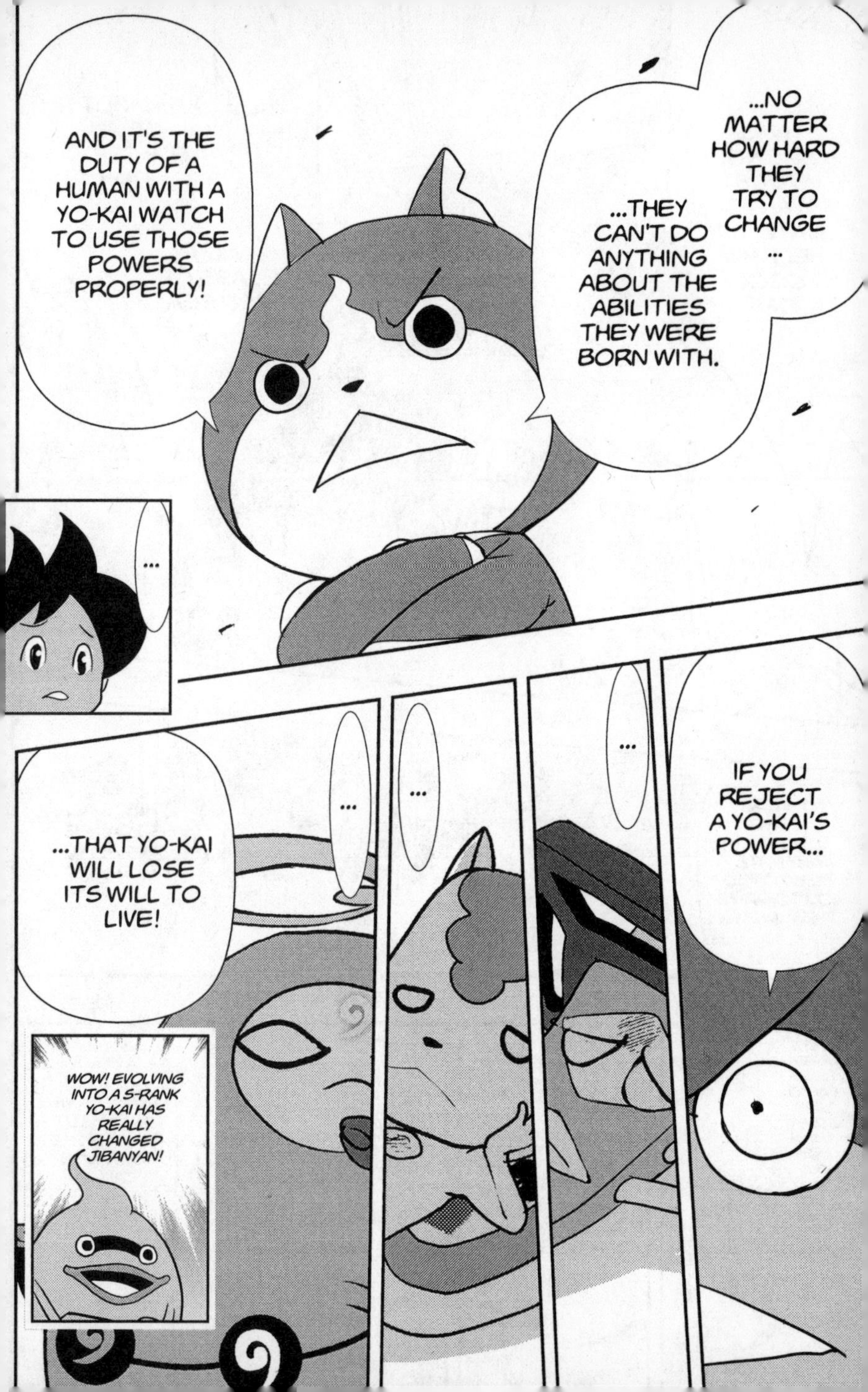
...NO MATTER HOW HARD THEY TRY TO CHANGE ...
...THEY CAN'T DO ANYTHING ABOUT THE ABILITIES THEY WERE BORN WITH.
AND IT'S THE DUTY OF A HUMAN WITH A YO-KAI WATCH TO USE THOSE POWERS PROPERLY!
...
IF YOU REJECT A YO-KAI'S POWER...
...
...
...
...THAT YO-KAI WILL LOSE ITS WILL TO LIVE!
WOW! EVOLVING INTO A S-RANK YO-KAI HAS REALLY CHANGED JIBANYAN!

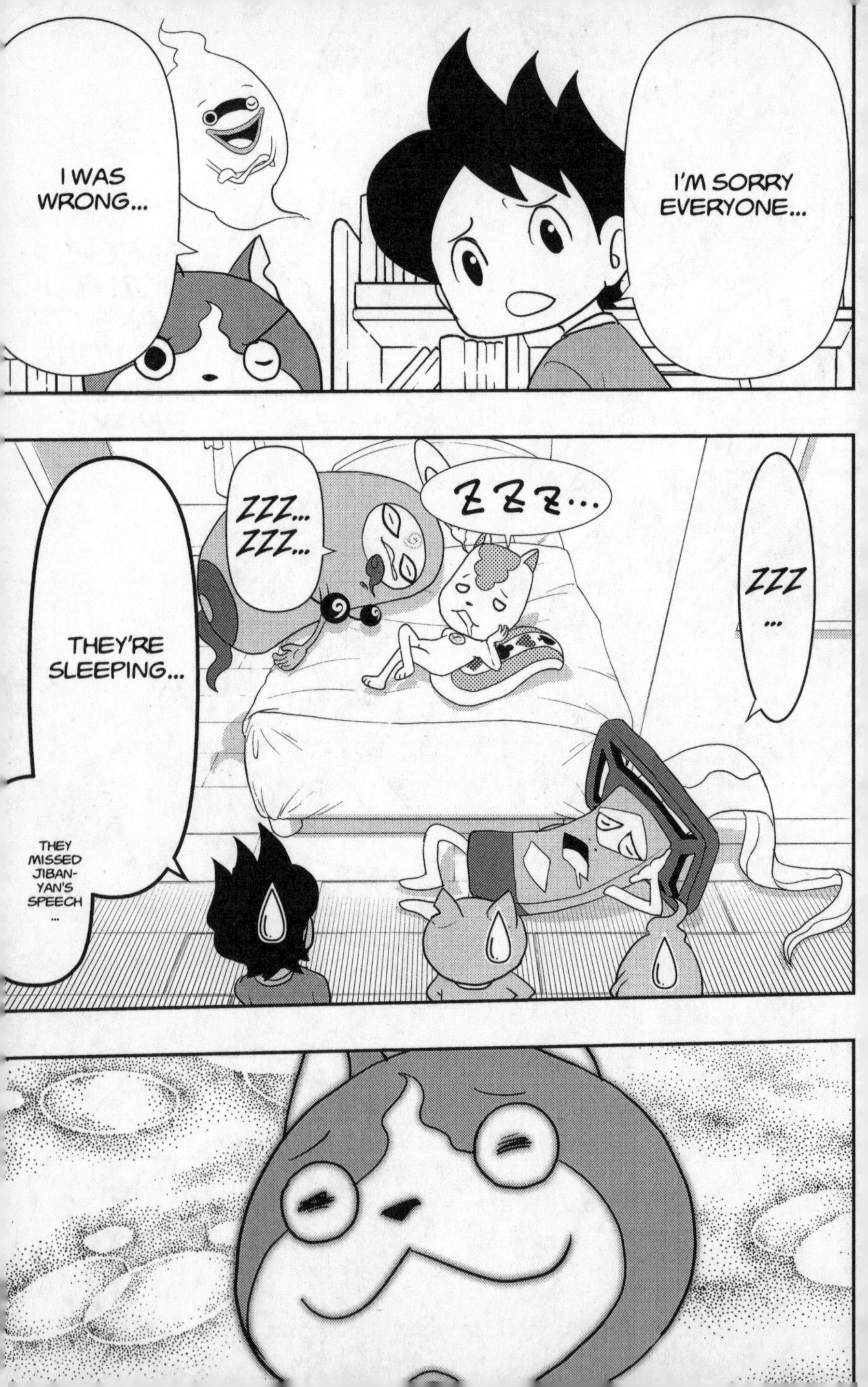
I'M SORRY EVERYONE...
I WAS WRONG...
ZZZ ...
Z Z Z...
ZZZ... ZZZ...
THEY'RE SLEEPING...
THEY MISSED JIBAN-YAN'S SPEECH ...

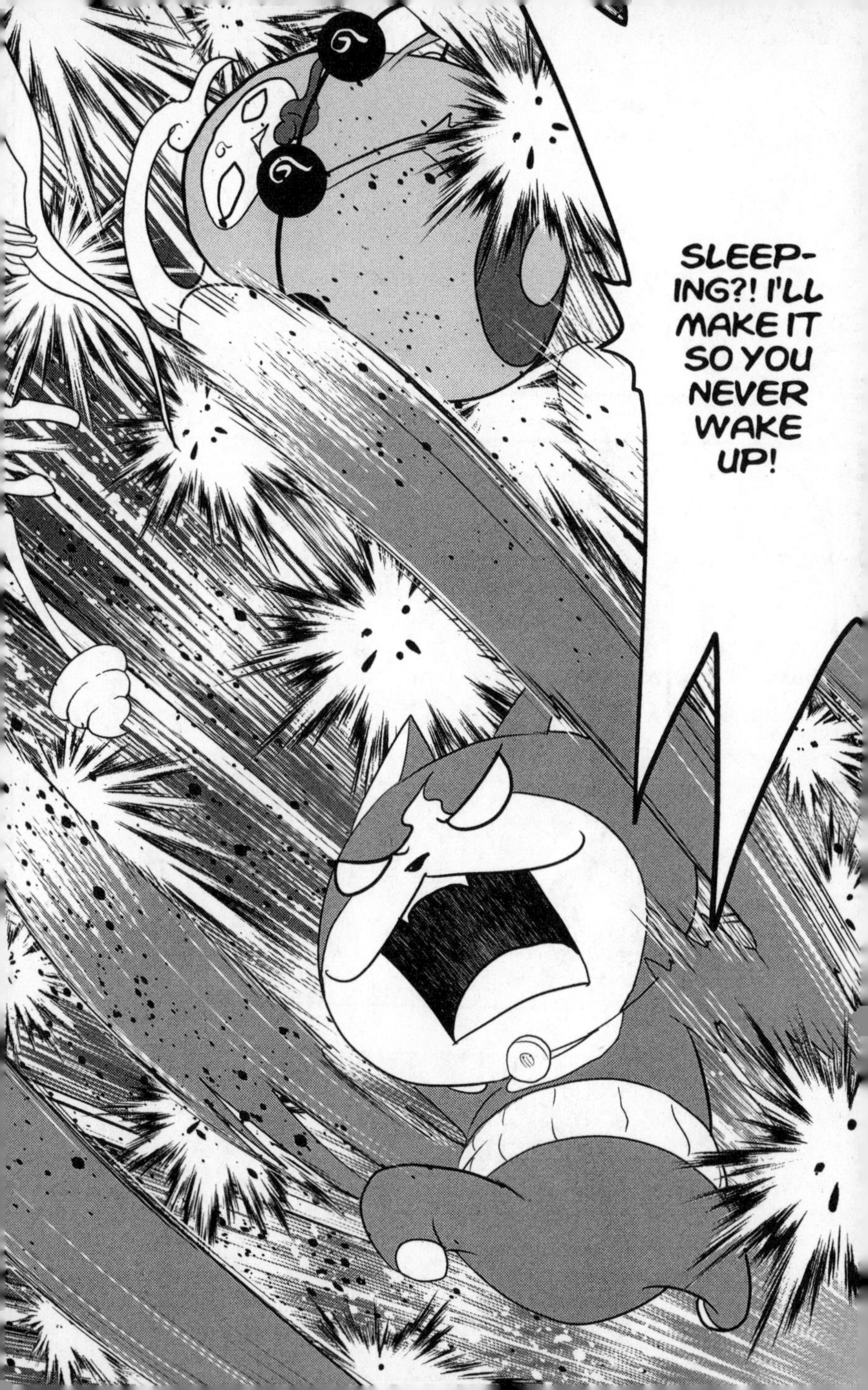
SLEEP-ING?! I'LL MAKE IT SO YOU NEVER WAKE UP!

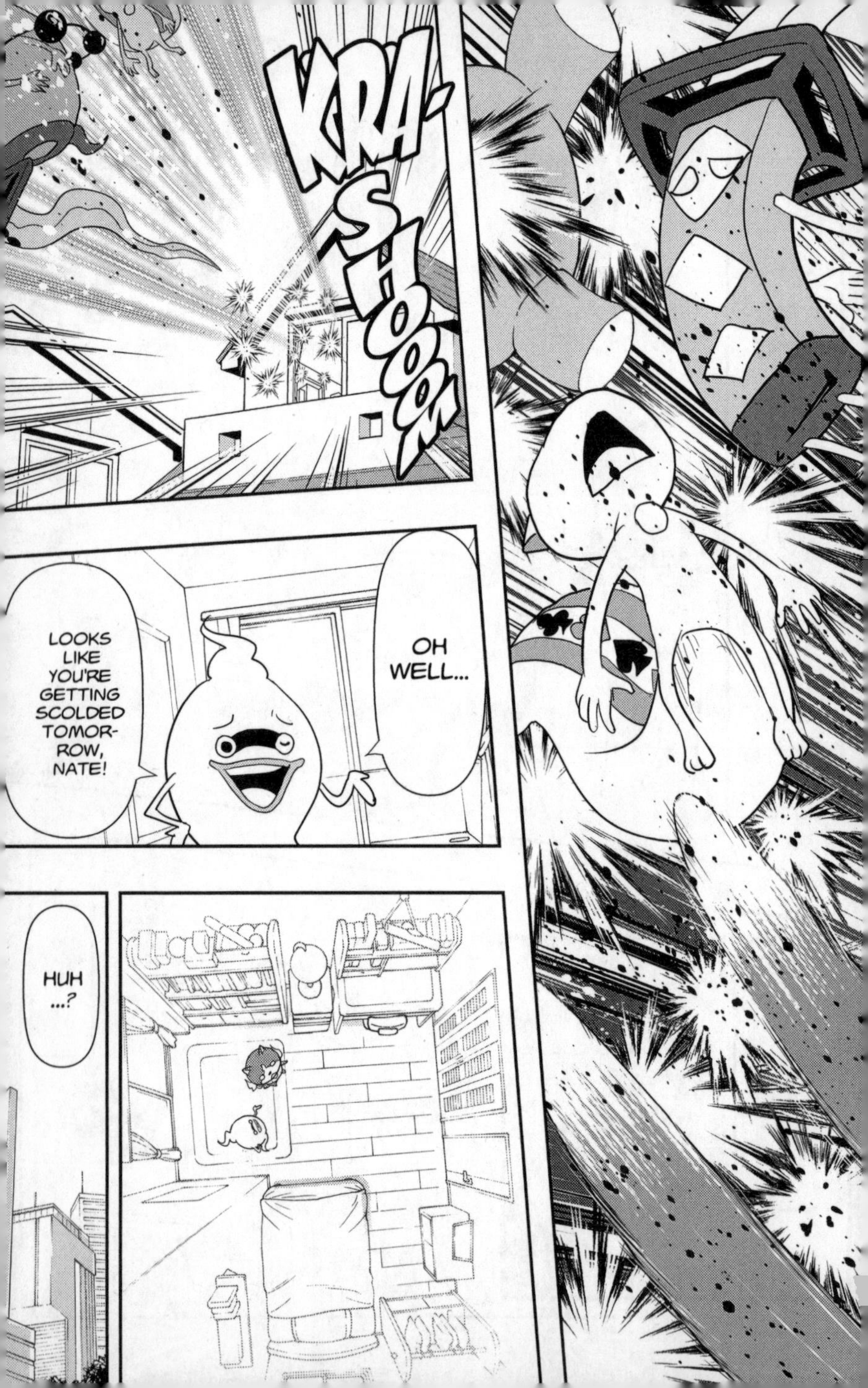
KRA-SHOOOM
OH WELL...
LOOKS LIKE YOU'RE GETTING SCOLDED TOMOR-ROW, NATE!
HUH ...?

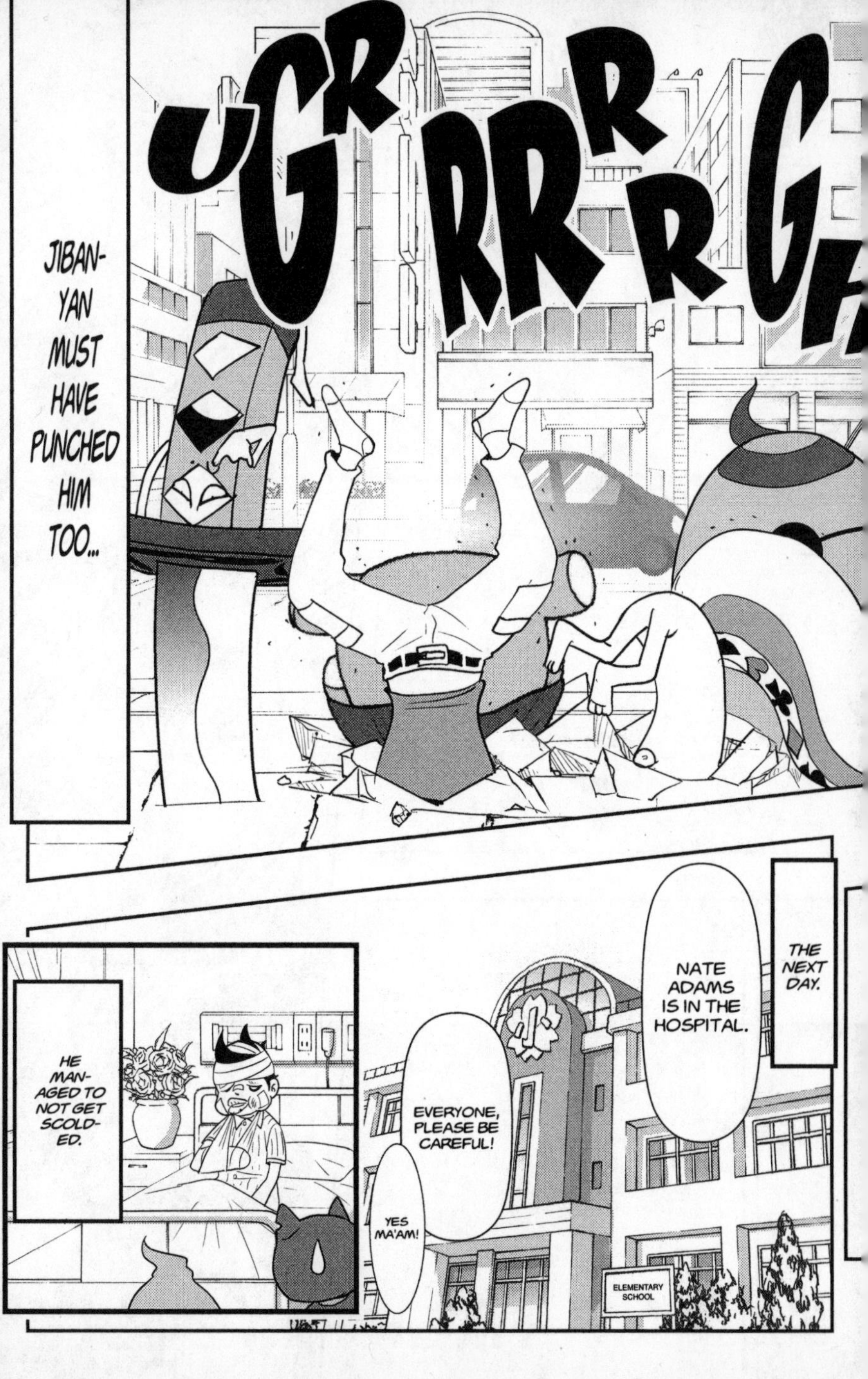
UGRRRRRGH
JIBAN-YAN MUST HAVE PUNCHED HIM TOO...
THE NEXT DAY.
NATE ADAMS IS IN THE HOSPITAL.
EVERYONE, PLEASE BE CAREFUL!
YES MA'AM!
ELEMENTARY SCHOOL
HE MANAGED TO NOT GET SCOLDED.

CHAPTER 144
INVENTION YO-KAI T. ENERGISON

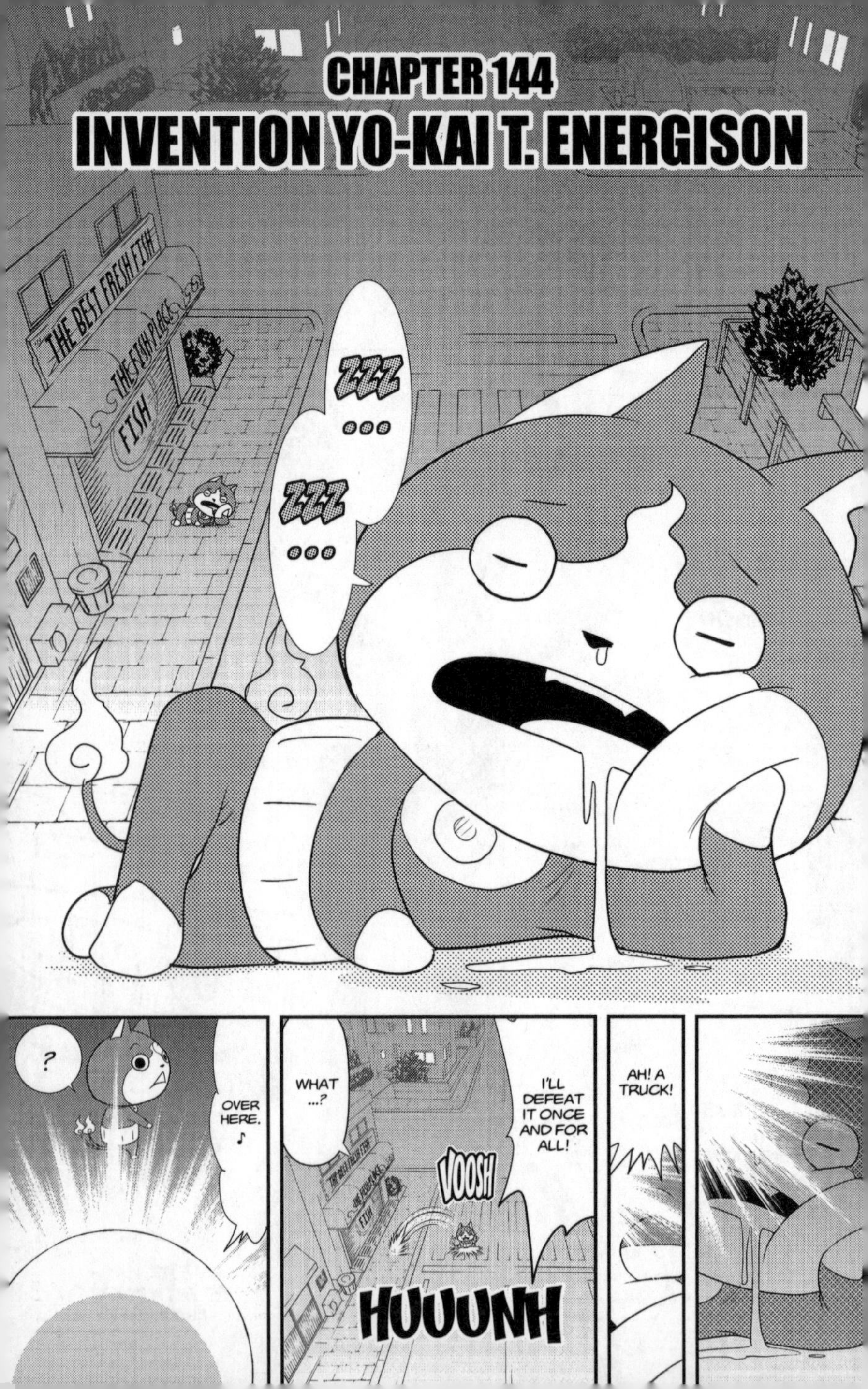
THE BEST FRESH FISH
THE FISH PLACE
FISH
ZZZ...
ZZZ...
AH! A TRUCK!
I'LL DEFEAT IT ONCE AND FOR ALL!
WHAT ...?
VOOSH
HUUUNH
OVER HERE. ♪
?

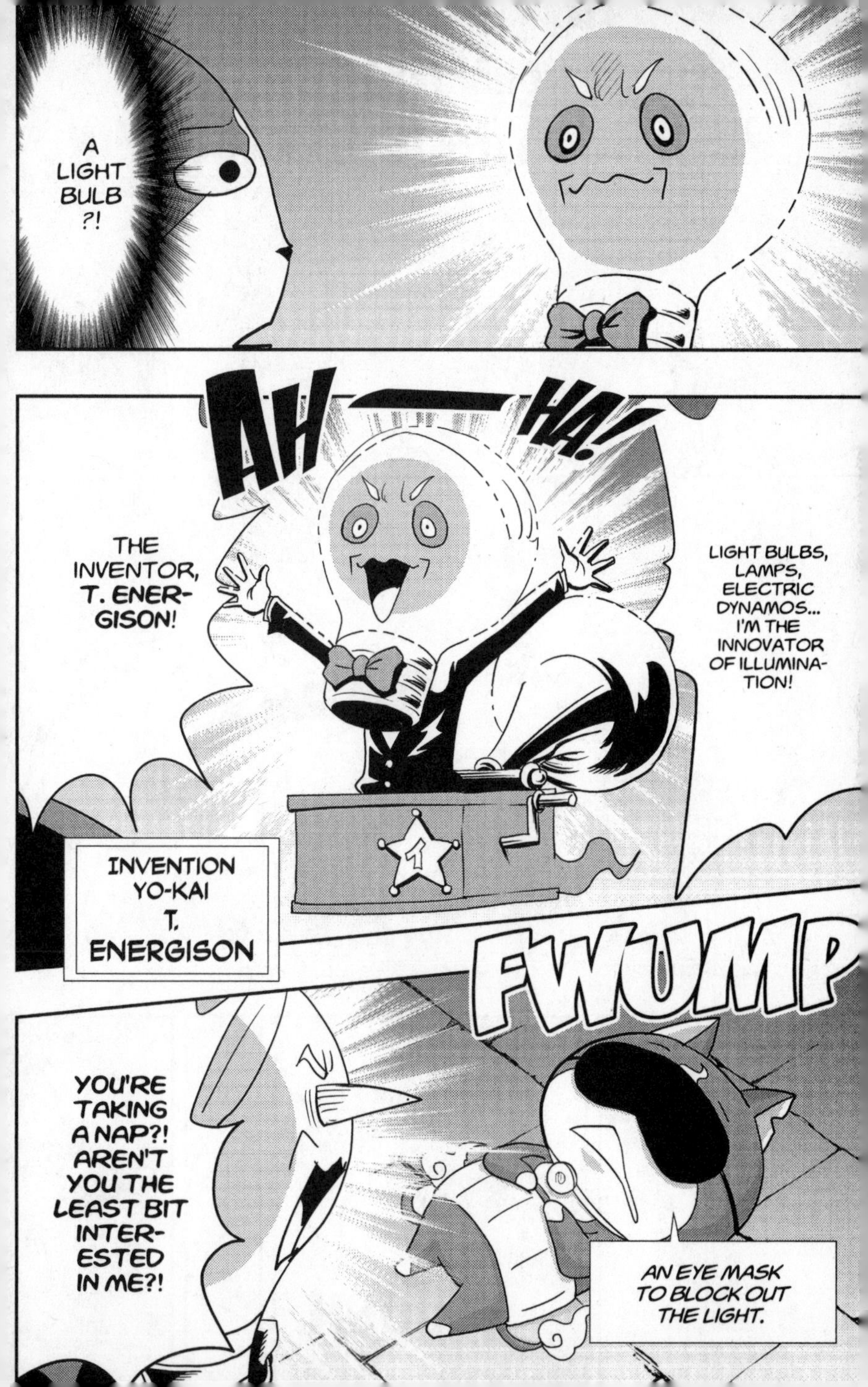
A LIGHT BULB ?!
AH—HA!
LIGHT BULBS, LAMPS, ELECTRIC DYNAMOS... I'M THE INNOVATOR OF ILLUMINATION!
THE INVENTOR, T. ENERGISON!
INVENTION YO-KAI T. ENERGISON
FWUMP
AN EYE MASK TO BLOCK OUT THE LIGHT.
YOU'RE TAKING A NAP?! AREN'T YOU THE LEAST BIT INTERESTED IN ME?!

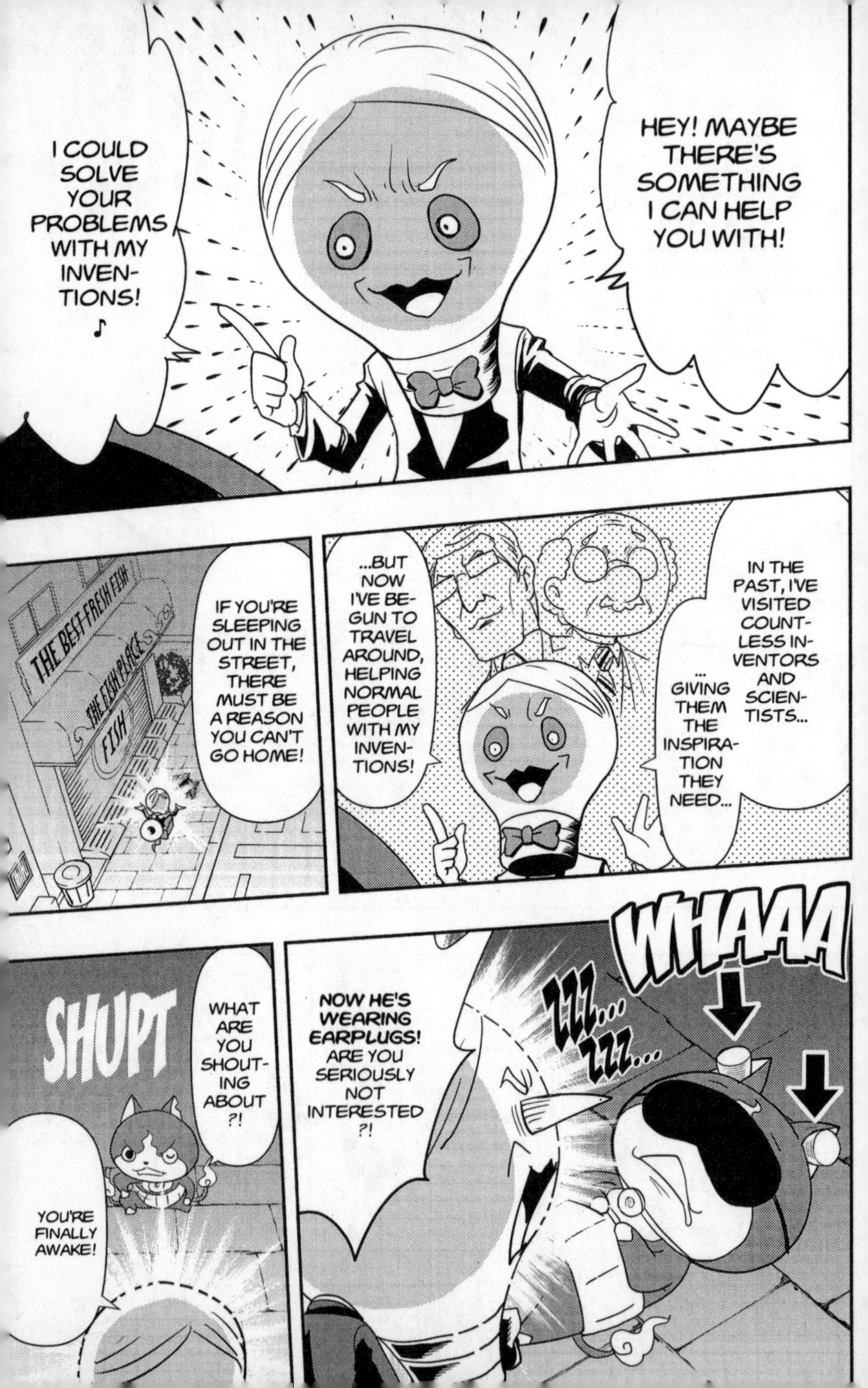
HEY! MAYBE THERE'S SOMETHING I CAN HELP YOU WITH!
I COULD SOLVE YOUR PROBLEMS WITH MY INVEN-TIONS! ♪
IN THE PAST, I'VE VISITED COUNT-LESS IN-VENTORS AND SCIEN-TISTS...
...GIVING THEM THE INSPIRA-TION THEY NEED...
...BUT NOW I'VE BE-GUN TO TRAVEL AROUND, HELPING NORMAL PEOPLE WITH MY INVEN-TIONS!
THE BEST FRESH FISH
THE FISH PLACE
FISH
IF YOU'RE SLEEPING OUT IN THE STREET, THERE MUST BE A REASON YOU CAN'T GO HOME!
WHAAAA
ZZZ... ZZZ...
NOW HE'S WEARING EARPLUGS! ARE YOU SERIOUSLY NOT INTERESTED ?!
WHAT ARE YOU SHOUT-ING ABOUT ?!
SHUPT
YOU'RE FINALLY AWAKE!

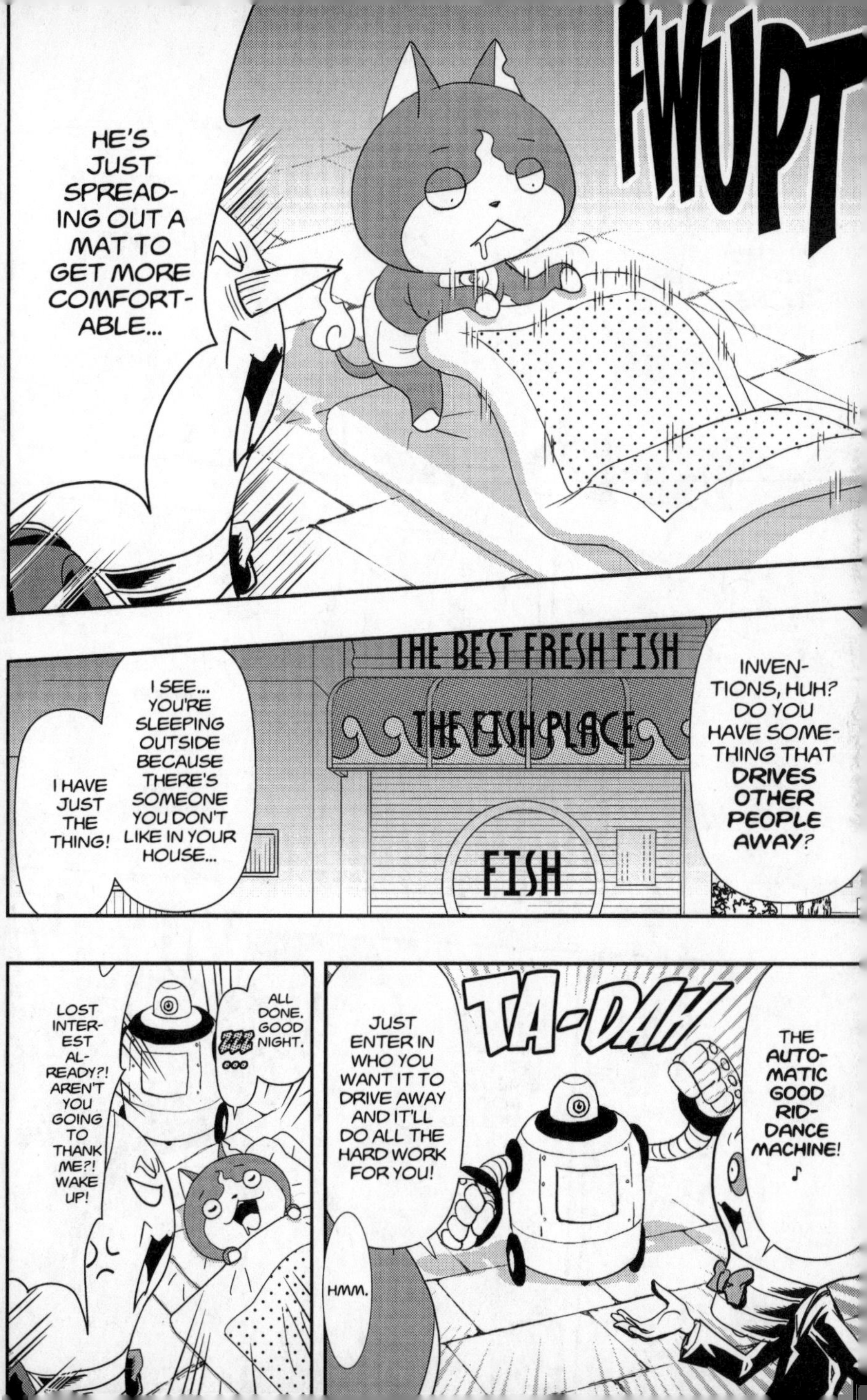
FWUPT
HE'S JUST SPREADING OUT A MAT TO GET MORE COMFORTABLE...
INVENTIONS, HUH? DO YOU HAVE SOMETHING THAT DRIVES OTHER PEOPLE AWAY?
THE BEST FRESH FISH
THE FISH PLACE
FISH
I SEE... YOU'RE SLEEPING OUTSIDE BECAUSE THERE'S SOMEONE YOU DON'T LIKE IN YOUR HOUSE...
I HAVE JUST THE THING!
THE AUTOMATIC GOOD RIDDANCE MACHINE! ♪
TA-DAH
JUST ENTER IN WHO YOU WANT IT TO DRIVE AWAY AND IT'LL DO ALL THE HARD WORK FOR YOU!
HMM.
ALL DONE. GOOD NIGHT.
LOST INTEREST ALREADY?! AREN'T YOU GOING TO THANK ME?! WAKE UP!

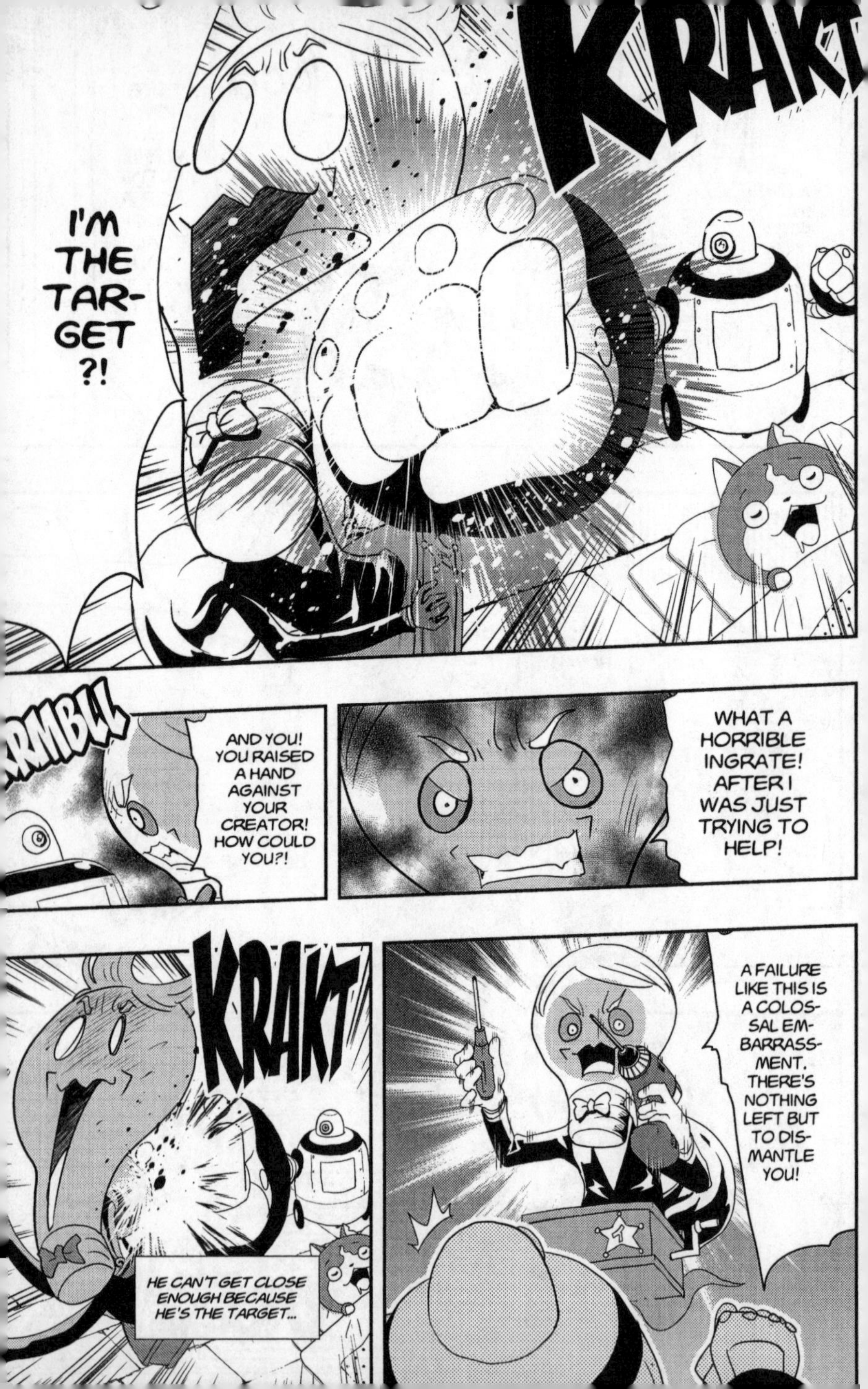
KRAKT
I'M THE TAR-GET?!
WHAT A HORRIBLE INGRATE! AFTER I WAS JUST TRYING TO HELP!
RMBLL
AND YOU! YOU RAISED A HAND AGAINST YOUR CREATOR! HOW COULD YOU?!
A FAILURE LIKE THIS IS A COLOS-SAL EM-BARRASS-MENT. THERE'S NOTHING LEFT BUT TO DIS-MANTLE YOU!
KRAKT
HE CAN'T GET CLOSE ENOUGH BECAUSE HE'S THE TARGET...

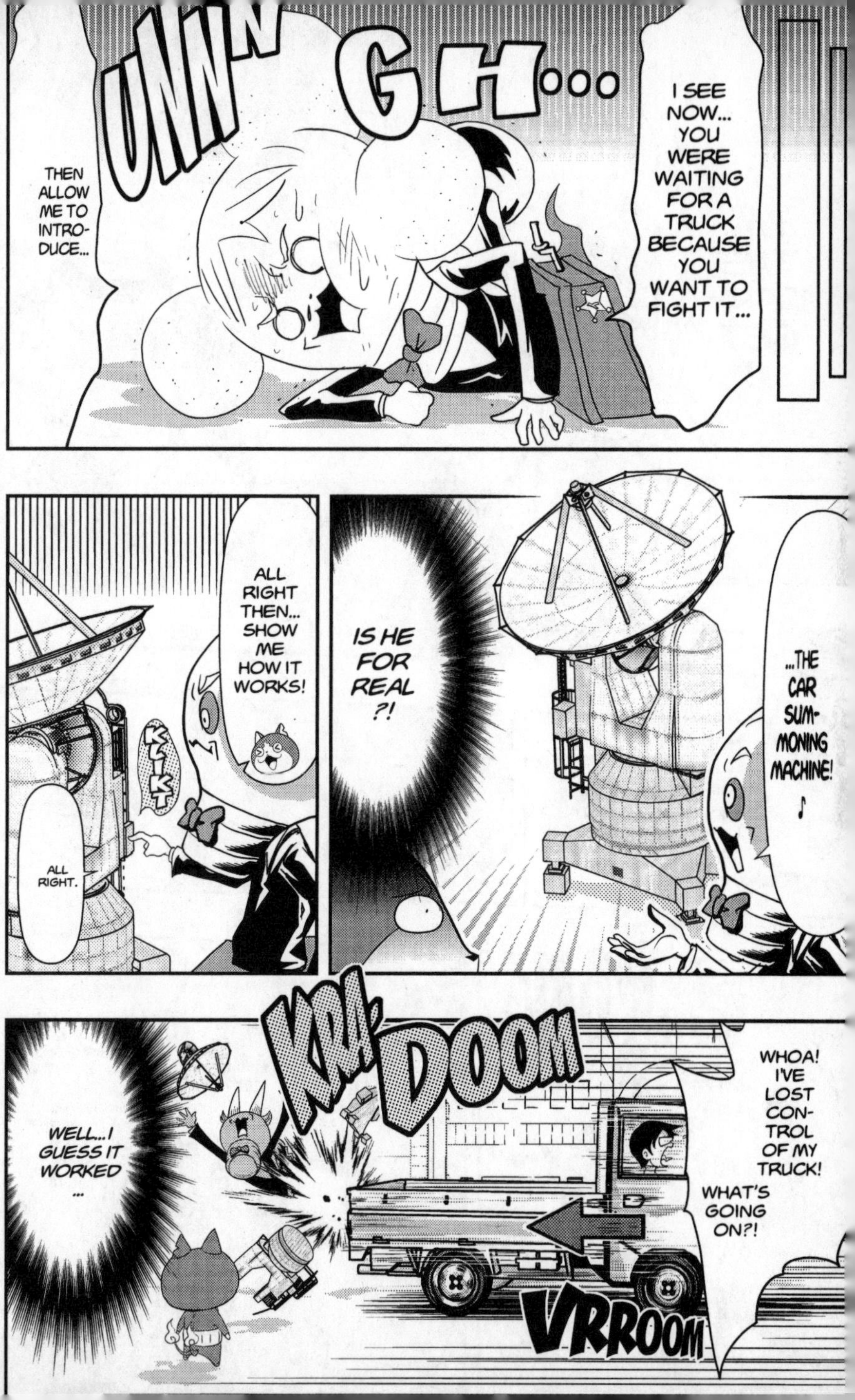
I SEE NOW... YOU WERE WAITING FOR A TRUCK BECAUSE YOU WANT TO FIGHT IT...
UNNNGH...
THEN ALLOW ME TO INTRO-DUCE...
...THE CAR SUM-MONING MACHINE! ♪
IS HE FOR REAL?!
ALL RIGHT THEN... SHOW ME HOW IT WORKS!
KLIKT
ALL RIGHT.
WHOA! I'VE LOST CON-TROL OF MY TRUCK!
WHAT'S GOING ON?!
VRROOM
KRA-DOOM
WELL... I GUESS IT WORKED...

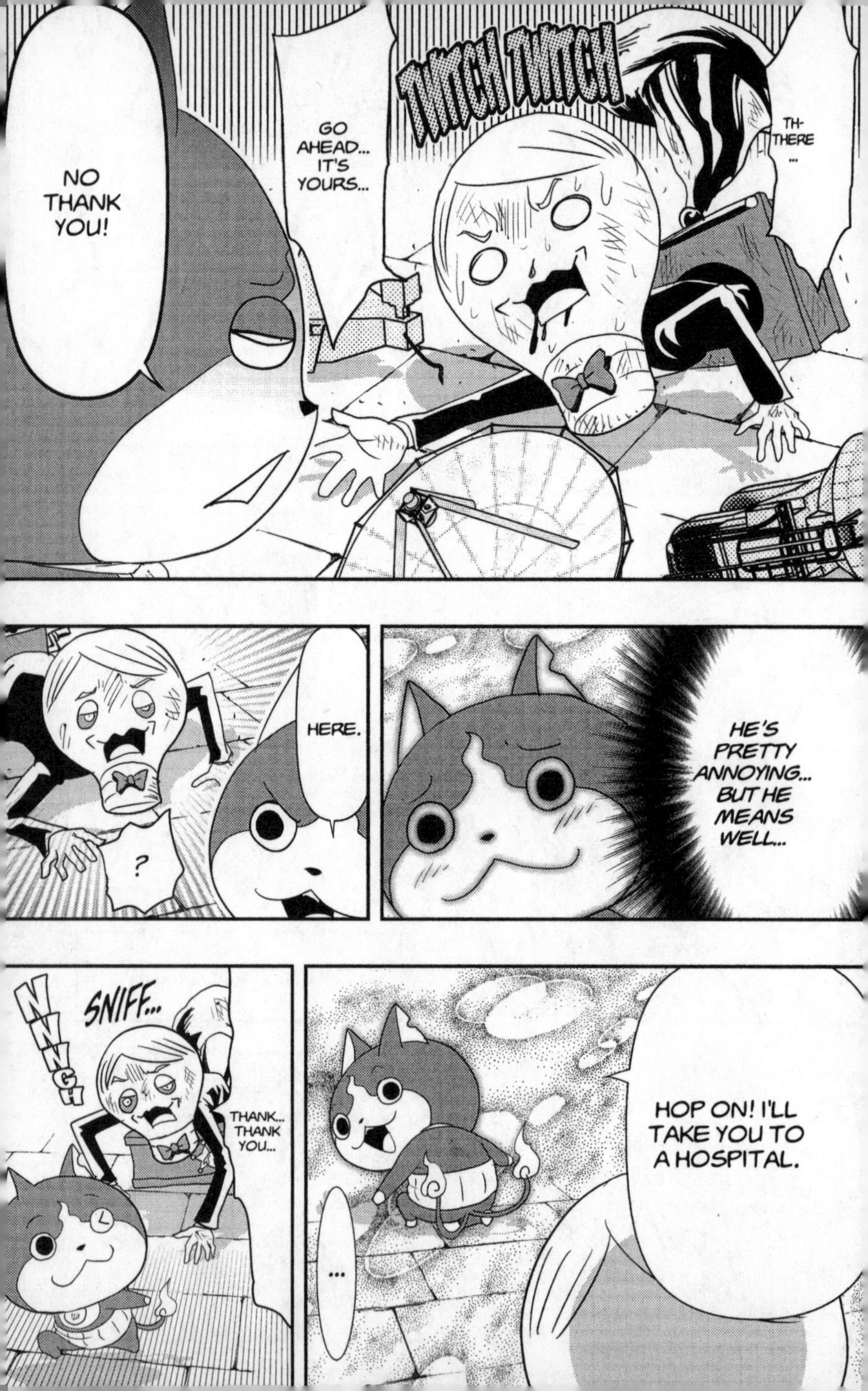
TWITCH TWITCH
TH-THERE ...
GO AHEAD... IT'S YOURS...
NO THANK YOU!
HE'S PRETTY ANNOYING... BUT HE MEANS WELL...
HERE.
?
HOP ON! I'LL TAKE YOU TO A HOSPITAL.
...
SNIFF...
NNNGH
THANK... THANK YOU...

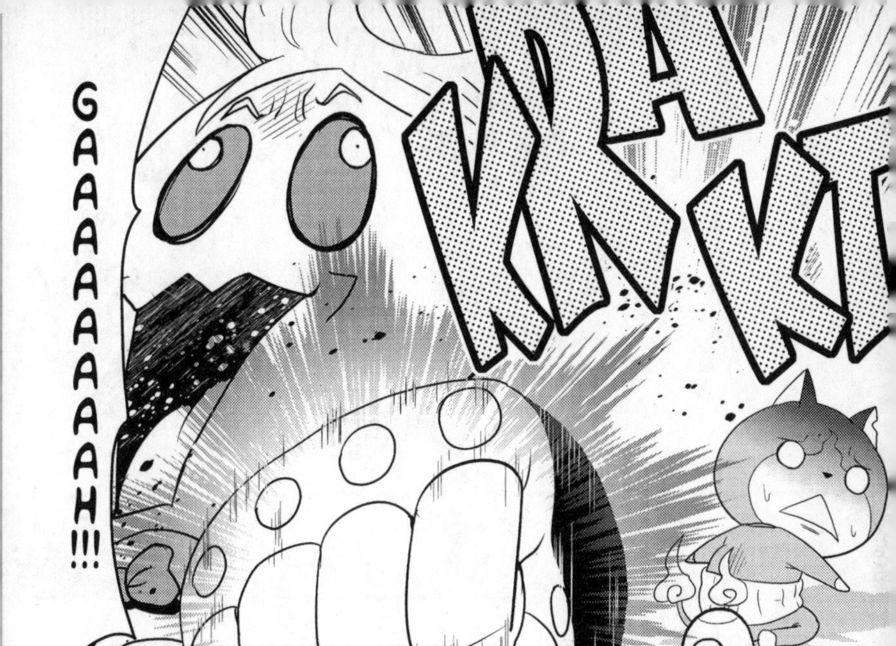
GAAAAAAAAAAH!!!
TARGET ACQUIRED

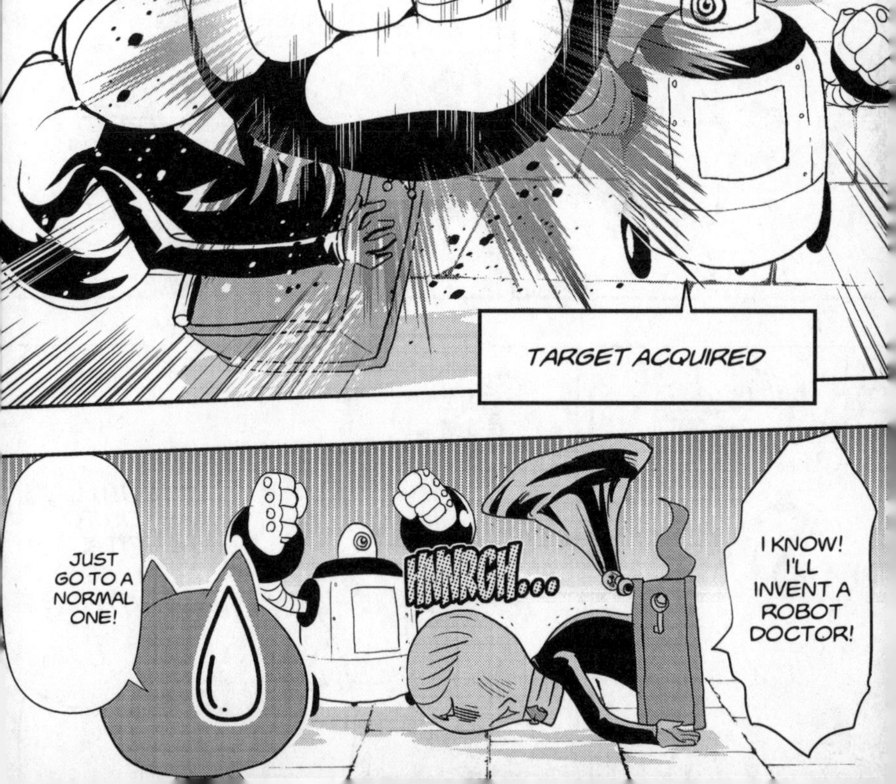
I KNOW! I'LL INVENT A ROBOT DOCTOR!
HNNRCH...
JUST GO TO A NORMAL ONE!

CHAPTER 145
SCHOLAR YO-KAI STARWIN

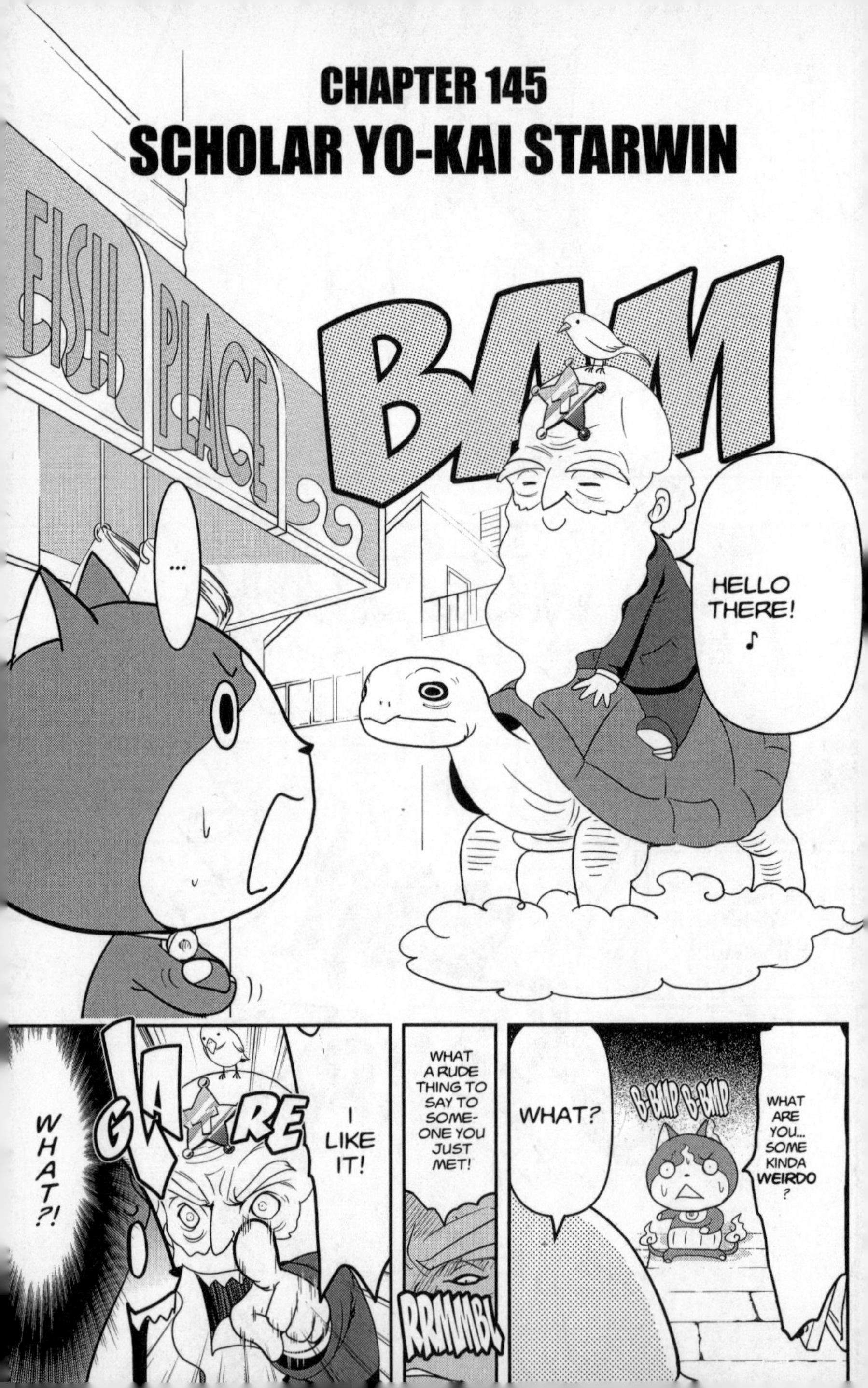
FISH PLACE
HELLO THERE! ♪
BAM
...
WHAT ARE YOU... SOME KINDA WEIRDO?
B-BMP B-BMP
WHAT?
WHAT A RUDE THING TO SAY TO SOME-ONE YOU JUST MET!
RRMMBL
I LIKE IT!
WHAT?!

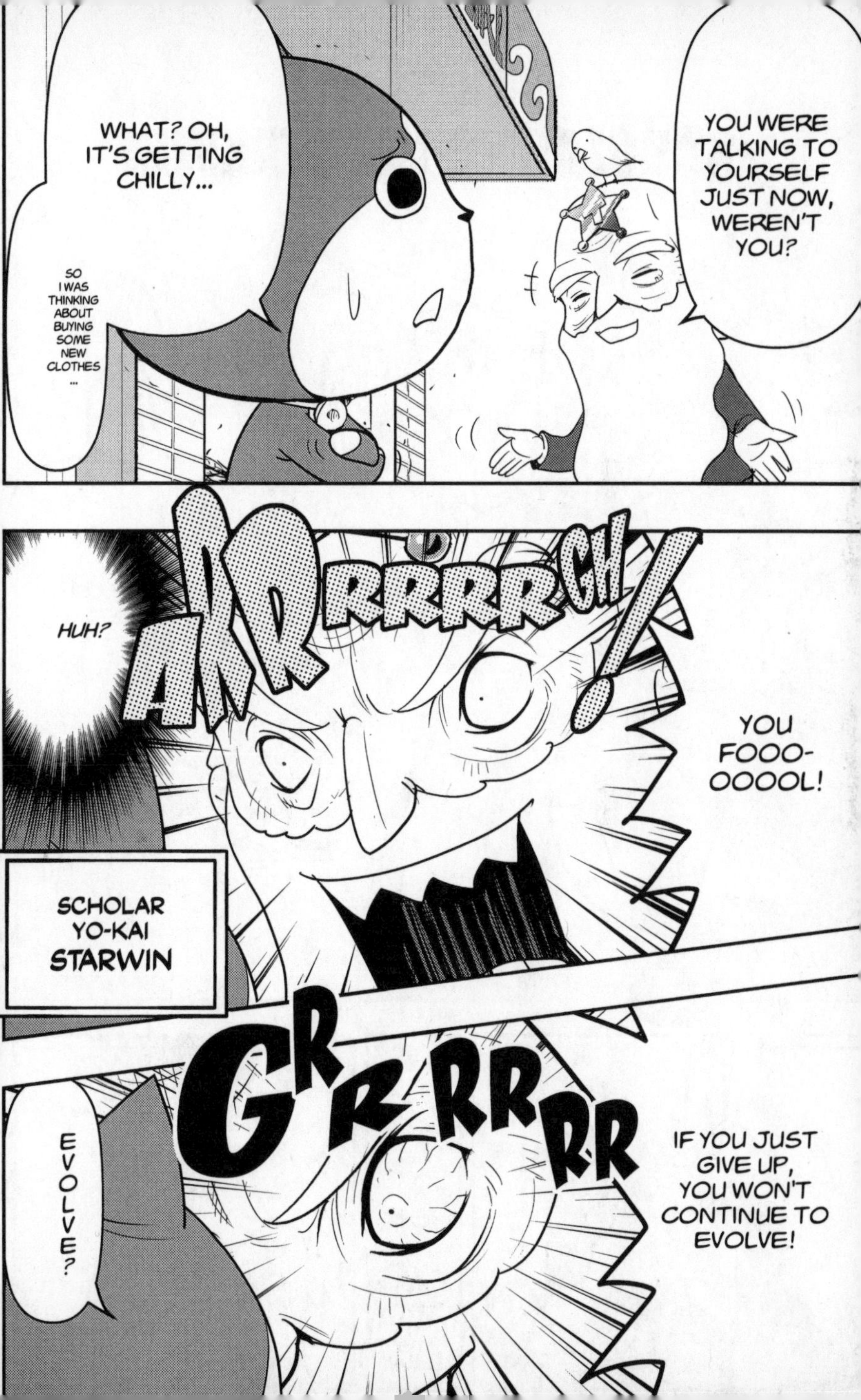
YOU WERE TALKING TO YOURSELF JUST NOW, WEREN'T YOU?
WHAT? OH, IT'S GETTING CHILLY...
SO I WAS THINKING ABOUT BUYING SOME NEW CLOTHES ...
ARRRRRRRGH!
YOU FOOO-OOOOL!
HUH?
SCHOLAR YO-KAI STARWIN
GRRRRRRR
IF YOU JUST GIVE UP, YOU WON'T CONTINUE TO EVOLVE!
EVOLVE?

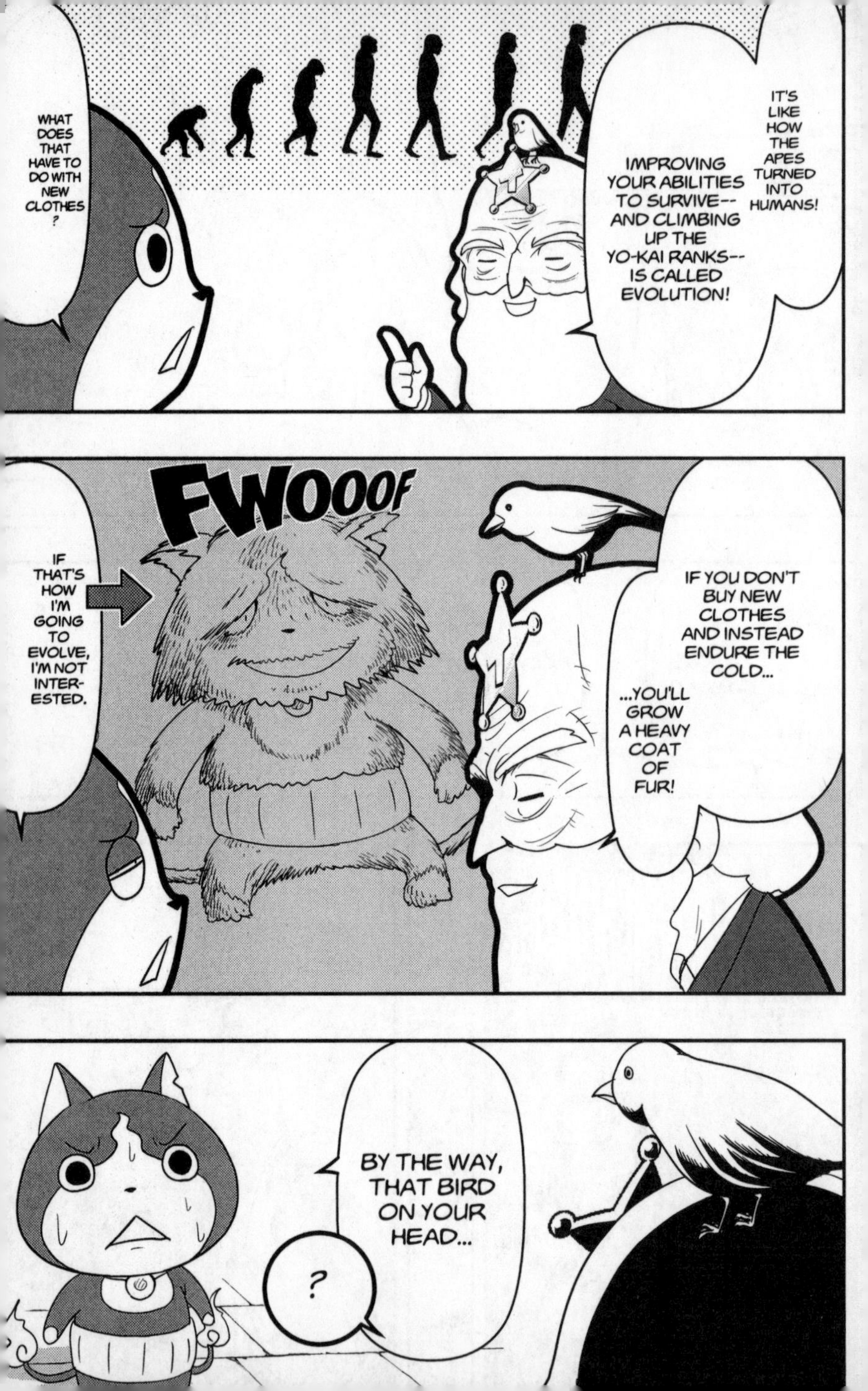
IMPROVING YOUR ABILITIES TO SURVIVE-- AND CLIMBING UP THE YO-KAI RANKS-- IS CALLED EVOLUTION! IT'S LIKE HOW THE APES TURNED INTO HUMANS!
WHAT DOES THAT HAVE TO DO WITH NEW CLOTHES?
IF YOU DON'T BUY NEW CLOTHES AND INSTEAD ENDURE THE COLD... ...YOU'LL GROW A HEAVY COAT OF FUR!
FWOOOF
IF THAT'S HOW I'M GOING TO EVOLVE, I'M NOT INTER-ESTED.
BY THE WAY, THAT BIRD ON YOUR HEAD...
?

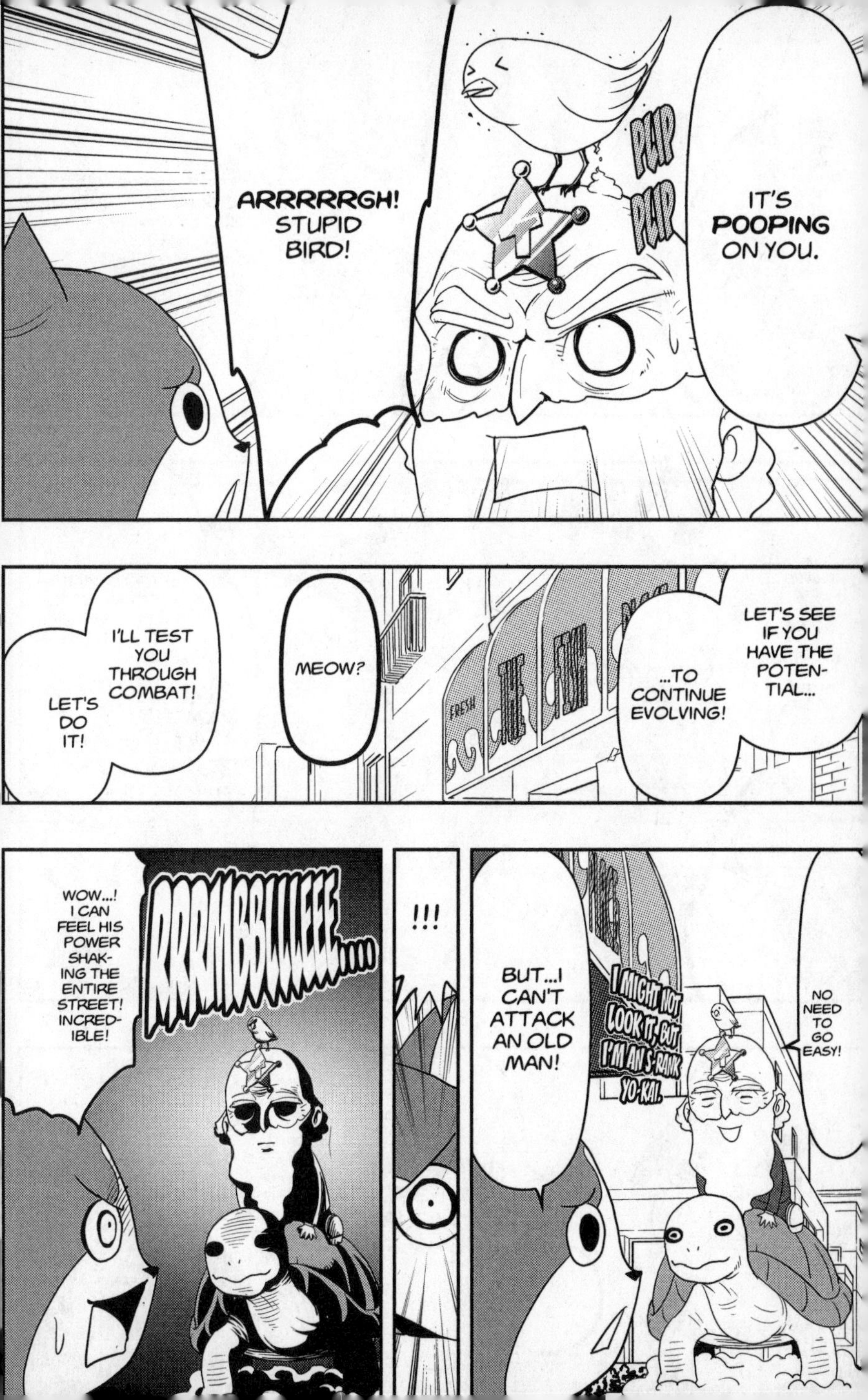
IT'S POOPING ON YOU.
PLIP PLIP
ARRRRRGH! STUPID BIRD!
LET'S SEE IF YOU HAVE THE POTEN-TIAL...
...TO CONTINUE EVOLVING!
MEOW?
I'LL TEST YOU THROUGH COMBAT!
LET'S DO IT!
NO NEED TO GO EASY!
I MIGHT NOT LOOK IT, BUT I'M AN S-RANK YO-KAI.
BUT...I CAN'T ATTACK AN OLD MAN!
!!!
RRRMBBLLLEEE.....
WOW...! I CAN FEEL HIS POWER SHAK-ING THE ENTIRE STREET! INCRED-IBLE!

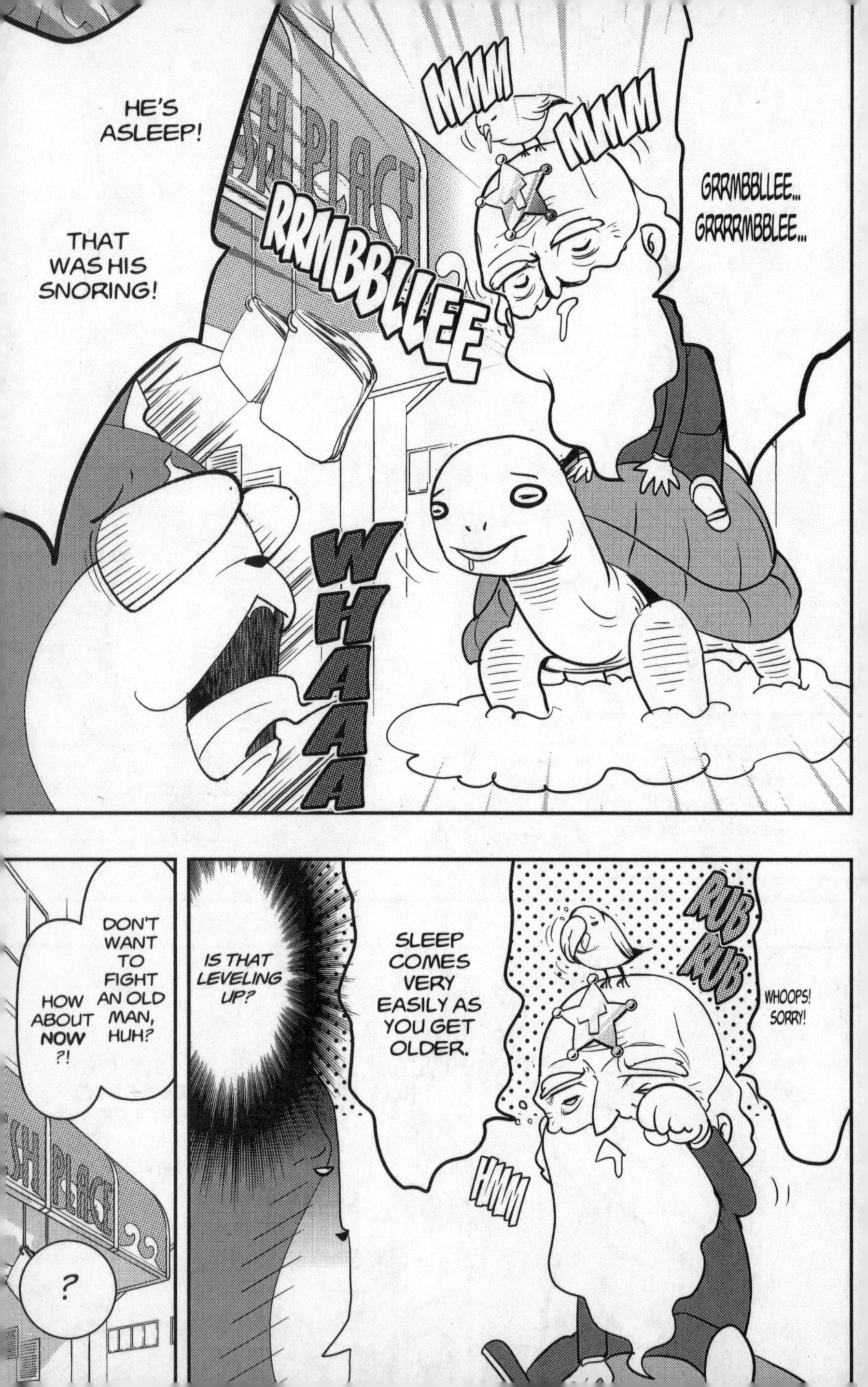
MMM
MMM
GRRMBBLLEE... GRRRRMBBLEE...
RRMBBLLEE
HE'S ASLEEP!
THAT WAS HIS SNORING!
WHAAAA
WHOOPS! SORRY!
RUB RUB
SLEEP COMES VERY EASILY AS YOU GET OLDER.
HMM
IS THAT LEVELING UP?
DON'T WANT TO FIGHT AN OLD MAN, HUH?
HOW ABOUT NOW?!
?

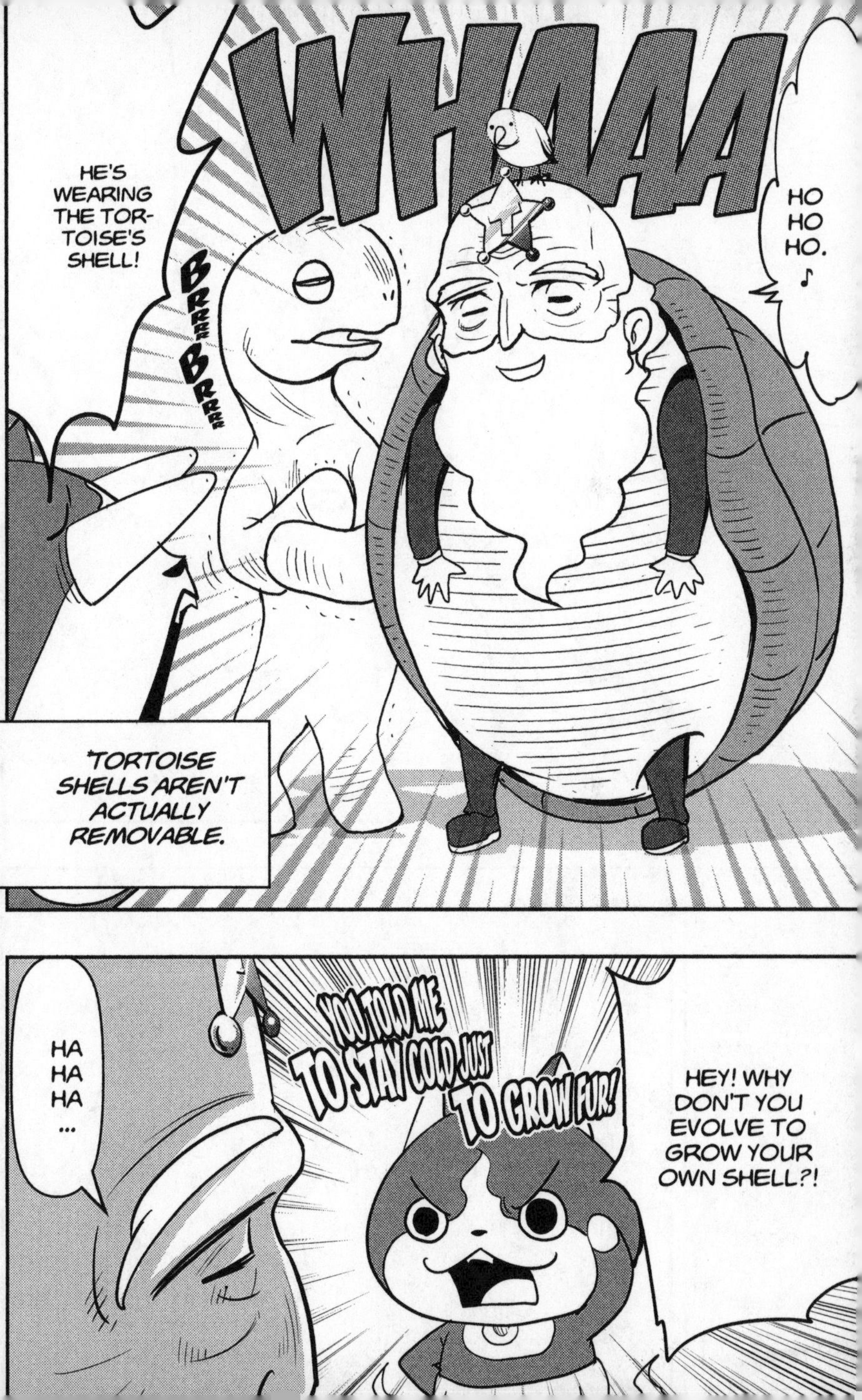
WHAAA
HO HO HO. ♪
HE'S WEARING THE TOR-TOISE'S SHELL!
BRRRR BRRRR
*TORTOISE SHELLS AREN'T ACTUALLY REMOVABLE.
HEY! WHY DON'T YOU EVOLVE TO GROW YOUR OWN SHELL?!
YOU TOLD ME TO STAY COLD JUST TO GROW FUR!
HA HA HA ...

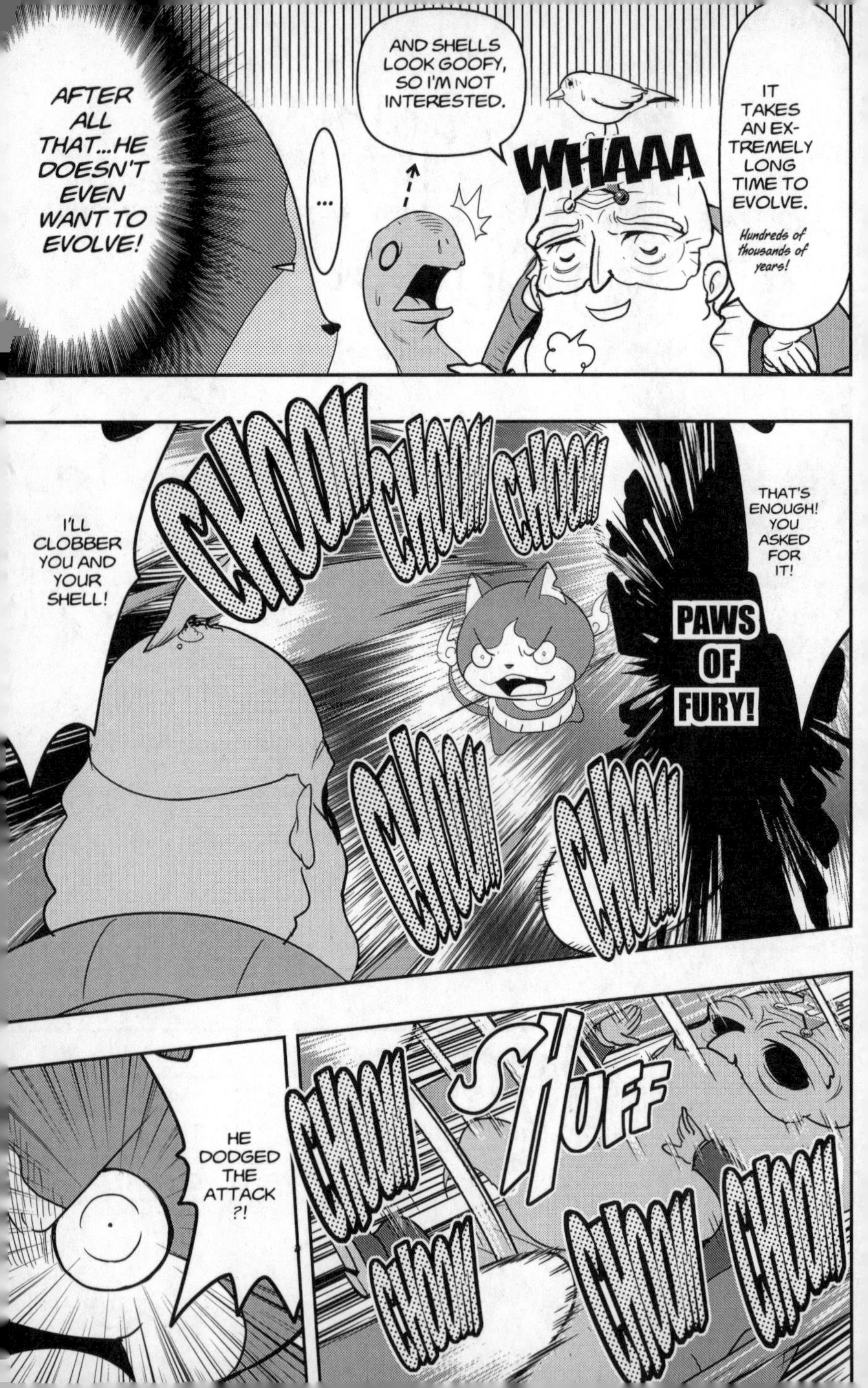
IT TAKES AN EXTREMELY LONG TIME TO EVOLVE.
Hundreds of thousands of years!
WHAAA
AND SHELLS LOOK GOOFY, SO I'M NOT INTERESTED.
...
AFTER ALL THAT...HE DOESN'T EVEN WANT TO EVOLVE!
THAT'S ENOUGH! YOU ASKED FOR IT!
PAWS OF FURY!
CHOOM CHOOM CHOOM
CHOOM CHOOM
I'LL CLOBBER YOU AND YOUR SHELL!
SHUFF
CHOOM CHOOM CHOOM CHOOM
HE DODGED THE ATTACK?!

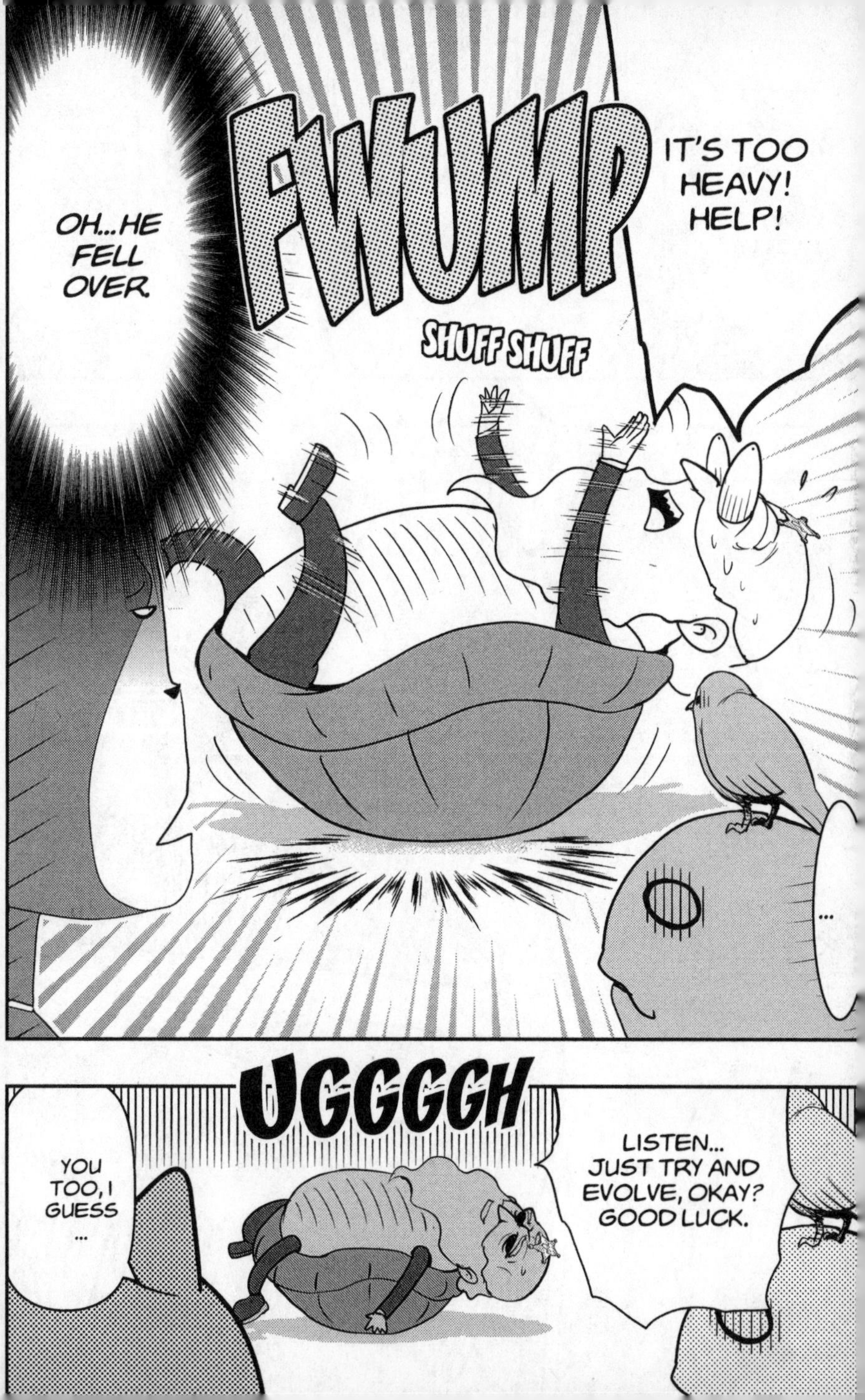
IT'S TOO HEAVY! HELP!
FWUMP
OH...HE FELL OVER.
SHUFF SHUFF
...
UGGGGH
LISTEN... JUST TRY AND EVOLVE, OKAY? GOOD LUCK.
YOU TOO, I GUESS ...

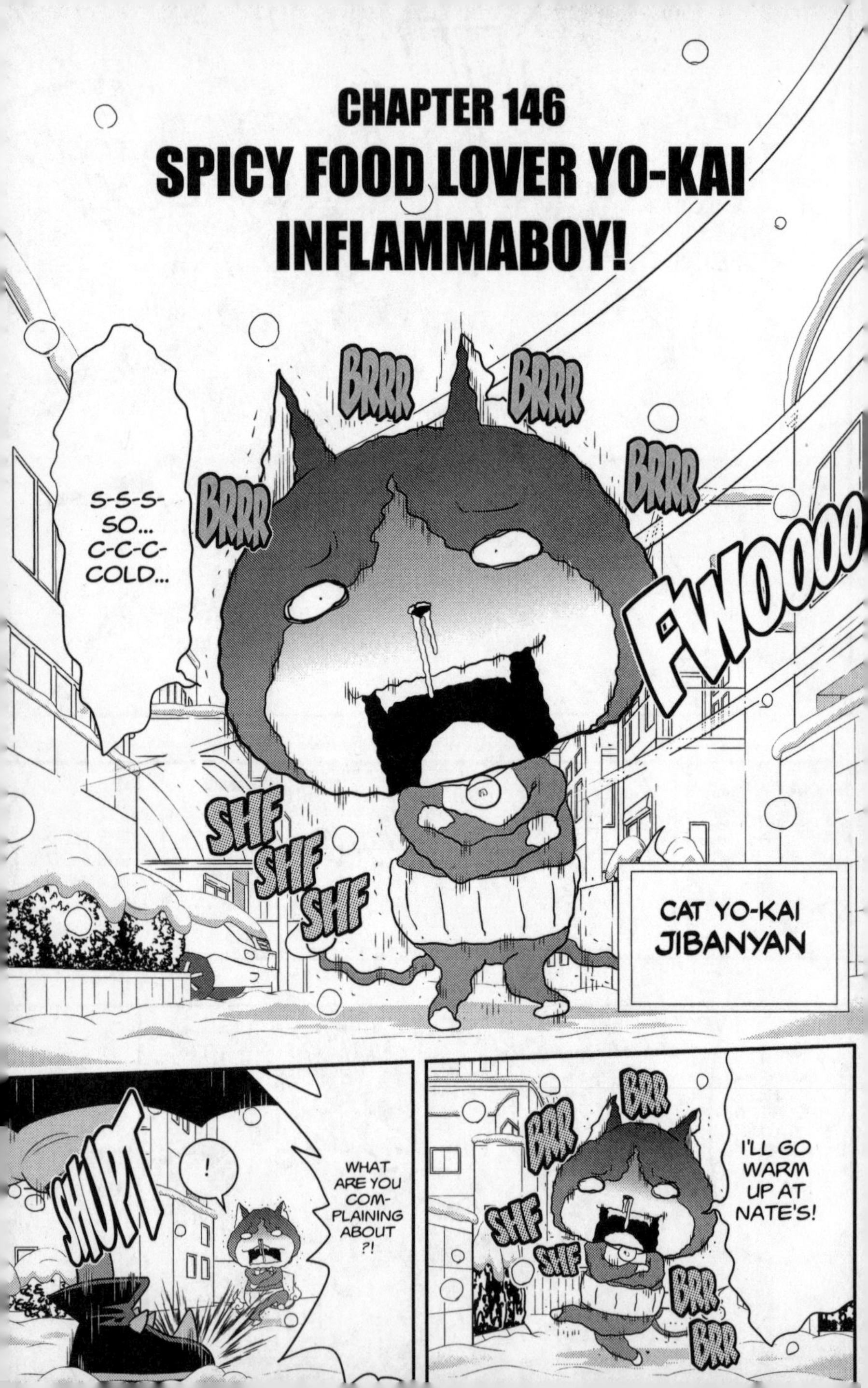
CHAPTER 146
SPICY FOOD LOVER YO-KAI INFLAMMABOY!
BRRR
BRRR
BRRR
BRRR
S-S-S-SO... C-C-C-COLD...
FWOOOO
SHF
SHF
SHF
CAT YO-KAI JIBANYAN
BRR
BRR
I'LL GO WARM UP AT NATE'S!
SHF
SHF
BRR
BRR
WHAT ARE YOU COM-PLAINING ABOUT ?!
!
SHUPT

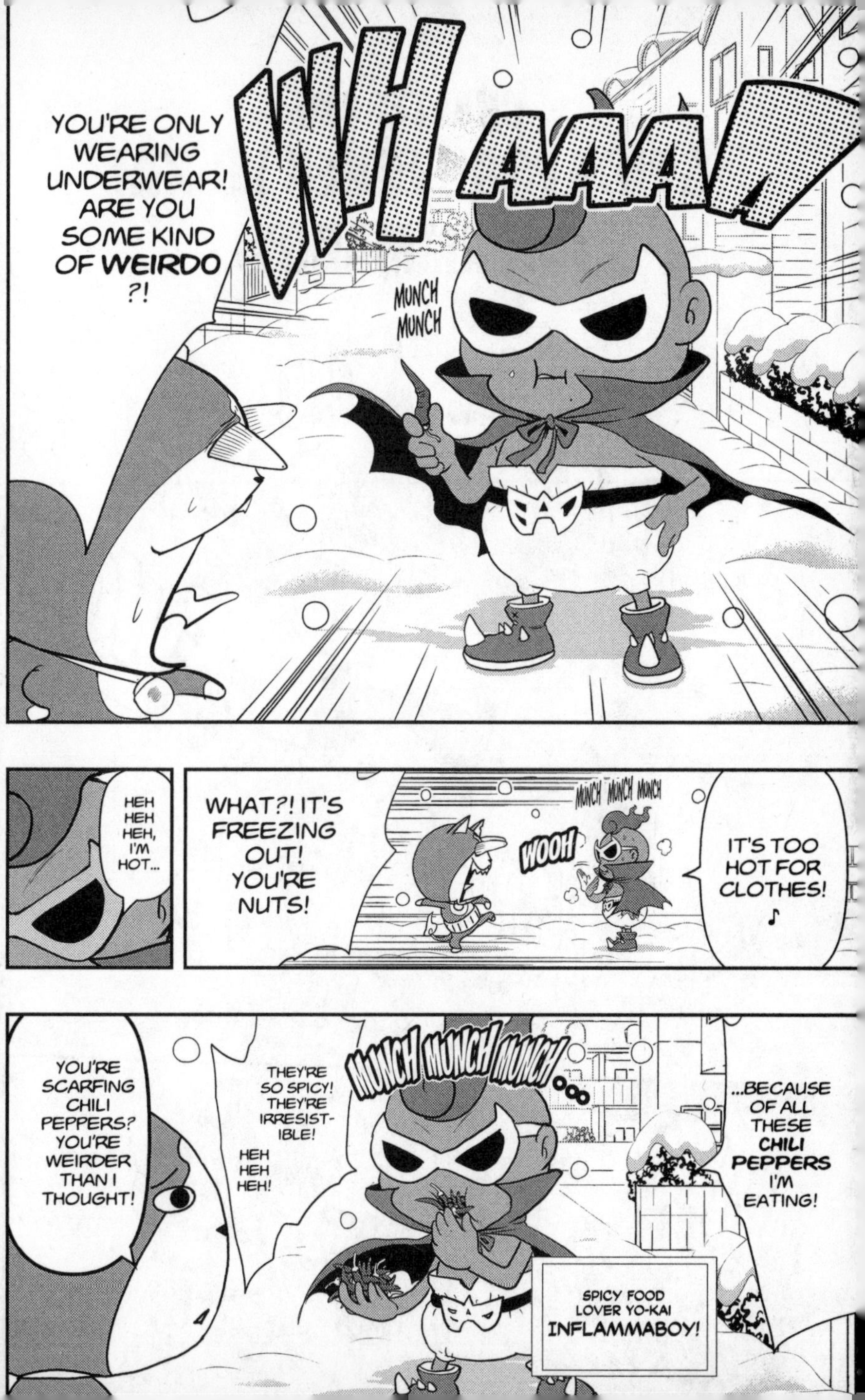
WHAAAAN
MUNCH MUNCH
YOU'RE ONLY WEARING UNDERWEAR! ARE YOU SOME KIND OF WEIRDO ?!
IT'S TOO HOT FOR CLOTHES! ♪
MUNCH MUNCH MUNCH
WOOH
WHAT?! IT'S FREEZING OUT! YOU'RE NUTS!
HEH HEH HEH, I'M HOT...
...BECAUSE OF ALL THESE CHILI PEPPERS I'M EATING!
MUNCH MUNCH MUNCH
THEY'RE SO SPICY! THEY'RE IRRESIST-IBLE!
HEH HEH HEH!
YOU'RE SCARFING CHILI PEPPERS? YOU'RE WEIRDER THAN I THOUGHT!
SPICY FOOD LOVER YO-KAI INFLAMMABOY!

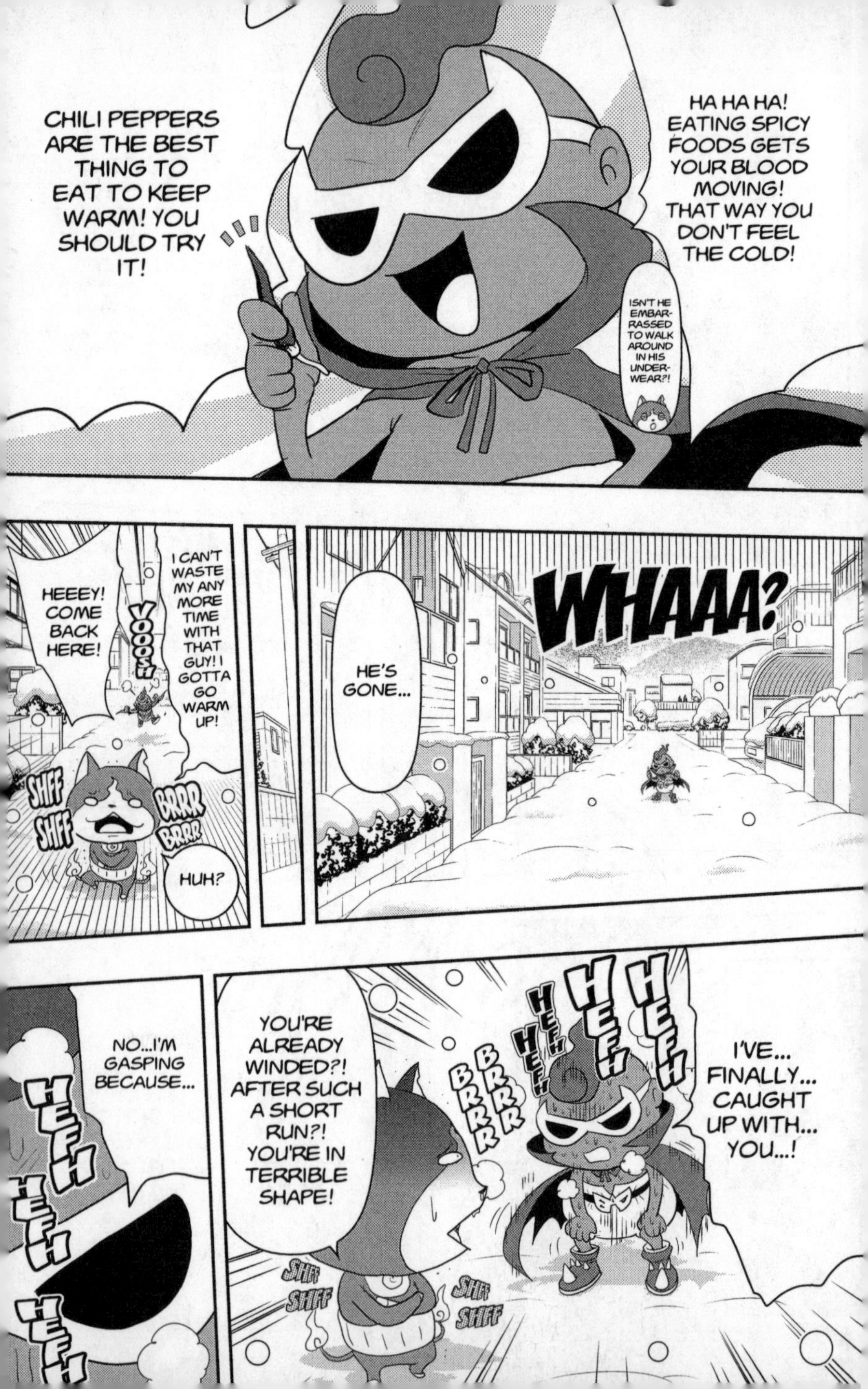
HA HA HA! EATING SPICY FOODS GETS YOUR BLOOD MOVING! THAT WAY YOU DON'T FEEL THE COLD!
CHILI PEPPERS ARE THE BEST THING TO EAT TO KEEP WARM! YOU SHOULD TRY IT!
ISN'T HE EMBAR-RASSED TO WALK AROUND IN HIS UNDER-WEAR?!
WHAAAA?!
HE'S GONE...
I CAN'T WASTE MY ANY MORE TIME WITH THAT GUY! I GOTTA GO WARM UP!
VOOOSH
HEEEY! COME BACK HERE!
SHFF SHFF
BRRR BRRR
HUH?
I'VE... FINALLY... CAUGHT UP WITH... YOU...!
HEFH HEFH
HEFH HEFH
BRRR BRRR
YOU'RE ALREADY WINDED?! AFTER SUCH A SHORT RUN?! YOU'RE IN TERRIBLE SHAPE!
SHFF SHFF
SHFF SHFF
NO...I'M GASPING BECAUSE...
HEFH HEFH HEFH HEFH

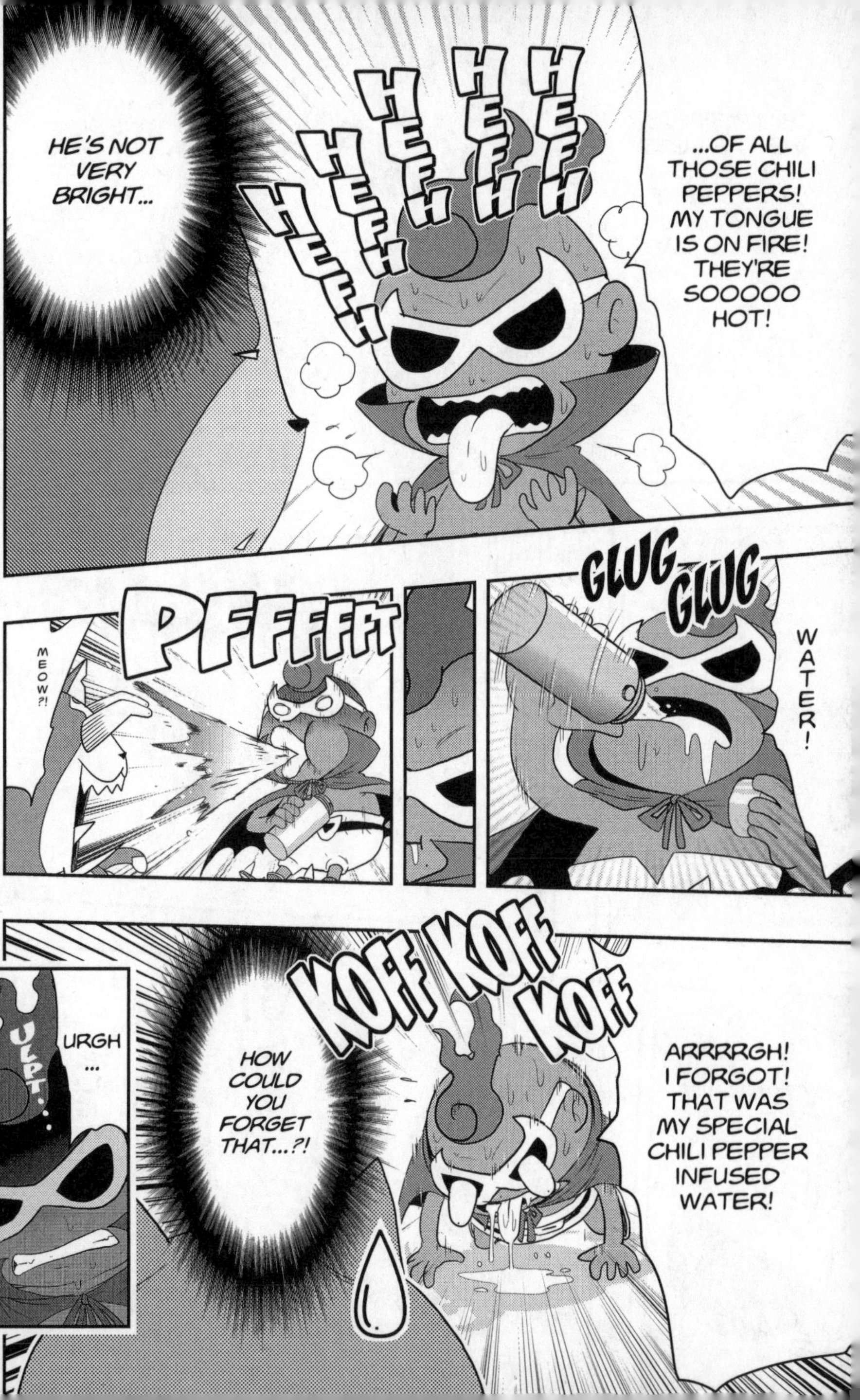
HEFFH HEFFH HEFFH HEFFH HEFFH
...OF ALL THOSE CHILI PEPPERS! MY TONGUE IS ON FIRE! THEY'RE SOOOOO HOT!
HE'S NOT VERY BRIGHT...
GLUG GLUG
WATER!
PFFFFFT
MEOW?!
KOFF KOFF KOFF
ARRRRGH! I FORGOT! THAT WAS MY SPECIAL CHILI PEPPER INFUSED WATER!
HOW COULD YOU FORGET THAT...?!
URGH...
ULPT.

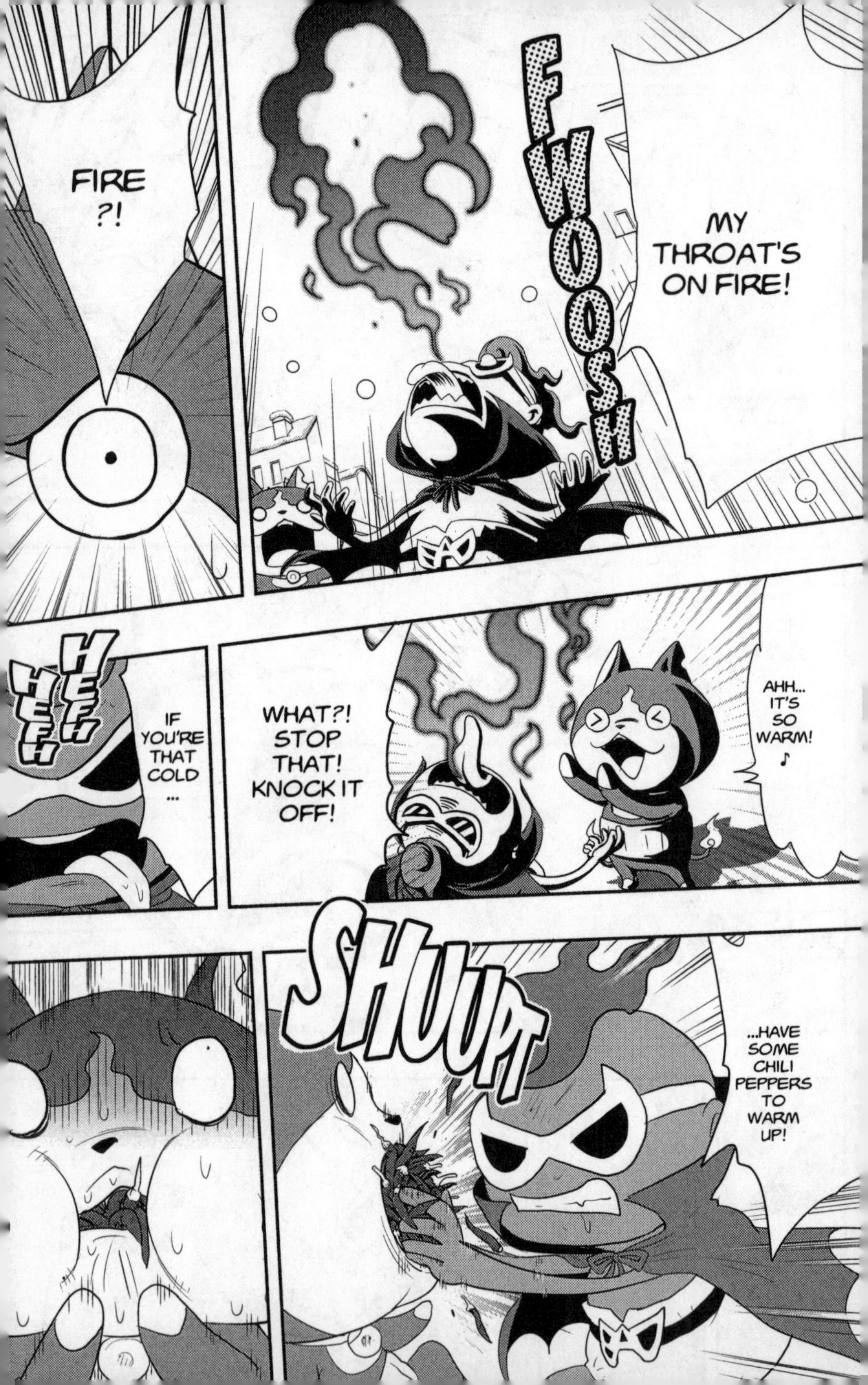
FWOOSH
MY THROAT'S ON FIRE!
FIRE ?!
AHH... IT'S SO WARM! ♪
WHAT?! STOP THAT! KNOCK IT OFF!
HEFH HEFH
IF YOU'RE THAT COLD ...
SHUUPT
...HAVE SOME CHILI PEPPERS TO WARM UP!

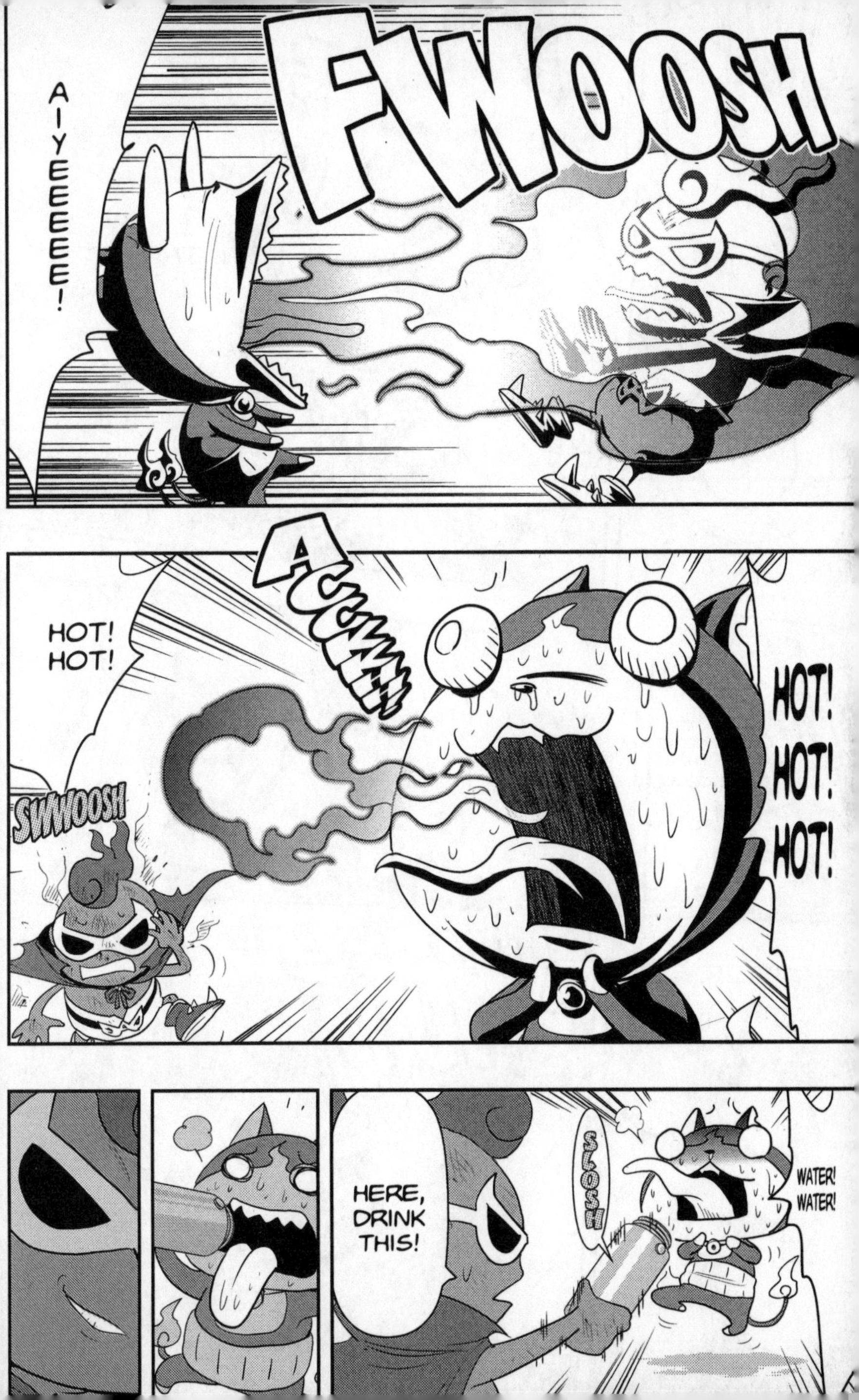
F'WOOSH
AIYEEEEEE!
HOT! HOT! HOT!
HOT! HOT!
SWWOOSH
WATER! WATER!
SLOSH
HERE, DRINK THIS!

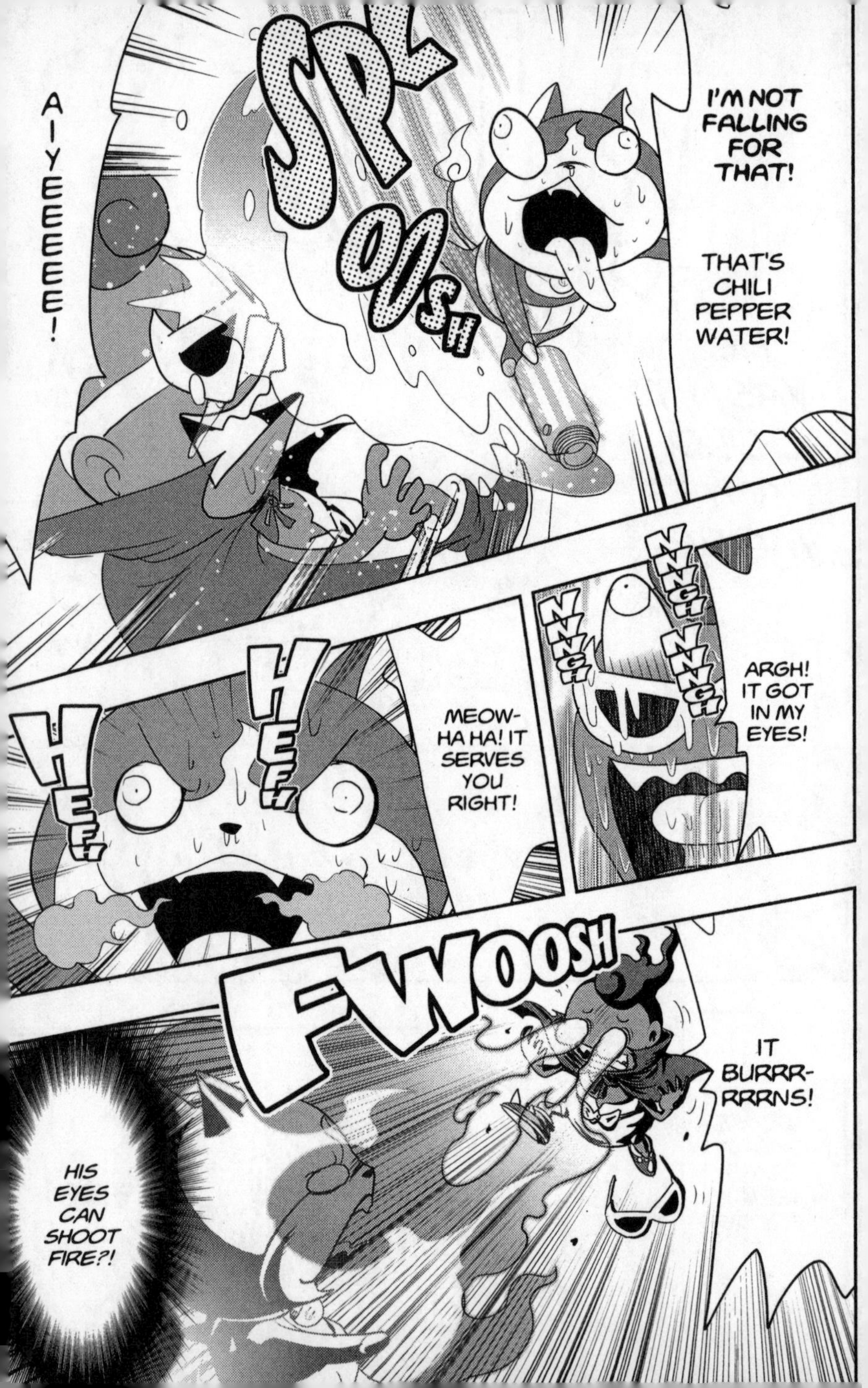
I'M NOT FALLING FOR THAT!
THAT'S CHILI PEPPER WATER!
SPOOSH
AIYEEEEEE!
NNNGH NNNGH
NNNGH
ARGH! IT GOT IN MY EYES!
MEOW-HA HA! IT SERVES YOU RIGHT!
HEH HEH
IT BURRRR-RRRNS!
FWOOSH
HIS EYES CAN SHOOT FIRE?!

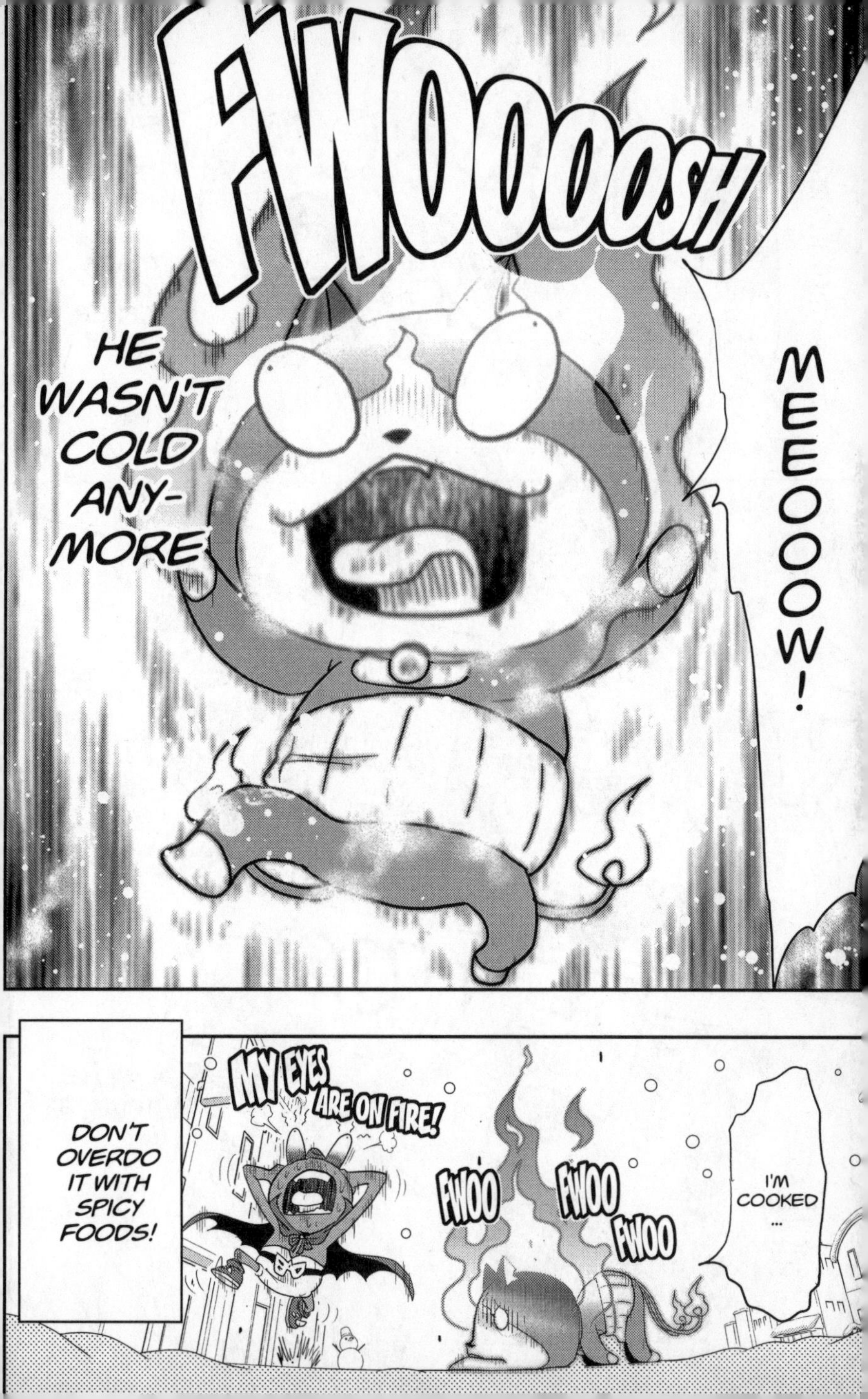
FWOOOOSH
MEEOOOOW!
HE WASN'T COLD ANY-MORE
I'M COOKED ...
FWOO FWOO FWOO
MY EYES ARE ON FIRE!
DON'T OVERDO IT WITH SPICY FOODS!

CHAPTER 147
SONIC SPEED YO-KAI DOUBLE TIME

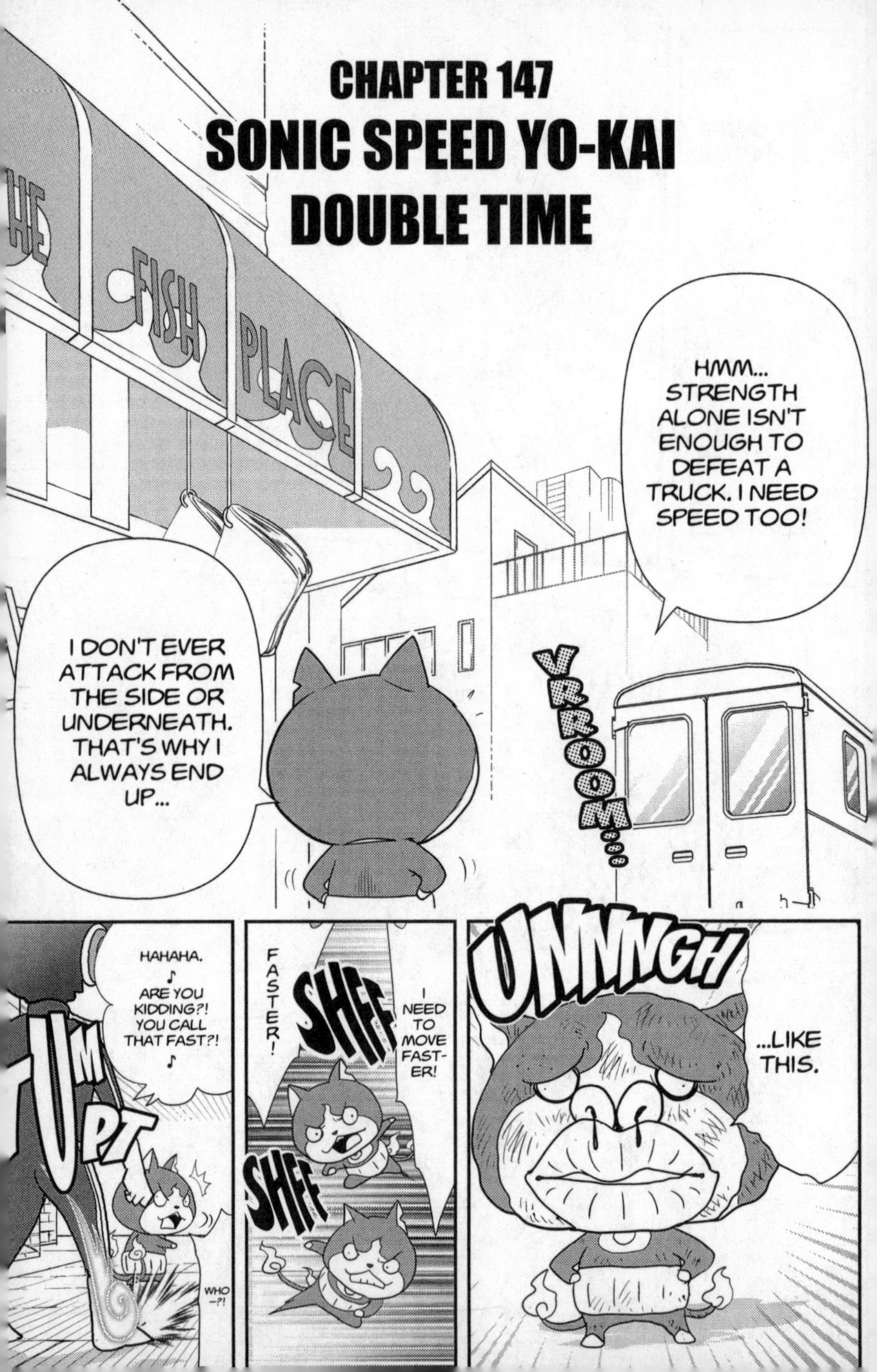
THE FISH PLACE
HMM... STRENGTH ALONE ISN'T ENOUGH TO DEFEAT A TRUCK. I NEED SPEED TOO!
VRROOM...
I DON'T EVER ATTACK FROM THE SIDE OR UNDERNEATH. THAT'S WHY I ALWAYS END UP...
UNNNGH
...LIKE THIS.
I NEED TO MOVE FAST-ER!
SHFF
FASTER!
SHFF
HAHAHA. ♪ ARE YOU KIDDING?! YOU CALL THAT FAST?! ♪
TUMPT
WHO—?!

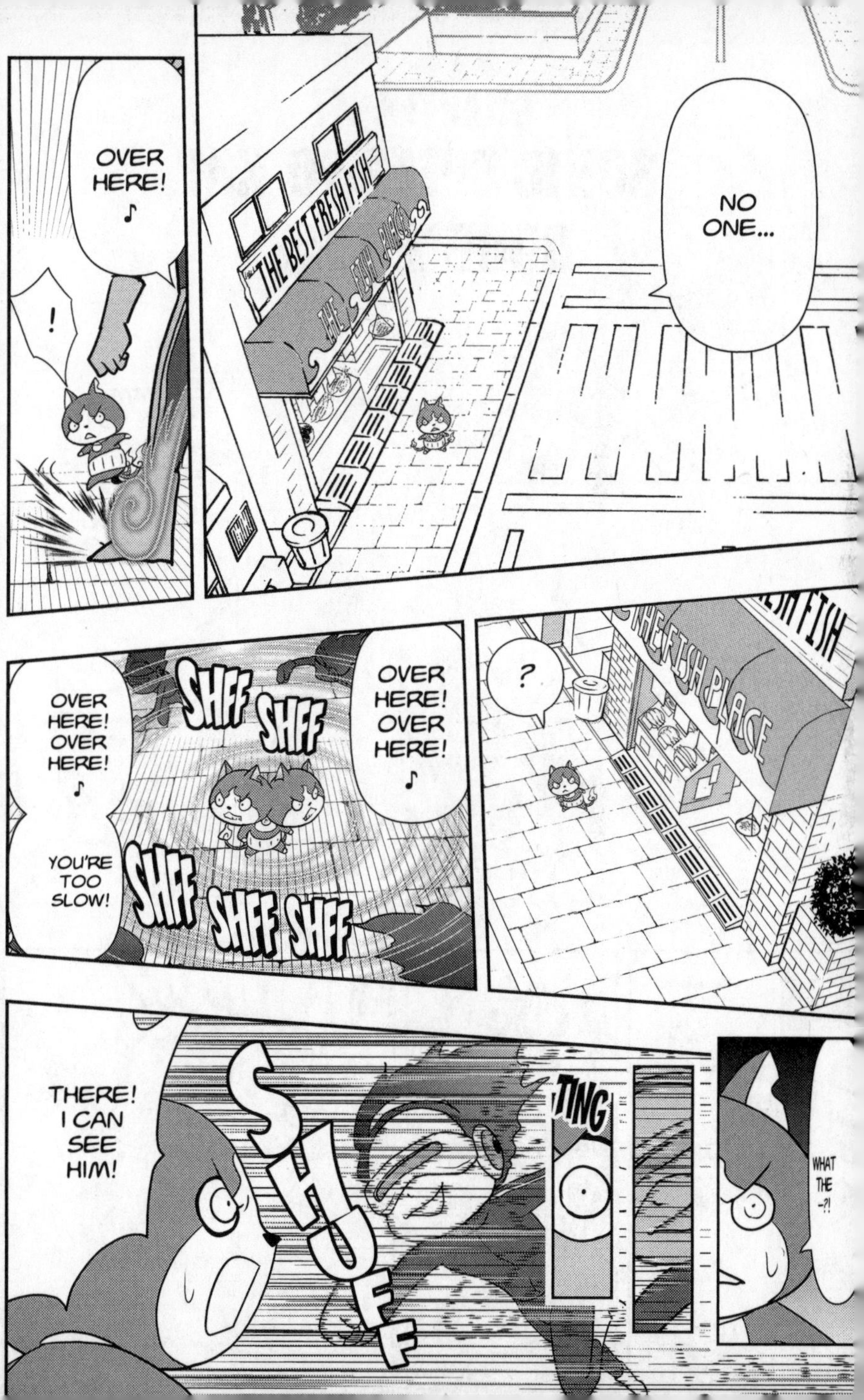
NO ONE...
THE BEST FRESH FISH
THE FISH PLACE
OVER HERE! ♪
!
?
THE FISH PLACE
OVER HERE! OVER HERE! ♪
SHFF SHFF
OVER HERE! OVER HERE! ♪
SHFF SHFF SHFF
YOU'RE TOO SLOW!
WHAT THE -?!
TING
SHUFF
THERE! I CAN SEE HIM!

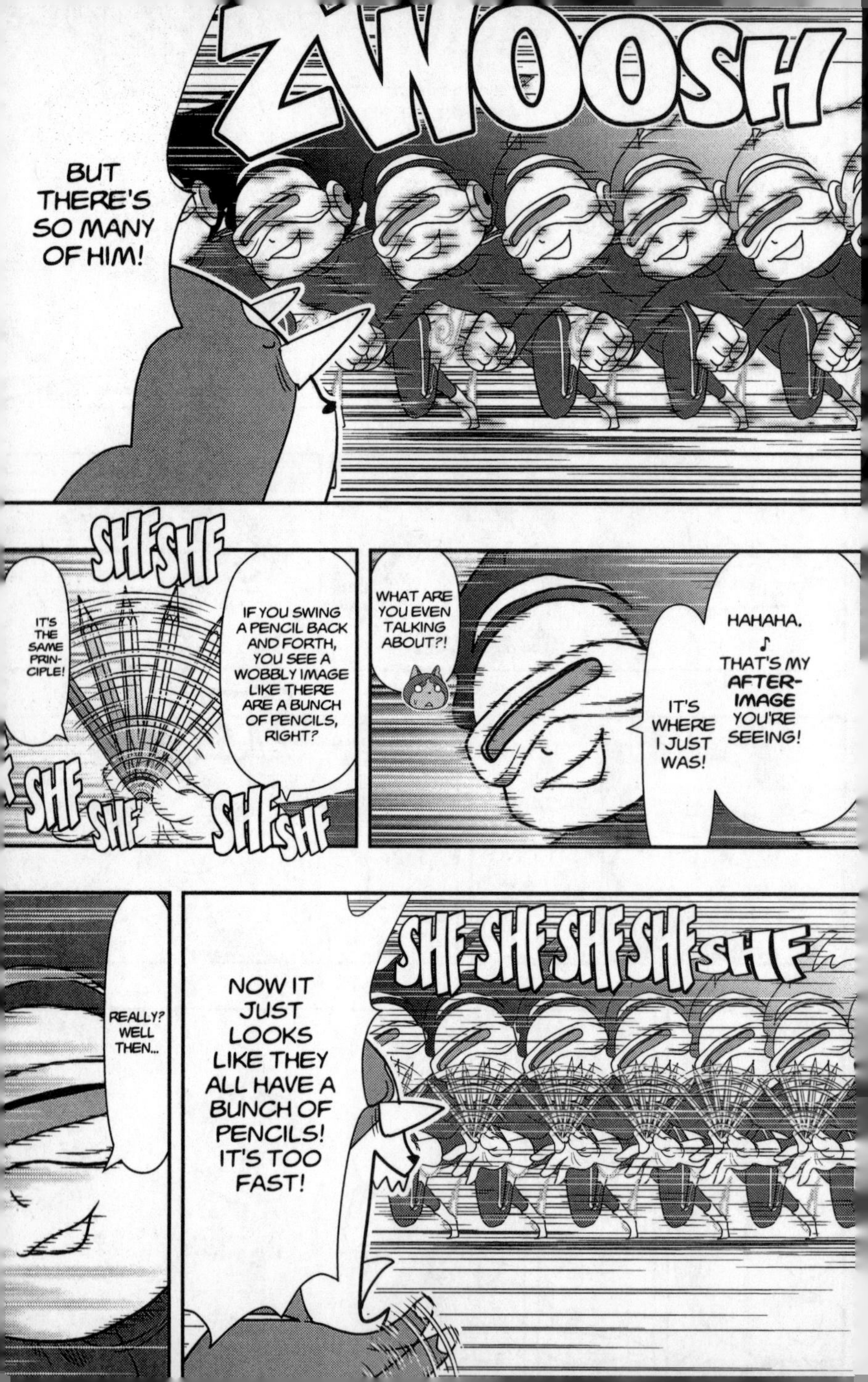
ZWOOSH
BUT THERE'S SO MANY OF HIM!
HAHAHA. ♪ THAT'S MY AFTER-IMAGE YOU'RE SEEING!
IT'S WHERE I JUST WAS!
WHAT ARE YOU EVEN TALKING ABOUT?!
SHF SHF
IF YOU SWING A PENCIL BACK AND FORTH, YOU SEE A WOBBLY IMAGE LIKE THERE ARE A BUNCH OF PENCILS, RIGHT?
IT'S THE SAME PRIN-CIPLE!
SHF SHF
SHF SHF
SHF SHF SHF SHF SHF
NOW IT JUST LOOKS LIKE THEY ALL HAVE A BUNCH OF PENCILS! IT'S TOO FAST!
REALLY? WELL THEN...

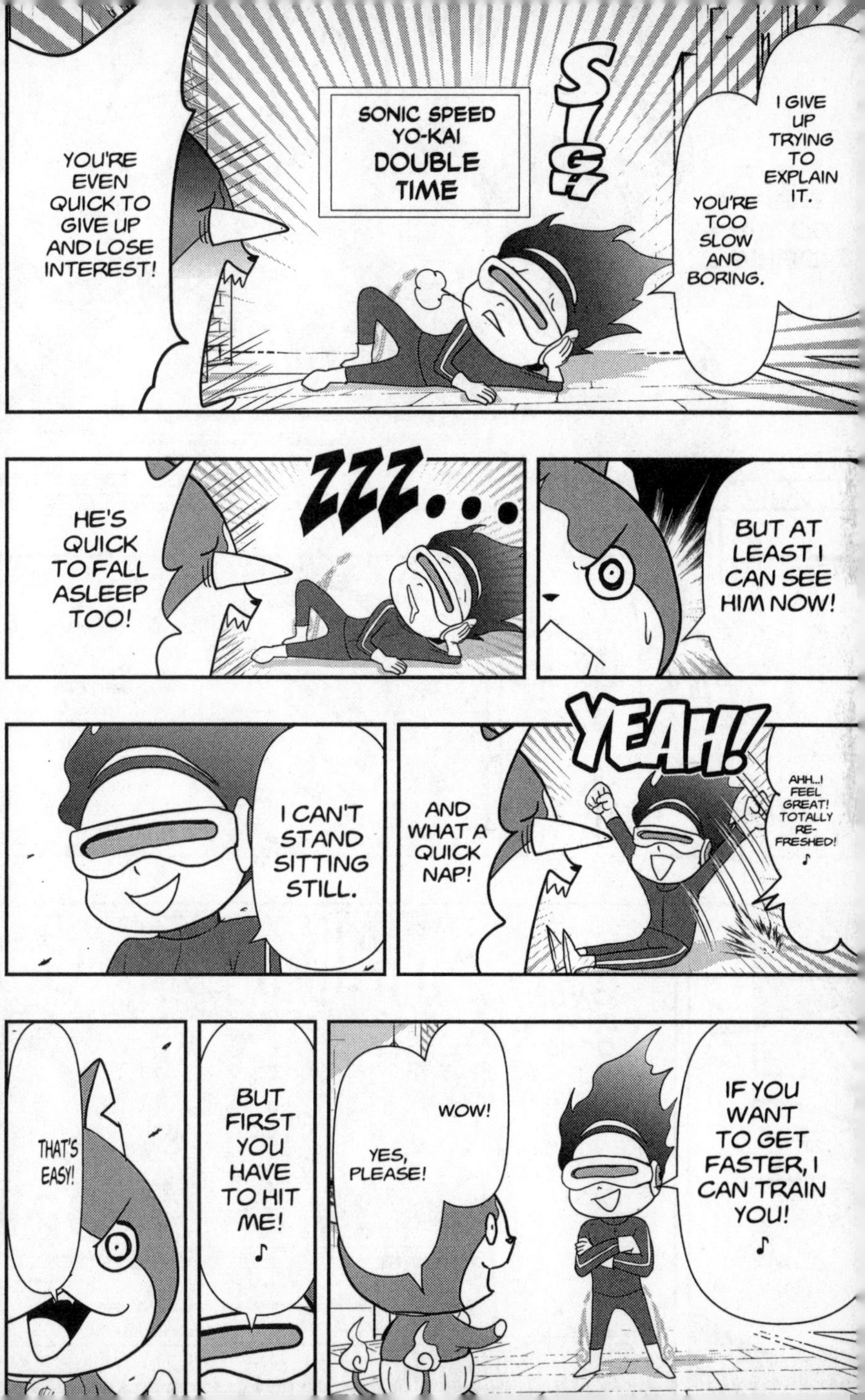
I GIVE UP TRYING TO EXPLAIN IT.
YOU'RE TOO SLOW AND BORING.
SIGH
SONIC SPEED YO-KAI DOUBLE TIME
YOU'RE EVEN QUICK TO GIVE UP AND LOSE INTEREST!
BUT AT LEAST I CAN SEE HIM NOW!
ZZZ...
HE'S QUICK TO FALL ASLEEP TOO!
AHH...I FEEL GREAT! TOTALLY RE-FRESHED! ♪
YEAH!
AND WHAT A QUICK NAP!
I CAN'T STAND SITTING STILL.
IF YOU WANT TO GET FASTER, I CAN TRAIN YOU! ♪
WOW!
YES, PLEASE!
BUT FIRST YOU HAVE TO HIT ME! ♪
THAT'S EASY!

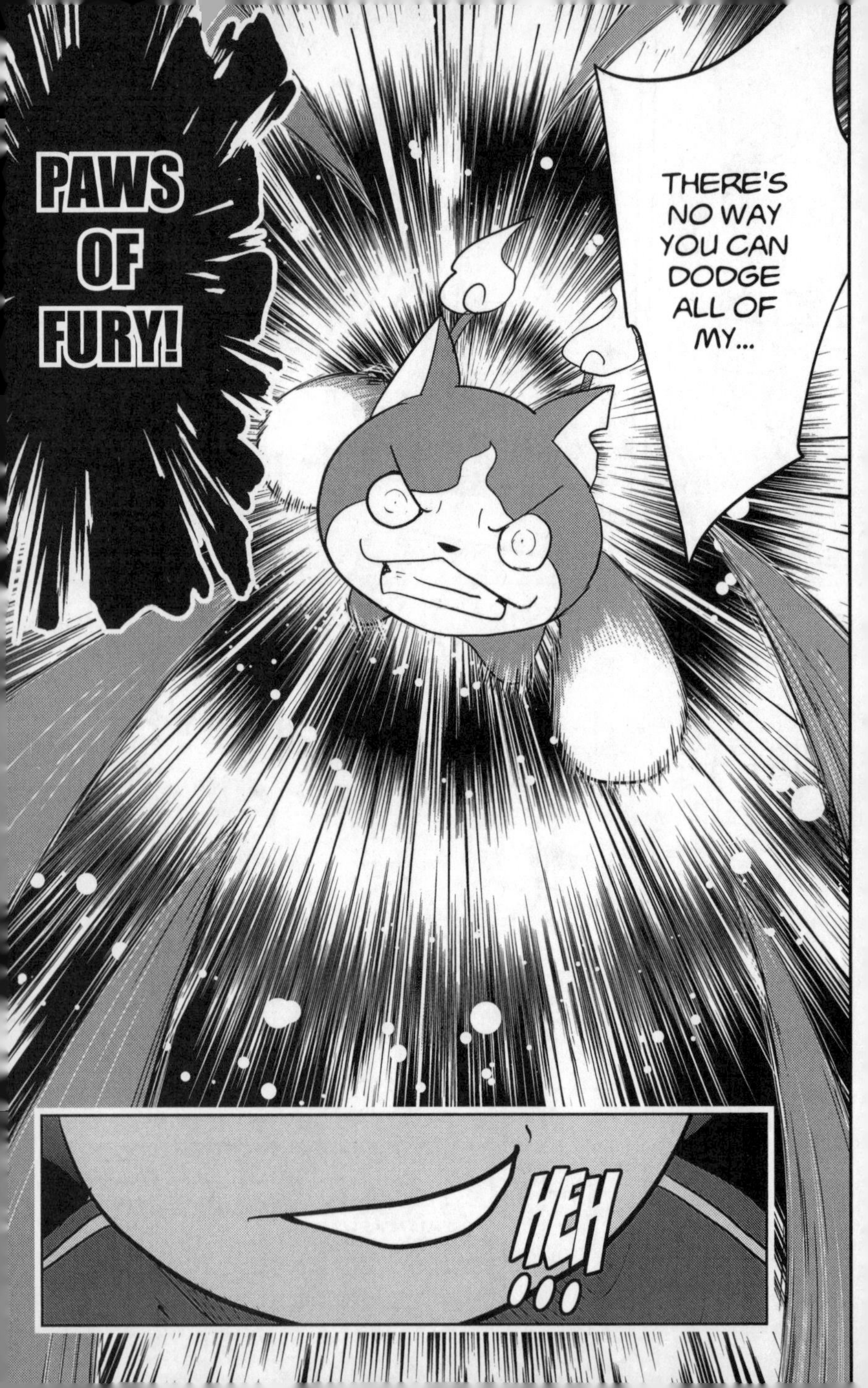
THERE'S NO WAY YOU CAN DODGE ALL OF MY...
PAWS OF FURY!
HEH...

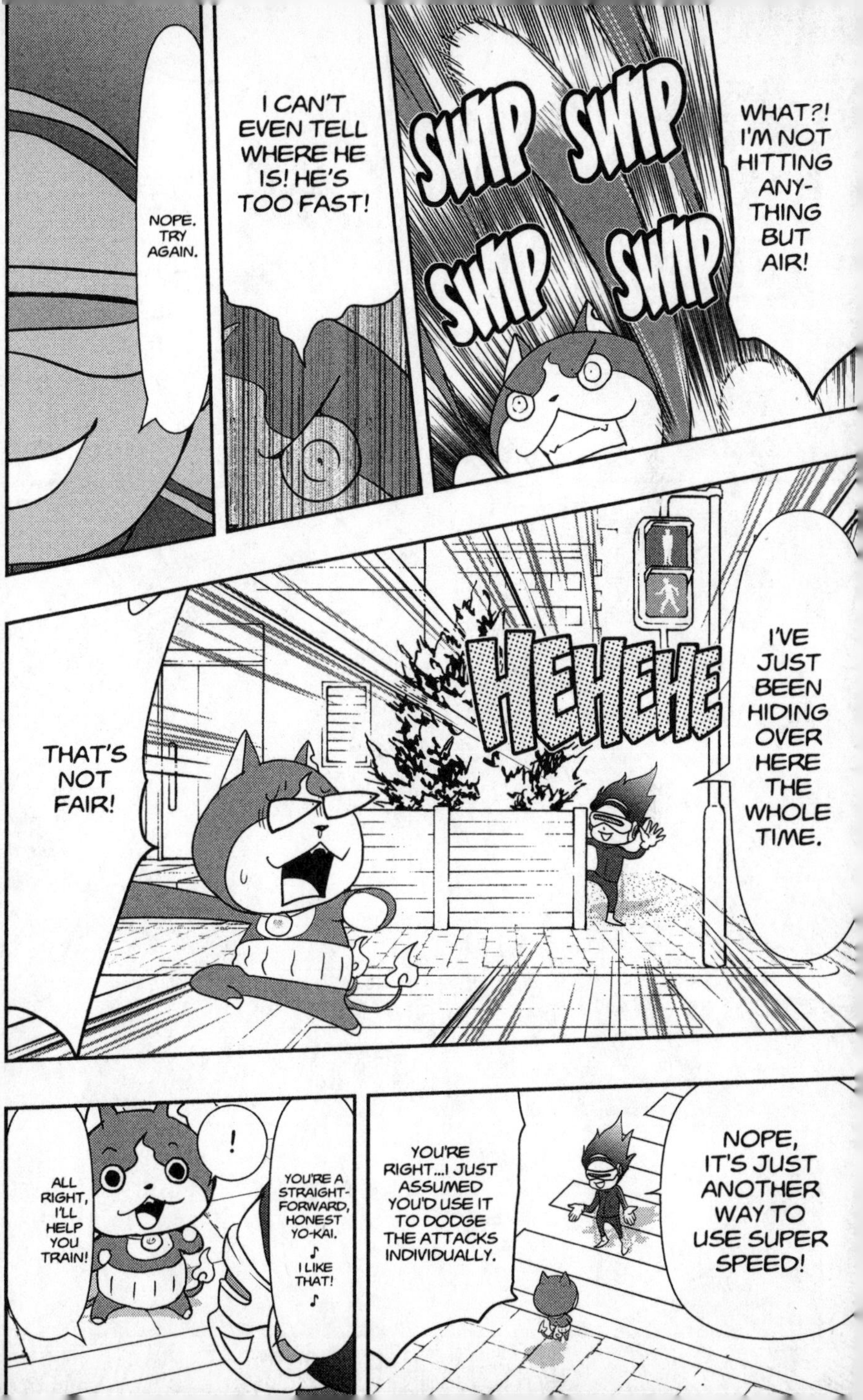
WHAT?! I'M NOT HITTING ANY-THING BUT AIR!
SWIP SWIP
SWIP SWIP
I CAN'T EVEN TELL WHERE HE IS! HE'S TOO FAST!
NOPE. TRY AGAIN.
I'VE JUST BEEN HIDING OVER HERE THE WHOLE TIME.
HEHEHE
THAT'S NOT FAIR!
NOPE, IT'S JUST ANOTHER WAY TO USE SUPER SPEED!
YOU'RE RIGHT...I JUST ASSUMED YOU'D USE IT TO DODGE THE ATTACKS INDIVIDUALLY.
YOU'RE A STRAIGHT-FORWARD, HONEST YO-KAI. ♪ I LIKE THAT! ♪
!
ALL RIGHT, I'LL HELP YOU TRAIN!

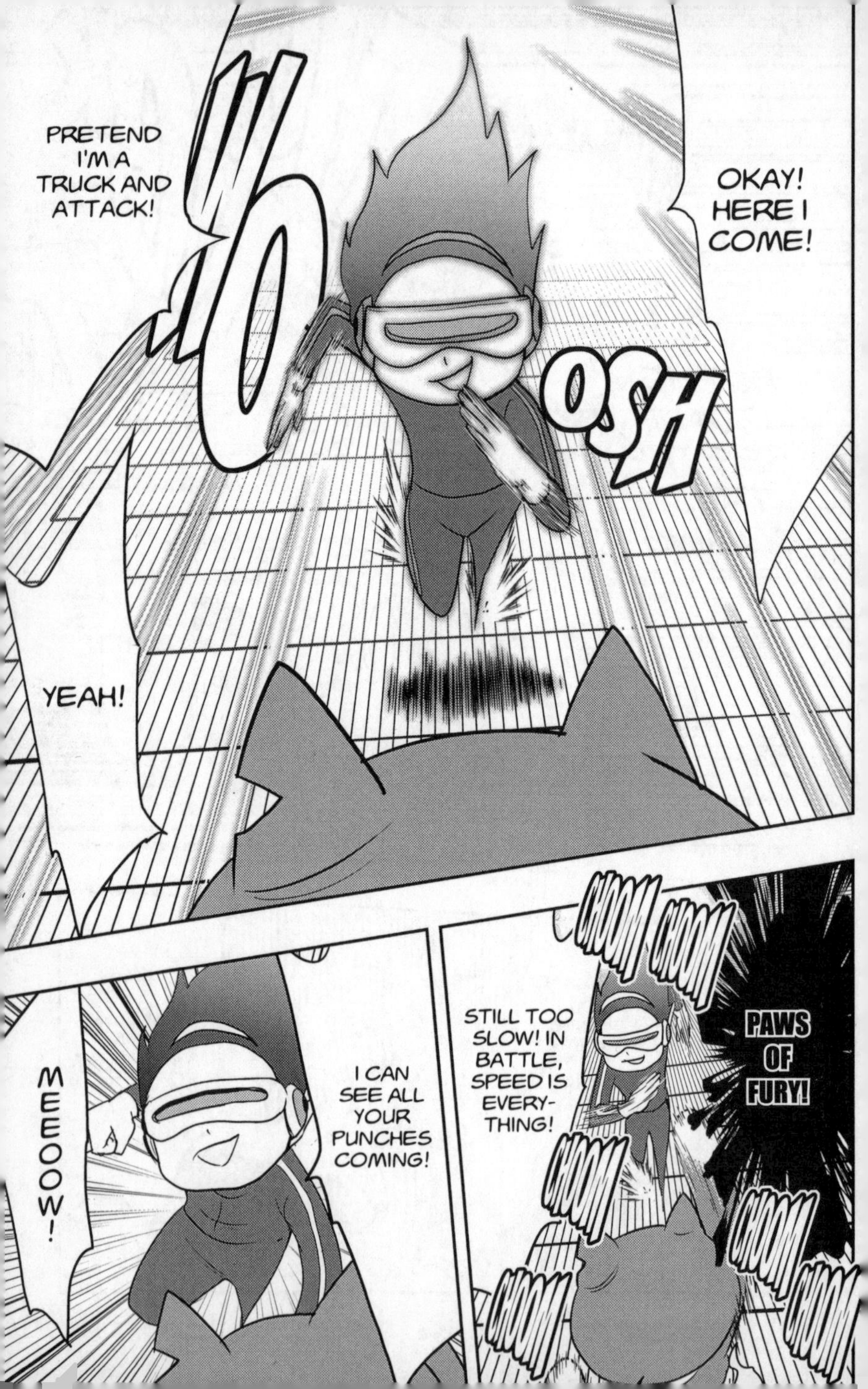
OKAY! HERE I COME!
WHOOSH
PRETEND I'M A TRUCK AND ATTACK!
YEAH!
CHOOM CHOOM
PAWS OF FURY!
STILL TOO SLOW! IN BATTLE, SPEED IS EVERY-THING!
CHOOM
CHOOM
CHOOM
CHOOM
I CAN SEE ALL YOUR PUNCHES COMING!
MEEOOOW!

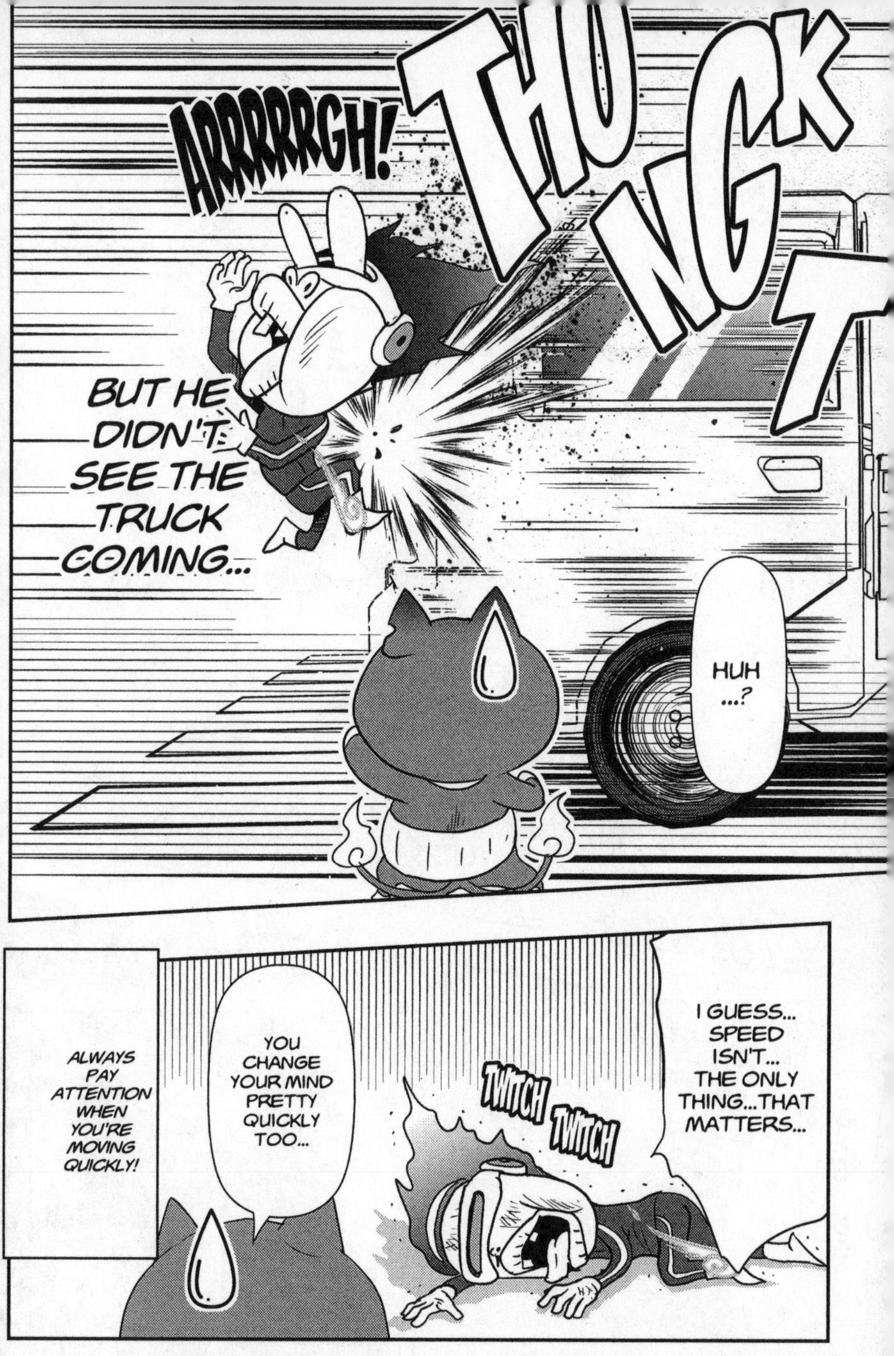
THUNGK
ARRRRRGH!
BUT HE DIDN'T SEE THE TRUCK COMING...
HUH ...?
I GUESS... SPEED ISN'T... THE ONLY THING...THAT MATTERS...
TWITCH TWITCH
YOU CHANGE YOUR MIND PRETTY QUICKLY TOO...
ALWAYS PAY ATTENTION WHEN YOU'RE MOVING QUICKLY!

CHAPTER 148
CRYSTAL YO-KAI CRYSTAL SHOGUNYAN

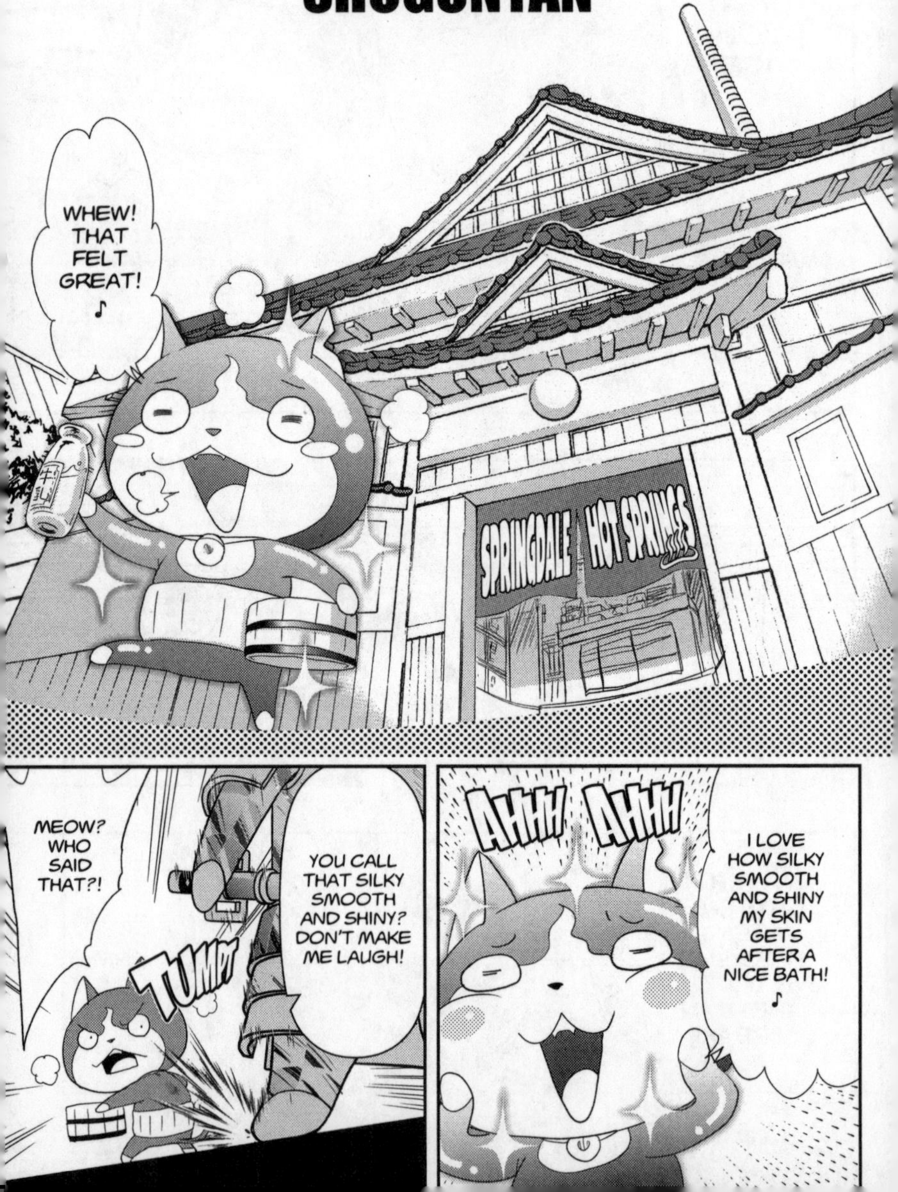
WHEW! THAT FELT GREAT! ♪
SPRINGDALE HOT SPRINGS
AHHH AHHH
I LOVE HOW SILKY SMOOTH AND SHINY MY SKIN GETS AFTER A NICE BATH! ♪
YOU CALL THAT SILKY SMOOTH AND SHINY? DON'T MAKE ME LAUGH!
MEOW? WHO SAID THAT?!
TUMP

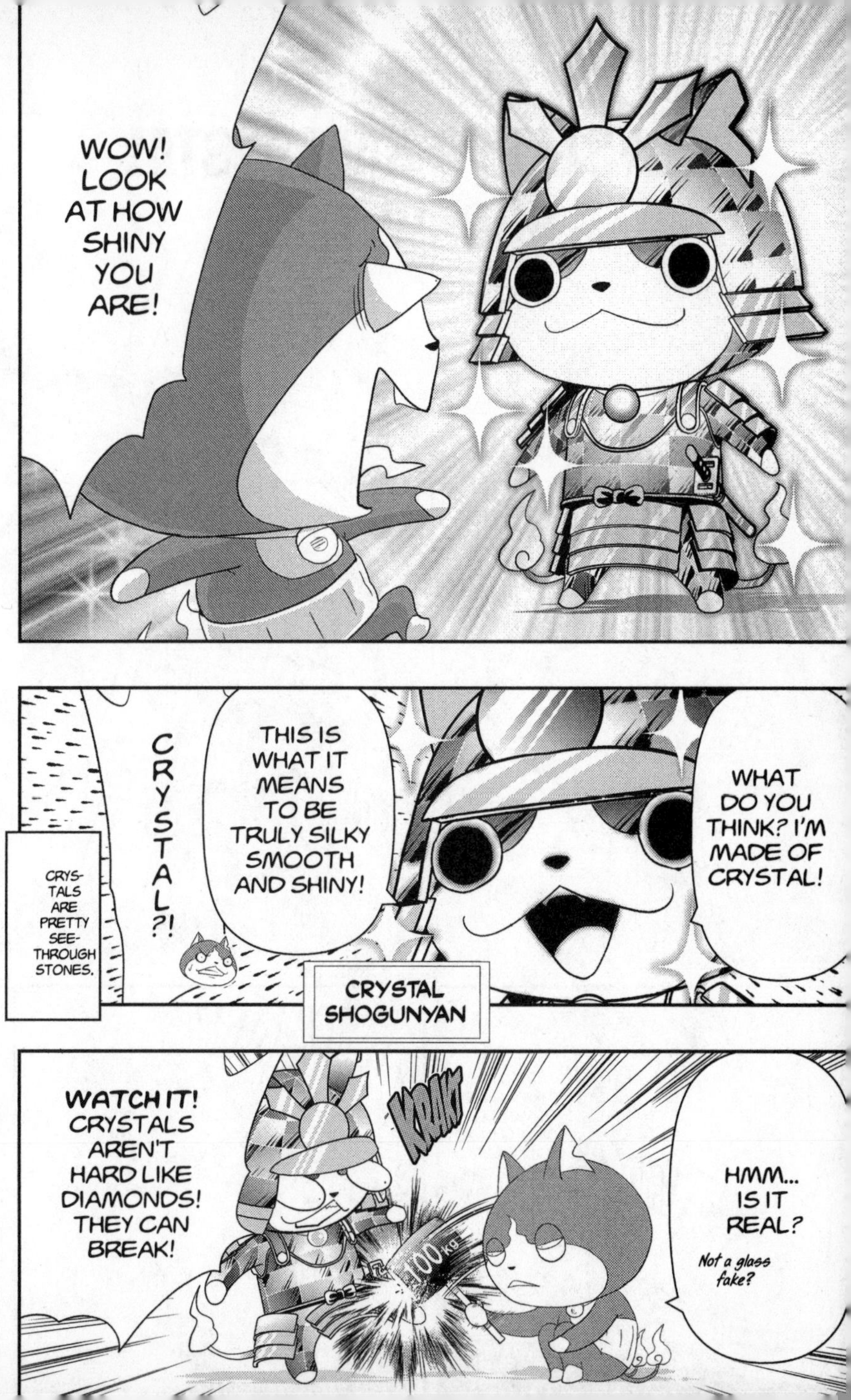
WOW! LOOK AT HOW SHINY YOU ARE!
WHAT DO YOU THINK? I'M MADE OF CRYSTAL!
THIS IS WHAT IT MEANS TO BE TRULY SILKY SMOOTH AND SHINY!
CRYSTAL SHOGUNYAN
CRYSTAL?!
CRYSTALS ARE PRETTY SEE-THROUGH STONES.
HMM... IS IT REAL?
Not a glass fake?
KRAKT
100kg
WATCH IT! CRYSTALS AREN'T HARD LIKE DIAMONDS! THEY CAN BREAK!

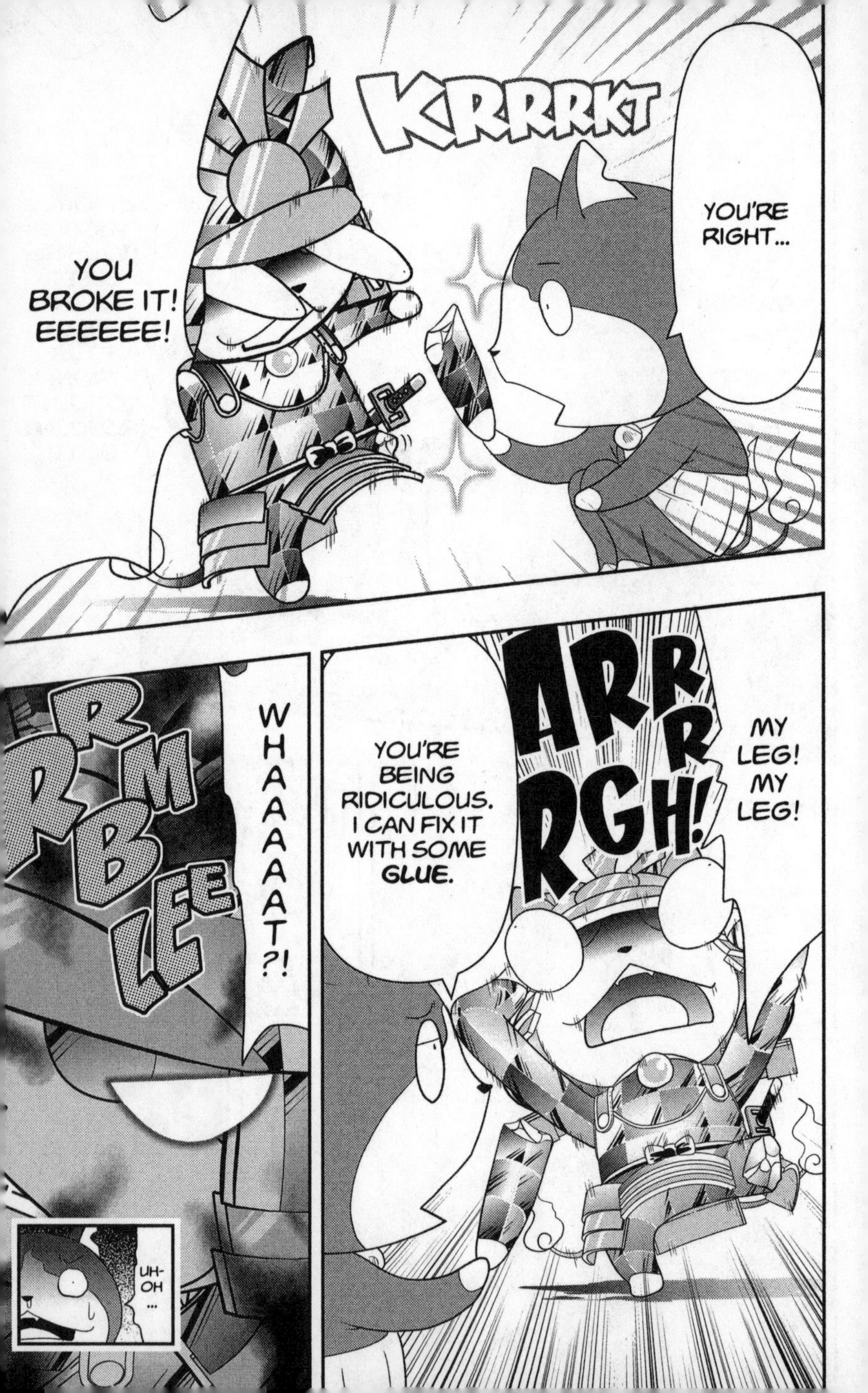
YOU'RE RIGHT...
KRRRRKT
YOU BROKE IT! EEEEEE!
MY LEG! MY LEG!
ARRRRGH!
YOU'RE BEING RIDICULOUS. I CAN FIX IT WITH SOME **GLUE.**
WHAAAAAAT?!
RRMBLEE
UH-OH...

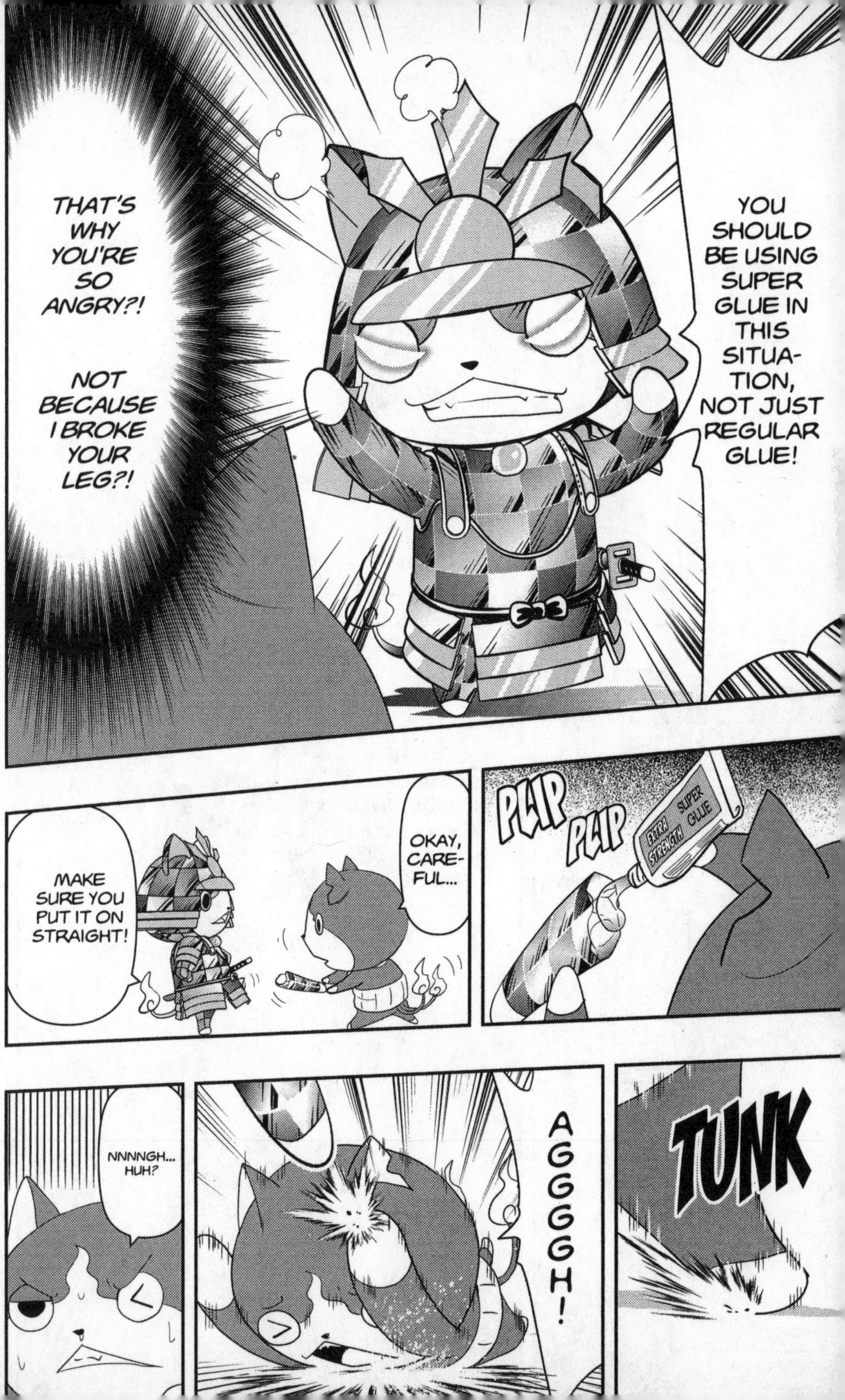
YOU SHOULD BE USING SUPER GLUE IN THIS SITUATION, NOT JUST REGULAR GLUE!
THAT'S WHY YOU'RE SO ANGRY?!
NOT BECAUSE I BROKE YOUR LEG?!
PLIP
PLIP
EXTRA STRENGTH SUPER GLUE
OKAY, CAREFUL...
MAKE SURE YOU PUT IT ON STRAIGHT!
TUNK
AGGGGH!
NNNNGH... HUH?

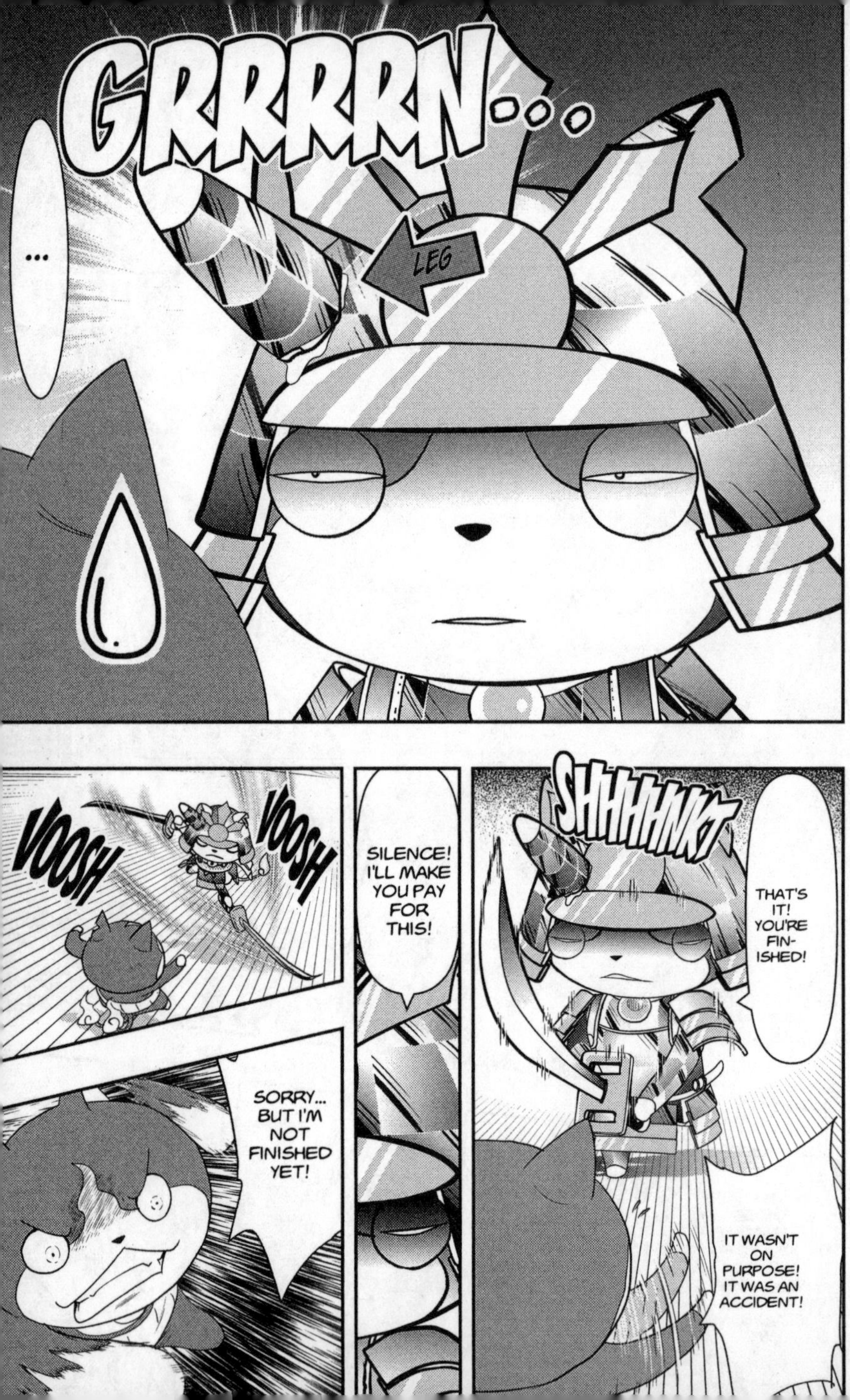
GRRRRRN...
LEG
...
SHHHHNKT
THAT'S IT! YOU'RE FIN-ISHED!
IT WASN'T ON PURPOSE! IT WAS AN ACCIDENT!
SILENCE! I'LL MAKE YOU PAY FOR THIS!
VOOSH
VOOSH
SORRY... BUT I'M NOT FINISHED YET!

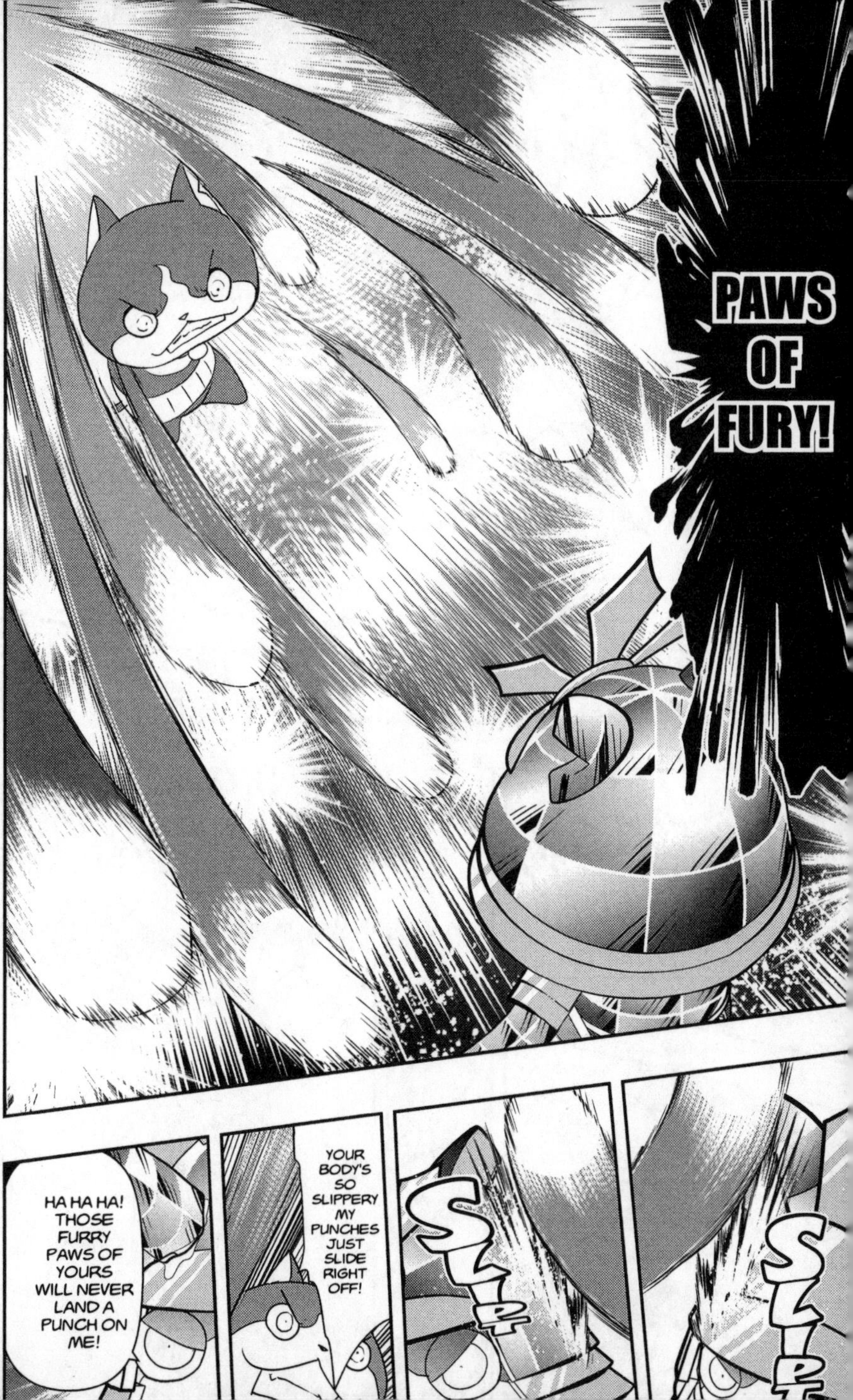
PAWS OF FURY!
SLIP
SLIP
YOUR BODY'S SO SLIPPERY MY PUNCHES JUST SLIDE RIGHT OFF!
HA HA HA! THOSE FURRY PAWS OF YOURS WILL NEVER LAND A PUNCH ON ME!

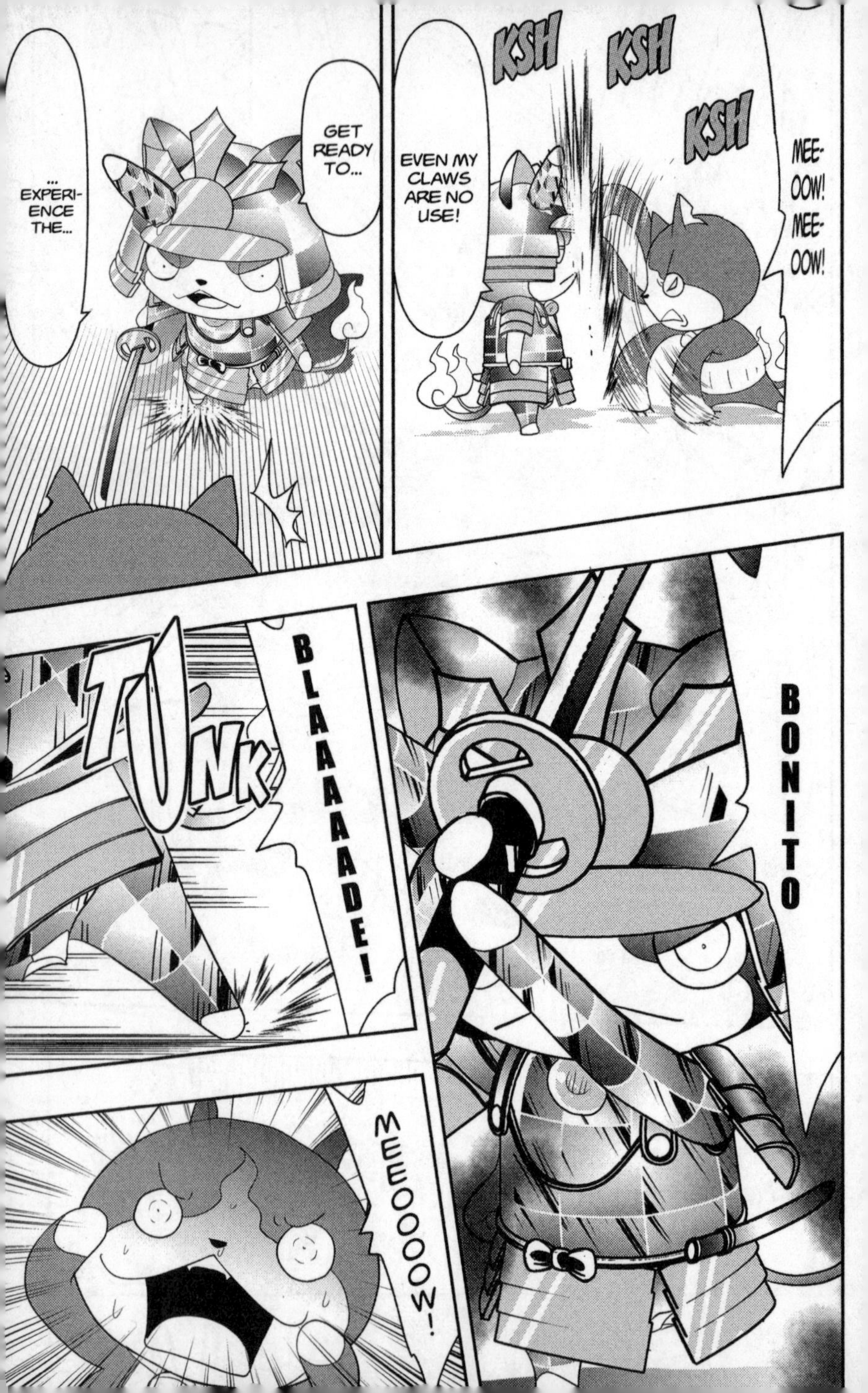
MEE-OOW! MEE-OOW!
KSH
KSH
KSH
EVEN MY CLAWS ARE NO USE!
GET READY TO...
... EXPERIENCE THE...
BONITO
BLAAAAADE!
TUNK
MEEOOOOOW!

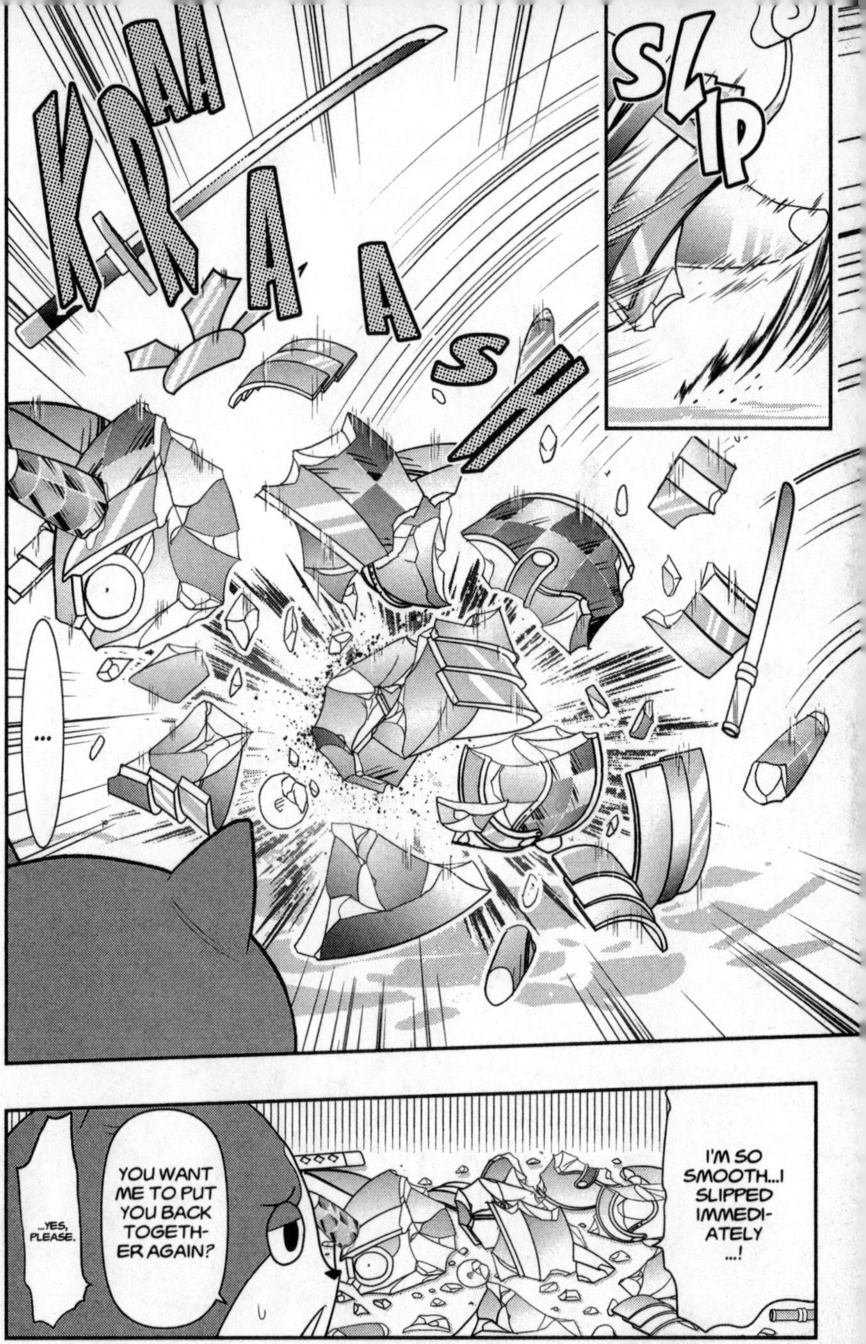
SLIP
KRAAAASH
...
I'M SO SMOOTH...I SLIPPED IMMEDIATELY...!
YOU WANT ME TO PUT YOU BACK TOGETHER AGAIN?
...YES, PLEASE.

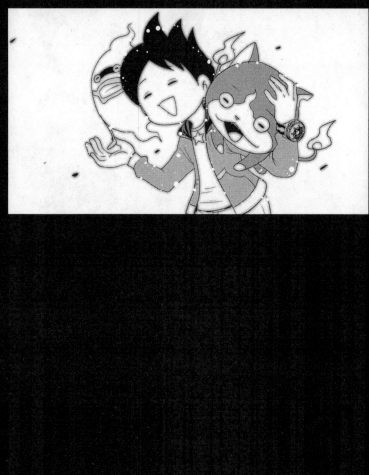

CHAPTER 149
FRIENDS AND SECRETS

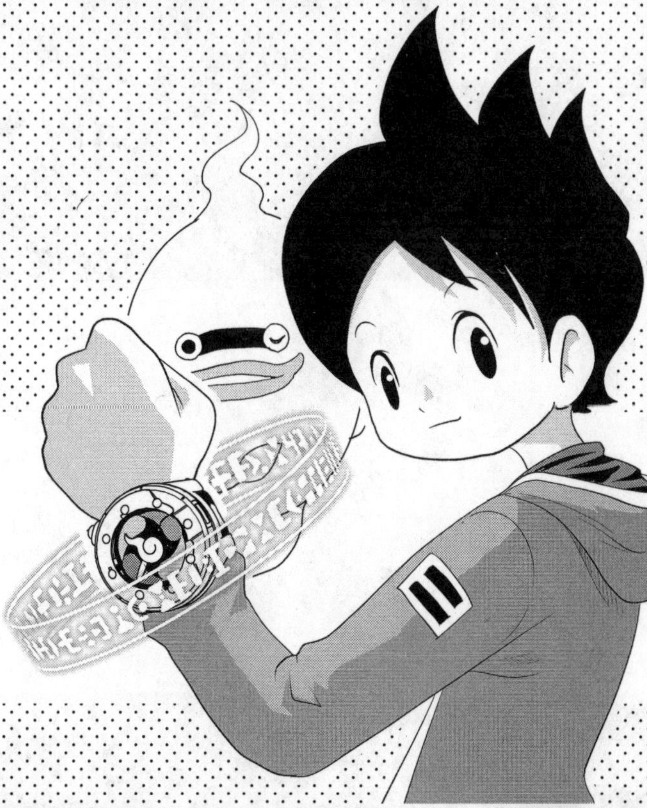

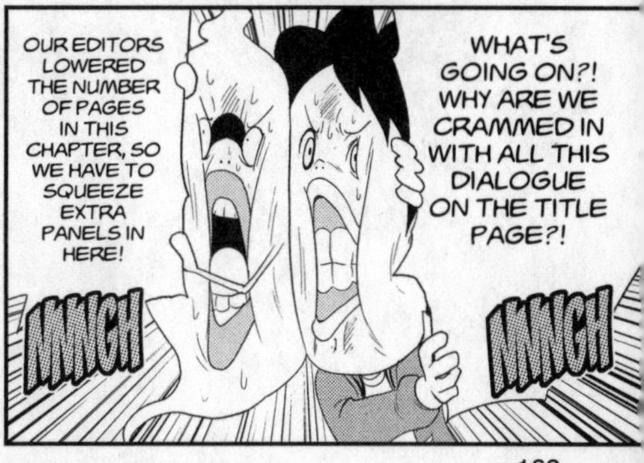
WHAT'S GOING ON?! WHY ARE WE CRAMMED IN WITH ALL THIS DIALOGUE ON THE TITLE PAGE?!
OUR EDITORS LOWERED THE NUMBER OF PAGES IN THIS CHAPTER, SO WE HAVE TO SQUEEZE EXTRA PANELS IN HERE!
MMNCH
MMNCH

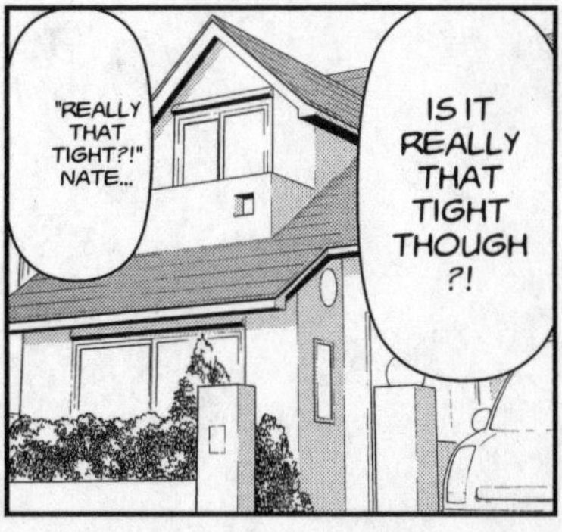
IS IT REALLY THAT TIGHT THOUGH?!
"REALLY THAT TIGHT?!" NATE...

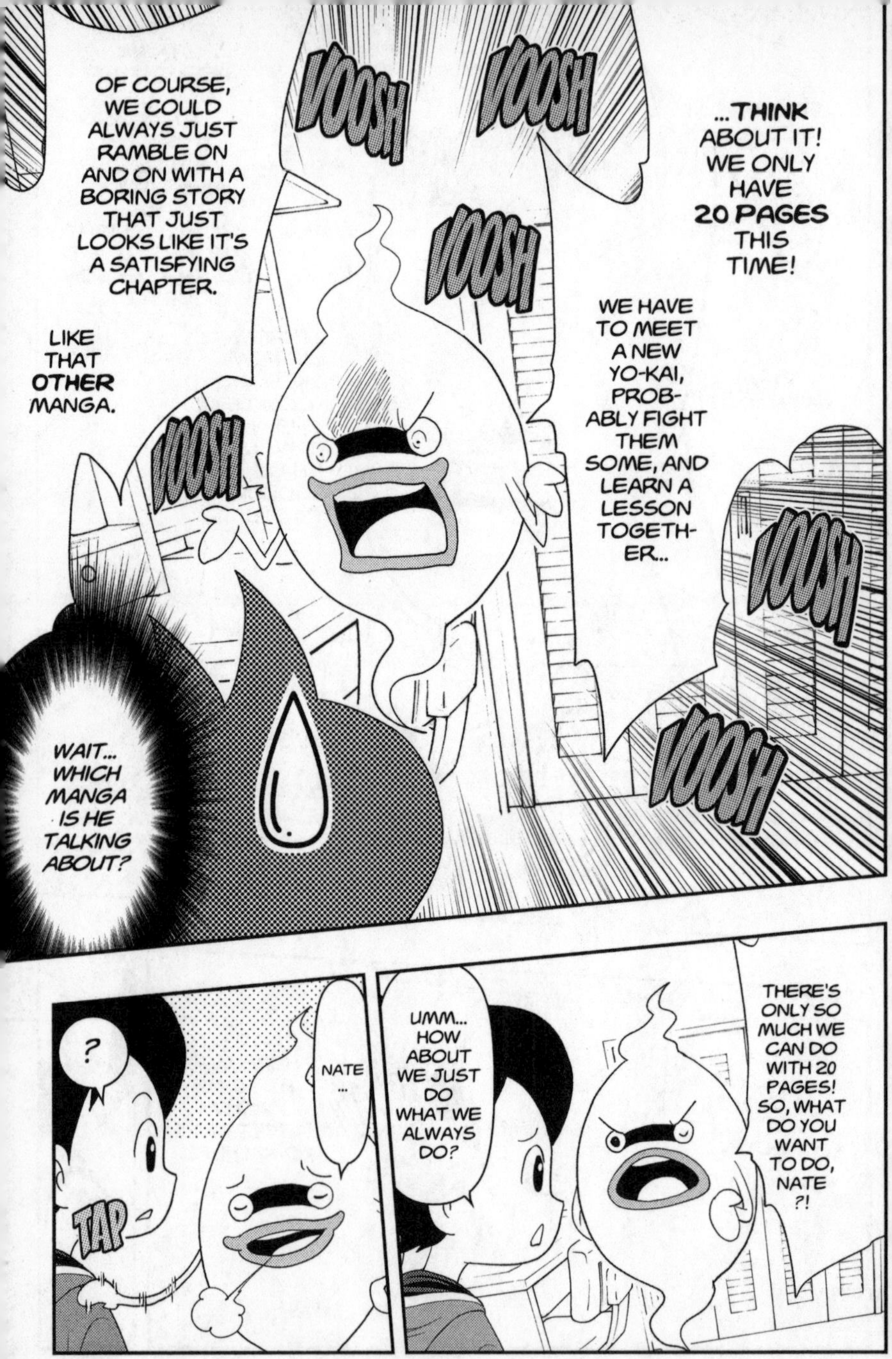
...THINK ABOUT IT! WE ONLY HAVE 20 PAGES THIS TIME!
VOOSH
VOOSH
VOOSH
WE HAVE TO MEET A NEW YO-KAI, PROBABLY FIGHT THEM SOME, AND LEARN A LESSON TOGETHER...
OF COURSE, WE COULD ALWAYS JUST RAMBLE ON AND ON WITH A BORING STORY THAT JUST LOOKS LIKE IT'S A SATISFYING CHAPTER.
LIKE THAT OTHER MANGA.
VOOSH
VOOSH
VOOSH
WAIT... WHICH MANGA IS HE TALKING ABOUT?
THERE'S ONLY SO MUCH WE CAN DO WITH 20 PAGES! SO, WHAT DO YOU WANT TO DO, NATE ?!
UMM... HOW ABOUT WE JUST DO WHAT WE ALWAYS DO?
NATE ...
?
TAP

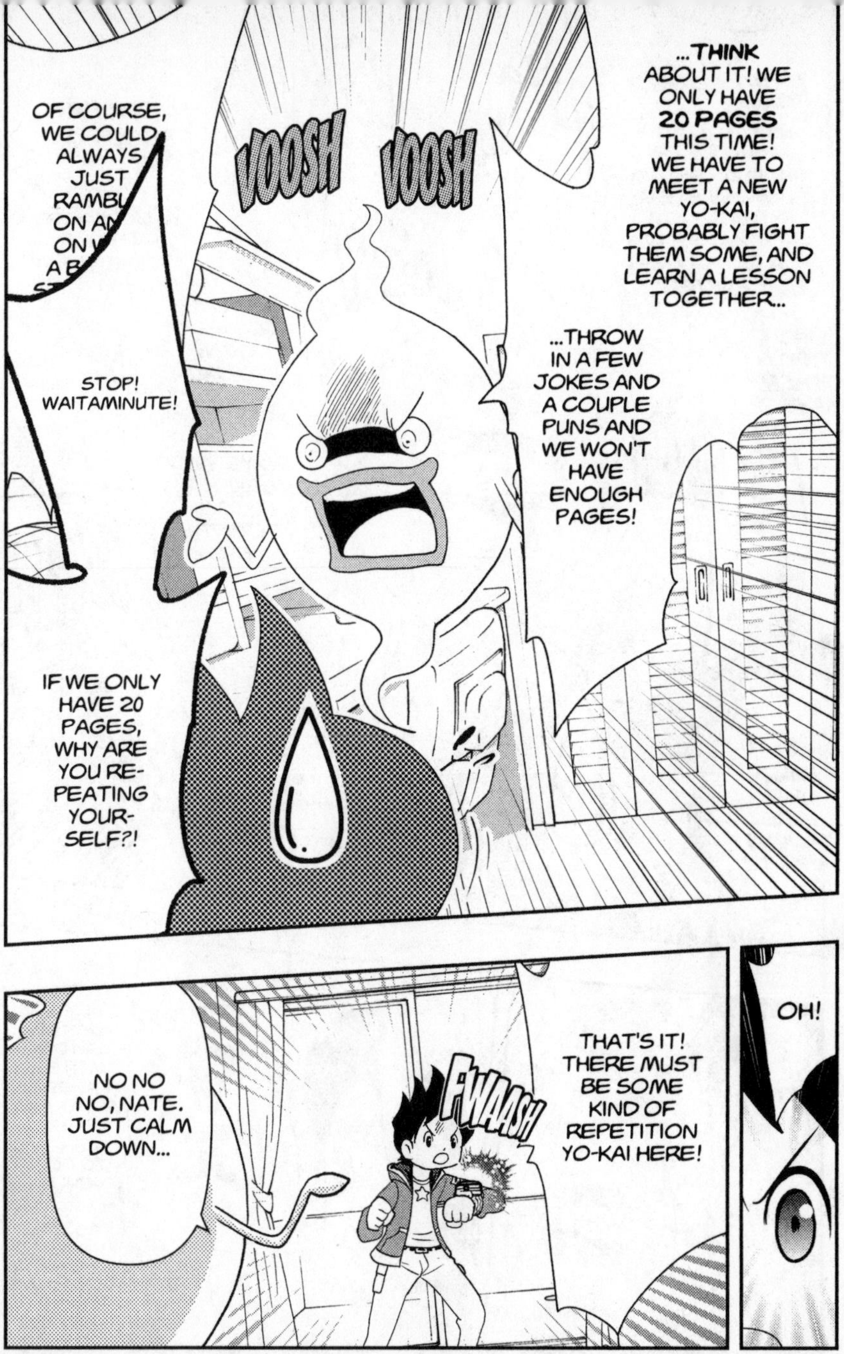
...THINK ABOUT IT! WE ONLY HAVE **20 PAGES** THIS TIME! WE HAVE TO MEET A NEW YO-KAI, PROBABLY FIGHT THEM SOME, AND LEARN A LESSON TOGETHER...
...THROW IN A FEW JOKES AND A COUPLE PUNS AND WE WON'T HAVE ENOUGH PAGES!
VOOSH VOOSH
OF COURSE, WE COULD ALWAYS JUST
STOP! WAITAMINUTE!
IF WE ONLY HAVE 20 PAGES, WHY ARE YOU RE-PEATING YOUR-SELF?!
OH!
THAT'S IT! THERE MUST BE SOME KIND OF REPETITION YO-KAI HERE!
FWAASH
NO NO NO, NATE. JUST CALM DOWN...

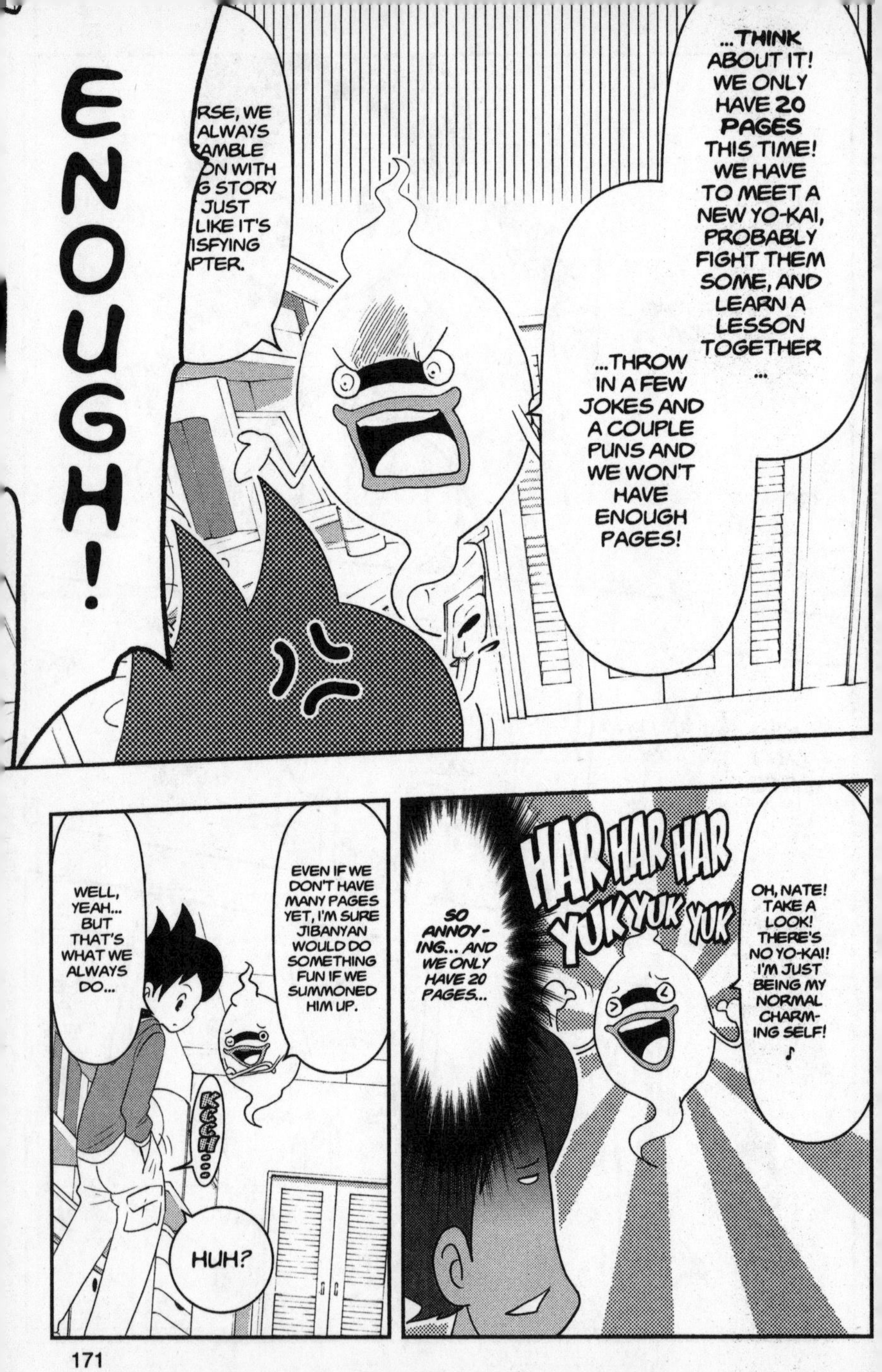

...THINK ABOUT IT! WE ONLY HAVE 20 PAGES THIS TIME! WE HAVE TO MEET A NEW YO-KAI, PROBABLY FIGHT THEM SOME, AND LEARN A LESSON TOGETHER ...
...THROW IN A FEW JOKES AND A COUPLE PUNS AND WE WON'T HAVE ENOUGH PAGES!
RSE, WE ALWAYS AMBLE ON WITH G STORY JUST LIKE IT'S ISFYING PTER.
ENOUGH!
OH, NATE! TAKE A LOOK! THERE'S NO YO-KAI! I'M JUST BEING MY NORMAL CHARM-ING SELF! ♪
HAR HAR HAR YUK YUK YUK
SO ANNOY-ING... AND WE ONLY HAVE 20 PAGES...
EVEN IF WE DON'T HAVE MANY PAGES YET, I'M SURE JIBANYAN WOULD DO SOMETHING FUN IF WE SUMMONED HIM UP.
WELL, YEAH... BUT THAT'S WHAT WE ALWAYS DO...
KCCH...
HUH?

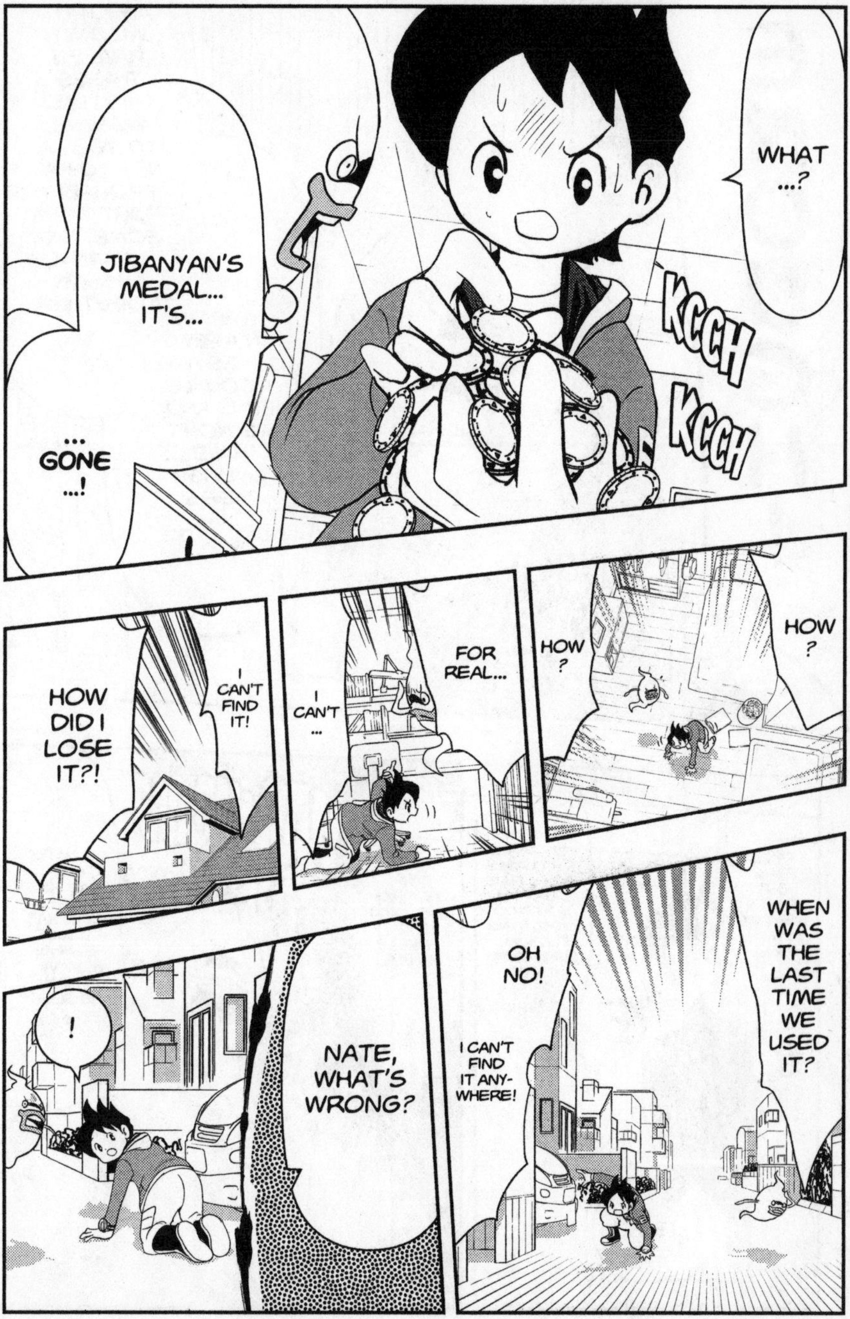
WHAT ...?
KCCH
KCCH
JIBANYAN'S MEDAL... IT'S...
... GONE ...!
HOW ?
HOW ?
FOR REAL...
I CAN'T ...
I CAN'T FIND IT!
HOW DID I LOSE IT?!
WHEN WAS THE LAST TIME WE USED IT?
OH NO!
I CAN'T FIND IT ANY-WHERE!
NATE, WHAT'S WRONG?
!

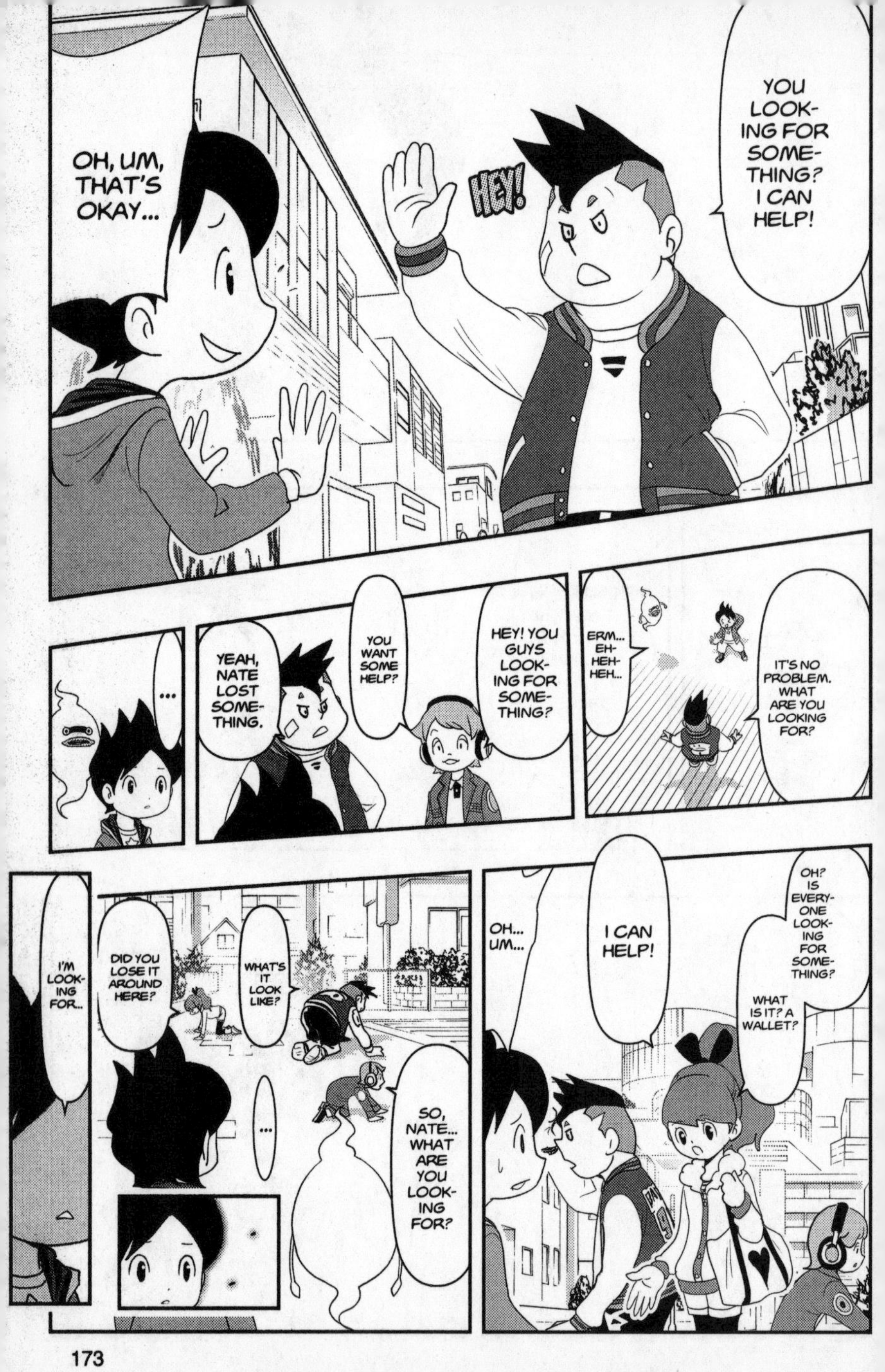
YOU LOOKING FOR SOMETHING? I CAN HELP!
HEY!
OH, UM, THAT'S OKAY...
IT'S NO PROBLEM. WHAT ARE YOU LOOKING FOR?
ERM... EH-HEH-HEH...
HEY! YOU GUYS LOOKING FOR SOMETHING?
YOU WANT SOME HELP?
YEAH, NATE LOST SOMETHING.
...
OH? IS EVERYONE LOOKING FOR SOMETHING?
WHAT IS IT? A WALLET?
I CAN HELP!
OH... UM...
SO, NATE... WHAT ARE YOU LOOKING FOR?
...
WHAT'S IT LOOK LIKE?
DID YOU LOSE IT AROUND HERE?
I'M LOOKING FOR...

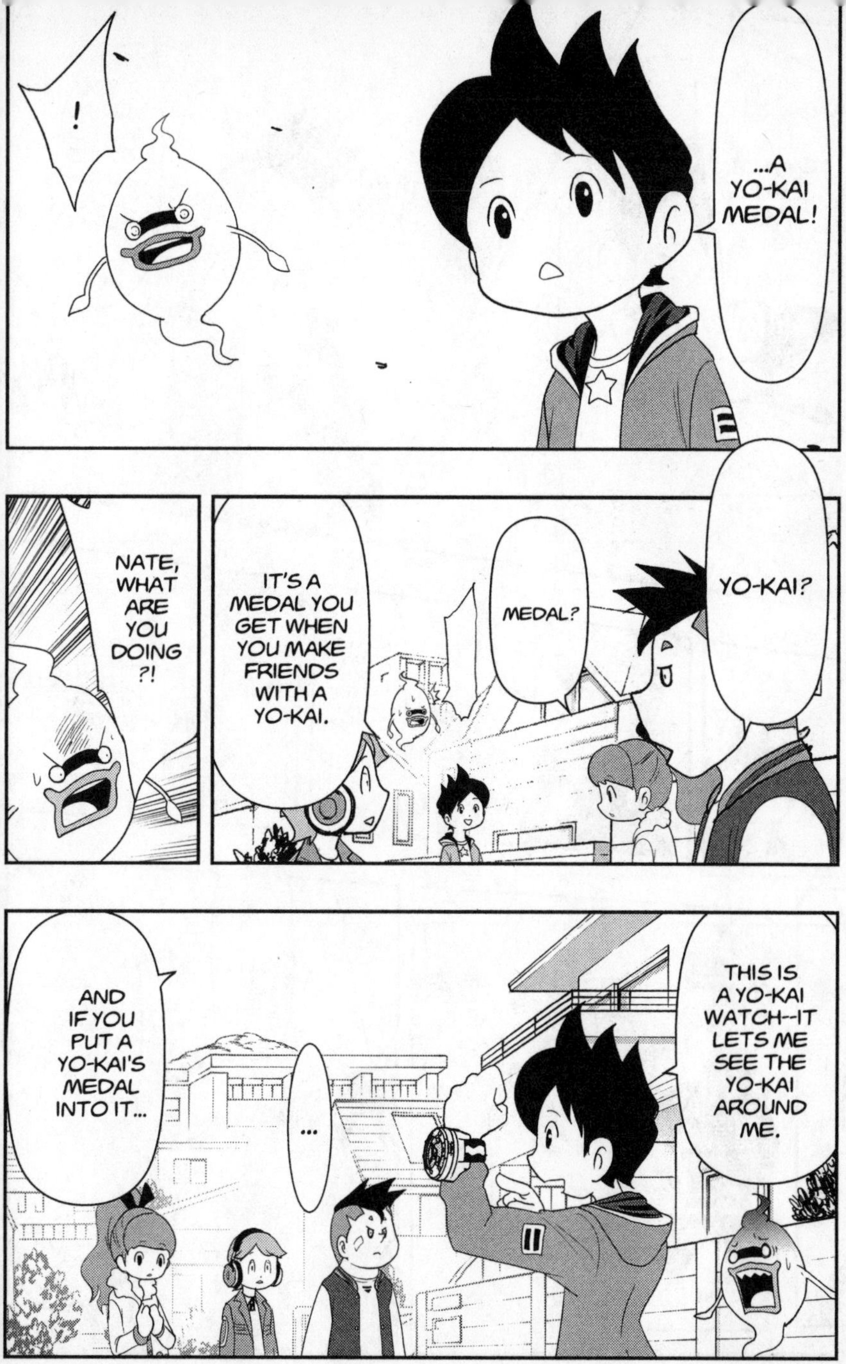
...A YO-KAI MEDAL!
!
YO-KAI?
MEDAL?
IT'S A MEDAL YOU GET WHEN YOU MAKE FRIENDS WITH A YO-KAI.
NATE, WHAT ARE YOU DOING ?!
THIS IS A YO-KAI WATCH--IT LETS ME SEE THE YO-KAI AROUND ME.
...
AND IF YOU PUT A YO-KAI'S MEDAL INTO IT...

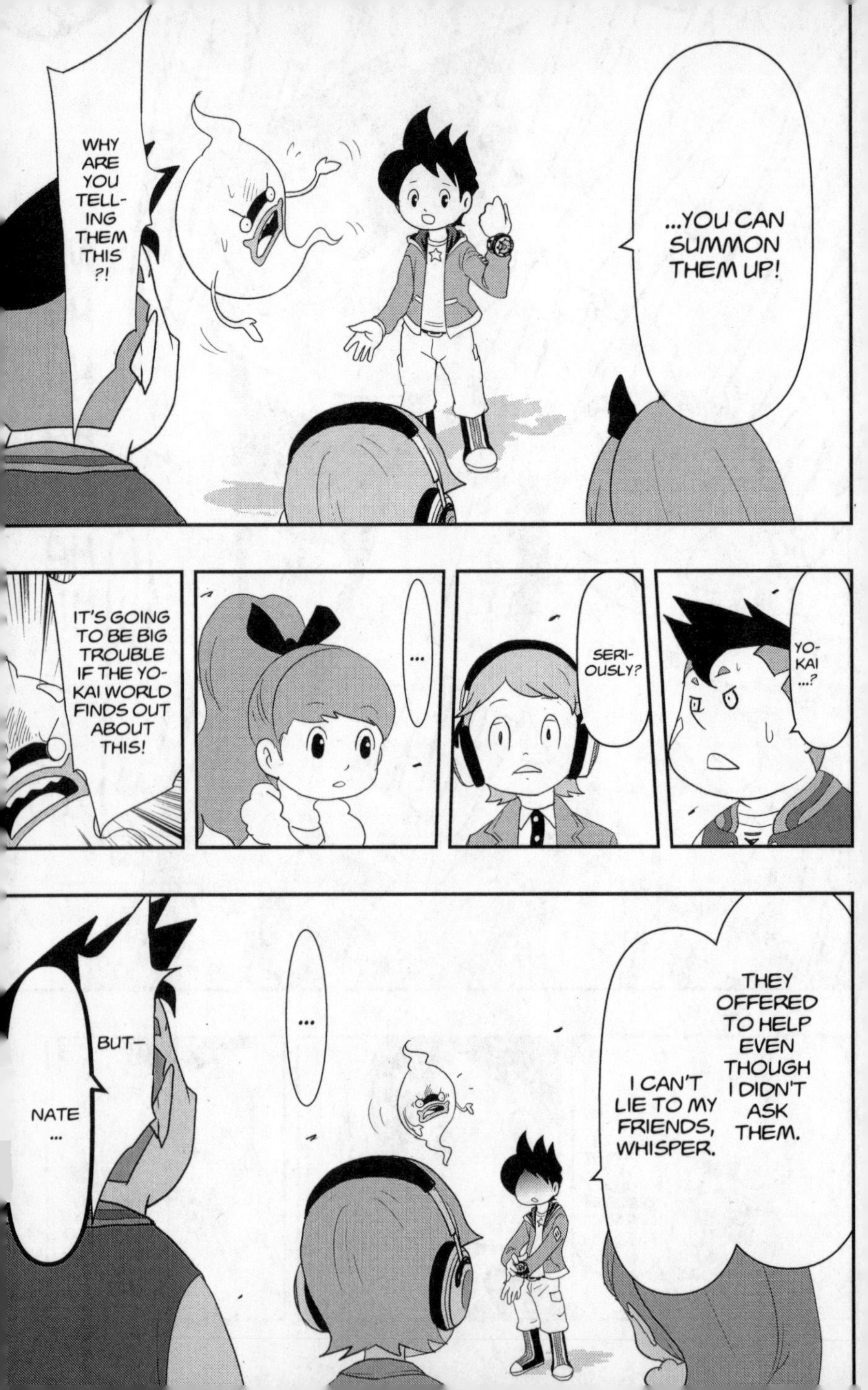
...YOU CAN SUMMON THEM UP!
WHY ARE YOU TELL-ING THEM THIS?!
YO-KAI ...?
SERI-OUSLY?
...
IT'S GOING TO BE BIG TROUBLE IF THE YO-KAI WORLD FINDS OUT ABOUT THIS!
THEY OFFERED TO HELP EVEN THOUGH I DIDN'T ASK THEM.
I CAN'T LIE TO MY FRIENDS, WHISPER.
...
BUT—
NATE ...

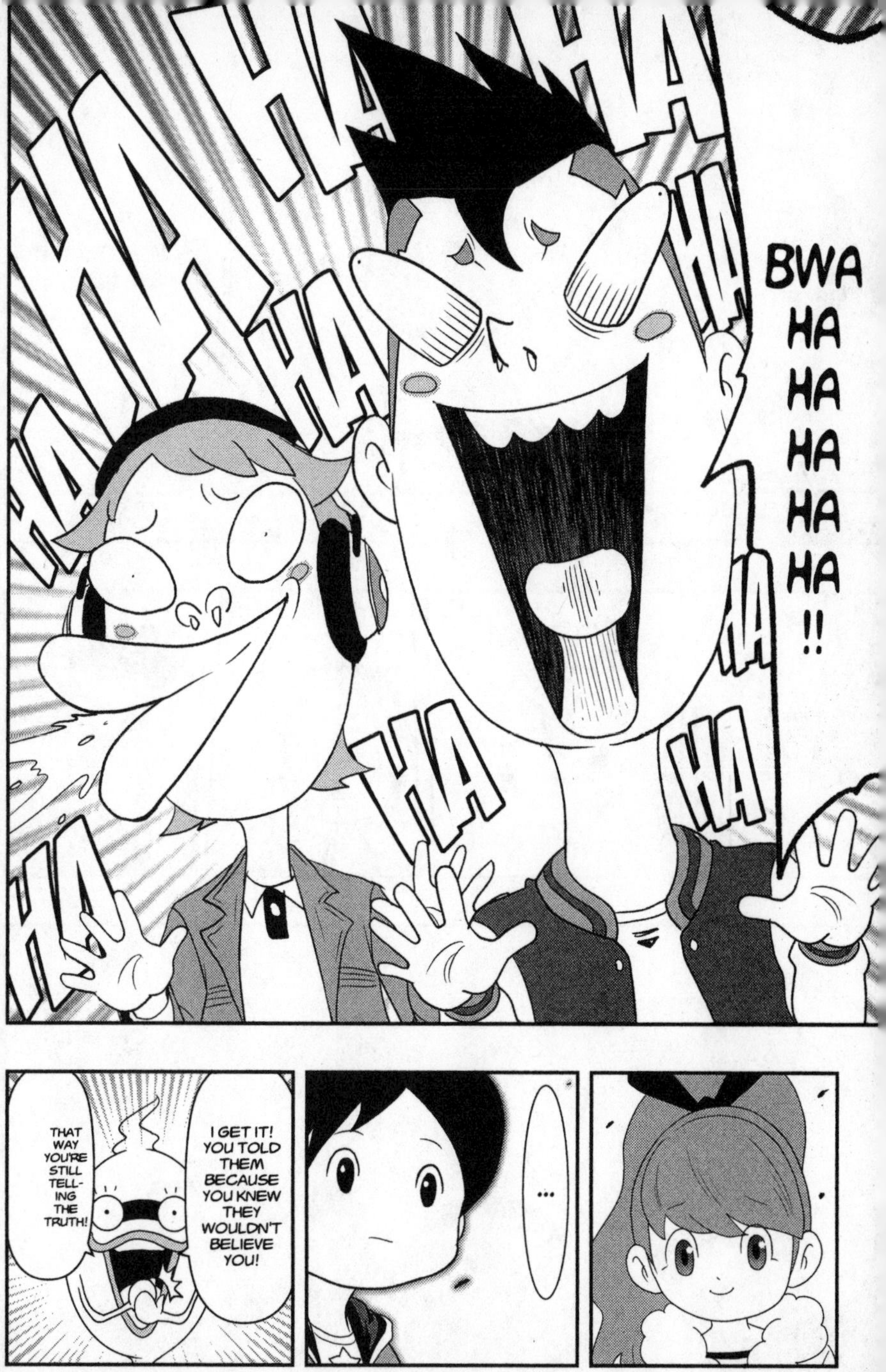
BWA HA HA HA HA HA!!
HA HA HA HA
HA HA HA
...
I GET IT! YOU TOLD THEM BECAUSE YOU KNEW THEY WOULDN'T BELIEVE YOU!
THAT WAY YOU'RE STILL TELL-ING THE TRUTH!

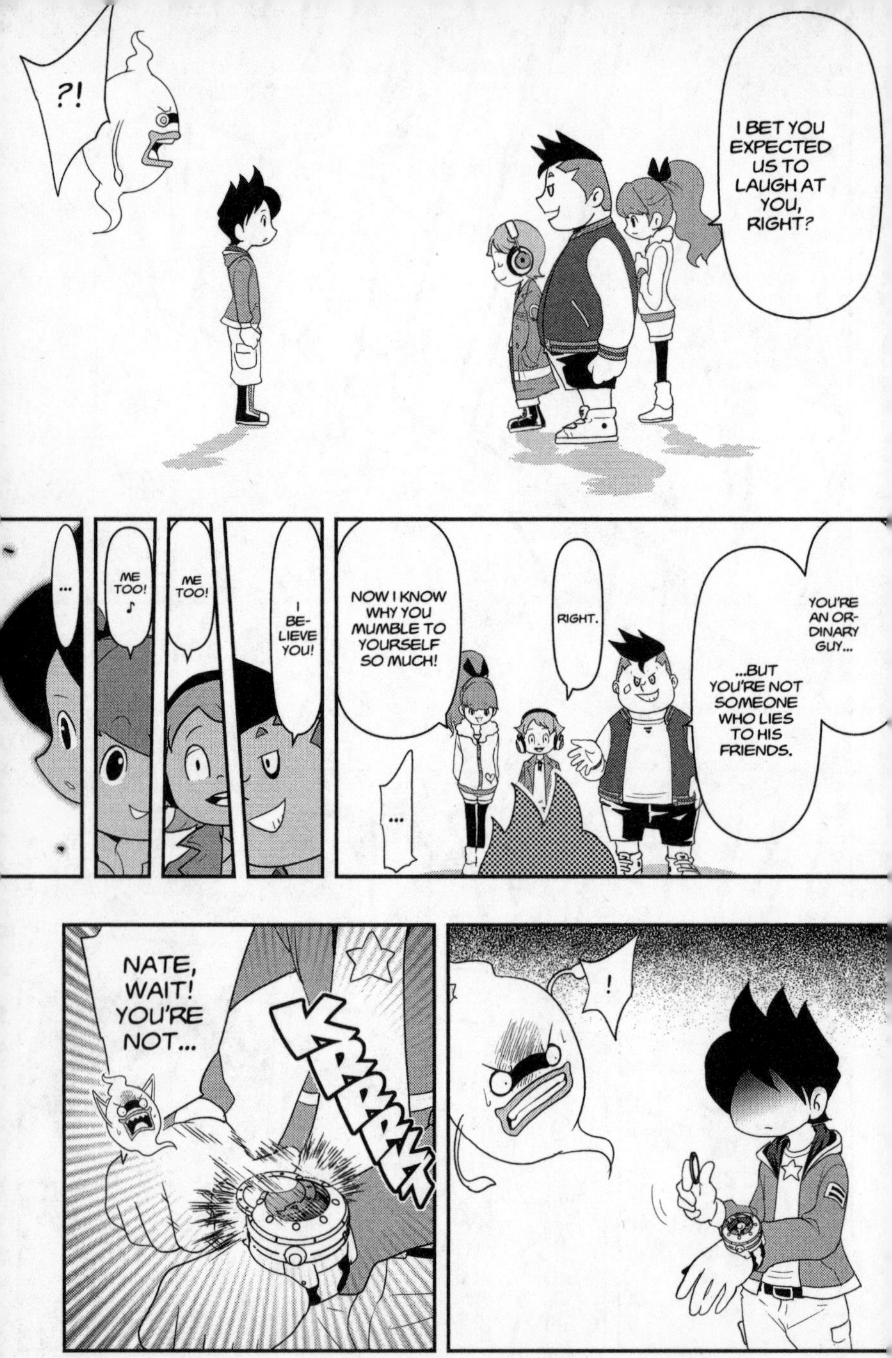
I BET YOU EXPECTED US TO LAUGH AT YOU, RIGHT?
?!
YOU'RE AN ORDINARY GUY...
...BUT YOU'RE NOT SOMEONE WHO LIES TO HIS FRIENDS.
RIGHT.
NOW I KNOW WHY YOU MUMBLE TO YOURSELF SO MUCH!
...
I BELIEVE YOU!
ME TOO!
ME TOO! ♪
...
!
NATE, WAIT! YOU'RE NOT...
KRRRKK

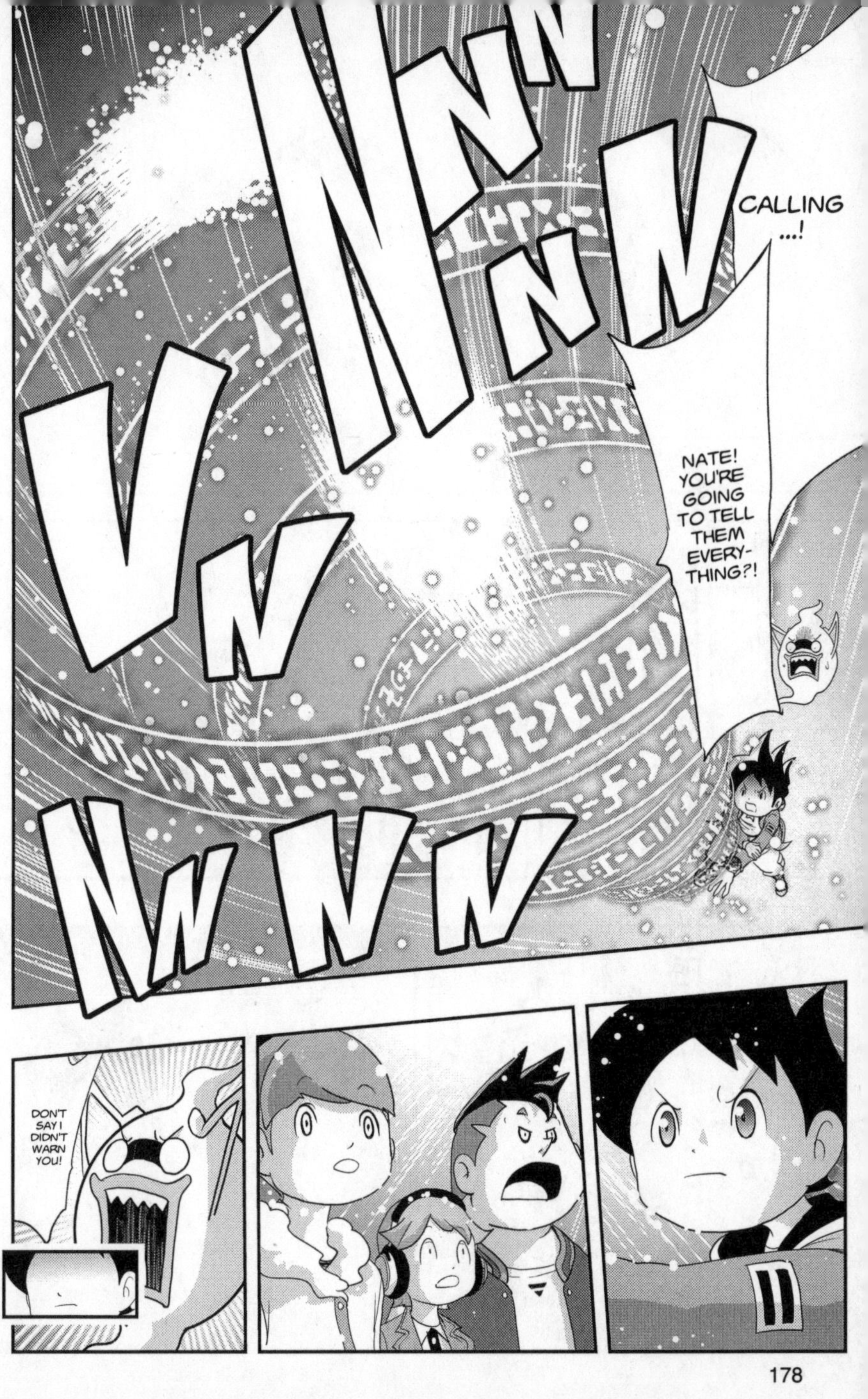
CALLING ...!
NATE! YOU'RE GOING TO TELL THEM EVERY-THING?!
VNNNNNNNN
NNNN
DON'T SAY I DIDN'T WARN YOU!

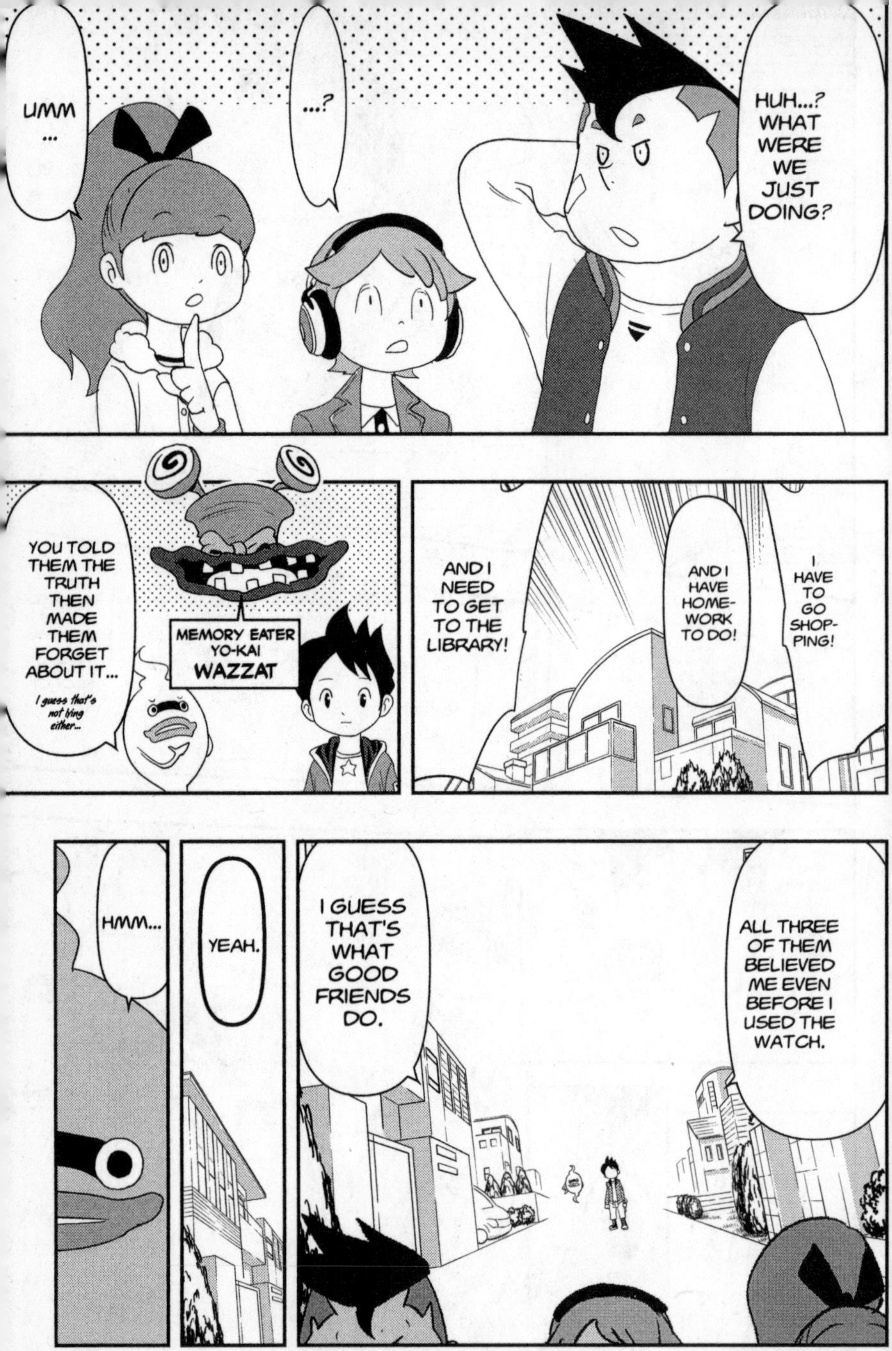
HUH...? WHAT WERE WE JUST DOING?
...?
UMM ...
I HAVE TO GO SHOP-PING!
AND I HAVE HOME-WORK TO DO!
AND I NEED TO GET TO THE LIBRARY!
MEMORY EATER YO-KAI WAZZAT
YOU TOLD THEM THE TRUTH THEN MADE THEM FORGET ABOUT IT...
I guess that's not lying either...
ALL THREE OF THEM BELIEVED ME EVEN BEFORE I USED THE WATCH.
I GUESS THAT'S WHAT GOOD FRIENDS DO.
YEAH.
HMM...

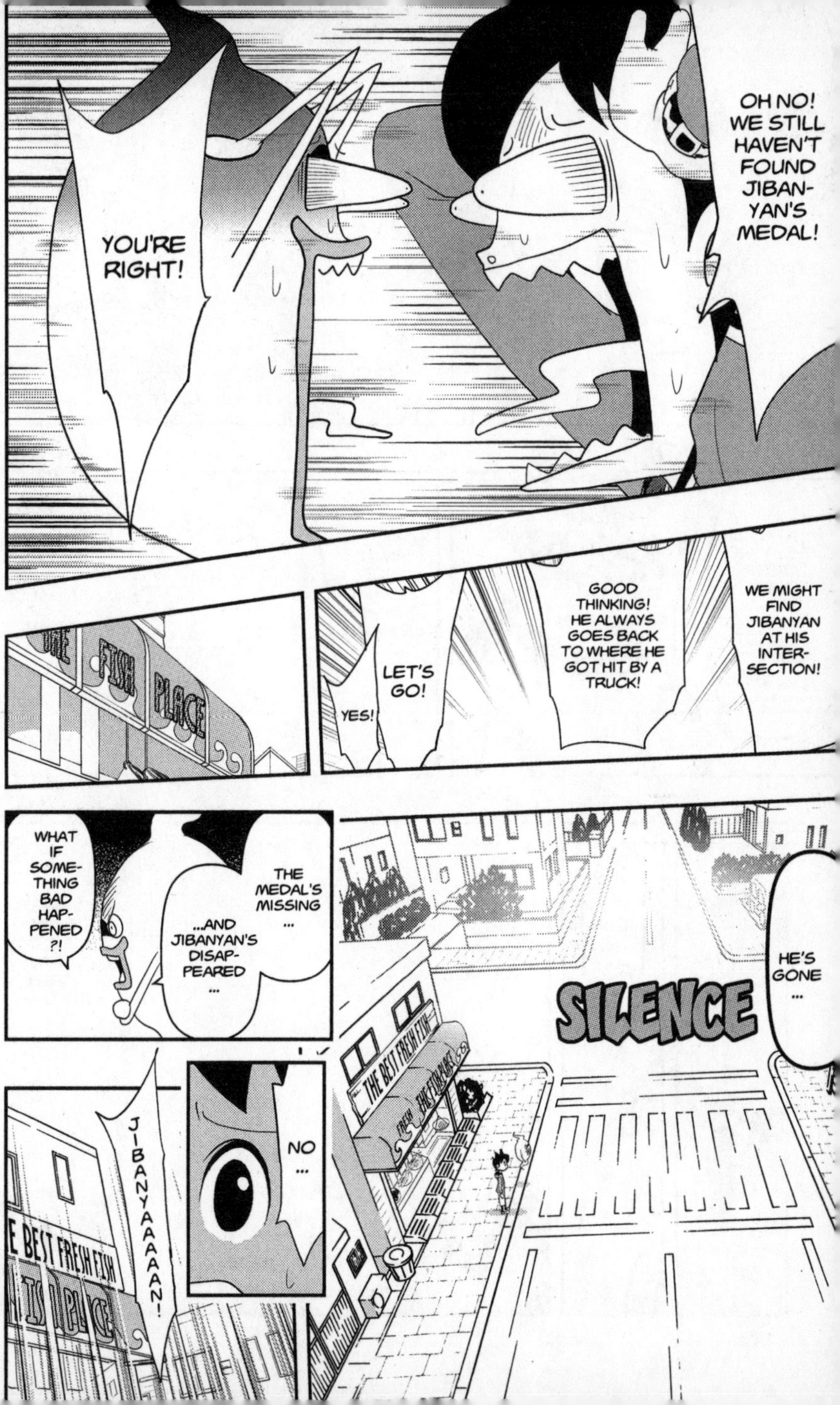
OH NO! WE STILL HAVEN'T FOUND JIBAN-YAN'S MEDAL!
YOU'RE RIGHT!
WE MIGHT FIND JIBANYAN AT HIS INTER-SECTION!
GOOD THINKING! HE ALWAYS GOES BACK TO WHERE HE GOT HIT BY A TRUCK!
LET'S GO!
YES!
HE'S GONE ...
SILENCE
THE MEDAL'S MISSING ...
...AND JIBANYAN'S DISAP-PEARED ...
WHAT IF SOME-THING BAD HAP-PENED?!
NO ...
JIBANYAAAAAAN!

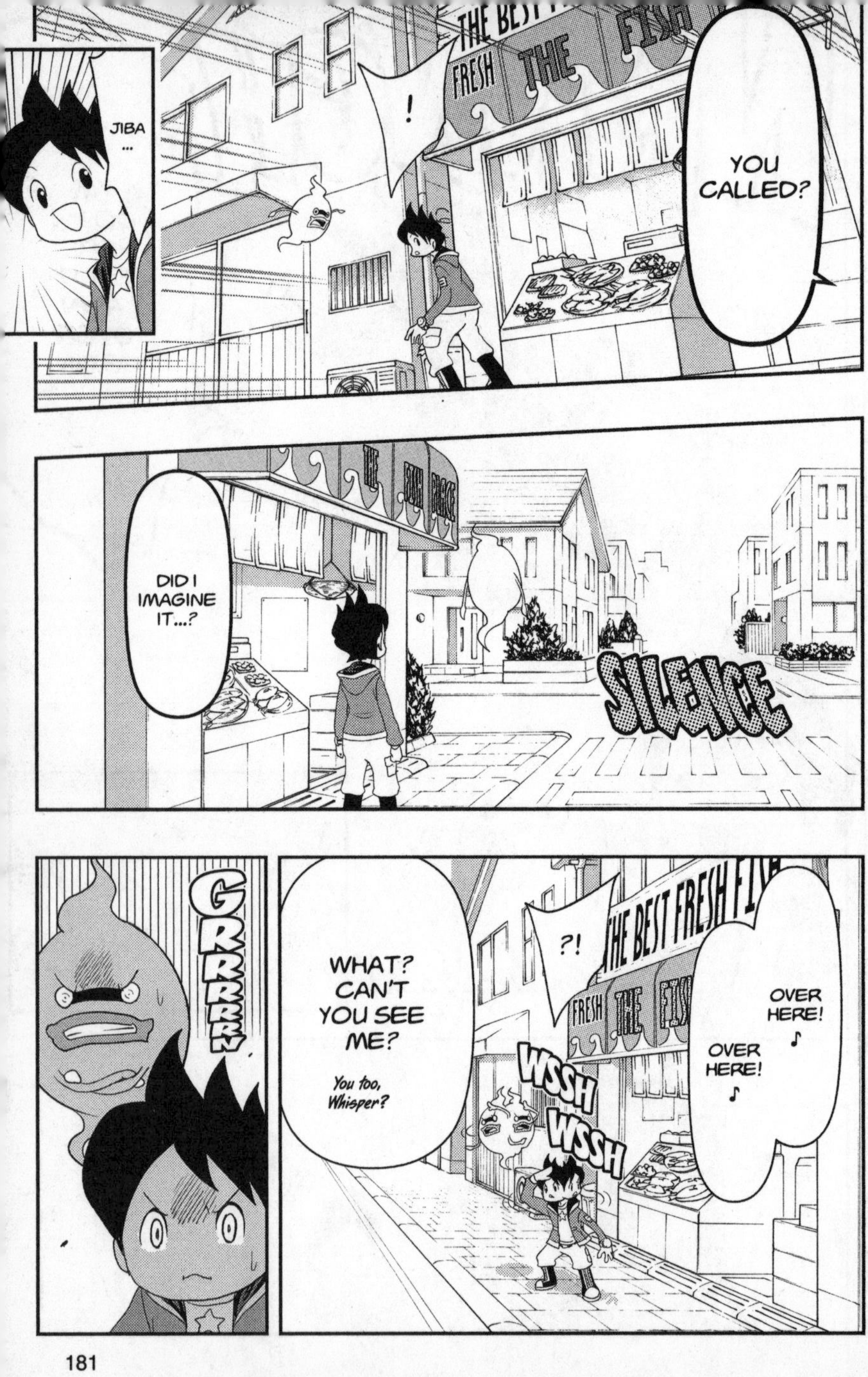

YOU CALLED?
!
FRESH
THE
JIBA ...
DID I IMAGINE IT...?
SILENCE
OVER HERE! ♪
OVER HERE! ♪
?!
THE BEST FRESH FISH
FRESH
THE
WHAT? CAN'T YOU SEE ME?
You too, Whisper?
WSSH WSSH
GRRRRN

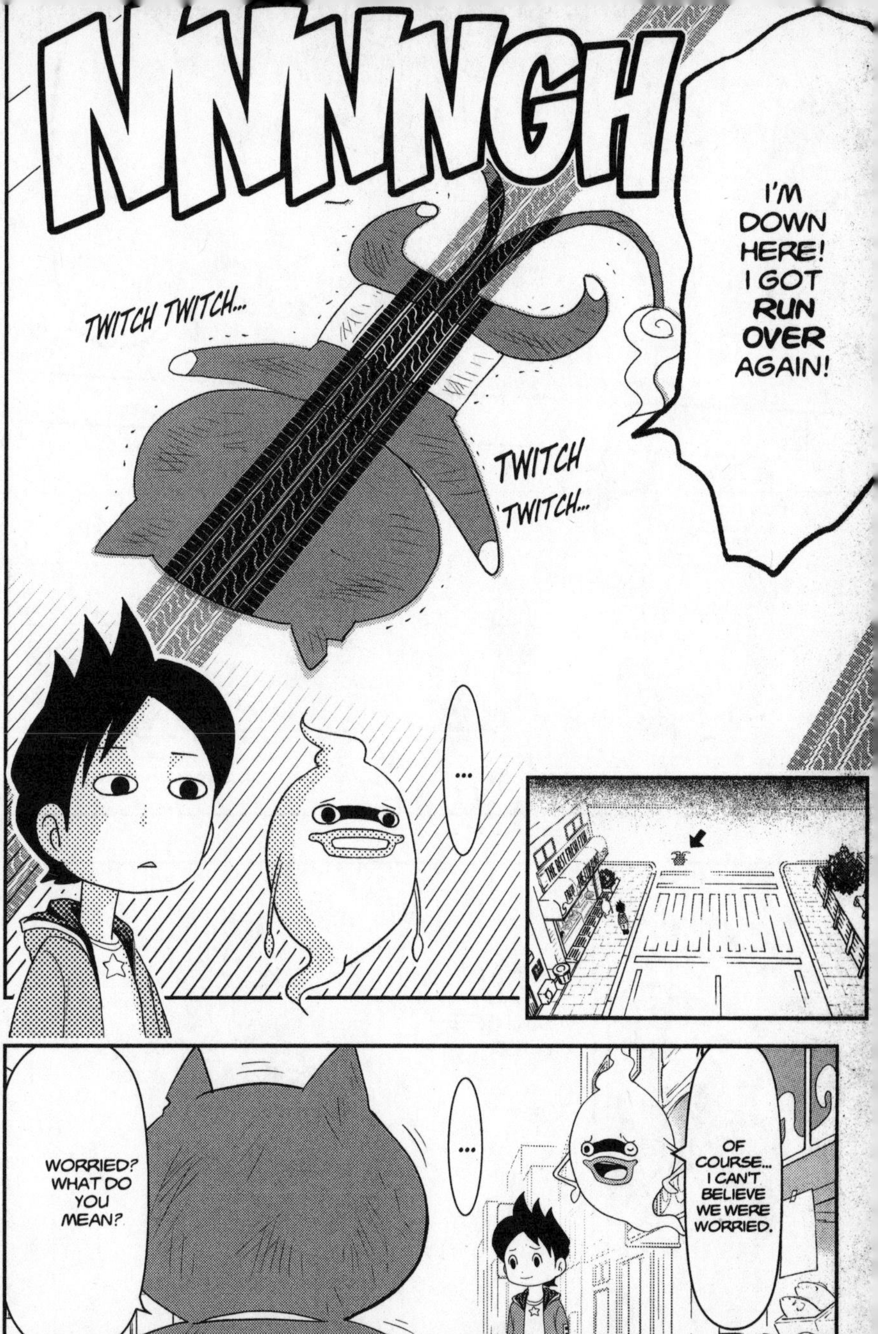
NNNNNGH
I'M DOWN HERE! I GOT RUN OVER AGAIN!
TWITCH TWITCH...
TWITCH TWITCH...
...
OF COURSE... I CAN'T BELIEVE WE WERE WORRIED.
...
WORRIED? WHAT DO YOU MEAN?

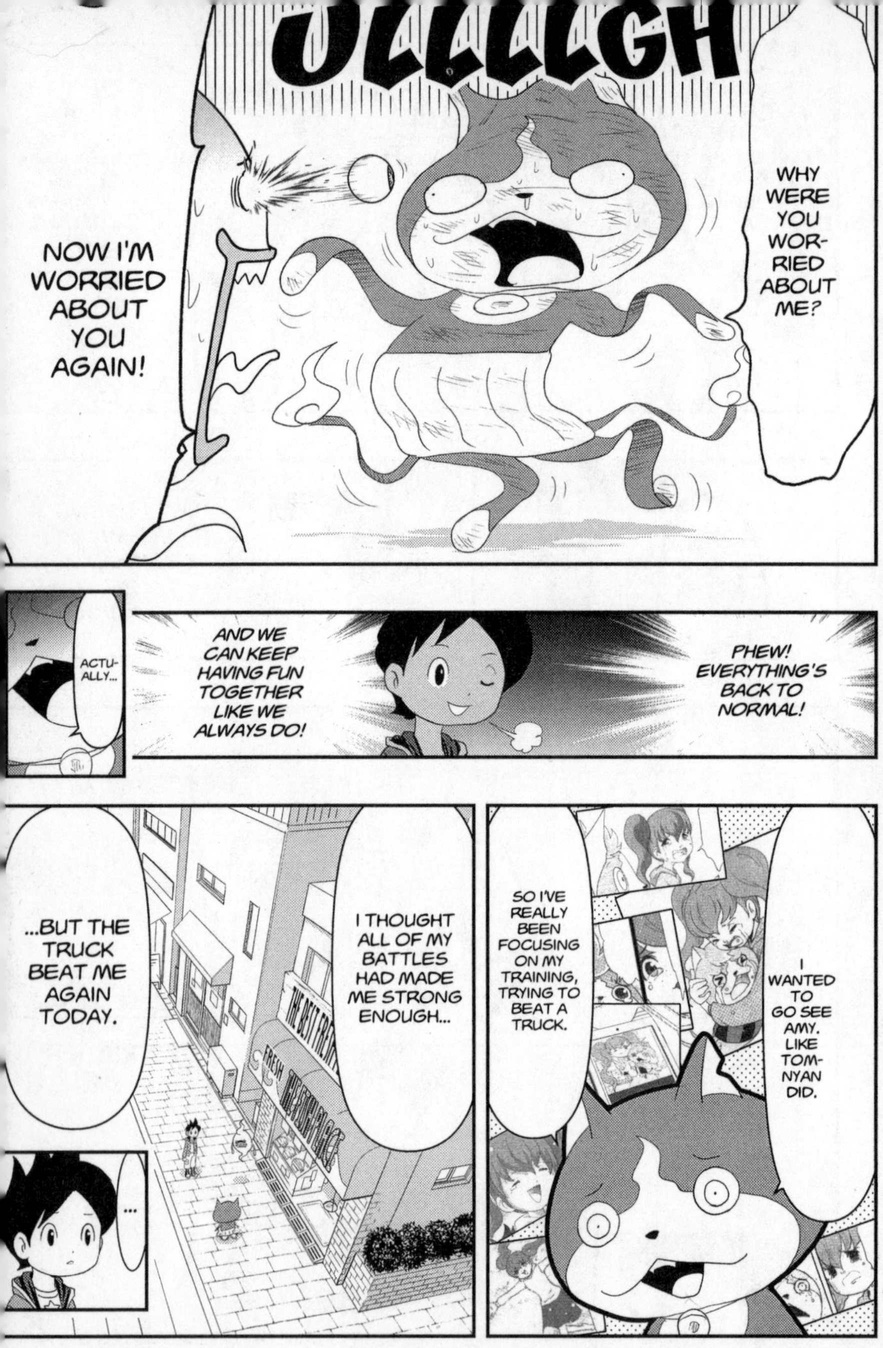
ULLLLGH
WHY WERE YOU WORRIED ABOUT ME?
NOW I'M WORRIED ABOUT YOU AGAIN!
PHEW! EVERYTHING'S BACK TO NORMAL!
AND WE CAN KEEP HAVING FUN TOGETHER LIKE WE ALWAYS DO!
ACTUALLY...
I WANTED TO GO SEE AMY. LIKE TOMNYAN DID.
SO I'VE REALLY BEEN FOCUSING ON MY TRAINING, TRYING TO BEAT A TRUCK.
I THOUGHT ALL OF MY BATTLES HAD MADE ME STRONG ENOUGH...
...BUT THE TRUCK BEAT ME AGAIN TODAY.
...

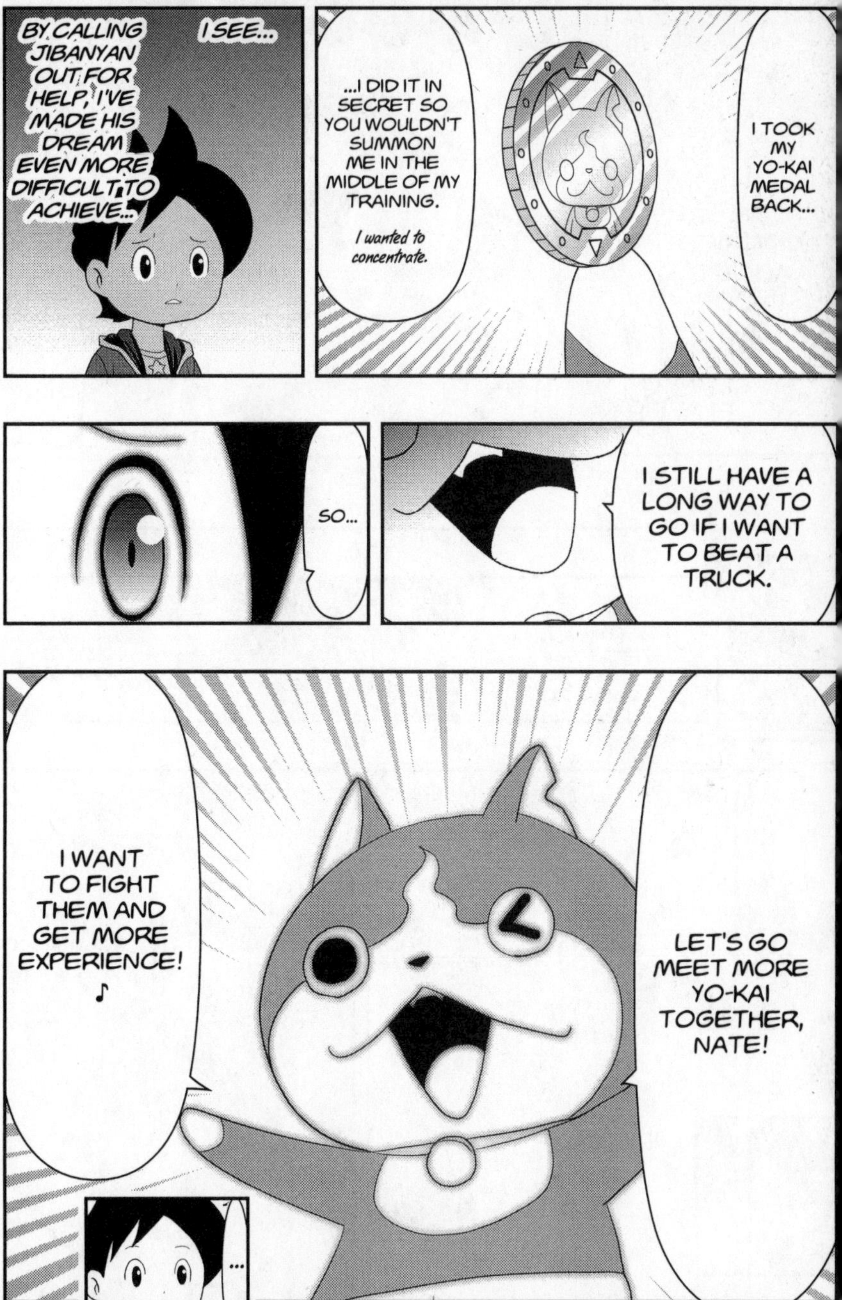
I TOOK MY YO-KAI MEDAL BACK...
...I DID IT IN SECRET SO YOU WOULDN'T SUMMON ME IN THE MIDDLE OF MY TRAINING.
I wanted to concentrate.
I SEE...
BY CALLING JIBANYAN OUT FOR HELP, I'VE MADE HIS DREAM EVEN MORE DIFFICULT TO ACHIEVE...
I STILL HAVE A LONG WAY TO GO IF I WANT TO BEAT A TRUCK.
SO...
LET'S GO MEET MORE YO-KAI TOGETHER, NATE!
I WANT TO FIGHT THEM AND GET MORE EXPERIENCE! ♪
...

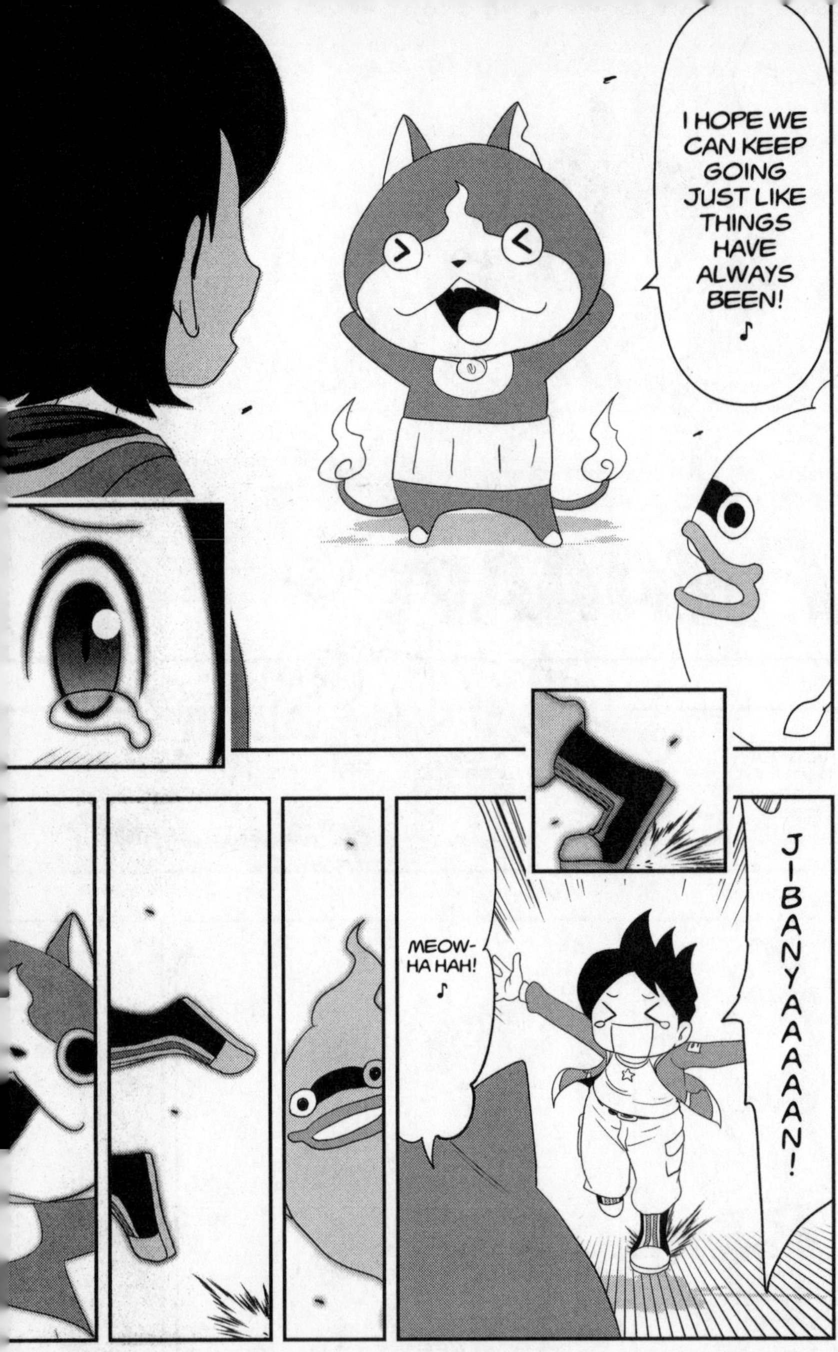
I HOPE WE CAN KEEP GOING JUST LIKE THINGS HAVE ALWAYS BEEN! ♪
JIBANYAAAAAAN!
MEOW-HA HAH! ♪

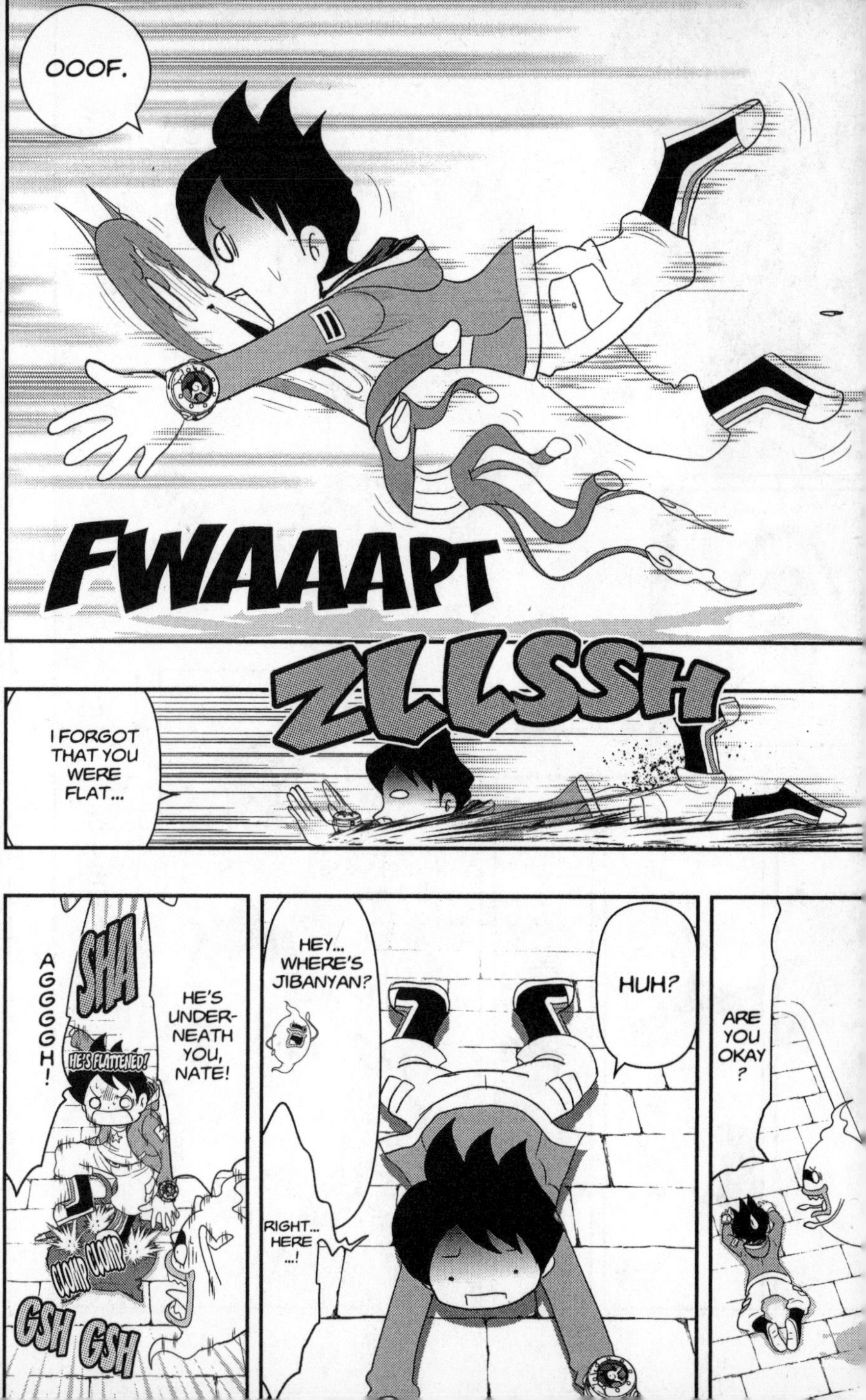
OOOF.
FWAAAPT
ZLLSSH
I FORGOT THAT YOU WERE FLAT...
ARE YOU OKAY?
HUH?
HEY... WHERE'S JIBANYAN?
RIGHT... HERE ...!
HE'S UNDERNEATH YOU, NATE!
AGGGGH!
SHA
HE'S FLATTENED!
CLOMP CLOMP
GSH GSH

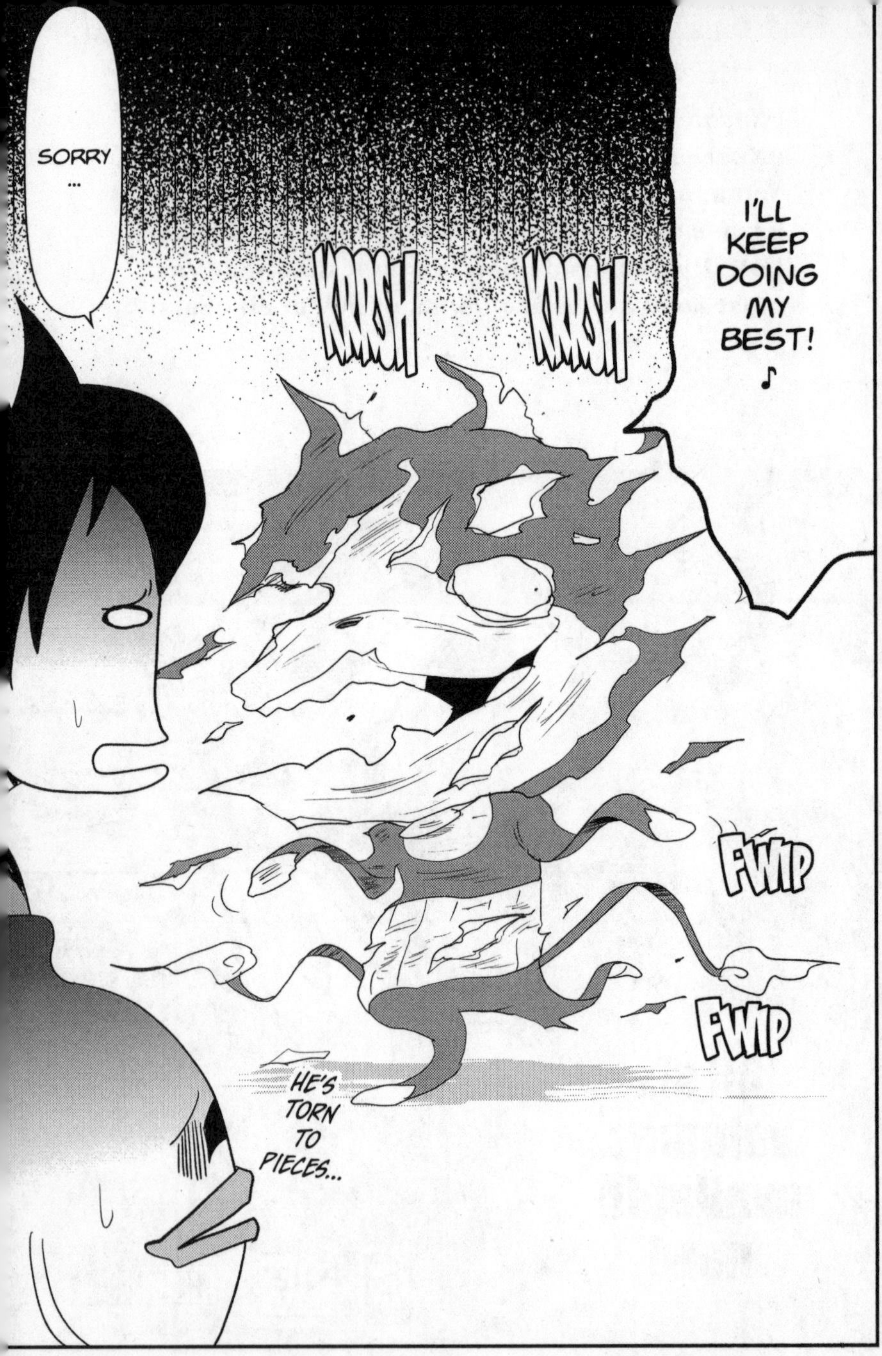
I'LL KEEP DOING MY BEST! ♪
KRRSH KRRSH
SORRY ...
FWIP
FWIP
HE'S TORN TO PIECES...

Welcome to the world of Little Battlers eXperience! In the near future, a boy named Van Yamano owns Achilles, a miniaturized robot that battles on command! But Achilles is no ordinary LBX. Hidden inside him is secret data that Van must keep out of the hands of evil at all costs!

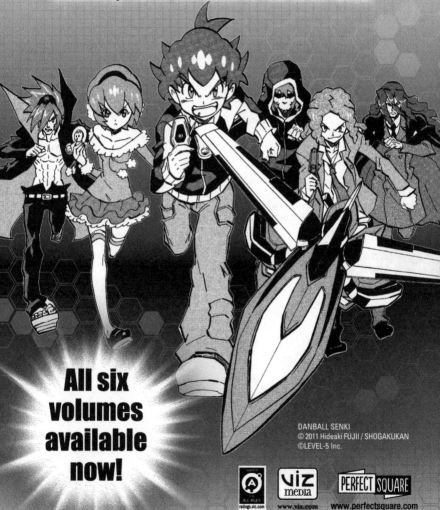

All six volumes available now!

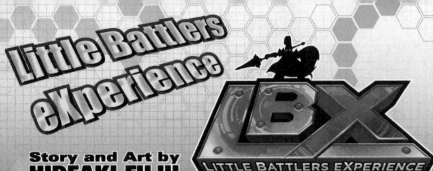

Little Battlers eXperience

LBX
LITTLE BATTLERS EXPERIENCE

Story and Art by HIDEAKI FUJII

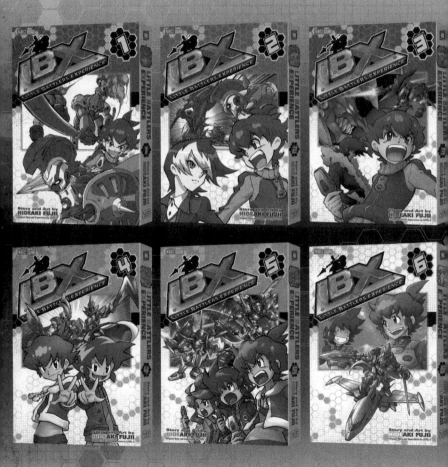

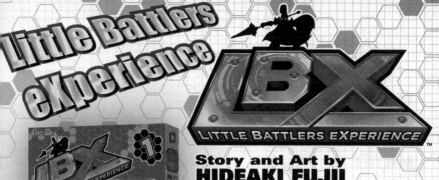

Little Battlers eXperience

LBX

LITTLE BATTLERS eXPERIENCE™

Story and Art by HIDEAKI FUJII

Welcome to the world of Little Battlers eXperience! In the near future, a boy named Van Yamano owns Achilles, a miniaturized robot that battles on command! But Achilles is no ordinary LBX. Hidden inside him is secret data that Van must keep out of the hands of evil at all costs!

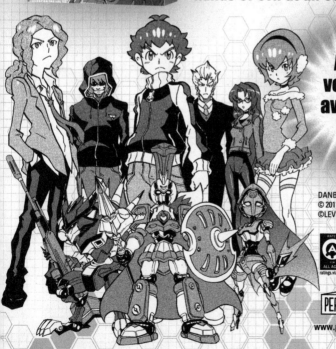

All six volumes available now!

AUTHOR BIO

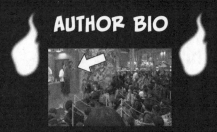

I am busy meeting fans and with other projects, but the Nate Arc is running in Monthy *Coro Coro Ichiban* magazine, which you can read in the upcoming volume 16. "I appreciate your support by picking it up whenever you see the series!"

*This was written in 2018

Noriyuki Konishi hails from Shimabara City in Nagasaki Prefecture, Japan. He debuted with the one-shot *E-CUFF* in *Monthly Shonen Jump Original* in 1997. He is known in Japan for writing manga adaptations of *AM Driver* and *Mushiking: King of the Beetles*, along with *Saiyuki Hiro Go-Kū Den!*, *Chōhenshin Gag Gaiden!! Card Warrior Kamen Riders*, *Go-Go-Go Saiyuki: Shin Gokūden* and more. Konishi was the recipient of the 38th Kodansha manga award in 2014 and the 60th Shogakukan manga award in 2015.

THIS IS THE END OF THIS GRAPHIC NOVEL!

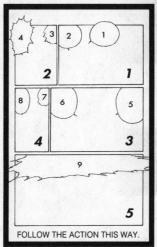

FOLLOW THE ACTION THIS WAY.

To properly enjoy this graphic novel, please turn it around and begin reading from right to left.